THE LE
THORGRIM LONGBEARD
VOL. ONE

"Dwarf Extraordinaire"

'THE EARLY YEARS'

A prequel (more or less) to
The Greatest Treasure in the World.

by

Scott Curtiss Tucker

ISBN: 9781676873822

Updated: May 27, 2021
Ver: 5-27-21B

For my young friend, Italia Durant.

Your love of my first book,
The Greatest Treasure in the World . . .
inspired me to write another one.

A special thank you to my dear friend, Nancy Brown. This book might not have been possible without your hard work in editing the manuscript. Rereading my changes and hunting down typos, rereading, editing, etc., over and over. I'm sure you've read the text so many times that you've memorized it.

If you are interested in full-color artwork from the novel or have questions regarding my work, please contact me. If you see any typos, please let me know!

My author page:
https://www.facebook.com/TheGreatestTreasureintheWorld/

My email addresses:
Scott@Tuckerscomputerdoctor.com.

Stucker868@yahoo.com

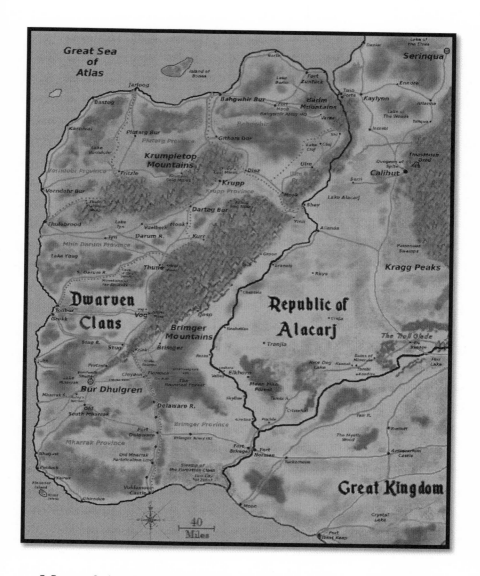

Map of the Dwarven Clans and surrounding areas.

Miscellaneous information:

For calendar years, the Dwarven historical timeline is used. BFD means 'Before the First Dwarves.' AFD means 'After the First Dwarves.'
(Note: If AFD is not specified with a year, then it is presumed to be AFD.)

In the Dwarven historical timeline, year 1 would be approximately the same as 13,000 BC, in the modern historical timeline.

To aid the reader and avoid confusion, the names of the Dwarven months and days have been replaced with their modern equivalents.

For distances, miles are used instead of the nearly identical, Dwarven 'leagues.'

For clock time, the modern abbreviations of a.m. and p.m. are used.

"A dwarf without a beard is like an axe without a head, an elf, and an empty ale mug.
All of them are worthless, pathetic, and lonely."
— Author unknown.

"The past does not repeat itself, but it rhymes."
— Mark Twain.

Contents:

Part One

**"You must go out into the world
and create your own destiny."**

I. Of Dwarves, etc.

Dwarves. Those feisty, beer-loving, elf-hating, barely five-foot-tall, bearded humanoids. Proud, though egotistical, honorable, yet unforgiving, and incredibly strong, but tenderhearted; none were braver, kinder, or more stubborn than those clever, spirited, industrious people known as dwarves.

This is the story of one of those dwarves. An extraordinary individual by the name of Thorgrim Longbeard.

Thorgrim lived a long, long time ago. He was born ten thousand years before Plato, eight thousand years before the ancient Egyptians built the Great Pyramids of Giza, and six thousand years before the Sumerians created the first stone tablets.

During that time so long ago, struggling to survive, most human beings were still nomadic, hunter-gatherers. However, unknown to the rest of the world, there existed a special land in the middle of a great ocean that was home to an advanced civilization . . . and Thorgrim Longbeard.

In this special land, a place where magic was real, there lived several million humanoids. Races of humans, dwarves, elves, orcs, halflings, and togglins co-existed with a wide variety of common land, air, and sea animals. Additionally, though less common and often considered monsters by many, groups of trolls, ogres and giants wandered the woods, hills, and mountains.

Though extremely rare, creatures of myth and legend also existed. Great dragons hoarded vast treasures deep within mysterious forests, caves or on high mountaintop lairs. Magical unicorns (the rarest of all mythical creatures and a symbol of purity and good) roamed the thick forests of the elven northlands.

It was a time when the land, air, and water were clean, the people were happy and life was good.

But . . . hidden in the cold darkness, and unseen by most, were the true monsters of the realm. During the day, supernatural, black-hearted creatures lurked in the shadows, jealous of the happiness and freedom of the sunlit world. There, sinister forces waited for nightfall, while they slowly and patiently plotted mankind's demise.

However, one day, a few hundred years after Thorgrim had lived, the special land was destroyed in a cataclysmic disaster, wiping out everyone and everything. The inhabitants, their technologies, their history . . . all lost forever.

Almost.

Several years ago, while searching for the lost continent of Atlantis, deep-sea explorers discovered the ruins of a lost civilization at the bottom of the mid-Atlantic Ocean. Among the artifacts recovered was a waterproof, steel vault. Inside, scientists found a wooden chest filled with gold and jewels. The ancient vault also contained hundreds of books and scrolls including over ten thousand pages of Thorgrim Longbeard's notes and diaries, all written in a strange language.

A team of over one hundred scholars and scientists, using powerful computers and state of the art scanning systems, made some remarkable discoveries.

The recovered items were tested and found to be between twelve to fifteen thousand years old.

After extensive analysis, several different languages were deciphered. The researchers then determined that the books and scrolls contained the history of a previously unknown, advanced civilization that was ultimately destroyed in a terrible calamity.

Although the research is still ongoing, only recently have some of the stories of this special land and its people become available to the public.

Unfortunately, some of the texts were heavily damaged due to their advanced age. However, enough material survived to allow us a glimpse into the lives of the people, and the special land they lived in.

Including the story of Thorgrim Longbeard.

Thorgrim Longbeard was an extraordinary dwarf; some might even say he was unique. There were many reasons he was special, one of which was that he was born with a beard. A very long, honest to goodness, full beard.

A baby born with a beard? Apparently true, and that fact alone made Thorgrim unique.

The recovered texts mention that beards, the longer, the better, were a symbol of pride and strength for any dwarf, especially males. Considered a mark of beauty, female dwarves also had beards, though typically not as long or heavy as that of a male.

Another reason Thorgrim was extraordinary was that he lived an unusually long life, even for a dwarf. He survived to the age of two hundred and two, which was over forty years beyond the average dwarven lifespan.

From birth, all races of humanoids aged at the same rate until reaching young adulthood at twenty-one, when for unknown reasons, the aging process began to slow down in both dwarves and elves.

Typically, after twenty-one, dwarves continued to age at about one-third the rate of humans, whereas elves aged at about one-fourth . . . and the elves always enjoyed reminding everyone of this fact. The favorite dwarven response was 'Better to live only one day as a dwarf, than three hundred years as a skinny, pointy-eared elf!'

Obviously, dwarves and elves disliked each other. There were several races of elves, with dwarves especially hating the grey variety.

The reader will soon discover why.

Stubborn as a mountain, egotistical but proud of their heritage, dwarves preferred to mingle with only themselves, typically shying away from inter-racial gatherings of any kind . . . unless it was a party. Dwarven drinking parties were legendary, and the dwarves did not care who joined them (unless you were an elf), as long as large quantities of malted beverages were available, particularly ale, the dwarven drink of choice.

Never would you find a feistier character than a heavily inebriated dwarf, and it was woe to those who tried to tell them that they were too drunk to have any more beer, or that all of the kegs had been emptied. Through the centuries, many pubs met their demise whenever all-night, rowdy, dwarven drinking parties were halted by the pub owner or the police.

Unlike most dwarves, Thorgrim avoided alcohol during much of his early adulthood, although later, his ale mug would become a constant and beloved companion.

Thorgrim was a rather shy, soft-spoken person and did not care for violence, although he was no one to mess with if cornered.

Anyone who has ever had to deal with dwarves on a field of battle, or even in a pub brawl, soon realized it was a serious mistake. Enemies of the dwarves quickly learned that the 'short, bearded grumblers' never forgot when dishonored or cheated, and they usually exacted a heavy price for any transgressions.

The elves faced the wrath of the dwarves on many occasions.

It is written in the history of the special land that the elves and dwarves waged war with each other, on and off, for centuries. Most were small, local conflicts, with the elves, usually receiving the worst of it.

However, between the years 1798 to 1800, several centuries before Thorgrim was born, a massive, bitter war was fought between the elves and dwarves. Started by the treacherous deeds of grey elves, the Great War, as some called it, was a bloody, take-no-prisoners clash.

One night, a few thieves snuck into the dwarven capital city of Bur Dhulgren and broke into the Grand Hall of the Dwarves, a museum of treasures and relics that dated back to the time of the first, ancient dwarves. Once inside, the thieves stole the dwarve's most prized and beloved treasure; the Aurumsmiter (smite with gold) Hammer. A giant sledgehammer made of solid gold, forged by the first dwarves for the Father God and creator of all, Moridon.

A few days later, evidence surfaced implicating grey elves in the crime. A week after the theft of the hammer, hundreds of grey elves raided several Dwarven Clan border towns and villages, stealing gold and other goods to fund their civil war against the moon and wood elves in the adjacent elven Kingdom of Alacarj.

The theft of the beloved hammer, the ultimate symbol of pride for all dwarves, and the violent, murderous raids, were acts of war. The Dwarven Clans responded by sending the Army across the border in a massive invasion of the Kingdom of Alacarj. During the fighting, there was much bloodshed and destruction, most of it suffered by the elves. Eventually, the Great Kingdom intervened and negotiated a peace agreement before the war spread across the entire realm.

After the war, for the Dwarven people, the grey elf became a symbol of evil and hatred. Unfairly, over time, this loathing would eventually spread to include all types of elves, most of them innocent of any transgressions towards the dwarves. Even the wood and moon elves, who fought with the dwarves against the greys, were called 'typical, despicable, skinny, pointy-eared elves.'

Even hundreds of years after the war had ended, dwarves were still taught to despise elves. Sadly, this included Thorgrim's generation, and thus, he would spend his entire life disliking most elves, especially hating the 'grey-skins.' However, around the age of twenty, he would discover that some elves were actually trustworthy, generous, kind-hearted folks. It would take an extraordinary dwarf to admit that.

An extraordinary dwarf, like Thorgrim Longbeard.

Dear friend, I present to you The Legend of Thorgrim Longbeard. 'Dwarf Extraordinaire.' Volume One: The Early Years. The first in a series of four books that will cover Thorgrim Longbeard's entire life.

***

On a cold winter morning, many, many years ago, in a land now lost and forgotten in time, a baby boy was born to a pair of proud and happy dwarven parents.

The parents, Luthor and Marjorie Longbeard, were shocked to discover that their firstborn had come into the world with a full, very long, dark-red beard. They named him Thorgrim (after Marjorie's father).

While it was a strange coincidence that Thorgrim's last name happened to be Longbeard, he was indeed born with a long beard and his parents were extremely proud of it. Perhaps having fun with an old, elven-authored rumor . . . later in his life, Thorgrim would often joke that dwarven babies were born with beards. He would never admit that he was the lone exception.

Thorgrim Longbeard, the bearded baby, started out life as a local celebrity of sorts and then would go on to become one of the most famous dwarves in the history of the special land.

The intriguing part of Thorgrim's life and the focus of this book begins in the summer of his nineteenth year, about a month after he graduated from high school.

What about the years before that?

Thorgrim Longbeard, the eldest of thirteen children, was born on January 1, 2229, in the small, silver mining town of Vog, located in Mharrak, which is the largest province in the Dwarven Clans and the ancient land of the original, first dwarves.

Mharrak Province was also home for the capital city of the eight major clans of dwarves: Bur Dhulgren. Previously known as Mharrak Bur, when the clans were united as a kingdom in the year 8 under the first Dwarven ruler, King Authumus Oakenhorn, the city's name was changed to Bur Dhulgren (which means City of the Dwarves, in the Dwarven language).

Thorgrim's mother, Marjorie, stayed at home and cared for her bearded son, while his father, Luthor, toiled in the nearby silver mine.

Thorgrim's ancestry lists two dwarves of notability. His fifth-great grandfather, Otum Longbeard, and Otum's father, Vog Longbeard.

Otum Longbeard became famous and wealthy when he discovered silver in the Brimger Mountains in the year 1801. He soon founded a settlement nearby, naming it 'Vog' (after his father, the famous General Vog Longbeard). Otum later became infamous when he secretly and illegally married a grey elf and had several children with her.

Whenever the subject came up about the possibility that one of his ancestors was a grey elf, Thorgrim would cringe and then laugh it off.

16

Of course, the Longbeard family always vehemently denied that they had any elf blood running through their veins.

Growing up in Vog, Thorgrim's childhood was like that of any other dwarf, although his beard occasionally caused problems. Most folks, who saw Thorgrim for the first time, mistook him for a very short, baby-faced, adult dwarf. When people discovered he was really a kid with a beard, some teased him, calling him rude names such as 'freak' or 'werewolf', while others admired the youngster's hairy chin.

Many people affectionately called Thorgrim, 'Beardby' (short for 'bearded baby'), a name his father and mother despised, however.

Thorgrim, ever the naïve one, did not know how to respond to reactions to his beard, nice or not. He usually replied with a shrug of his shoulders and a smile.

Perhaps jealous of the attention directed towards Thorgrim, some tried to bully him, but they quickly learned the hard way that it was best not to tangle with the kid with the beard.

When Thorgrim entered his early teens, a time when all dwarves begin to sprout beards, his birth 'defect' became less of an issue. Unfortunately, for some reason, a few troublemaking classmates hated him, and they would never let him forget that he was born with a beard.

Thorgrim's high school years were typical, and although he did well in his studies and with the girls, it was around this time that he discovered something terribly unfortunate about himself.

He was claustrophobic.

For a dwarf, claustrophobia was unacceptable. Male dwarves growing up in the mining towns were expected to begin working in the ore mines upon graduation from high school, which would obviously be a problem for anyone that was claustrophobic. In order to avoid trouble, he kept it a secret.

***

The service in the mines was mandatory although exceptions were allowed for those physically unfit or anyone that worked in a family-owned business, farmed, attended a university, or joined the all-volunteer military.

Female dwarves were luckier. Although girls could enter a university, they were not permitted to work in the mines or join the military. All females were expected to remain at home to help on the farm or to learn housekeeping, and how to be a good mother.

17

Minimum time in the mines for a dwarf was twenty years after which they would be granted official discharge from service to pursue other interests. They could leave earlier, though only if they entered into one of the aforementioned fields.

***

While he attended high school, Thorgrim became fascinated with history. However, unfortunately for him, the focus of Vog's small, single room high school, and its lone, volunteer teacher, was basic reading, writing, and mathematics. Thus, very little was taught about the past, with many important events in Dwarven history ignored or only glossed over. Even the Great War was only briefly summarized in class, which was ironic because the war was the root of dwarven hatred towards elves. Despite above-average grades in the courses provided, Thorgrim did not qualify for a university scholarship simply because the little school did not offer any.

Sadly, the Longbeard's could not afford to send Thorgrim to the university in Bur Dhulgren, where he hoped to attend, nor did they desire to send him off to the military. The Vog Silver Mine was part of the family heritage and it was here that Thorgrim belonged. At least it was his father's preference.

In truth, Thorgrim's real love was books. His dream was to one-day visit the Supreme Library in Bur Dhulgren. Every chance he could, he would walk down to the little Vog library and spend hours scouring over every publication available. He especially loved books about history, lost treasures and ancient relics, but the library only had a few books available regarding those subjects. He also enjoyed reading the classics. Often, he would check out favorites but forget to return them . . . perhaps on purpose.

As Thorgrim's high school days ended, he had to accept the fact that at least for the immediate future, he would have to work in the silver mine alongside his father and would only be able to dream about working with books.

For various reasons, Thorgrim hated the Vog Silver Mine before ever stepping foot inside it. As a practical joke, some of his friends told him several creepy stories claiming that the angry ghosts of long-dead miners haunted the mine. Those stories and other supernatural tales would cause Thorgrim much grief, and a lifetime of phasmophobia.

Having read several books on the paranormal, throughout his entire life, Thorgrim would always argue for the existence of spooks, haunts, ghosts and other supernatural phenomena. Whenever asked if he had ever seen a ghost, his eyes would widen. Though it contradicted his view that you cannot prove the existence of anything you cannot see, Thorgrim would reply, 'No, never seen one. But I've seen and heard some strange things, like doors opening by themselves, or footsteps walking in the middle of the night. Have no doubts, spooks are real. We just can't see them because they're usually invisible.'

Wrongly assuming that Thorgrim's spook paranoia was due to excess ale consumption, most would shrug and walk away muttering, 'How do you argue with that?'

Ghosts or not, although Thorgrim would later admit that he was a bit lazy, too, the main reason that he did not want to work in the silver mine was that he feared suffocation, often having nightmares about being buried alive in a cave-in. At first, he tried to hide his claustrophobia and fear of ghosts, but it soon became impossible.

***

It is dawn, Monday, July 1, 2248, over twelve thousand years ago. For the recent high school graduate, nineteen-year-old Thorgrim Longbeard, it is time to climb out of bed and get ready for work, but he will have none of it.

II. Thorgrim's Dilemma

Seventy-four-year-old Luthor Longbeard, still young and in the prime of his life, stood at the entryway of his son's bedroom, tugging on his beard and tapping his foot. He was not happy.

"Thorgrim! What da hell is da matta wit ya? You still sick, is it? Git yer arse outta dat bed, now! It's a quarter past six and we've got to git to da mine by seven!"

Afraid to reply, Thorgrim always knew he was in trouble whenever his father lowered the tone of his voice and clipped his words when he spoke.

Getting no response from his son, Luthor roared, "Well, Are ya sick or not? Answer me!"

Thorgrim rolled over, and as he did, his massive beard toppled out of his bunk and on to the floor.

Concerned that his father's anger was reaching the boiling point, Thorgrim finally replied, "Uh, yes, that's it. I'm still sick, Papa. Ugh! Cough!-Cough! I'm sorry, but I can't work in the mine today."

Luthor exploded. "What da hell! You've been sick or had one blah, blah, blah excuse or another since you graduated from school a month ago! Are ya really sick or just lazy, boy? Margie! Our son says he's sick again un won't go to work!"

A moment later, Thorgrim's mother entered his bedroom. She was very pregnant, and her hair and beard were still in curlers.

Concerned, Marjorie said, "Son, are you still not feeling well? I think we better contact Dr. Thacker and have him come to look you over."

Walking over to Thorgrim's bed, she felt her son's forehead. "Hmmmm. I don't think you have a fever. Is yer stomach upset again? I told you to stop eating those purple 'shrooms!"

Thorgrim grimaced and rubbed his belly. "No, Mother, no 'shrooms this time, I'm just sick to my stomach."

Wearing a stern expression, Thorgrim's father pointed a plump index finger straight at him. Never before had Thorgrim seen his father's monobrow so crumpled.

"If yer really sick, I'm sorry to hear dat, but how come none of yer brothers and sisters are ever sick?" said Luthor, still tapping his foot. "Have ya been sneakin' around like an elf un gettin' into some of muh private ale stock, boy? It seems dat some's a missin'!"

Thorgrim rapidly shook his head and pulled the blankets up to his face.

His father continued to rant. "Ya know dat yer not old enough to be drinkin' or smokin' yet. Not 'til next year! Yer still a minor un could be arrested for doin' dat! So, if I catch ya smokin' or drinkin, I'll tan yer hide 'til da end of time. Maybe even longer!"

Thorgrim was still shaking his head. "No, Papa, I haven't been sneakin' any of yer ale," he replied. "I know I'm not old enough to be smokin', or drinkin' beer. I don't even like either of it very much."

Luthor bellowed, "Well, how do ya know if ya don't like either of it very much unless you've been doin' it?"

"I haven't been, I promise!"

"You betta be tellin' da truth, cuz like I said, I'll —"

Marjorie offered her husband a scowl. "Luthor, please settle down, we can barely understand a word yer sayin'! And you won't need to tan his hide. I'm sure that Thorgrim's a good boy and is not drinkin' yer ale or smokin' tobaccee. Isn't that right, Thorgrim?"

Still peeking out from under the blankets, Thorgrim offered a quick, triple-nod of his head.

Mrs. Longbeard continued, "Husband, if there's any ale missing it's because you've been drinking it! Now, you're going to be late. You won't have time to finish yer breakfast!"

Luthor shrugged, though his brow remained furrowed. "Okay, okay. But you get Dr. Thacker in here today and find out what's goin' on with dis boy! He has to come to work in the silver mine! The management is askin' questions every day, wantin' to know where dis kid is!"

She nodded. "Okay, I'll contact the doctor today."

Luthor shook his finger. "Thorgrim, I don't care how sick ya are tomorrow. Ya **are** goin' into da mine un work!"

"Shoo, shoo, husband!" said Marjorie, gesturing with her hands. "Get going! I love you and I'll see you tonight. I'll have a hot 'n spicy venison and possum snout stew waiting for you!"

Luthor grinned. His wife always knew she could calm him down by using the kitchen. "Mmmm! I can taste it already!" he replied. "Extra crispy on the snouts un extra spicy, too!"

She smiled. "Of course, now out or you'll be late again!"

"Okay, okay! I'm goin'! Un honey, don't overdo it today! Consider yer condition! If anything happens, make sure that ya have someone send word for me, un I'll come at once!"

Luthor rubbed her belly and smiled. Exiting the bedroom, he paused briefly to offer Thorgrim a wag of his index finger.

Hungry and anxious to get to work, Luthor scurried down the hall and into the kitchen. There, seated around a big table, were the rest of his children. Eleven smiling faces, all of them with curly locks of auburn hair piled on top of their heads. Ranging in age from two to fifteen, the kids were eagerly eating their sausage and flapjack breakfast. With a double-take towards his own plate, Luthor noticed that his sausages were missing.

"Hey, who ate my breakfast?" he asked. Leaning down towards the cute, chubby face of his youngest boy, Trancy, he said, "Hmmm was it **you**? I don't know, but you sure look guilty!"

The other children giggled.

Looking up at his father, the two-year-old toddler grinned and nodded his head. Still chewing on a juicy sausage, grease covered his fat cheeks and hands.

"Yeah, I suspected so," chuckled Luthor before giving Trancy a kiss on his little pug nose.

Patting his potbelly, Luthor smiled and said, "Well, my pants are fittin' a bit tight anyway and besides that, I'm almost late for work, so I don't have time to eat! I love you all. Take care of yer momma for me! Remember, yer new brother or sister is comin' soon! And, uh, take care of yer big brother, Thorgrim. I'm worried about him. Bye!"

"Bye Papa!" they all called out.

With a quick turn, Luthor pilfered a sausage from the plate of his sixth eldest, nine-year-old daughter, Hannah, and shoved it into his mouth. Next, from the kitchen counter, he grabbed his old lunchbox full of goodies that his wife lovingly packed for him each morning.

Making his way to the front door, the father of twelve, soon to be thirteen children, grabbed his pickaxe from the wall and along with his lunchbox, hat, and lantern exited the little house. As usual, Luthor was going to be late for work, and a long day in the silver mine awaited him.

The supervisor of a crew of twelve dwarves, Luthor was extremely concerned and disappointed that again, due to illness, Thorgrim was unable to join him at work. Disappointed or not, Luthor had a job to do, and even after fifty-five years of service, it was a job he still loved.

***

Peering out from the window of the small wooden shack that stood in front of the Vog Silver Mine entrance, the time clock manager, Biff

Knickers, scolded Luthor Longbeard and several other dwarves for being late again.

"It's after seven! Yer all late! Do you want to keep yer jobs or not?" Angrily, Biff turned to Luthor, who was next in line to clock in for his shift.

"Luthor, your late again, and where's your boy, Beardby? Is he still sick? And why do you keep bringing your pickaxe? You're a supervisor. You're supposed to supervise, not mine silver ore!"

Luthor resented the time clock manager, as well as any manager, for that matter. Biff Knickers was the skinniest dwarf Luthor had ever seen and someone who always did everything by the book. If there was a problem such as tardiness or lack of performance, he never gave an employee a break, no matter the excuse. Behind Biff's back, Luthor often called him a 'twig-boy elf.'

Wearing a look of disappointment, Luthor presented his identification card, then said sheepishly, "Uh, ya, he's still sick, I guess. We're gonna have the doc check him over today. By da way, I bring my pickaxe because I won't have my crew doing something I won't do. I lead by example."

While waiting for Biff to record his start time, Luthor's face turned red with anger. With his words clipping, he roared. "Oh, un for da last time, will ya please stop callin' muh son, Beardby? I hate dat name! His name is Thorgrim!"

"But everyone calls him Beardby, don't they?" replied Biff, startled by Luthor's sudden outburst.

Furrowing his heavy monobrow, Luthor stuck his head through the shack's open window and glared at the surprised manager. Biff wisely took a step back.

Luthor growled, "Well, everyone but me. Un if I don't call him dat name, I don't want anyone else doin' it either. Got it, twig . . . err, I mean, Mr. Knickers?"

"Yes, I got it," replied Biff. "I'm sorry, I'm sorry. Thorgrim it is." Biff quickly clocked Luthor into the system and returned his ID card.

Biff cleared his voice and said. "Just make sure he gets to work as soon as possible. You know the law. You don't want the authorities hounding you, do you? Now get to work. Your crew is waiting for you inside."

Looking past Luthor, Biff waved at the long line of late to work dwarves. "Damn ya! You're all late! Next!"

Luthor, still miffed, flapped the end of his long beard (considered an insult by dwarves) in the direction of Biff.

Outranked by Biff, Luthor risked his job with such a display. However, he also knew that having served over fifty-five years in the mine that had been founded by his ancestor, gave him some clout. If he were to be dismissed for any reason, it likely would cause a riot with the rest of the three hundred miners who worked in the Vog Silver Mine. In other words, Luthor Longbeard was highly respected and beloved by everyone. He had little to fear from his employer for almost any transgression.

With his equipment in hand, Luthor trudged on ahead and approached the mine entrance, grumbling something about the lack of respect by the 'big shots', a name that he liked to call everyone on the mining company's management team.

Once inside, Luthor found his crew patiently waiting, holding on to their lunchboxes, lanterns, and pickaxes. He could hear the faint clanking of pickaxes from teams already at work, some of them more than a mile deep inside the Brimger Mountains.

Luthor nodded and paused to look at his twelve-man crew, most of whom had been with him several decades. They already looked weary, although the workday had just begun.

"Good morning, boss," said one of them to Luthor.

"Sorry I'm late again, boys," replied Luthor. "Are ya ready to start?"

Some nodded, and a few muttered, "Yes."

"Let's get at it then!" said Luthor excitedly.

Together, they began the long stroll into the heart of the mountain, their great beards swaying back and forth. Led by Luthor, they began singing a song about going off to work.

***

"Please, come in Dr. Thacker!" said Marjorie, holding the door to the little bungalow open. "I'm so glad you're here!"

"Certainly! I got the message that your son, Thurston, had dropped off at my clinic this morning," replied the doctor as he stepped through the door with his medical bag in hand. "I realize that now it's a bit late in the afternoon, but I got here as soon as I could. Been a busy day for me."

Gesturing towards the living room, she replied, "I understand, and my husband and I both appreciate you taking the time to stop and see Thorgrim. We're very concerned about his health."

After entering the living room, Dr. Thacker glanced around and tugged on his salt and pepper beard. He was amazed at how clean the little place was and doubly amazed that so many people could fit inside.

The Longbeard hovel originally had only two small bedrooms, an eat-in kitchen, laundry, bath, and living room. Over time, with his own hands, Luthor expanded the home by adding more rooms to accommodate his growing family. Now the home had a total of eight bedrooms and an extra bath. Mr. and Mrs. Longbeard's bedroom was the largest at eight by nine feet. Thorgrim, the oldest child, as per tradition, had a private room, which measured seven by seven feet. Stocked with makeshift bunkbeds and each shared by two children, the rest of the bedrooms measured six by seven feet.

The doctor knew the Longbeard family was very poor, and he had never charged them a copper for any of his services through the years. In fact, Dr. Thacker had happily delivered every one of the Longbeard children, provided annual checkups, and treated them for the typical childhood maladies when needed. He was preparing to do the same for a new baby that was almost due.

Studying Mrs. Longbeard's protruding belly, Dr. Thacker said, "I know I'm here to see Thorgrim, but first, I want to know how you're doing! You're what, two weeks away from your due date? How have you been?"

She smiled. "Oh, I'm fine. Yes, two weeks. The little one is kicking like crazy! It's almost like he's knocking on the door wanting out!"

"Oh, you're sure it's a he, this time? You have six of each, correct?"

"Yes, six of each!" she replied with a big smile. "And ask Luthor. I haven't been wrong yet!"

Dr. Thacker returned the smile. "Indeed! Well, I'll be checking in on you from time to time, and please, contact me if you need anything."

The doctor had just finished his sentence, when, from out of nowhere, eleven dwarven children, laughing and screaming, ran past, almost knocking him to the floor.

Regaining his balance, Dr. Thacker commented, "So, I can see that your children are enjoying their summer break from school!"

Marjorie shouted, "Children! Outside this instant or there won't be any supper for you!"

"Okay, Mama!" most replied, as they left the little house at various exits, including some of the windows.

"Please, keep an eye on Trancy! He's too little to be outside alone!"

"Okay, Mama!" some of them hollered.

25

Glancing around on the floor, Dr. Thacker said, "Uh, I'm afraid that when they flew through here, I think one of them took my medical bag."

Marjorie covered her mouth, embarrassed. "Oh, I'm so sorry! It was probably my fifteen-year-old. He wants to be a doctor, you know. **Thurston! Bring Dr. Thacker's bag back here right now, or your father will tan your hide when he gets home!**"

In an instant, a black bag came flying through an open window. Striking the floor, it bounced twice before coming to rest next to the doctor's boots.

"There you go!" Marjorie said, still embarrassed. "Again, Dr. Thacker, I apologize!"

"Not a problem." Bending down, the doctor picked up his bag. When he stood up, he checked his pockets and said, "Oh, and it appears that my pipe and tobaccee are missing, too."

Marjorie shouted, "**Thurston! The pipe!**"

Without warning, a smoking pipe, still burning with a fresh load of tobacco recently lit by Thurston, flew in through the window and landed on the floor.

"And the tobaccee, please!" she yelled.

A couple of seconds later, a small package of greenish-brown leaf tobacco flew in, landing at the doctor's feet before sliding into a wall.

Marjorie continued to yell at her second-oldest, "**Thurston! What did I tell you about smokin' at yer age, Thurston? Are you listening to me?**"

She continued, "I'm so sorry for all of that, Doctor! These children nowadays!"

After snuffing out the pipe, Dr. Thacker picked up the tobacco package and put the items back into his suit jacket. He then smiled and replied, "Uh, it's okay! Had kids of my own, you know! They can be as quick as elves when they're that young, can't they!"

She giggled. "Yes, and perhaps just as sneaky, too!"

Dr. Thacker said, "Of course. Uh, so shall we have a look at Thorgrim? Where is he?"

"He's in his bedroom where he always stays, except when he sneaks out and goes down the street to the library. Please, follow me."

She led the doctor down the hallway towards Thorgrim's bedroom. When they reached it, she gently rapped on the closed door.

"Thorgrim. Dr. Thacker is here to see you."

There was a brief pause, then Thorgrim replied, "I'm fine, Mama. Feelin' much better. I don't need to see the doctor."

26

She replied, "Good! Since you're feeling better, you can grab your pickaxe and lantern! I'm sure your father will be happy when you show up to work in the mine today!"

Thorgrim moaned. "Uh, ohhhhh. I'm not feelin' so good, I guess! My stomach!"

"I thought so. I'm bringing the doctor in now, so I hope you're dressed!"

"I'm still in bed, Mama,"

Turning to the doctor, she whispered. "You've got to find out what's wrong with him! Every day Thorgrim has an excuse that he doesn't feel well enough to go to work in the mine! He's a month out of graduation, and he hasn't gone to work even once! We gave him a shiny new pickaxe for one of his graduation gifts, and he hasn't touched it. Needless to say, his father is beside himself."

"I understand," replied Dr. Thacker in a quiet voice. "I'll see what I can do."

"Thank you," she said, before turning the knob and slowly opening the door.

Peering into Thorgrim's dimly lit bedroom, Dr. Thacker saw dozens of leather-bound books scattered everywhere, along with a dresser, a couple of chairs, various piles of clothes, and other belongings. A single bed was shoved in the corner beneath a small window. The bed was piled high with a mountain of blankets making it difficult to know for certain that Thorgrim was lying in it. The only evidence was a dark-red beard that draped off the side of the bed and onto the floor. Somewhere, hidden deep inside the covers was nineteen-year-old, Thorgrim Longbeard.

On an emotional rollercoaster due to her pregnancy, Margorie hollered, "**Thorgrim!** Get out of bed this instant so Dr. Thacker can examine you!"

"Okay," he mumbled from beneath the blankets.

"Doctor, I told Thorgrim to quit eating those purple 'shrooms that the old hippy is growing in his garden next door! But he claims that's not the reason he's sick. He says his stomach is upset."

Dr. Thacker's bushy monobrow dropped. "He's been eating purple mushrooms? Hmmm."

"**Thorgrim!**" she shrieked, causing the doctor to jump. "**Get up!**"

For a moment, nothing stirred from the bed, but then the blanket mountain shifted and tumbled onto the floor. Swinging his legs over the side, Thorgrim sat up on the edge and smiled.

His mother, noticing that her son was fully clothed, scowled.

She placed her hands on her hips and began her bombardment. "Thorgrim! You're not sick! And here I'm always tellin' your father that you're such a good boy! You snuck out again and went down to the library, didn't you! Don't deny it, because I see a new stack of books next to yer bed! Don't give me any excuses or any other blah, blah, blah like you always do! Just wait 'til yer father gets home!"

Thorgrim dropped his head.

Looking at the many books lying around, she yelled, "**By Moridon's beard, how many books have you checked out of the library?** Do they have any left? How many are overdue? If you don't stop—"

Dr. Thacker interrupted her rant. "Ma'am," he said calmly. "Please, if you don't mind, I'll take it from here."

Taking a step back, she nodded and said, "Oh, I'm sorry, of course. Please excuse my yelling, Doctor, but these kids!"

Marjorie wagged her finger at her son and as she exited, said, "We'll finish this later, Thorgrim!"

Thorgrim looked at the doctor and offered a shrug along with a toothy grin.

A hard slam of the bedroom door by Mrs. Longbeard caused both Thorgrim and the doctor to flinch.

Thorgrim cringed. "Oofta! She's mad at me!"

"Yes, I would agree!" replied the doctor with a nod. "That might be an understatement. You've probably heard the old saying, 'hell hath no fury like that of a female dwarf's scorn,' haven't you?"

Thorgrim shook his head.

"You haven't heard that expression before? I would advise you to research that before you irritate your mother again . . . or any woman for that matter. It's a very important saying that all male dwarves should know and never, ever forget!"

"I'll try to remember that."

Clearing his throat the doctor continued, "Good. Well, anyway, don't mind her. It's the pregnancy. It can mess with a woman's emotions."

"Okay, I understand, I guess."

"So, I hear that you're not feeling well, is it?"

"Uh, not really the best, no," replied Thorgrim, swinging his boots back and forth.

"And, where do you feel ill?" the doctor asked, as he opened his bag.

"Uh, muh stomach, I guess."

"You guess? Relax. I'm going to do a routine examination."

Thorgrim sighed, "Okay."

For the next fifteen minutes, Dr. Thacker checked Thorgrim's temperature, listened to his heart and lungs, then examined his eyes, ears, and throat. Everything seemed fine.

"Lay down on your back, please. I'm going to take a look at your abdomen."

Thorgrim complied.

Moving Thorgrim's beard out of the way, as well as his own, the doctor reached down and gently pushed on various parts of Thorgrim's stomach.

"Tell me, does this hurt when I press here?" asked the doctor, pushing near Thorgrim's navel.

Chuckling, Thorgrim replied, "No, uh, I mean, yes. Well, no. I mean . . . it kinda tickles!"

As Dr. Thacker had suspected, there was nothing wrong with his teenage patient.

"Thorgrim, I think I know what's troubling you, and I have something right here that will fix it."

The doctor reached into his bag and pulled out a huge syringe with a six-inch needle. It was Dr. Thacker's go-to, cure-all, problem solver.

"Roll onto your right side please, and pull your pants down. I need to see your backside."

"Huh!" exclaimed Thorgrim. Sitting straight up in bed, he looked at the giant needle, while his eyes bugged out in horror. "Yer not gonna stick that thing into my butt, are you?"

"Well, of course, all six inches of it! Unless you want to tell me what's really making you feel ill."

Thorgrim squirmed. "What's really making me feel ill?"

"Uh, yes," replied the doctor as he moved the big needle towards Thorgrim.

"Okay, okay," moaned Thorgrim, nervously as he scooted further into the bed.

Putting the syringe back into his bag, Dr. Thacker wrinkled his brow and said, "So, between you and me, why aren't you going into the silver mine to work like you're supposed to? I know you're aware that if you don't go to the university, join the military, work on a farm, own a business, or have a serious health issue, that you must work in one of the mines. You know this. It's the way of the dwarves."

Thorgrim scooted towards the edge of the bed and swung his legs and beard off the side. Staring down at the floor, he said, "I know, I know, but . . . something's botherin' me."

Dr. Thacker shook his head. "Thorgrim, I can't find anything wrong with you. You're as healthy as a mountain ox. Now, I don't know how you can hide beneath all of those blankets every day in this summer heat without sweating to death, but . . . tell me, is what's troubling you, really **that** bad?"

Thorgrim looked up at Dr. Thacker. "Yeah. It's bad."

"Why won't you go to work with your father in the silver mine? You can tell me. Trust me. I won't repeat a word you say to anyone."

"Uh, I'm allergic to dust," came the quick reply.

"Really? Hmmm. Well, what I have in that syringe will fix that!" Doctor Thacker pointed towards his open medical bag. The top of the giant syringe was in clear view.

Thorgrim shuddered, then looked towards the bedroom door, concerned that his mother might overhear. He whispered, "No! Please, I don't want that shot! It's not the dust. I . . . I'm afraid to go into the mine, Doc." Embarrassed, the young dwarf dropped his head and twirled his beard.

Doctor Thacker raised his brow. "Afraid? Afraid of what?"

Continuing to whisper, Thorgrim replied, "Spooks, for one thing!"

"Spooks? Do you mean ghosts?"

Thorgrim became wild-eyed and said, "Yeah! I heard that some miners were killed in a cave-in, tons of years ago, un now they haunt the mine. I heard that the spooks are angry un will kill ya when they catch ya, un then you'll turn into a spook, too!"

Dr. Thacker frowned. "Thorgrim…"

Thorgrim dropped his head again and interrupted, "Not only that, but I'm . . . well, I'm . . ."

"Yes, you're what?"

"Claustra . . . claustro . . . claustri—"

"Are you trying to say that you're claustrophobic?"

Looking up, Thorgrim exclaimed, "Yeah!"

Shaking his head, the doctor replied, "Oh, Thorgrim. That is a problem. Especially for a miner!"

"I know."

The doctor sighed and placed his hand on Thorgrim's shoulder. "Look, first, there are no such things as spooks, ghosts, or whatever you want to call them. At least I can say that in my one hundred and twenty-one years of breathin' air, I've never set eyes on any ghost. Not one! And you understand in my line of work, I see a lot of dead things, right?"

"But, you can't see spooks! They're invisible! I've read all kinds of books on the subject! Like this one over here."

Thorgrim reached for an old hardcover book. Handing it to the doctor, he continued, "See, this book explains everything about spooks."

Dr. Thacker glanced down at the title and read it aloud. "Spooky Spooks, by I.M. Morbid. Hmmmm." He smiled and said, "Thorgrim, you've actually read this book?"

"Yeah, several times. Everything you want to know about spooks is in there! The author's description of the different kinds of spooks scared the wits out of me! To make things worse, the stories my friends told me about the spooks in the silver mine match up exactly with what the author wrote!"

Tipping the binding of the book towards Thorgrim, the doctor said, "I think I found a health problem with you after all! You might need glasses. Can you read that small print below the author's name and title?"

Thorgrim leaned forward and squinted. "Yeah, it says 'fiction."

The doctor's monobrow went so high it almost met his hairline.

After a moment, Thorgrim grinned. "Oh, I guess I missed that! But, it doesn't mean spooks aren't real!"

"Thorgrim, I'm not really worried about the spooks. I'm much more concerned about your claustrophobia. Are you sure you're claustrophobic?"

"Yeah. If I'm in an enclosed space, I feel trapped, un I can't breathe."

"But when I came in here, you were buried under a huge pile of blankets."

"That's different. I keep muh head out."

"Thorgrim, if anyone finds out, they'll ship you off to the Army or Navy, and if you refuse, you'll likely go to prison or in the least, be registered as an outcast. They could kick you out of the country and you'll never be allowed to return! You do realize this, don't you?"

Again, Thorgrim dropped his head. "Yeah," he mumbled. "Being an outcast or going to prison doesn't sound like much fun. I don't want to embarrass my family, either. I'm really worried. What else can I do?"

"You could always try to get a job working on a farm, but there aren't any near Vog. The other problem is that no one will hire you as a farmhand unless you have experience. Do you know anything about agriculture?"

"Have you met the neighbor next door, the one with the really long hair and the beads?"

"No, I haven't."

"Well, he showed me how to plant some funny-lookin' mushrooms un some other plants that look like weeds. Does that make me a farmer?"

"No, that ain't gonna cut it, I'm afraid. Forget that guy and listen to me."

The doctor sat down on the edge of the bed with Thorgrim. Placing his arm around the confused teen, he continued, "Thorgrim, you have nothing to fear in the silver mine. It's very rewarding work! I worked in one of the Krupp Province iron mines for ten years, saved my money, and then went to the university in Dartag Bur. Twelve years later, I walked out with my medical degree!"

Thorgrim was confused. "But yer supposed to serve twenty years in the mines, aren't ya?"

"You can leave anytime if you can afford to attend a university. You can also volunteer and join the Army or Navy. But it seems right now that the mines are the only option for you."

"But I'm afraid of being smothered! I don't want to go underground!"

"Well, technically I don't think your underground. If it's like the Krupp iron mines, you're barely inside the mountain."

Thorgrim shook his head. "Inside a mountain or underground is the same thing to me!"

Dr. Thacker patted Thorgrim on the back. "I understand, and I guess you have a good point. Have you always felt this way? When did this problem start?"

"Well, not always, but one night a few years ago, my beard got wrapped around my face really tight in the middle of the night, un it almost smothered me! I was dreamin' that I was working in the silver mine, un the whole place caved in on me. It was terrible! That's the big reason I'm afraid to go into the mine! I don't like spooks, but I don't want to be buried alive if the place caves in!"

Looking at Thorgrim's beard, the doctor said, "I see. Thorgrim, you know those stories your friends told you about the miners who died and are now haunting the mine? They were lying to you. They were probably just trying to scare you. And as far as I know, there's never been such an accident in the Vog Silver Mine. Never, at least to my knowledge. I've been told that the tunnels are solid and only a massive earthquake could shake 'em. We're not in a quake zone, so you have nothing to fear. Trust me!" He finished with a smile and another pat on Thorgrims back.

"I've got nothin' to fear?"

"Nothing!"

"Uh . . ."

"Thorgrim, look at me. Don't you trust me? I delivered you into this world nineteen years ago. I would never lie to you."

Thorgrim looked over to him. "Well, I don't remember you deliverin' me 'cuz I was a baby! But, I do trust ya."

"Well, I sure remember!" replied the doctor with a quick chuckle. "When I saw that amazing beard on your little face, I was stunned!"

Thorgrim twirled his beard and smiled.

Dr. Thacker nudged Thorgrim and said, "Now, I don't want you to get into any trouble. Please, promise me that tomorrow you'll go with your father, and at least try to enter the mine. Your father wouldn't let anything happen to you, would he?"

"No, he wouldn't."

"Of course, he wouldn't! You know, Thorgrim, you're basically an adult now. You have to start acting like one."

"My parents have said that before, many times."

Glancing around at all of the books, Dr. Thacker said, "Look, I know what your true desire is. It's obvious! If you work hard in the silver mine, you can save your money and then one day, fulfill your dreams. Tell me if I'm wrong. You want to write or at least work with books in some capacity. Am I correct? Maybe even become a teacher?"

"Yeah! Well, I don't know about becomin' a teacher, but I love books, un I want to work at the biggest library in the world in Bur Dhulgren!"

***

Thorgrim loved books for many reasons and one of them was that when he read stories, he was transported away from his rather mundane life in Vog. The books took him on adventures that he could only dream about.

Although the selection in the small Vog library was limited, Thorgrim still managed to find some favorite books of interest. As mentioned earlier, he especially loved history books and stories about lost treasures and ancient relics. He also enjoyed fiction, including tales about pirates, great battles between dwarves and elves, even demons, witches, wizards, and dragons. Because Thorgrim had never seen real magic or a dragon before, he believed those types of stories were made up to scare little children. Nevertheless, he found the tales exciting and fun.

Books about the paranormal also fascinated Thorgrim, but there were certain stories that frightened him. Ghost stories scared the wits out of him and most of all, anything regarding the undead. Horrifying tales about evil creatures such as vampires, liches, zombies, revenants, and others, kept him awake all night shuddering beneath his pile of blankets.

He had also learned in school that somewhere in the world, far away to the southeast, past the land of the orcs, there existed a place where the undead dwelled: The Bone Empire.

***

Continuing to look at the piles of books, Dr. Thacker said, "Yes, I can see you love books! Oh, and just so ya know . . . the Supreme Library in Bur Dhulgren is only the second largest library in the world. The Library of Shem in the Alacarjian city of Calibut is supposed to be the largest."

"Yeah, but that's an elf library, so it doesn't count. I was taught not to ever trust elves, so I won't go near the place."

Dr. Thacker laughed. "Yes, it is an elf library, but what do you mean it doesn't count? Compared to the Supreme Library, I heard the Library of Shem has more than twice as many books! For a book lover like you, such a place should be hard to resist."

In truth, the thought of all of those books excited Thorgrim.

His monobrow jumped. "Over twice as many? Hmmm. Elves or not, maybe I'd entertain the idea of going there one day. But, I'm only sayin', maybe."

"Thorgrim, have you ever met an elf?"

"No."

Dr. Thacker raised the corner of his monobrow. "Do you really know why elves are so despised by us dwarves? Especially the grey elves? Certainly, you're familiar with the Great War."

"Only what they taught us in school, which wasn't much. I think the teacher spent one day talkin' about the war. He told us that elves snuck in un stole the golden hammer, then they raided our lands un that's why we hate 'em. We went to war over it. That's about all I know."

"If your teacher only spent one day discussing the Great War, then he did you, and every other student in the class, a disservice. The war is an important part of Dwarven history."

Thorgrim nodded. "I like history un maybe one day I can learn more about the war."

"That's a good idea. Those who fail to study history are doomed to repeat it. Don't forget that. As far as the hammer, you know, it wasn't just a golden hammer. It was the Aurumsmiter Hammer of the first dwarves. You're aware that the ancient dwarves made the Aurumsmiter Hammer as a gift to the Father God, Moridon?"

34

"Yeah, I read a book about it. I know the history of how the goat herders found the hammer, the stone tablets, un some other things in the Cave of the Winds a couple thousand years ago."

"The theft of the hammer is only one of the reasons dwarves still despise elves. Are you familiar with the details of the raids that happened a week after the theft of the hammer?"

"Our teacher told us that some grey elves attacked un robbed some people."

"That's an understatement," replied Dr. Thacker with a frown. "Thorgrim, have you ever been to Bur Dhulgren?"

"No, it's over a hundred miles from here. Except for a school field trip to Lake Vog, I haven't left this town since the day I was born."

"If you ever get the chance to go to the capital, make sure you visit the Grand Hall of the Dwarves Historical Museum. It's right across the street from the Supreme Library in the City Center. Go there, and you'll see other reasons why dwarves still hate the grey elves to this day. When you're in the museum, be sure you spend a lot of time in the Hall of Tears. What you'll see in there will shock you."

"If I ever get the chance, I'll do that. I don't know how to ride a horse, so I'd have to walk."

Dr. Thacker chuckled. "Someday, you'll get to visit the capital. Regarding elves, and most specifically, the grey-skins, don't misunderstand me. I'm not claiming that all greys are bad people. I'm sure there are some good ones too, but I'll admit that I've never met any. Nevertheless, the fact is that to this day, even centuries after the war, grey elves are not trusted by dwarves. Sadly, through the many years, this mistrust has spread and now includes all types of elves."

Thorgrim nodded. "I understand. Like I said, I was taught to never trust 'em."

The doctor checked his timepiece and sighed. "Thorgrim, I have to leave now. No worries, I won't say a word to anyone about your claustrophobia. I'll leave that to you, but hopefully, there'll be no need for you to say anything about it!"

Rising from the bed's edge, he closed his medical bag and continued. "You'll be fine. Promise me you'll go to work tomorrow? Just go in there with your father, and take it slow. You have to relax, and stop thinking the place is going to fall in on you."

Thorgrim paused before answering. Taking a deep breath, he said, "Okay, I promise, Doc. I'll go. But there are no spooks in there, right?"

Dr. Thacker shook his head. "No spooks."

"Un the mine won't cave in on me?"

"Nope!"

Thorgrim sighed. "Thankee, Doc."

"You're welcome! I'll be back to see how you are in a week or so, okay? Bye for now. Hey, lay off those magic 'shrooms, won't you? And by the way, I checked on the inside cover of that spook book you showed me. It's two months past due. I'm sure there are other books in this room that are in the same situation."

Thorgrim laughed, "Okay, no shrooms, un I'll return the overdue books. Thanks again!"

After a quick wave of goodbye, Dr. Thacker opened the door. When it swung open, Thorgrim's eavesdropping brother, fifteen-year-old Thurston, had his ear pressed so close to the door, that he fell into the bedroom and onto the doctor's boots.

As the miffed doctor helped the snooping teen to his feet, Thurston said, "Thorgrim, I'm tellin' dad that yer claustro—"

Interrupting the troublemaking, second-oldest child, Dr. Thacker covered the kid's mouth and grabbed him by the short beard that was only recently starting to sprout. Thurston was quickly hustled out into the hallway.

Dr. Thacker glared. "You, young man, will do no such thing!"

Using the teenagers short, peach fuzz beard, the big doctor pulled the pimply-faced redhead closer and looked straight down into his eyes.

Speaking in a low monotone, he said, "Now you listen, and you listen well, boy. I don't have time for little, sneaky eavesdroppers like you. You do know that elves are infamous for eavesdropping, don't you?"

Thurston shook his head, his eyes wide with fright.

"Yes, they are! How would you like me to declare that I examined you and discovered that you're really an elf? Maybe I'll tell all of your friends. Do you want me to do that?"

The teen continued to shake his head.

"Good! Then you won't say a word about what you heard? We have a deal?"

Speechless, Thurston nodded his head, yes.

Pulling the kid closer, the doctor said gruffly, "Pay attention. If I find out that you repeated anything you overheard to anyone, I'll give you a shot of a drug that will really turn you into an elf. In fact, it will turn you into a skinny girl elf. After that, you can go to school in the fall wearing a skirt and try to explain to your friends why you're a girl elf instead of a boy dwarf. Do you understand?"

While peeing himself, Thurston nodded and exclaimed, "Yes, I understand! I'm sorry, I'm sorry!

At that instant, Mrs. Longbeard, who had just overheard Thurston's apology, appeared in the hallway.

"Oh, I see Thurston finally apologized for stealing yer things!"

"Yes, he did apologize!" replied Dr. Thacker, releasing his hold of the teen's beard while patting him on his head. "You said he wanted to be a doctor one day, so I was telling him about some of the things we doctors can do!"

The moment Dr. Thacker finished his sentence, the rest of the children, giggling and yelling, scrambled down the hallway, past the doctor, bumping into him again and trampling his boots.

Dr. Thacker straightened his beard and said, "Thurston's a good kid as are **all** of your kids, Mrs. Longbeard."

Blushing, she replied, "Oh, thank you, doctor, that is so kind of you to say."

"Certainly, I meant every word of it."

"So you examined Thorgrim? Does he have the flu or was it those 'shrooms?"

Slipping by Marjorie in the narrow hallway, the doctor headed towards the front door.

"It might have been a little of both! But he's feeling much better now and he says that he'll be ready to go to work tomorrow!"

She beamed a huge smile. "Oh, my! Luthor will be so happy! I can't thank you enough, Dr. Thacker!"

As Dr. Thacker opened the door and stepped through, he turned to her and said, "My pleasure, ma'am. Oh, by the way. Just a moment ago, when your children about ran us over in the hallway . . . well, one of them stole my pipe and tobaccee, again. But that's okay," he said with a wink. "I'm trying to quit!"

III. The Vog Silver Mine

Twenty minutes before sunrise, while the hungry Longbeard children waited impatiently around the table, their mother prepared to serve another delicious breakfast.

Lifting the sizzling hot skillet from the stove, she announced, "Rabbit eggs and bacon, everyone! Yer favorite!"

All of the children cheered happily, bouncing in their chairs.

Luthor leaned over and whispered, "Margie, for the sake of bushy monobrows, when are ya gonna finally tell them that rabbits don't lay eggs?"

She smirked, whispering, "Husband, if they find out these are chicken's eggs, they won't eat them. They'll run away in disgust and never trust me again!"

Luthor replied softly, "Well, don't ya think that they learned in school that chickens lay eggs and not rabbits?"

Sliding some eggs and bacon onto her husband's plate, she replied in a quiet voice, "Probably, but this past school year they all brought home low grades, so I don't think they're paying much attention in class!"

Luthor gave his wife a quick peck on her cheek, then carried his plate over to the table and sat down.

Taking a bite of his breakfast, Luthor said, "As usual, the food tastes wonderful, honey. Speaking of food, did I tell you how incredible that delicious, spicy venison and possum snout stew was last night? It was yer best yet! I couldn't stop eating it!"

Marjorie replied with a laugh, "Well, you didn't say either way, but with all of the gas you were passing last night, I assume you must have eaten yer share and then some . . . but those fumes! May Moridon help us all!"

Luthor shrugged his shoulders and offered a big, buck-toothed grin.

The children plugged their noses and laughed loudly. Several claimed that they could hear their father's loud farting sounds all night long. The only one who was not present in the kitchen to comment on the gassy subject was Thorgrim.

Amidst the roaring laugh-fest, Luthor said, "All right, settle down! I can assure every one of you, that I've smelled my share of yer stinky diapers when you were babies!"

The children immediately calmed down but continued to snicker.

Looking around concerned, Luthor became agitated. "Where's Thorgrim? It's already almost six-thirty. I hope he's not sick again, for God's sake. I thought he said dat he was feeling good and would be coming to work with me today. Please, don't tell me dat—"

Marjorie replied, "Relax, husband. I'm sure he's feelin' fine. He might still be in bed. You know how he always oversleeps."

"Good morning, everyone," shouted Thorgrim as he dashed into the kitchen. "Sorry, I'm a bit late, but I couldn't find my pants!"

Luthor commented with a chuckle, "Probably buried under those piles of books, weren't they."

"Yes, exactly!" replied Thorgrim, sniffing. "Mmmmm! That bacon smells delicious, Mother, but I'll pass on those chicken eggs . . . uh, I meant to say, I'll pass on those rabbit eggs."

Marjorie spun around with a scowl and a headshake. The kids noticed her and laughed. Strolling over to the table, she delivered two large plates, heaping with fried eggs and fresh bacon.

"There you go. Pass the food around, please."

Thurston took the plate of eggs and pulled a couple off before passing it to his left. He said, "Mother, we know that rabbits don't lay eggs. We know these are chicken eggs. Guess what! We like 'em!"

With Luthor nodding and grinning, his wife uttered a sigh.

Nine-year-old Hannah complained, "Mama, Trancy keeps shoving bacon up his nose, and then he takes it out and eats it. It's gross!"

Marjorie looked at her youngest who was sitting in a highchair next to her. "I know, but he's two years old. It's what two-year-olds do."

"He's throwing food around, too."

Marjorie looked at Trancy. "What am I going to do with you?"

Trancy grinned and scrunched his nose.

Turning to Thorgrim, who was working on his breakfast, Luthor said, in-between bites, "Better hurry up, Son, we don't want to be late! It will take us fifteen to twenty minutes to get to work by seven. The clock-manager will chew our butts if we're late, and they'll dock our pay!"

Thorgrim nodded and began eating as fast as he could. Soon, he and his father were finished, and after quick hugs to everyone, they attached their lanterns to their belts, grabbed their lunchboxes in one hand and pickaxes in the other. With a final goodbye, they went out the door.

✳✳✳

When Mr. Longbeard and son had started the half-mile trek to the silver mine, Luthor glanced over and looked towards the east. Noticing the bright morning sun well above the horizon, he checked his timepiece. He sighed and said, "Oh, boy, it's already ten to seven. We need to hurry."

Walking as fast as they could along the foothills of the Brimgers, down the narrow, dusty road, they encountered neighbors and others going off to work. Most were on their way to the silver mine or to their jobs at the few local businesses that dotted the main street in the small town of Vog.

Although Luthor was annoyed that he was late once again, he was also extremely happy. He was excited that his oldest boy was finally coming to work with him, thus fulfilling the time-honored tradition of a son joining his father in the ore mines.

With both of their great beards, swaying back and forth as they hurriedly walked, Luthor said, "You know, Son, I can't say how pleased I am that yer actually goin' to join me in the mine! I remember the first time I went into the mine with my father. I sure miss workin' with him!"

Fearful that he would soon be entering the dreaded mine, Thorgrim did his best to hide his nervousness by continuing the conversation. "Why doesn't Grandpa Pistachio work in the mine anymore?"

"Well, Grandpa's a hundred and thirty-six years old now. Mandatory retirement age is one hundred and thirty. Remember when we threw him that retirement party?"

"Yes, Father. He got so drunk, that he spent three days with us. I remember because he had to use my bed, and I had to sleep with Thurston! That kid smells funny. What a horrible experience."

Luthor studied his son as they walked. Although he was concerned that Thorgrim might not like working in the mine, he was proud of him and loved him very much.

Luthor, at seventy-four years of age, (the equivalent of a thirty-seven-year-old human) was still young. Very poor because of the size of his family, he wanted a better life for Thorgrim than what the mine could provide. Luthor knew his son wanted to go to the university to study and perhaps one day become a writer, but the enrollment costs were far beyond what he could afford.

"Son, you know if you work hard in the mine and save yer money, maybe in a few years you can enter the university."

Thorgrim, aware that they were getting closer to the mine entrance, could hardly breathe, but he managed to reply with a smile, "Dr. Thacker mentioned that to me yesterday. He said that he saved his money and did the same thing."

"Ah, Dr. Thacker. He's a good dwarf and very wise. See, if Dr. Thacker could save his money and go to the university, so can you. You don't have to be like me and Grandpa Pistachio. He worked his whole life in the silver mine, and it looks like I'm goin' to be doin' the same thing. But I love this kind of work, and it's important to do what you love. Hey, look! There's the entrance to the silver mine! Let's pick up the pace, Son, we're late!"

Thorgrim looked up and turned white as a sheet. Before him, about fifty yards ahead was the entrance to the Vog Silver Mine. Carved into the side of the Brimger Mountain range was a massive entrance seventy-five feet wide. Off to the right was the small shack of Biff Knickers, the timeclock manager. In front of the shack stood a long line of dwarves waiting their turn to check-in, all of them late for work like Luthor and Thorgrim.

Panic had already sunk its claws into Thorgrim. Woozy, he slowed his pace.

As they marched towards the entrance, Luthor glanced back to tell Thorgrim that they needed to get in line to clock in. He noticed his son's complexion had turned as white as a sheet.

"What's the matter?" Luthor asked, puzzled. You don't look so good. Oh, for Moridon's beard, you're not feelin' sick again, are you?"

Without warning, Thorgrim stopped in his tracks and stared down at the ground.

"No, I uh, um," he stammered.

Luthor, now several feet ahead, turned around and approached Thorgrim.

"Son, what's the matter?"

Trembling and unable to answer, Thorgrim slowly raised his head. Still pale-faced, he fearfully looked towards the mine entrance.

"My God, Thorgrim. Are you afraid to go into the mine? Has this been the problem the whole time?"

Embarrassed, Thorgrim replied, "Yes, I am afraid to go in there!"

Glancing around to make sure no one else could hear, Luthor said, "But, why?"

Not knowing what to say, Thorgrim stared down at his boots, mumbling something unintelligible.

"What? I can't understand what yer sayin'. Look up at me."

Thorgrim, tears forming in the corners of his eyes, slowly looked up at his father.

41

Luthor frowned. "For the love of a frosty mug of ale, you really are afraid to go in the mine! What are you afraid of?"

"Spooks," replied Thorgrim, only able to admit one of the reasons.

"Spooks? What do you mean, spooks?"

"Ghosts, I guess."

"Ghosts? In the mine? Hehe, Thorgrim there are no ghosts in there or anywhere else for that matter! Who told you that?"

Thorgrim's eyes were wild. "Some of my friends like Zippy Borknoi and Rumbler McGeever. They warned me that the place is haunted with the ghosts of some dead miners!"

"Zippy and Rumbler told you that nonsense? Son, there's no such things as ghosts. Now, I heard a story that around a hundred and fifty years ago, some miners got lost somewhere deep in the mine and were never heard from again. I can't say that it's a true story, because there are only a few records left over from that time. It might just be a story someone made up. Either way, the story I heard didn't mention that they died, only that they got lost and were never found. Who knows, maybe they eventually got out, or maybe the story is made up!"

"But, Zippy and Rumbler said—"

"Son, Zippy and Rumbler probably heard the same story from someone and then told you."

Thorgrim took a deep breath and nodded. "Yeah, I guess that could be. But they told me that the dead miners will get me and kill me!"

Luthor continued but now wore a heavy scowl. "Zippy and Rumbler told you that pile of B.S., did dey? Hmmmm. Well, they're working in the mine with another team at the deepest part of one of the shafts. When I see dem, I'll straighten dem out for trying to scare you!"

"No, please, don't say anything to them. I'll be okay."

Luthor raised his brow. "Yer sure?"

Unable to tell his father the bigger problem, the fact that he was claustrophobic, Thorgrim nodded, took another deep breath and said, "Yeah, don't say a thing. Let's go, Papa."

"Okay, be prepared to get yer butt chewed by the clock manager, Mr. Knickers, though. We're already five minutes late for work! Hey, I almost forgot! Here's yer official Vog Silver Mine identification card! You'll present this card whenever you clock in and out for yer shift! Don't lose it!"

Thorgrim took the card from his father and nodded. Glancing at the card that had been filled out for him, he saw his name and other personal information.

Walking towards the entrance again, Luthor said, "Now, when we get in there, I'll show you the ropes, okay?"

"The ropes? Why do you use ropes in a silver mine?" asked Thorgrim naively.

"No, not real ropes, I mean, I'll teach you how to swing yer pickaxe to chip away at the ore and other things that you need to know."

"Oh, okay."

Getting into line, Luthor looked up and counted twenty dwarves in front of him. He and Thorgrim were last.

"By the gods, when we get up there, we'll really be in for it," warned Luthor. "But don't worry, the manager is all bark and no bite, however, he will dock our pay. Starting tomorrow, we're up an moving fast at dawn. No messin' around. We eat and then get our butts down here, okay?"

Thorgrim, still white-faced, nodded.

After ten minutes, it was finally Luthor and Thorgrim's turn to clock in for their shift.

Mr. Knickers looked up at both Luthor and Thorgrim. With a smirk and his monobrow furrowed, he said, "Well! Lookie here! Over fifteen minutes late! And if it ain't Beards— uh, I mean . . . Thorgrim! You finally made it! Feeling better, are we?"

Thorgrim mumbled, "Yes, better."

Frowning, Biff said, "Good! Well, here's some advice for ya, young one. Yer father is one of the best, so you learn what you can from him, okay? The only thing I don't want you to learn from him is how to be late for work every day! Your shift starts at 7:00 a.m. Please, remember that."

Thorgrim nodded, and Luthor grimaced.

Biff continued to frown. "Cards, please?"

Both presented their identification cards.

Biff worked the lever of the device that noted the time of their start of work, then waved them both on. "Lunch break is at noon. Yer father will explain the rest."

Luthor gestured to the mine entrance. "Son, go on ahead and wait for me by the front. I'll be right there."

Thorgrim slowly walked towards the mine entrance but only managed a few steps before coming to a stop, hardly able to breathe.

Turning to Biff, Luthor sneered and whispered, "You almost blew it! Don't you dare call him Beardby, or you'll be working that time clock from a hospital bed!"

Luthor, continuing to sneer, turned and walked towards his son, who was waiting near the entrance.

Biff was speechless and his complexion ashen. With a shrug of his shoulders, he swung his beard around and shouted, "Next! You're **all** late again, and—"

Biff stopped yelling suddenly when he realized there were no more dwarves in line. Shaking his head, he said to himself, "Ugh, I need a vacation."

Luthor overheard Biff and laughed. Pointing up towards the large opening, he said, "So, here we are, Son! Are ya ready? Now, remember, there are no spooks in here, so no worries! Follow me, and I'll introduce you to the crew!"

Thorgrim swallowed hard and followed behind Luthor, not looking up, watching his father's feet all the way in. Soon, they were inside the entrance.

Thorgrim knew it and tried to remain calm, although the thought of being beneath a billion tons of rock, horrified him. At least it was very cool inside, though he realized that once he started chipping away at the ore, he likely would be working up a good sweat.

Just inside the entrance was a large room. Here, at the beginning of the shift, all supervisors would meet with their crew before heading to their assigned areas.

Thorgrim counted three groups of twelve dwarves who had also arrived late for work. Two groups were entering a large mineshaft while being chewed out by their angry boss for being tardy. The last group belonged to his father. They were standing together, chatting. When they saw Luthor, they waved hello.

Luthor waved back as he approached them with Thorgrim. "Hey boys, sorry I'm late again, but ya know how things are.

One of them replied, "We dunna care if yer late, bawth! We're all clocked in un gettin' paid, either way!"

Luthor eyed the dwarf who had just spoken to him and said, "Hey, Kilgur, repeat what you just said, and slowly, please."

Kilgur shrugged and complied, "I said, we dunna care if yer late, bawth! We're all clocked in un gettin' paid, either way!"

Luthor stepped in close to Kilgur and sniffed. "You've been drinkin' that homemade brew of yers again dis morning? Don't deny it 'cuz I can smell it, and besides dat, yer not pronouncing some of yer words correctly! You know da rules. If yer wasted-drunk, clock out and go home!"

44

"But, yer not pronouncing some of yer words correctly either, bawth."

Luthor scowled heavily. "Dat's because I'm pissed off! How much have you had to drink?"

"Jus' a few tankards, dat's all, bawthy."

"Get out. I should fire yer butt right now. In fact, with my son comin' on board, one of you is going to get a transfer to make room for him. Likely, it will be you, Kilgur."

"Okay, okay, sorry bawth!" See ya tomorree, woohoo!"

Luthor bellowed. "Yeah, maybe. Lay off da booze during the workweek, ya fool!"

Kilgur offered a fat thumbs up, as he stumbled out of the mine.

"Okay, boys, come on! You all know da rules about coming to work drunk like he is! If any of the rest of you have been hitting the spirits hard already today, clock out and head home now!"

All of the crewmembers eyed each other and looked back at Luthor.

"Yer all sober? Every last one of ya? Last chance! If I find out later that any of ya is in an ale stupor, I'll beat the tar outta ya and den fire ya before ya hit the ground!"

Three of the remaining dwarves suddenly turned and headed for the exit, grumbling all the way, as dwarves always do.

Luthor yelled, "I lost four of ya today? By Moridon, you chaps need help! For the sake of bearded females everywhere, don't drink booze in the morning before coming to work! I suggest you all sign up for D.A. and attend every meeting!"

Thorgrim whispered to his father, "D.A. . . . what's D.A. mean?"

Luthor glanced back at his son and replied grimly, "Dwarfaholics Anonymous."

"Oh."

"The rest of ya pay attention because I would like ya to meet my son, Thorgrim Longbeard! He's nineteen years old and recently graduated from high school this past spring. I'm proud to announce that he's joining our crew today! He's been ill but is feelin' much better. Aren't ya, Son?"

Shy, Thorgrim could not look up from his own feet and innocently nodded his head.

"Son, I want ya to meet muh crew." Chuckling, he continued, "Well, what's left of 'em."

Pointing to each, Luthor introduced the remaining eight dwarves. "This is Yudelak, He's been with me the longest, and we like to call him Yoody."

"Yup, been working with yer papa over fifty years now!" said Yudelak, reaching towards Thorgrim for a handshake. "Pleasure to finally meet ya, Thorgrim."

Thorgrim shook Yudelak's hand. The veteran miner's hand was grizzled and so strong that it made Thorgrim wince when he gripped it.

Luthor continued, "This is Molky, Polis, Gaully, Thorn, Bloop, Jarv, and last but not least, Kregg. They've all been with me over forty years, now.

"Hello, Thorgrim! Good to have ya aboard," said Gaully. The rest came forward and each shook Thorgrim's hand.

"Thorgrim, if you can work half as hard as yer father, you'll be a bonus to this crew!" commented Bloop.

Luthor, proud as ever, smiled. "Son, when the rest of the guys sober up and come back to work tomorrow, I'll introduce them. Meanwhile, let's get at it! Son, follow me. We're going to walk to our assigned area in the mine. The rest of ya get in behind Thorgrim."

Gesturing towards the tunnel entrance straight ahead, Luthor said, "Thorgrim, this is called the Main Shaft. It's like the main highway into the mountain. Everything comes and goes through this mineshaft."

Thorgrim took a good look at the Main Shaft entrance, guessing it to be over twenty feet wide and eight feet high.

As Luthor led the way into the Main Shaft, Thorgrim followed behind his father, and though his claustrophobia teased him, he tried his best not to panic. The eight remaining sober crewmembers, marched behind Thorgrim as ordered.

As they went forward, Thorgrim looked around in the musty-smelling shaft, though he was afraid to look up at the heavy timber that helped support the mine's ceiling, fearing that as soon as he did, it would all come crashing down on everyone.

The well-lit Main Shaft was decorated top to bottom with many burning oil lanterns as well as a few signs warning employees about the dangers within. Thorgrim noticed that several attendants were checking the oil in the lamps, refilling some and relighting others. Far off in the distance, deep in the system, he could hear workers singing and the pinging of their pickaxes chipping away chunks of silver ore from the cavern's walls.

Thorgrim, trying his best to keep up with his father, whispered, "Papa, how did you know those guys were drunk back there?"

"When a dwarf drinks over his limit, he tends to talk a bit funny. Every dwarf is affected by this differently, so sometimes it's hard to tell."

"Oh, I see."

46

"One day, you'll develop a taste for malted beverages of one kind or another. Typically ale! I can guess you probably already have, but make sure you control it, or over-indulgence can get ya into all kinds of trouble . . . oh, and make sure ya don't tell yer mother! Remember, yer not legally old enough to drink or smoke until yer twenty!"

Like most teenagers, Thorgrim had experimented with alcohol and smoking but quickly discovered that he disliked both. Slightly embarrassed, he changed the subject.

"Hey, Papa, there are lanterns lit up all along the way in here. Why do we need to bring our own lantern?"

"Well, in case of an emergency. You never know when you might need some light down here."

"Don't ya mean **in** here?" asked Thorgrim, more nervous than ever. "What do you mean **down** here?"

"Well, Son, we are going down and in. On the Main Shaft, we actually go down into the ground. There are other shafts that branch off, most of them go up into the mountain. The silver ore veins flow in different directions. In this mine, the richest ore is typically below ground level."

The topic of the conversation was causing Thorgrim panic attacks. Dizzy, he did his best to hide his anxiety.

"But Dr. Thacker said that we don't go below ground level in the mines!"

"Well, Dr. Thacker is kinda wrong about that. In many mines, you won't go below ground level, but in this mine we do. What are you worried about? Look, I already told you that there are no ghosts in here."

"I'm not worried about anything," lied Thorgrim, still doing his best to hide his claustrophobia.

After several more minutes of trudging along, with the crew whistling some strange song, nervous and nauseated, he asked his father, "I feel like we've been walking for an hour! How much further?"

Yudelak, walking behind Thorgrim, overheard him and replied, "We've only been walking for about ten minutes! No worries, not much further. About a half-mile past Hub Three."

"About a half-mile! Are ya kiddin'?" asked the agitated teen. "And what's Hub Three?"

Pointing to a wide wooden door, up ahead on the left side of the Main Shaft, Luthor said, "Well, that's the entrance to Hub One and across from it on the other side of the shaft is Hub Two."

Thorgrim looked at both doors, which had large, steel ring handles and a number '1' and '2' painted on them, respectively.

"Hubs?"

"Our assigned Hub is number three," replied Luthor. "I'll explain what the hubs are when we get to ours in a few minutes."

Yudelak said, "Hey, Thorgrim, just be thankful we're not at the Main Shaft point! That's probably another half-mile beyond where we'll be

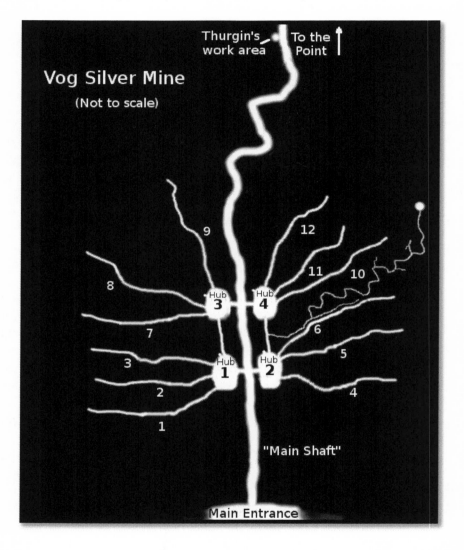

working. It's a crazy, winding tunnel and down below the ground another five hundred feet deeper!"

Anxious and dizzy with claustrophobia, Thorgrim grimaced and said, "It's crazy and winding, is it? Uh, well, why's it called the Main Shaft point?"

Yudelak replied, "There are technically several areas that we call the point. It's the furthest dug out area in any particular shaft. When an area is stripped of silver ore, we bring in heavy picks and dig deeper for a week or so to lengthen the shaft. The excavation usually exposes more silver ore. When not, we start digging in different directions until we find more. When we add to the length of the shaft, the very end of it is called the point."

Thorgrim, already frightened by the thought of being so far underground, now heard several squeaking sounds straight ahead. He had heard this sound before and stopped dead in his tracks, his blood running ice-cold with fear. The other dwarves, following close behind, took turns colliding with whoever was in front of them.

"Giant rats!" yelled Thorgrim.

Luthor, hearing the commotion, unsure about what was happening behind him, turned and saw that his son was frozen with fright and several of the crew were lying on the ground, struggling to get up.

"Giant rats?" said Luthor, pointing ahead, chuckling. "No, that's an ore cart, probably one of the night shift crews running a bit late trying to fill their ore quota."

Looking at the rest, he shouted, "Get up, ya fools, and watch where yer goin'!" He finished with a big laugh.

Ahead, in the dim light, three dwarves were seen pulling a large cart full of silver ore, en route to the entrance for distribution to horse-drawn wagons. When filled, the wagons would deliver the ore to the massive smelting facility in Vumfumik, on the outskirts of Bur Dhulgren. From there, the smelted silver, like all other metals mined in the Dwarven Clans, was used for multiple purposes including coinage, jewelry, or for trading in the markets.

Thorgrim, embarrassed because he caused an unneeded disturbance, watched in silence as the three weary dwarves pushed the heavy cart past him. Offering a nod, they went by Luthor's crew and then on to the mine's entrance, the wheels squeaking and sounding exactly like a few giant rats.

Luthor laughed again. "Giant rats! Ha! Well, one thing's fer sure; there aren't any giant rats in these mines, right boys?"

"Dat's right," cried out a couple of them as they got back in line behind Thorgrim.

"Why's that? Why no rats?" asked Thorgrim curiously.

"The giant snakes ate 'em all!" replied Kregg, jokingly.

Hating snakes, Thorgrim cried out loudly, "Giant snakes?"

Pointing back at his crew, Luthor said, "Knock it off, will ya?"

Looking at Thorgrim, he continued, "No worries, he's only kiddin', Son. There are no rats or snakes. All the noise and racket we make in here has scared off everything except a few bats and bugs. I assure ya, there's nothin' in here that can hurt any of us. Come on you guys, quit goofin' around, we've got work to do. Let's move it!"

Continuing along the Main Shaft, after a few minutes, Luthor stopped and pointed to two more doors that looked exactly like the two he saw earlier. This time, the one on the left had the number '3' painted on it, and the one on the right had the number '4.'

"Hub Three is ours," Luthor said, as he pushed open the heavy door. "Come on in, and I'll show you around."

Luthor entered first, with Thorgrim and the rest of the group following. They were now standing in an oblong-shaped area that was over fifty feet long, thirty feet wide, with a ten-foot-high, reinforced ceiling. The room was well-lit, having many burning lanterns hanging from hooks on the walls. Not including the main door, there were four large openings and a big, whitewashed door. The room also contained various tables and chairs and other items.

Luthor was about to explain what the area was used for when he noticed a group of a dozen dwarves entering Hub Three from a cut-out opening that was the entrance to Shaft Nine.

The dwarves were part of the night shift and had been working the point in Shaft Nine. They were on their way to clock out and head home for the day.

The lead dwarf, dirty and exhausted, waved his hand and said, "Morning, Luthor! Hello there, fellow miners!"

Luthor and his crew returned the friendly greeting.

Seeing a young, teenage dwarf standing next to Luthor, the lead dwarf continued, "Hey, Luthor, is that yer boy, Beardby?"

Trying to control his temper, Luthor responded, "Yes, it is, and his name is Thorgrim, not Beardby."

The lead dwarf nodded and the rest, who were following behind him, waved hello to everyone. However, a few chuckled or tugged on their beards, as they exited the hub and headed towards the mine entrance.

Luthor offered his son a half-grin. "Sorry, Son. You know, yer kinda famous."

"I know, it's okay. I don't mind."

Luthor rubbed his son's head. "Well, everyone deserves to be called by their proper name."

Looking around, Thorgrim noticed several sets of chairs and tables as well as extra lanterns, standard and heavy pickaxes, sledgehammers, medical kits, food, jugs of water and other supplies. There was a wide path in the middle, so the filled ore carts could be brought through on their way out to the front.

"So this is a hub?" asked Thorgrim. "What's this place used for?"

"I was about to tell you," replied Luthor. "Like I said, this is called Hub Three, and it is one of four primary areas that are connected to adjoining mineshafts. In each of these areas, there's room for over fifty dwarves to take breaks, eat lunch, et cetera. You'll notice that there are all kinds of supplies and other things here also. The path in the middle is where the filled ore carts are pulled through and then eventually outside where they are weighed and then unloaded."

Next to a whitewashed door, Thorgrim saw a large stack of corncobs sitting inside of a huge wooden crate. Several cobs were scattered on the floor next to it. He asked, "What's with the corncobs?"

Luthor grinned. "Oh, almost forgot to tell ya that each hub has its own Crapola." Pointing towards the white door, he continued, "It's right in there if ya need to go. Just take a corncob or two along, if ya feel the need. Just don't lean over too far and fall in. If ya do, well . . . just don't lean over too far. I'm serious. When using the Crapola, hang on to the handles."

Understanding the purpose of the room, Thorgrim's brow crumpled a bit, because he had never heard of the word 'crapola.'

"Crapola?"

"Yes, it's a latrine . . . ya know, like our outhouse back home, 'cept this one is huge. Ya just go in there and do yer thing, and all of it empties down a big hole and into an underground stream!"

Thorgrim wrinkled his face. "An underground stream? But, where does that go to?"

"Yes, there are several underground streams deep below us. As far as where everything goes, well, we don't know for sure, and I feel pity for whoever is at the other end of it! Earlier generations of miners built the crapolas tons of years ago, that's all I know."

Yudelak laughed. "There ya go again, Luthor. You Mharrakian dwarves sure have a funny way of talkin'! I'll never get over it."

"What'd I say that was funny?" Luthor asked, his brow low.

Yudelak shook his head, chuckled and replied, "You said, 'tons of years ago.' A ton is the weight of something, you know, like silver ore . . . not a number! How many times do I have to tell ya that? We Plutarg dwarves are taught that in the second grade! Tons of years . . . haha! Been workin' with ya for over fifty years and it still drives me nuts when you midwestern Mharraks talk like that!"

51

Luthor shook his head and said, "Elf crap. A ton is a huge number, and there is nothin' wrong with usin' the word, so shut yer flapper!" he finished with a loud belly laugh while slapping Yudelak on his cheek playfully.

Yudelak slid his pipe into his mouth, lit it and grinned.

Luthor looked back at his son. "Hmmmm, don't pay any attention to that guy. Okay, where was I? Oh, yes! So, Thorgrim, if ya have to go, that's the place. Just don't fall in!"

Thorgrim nodded, but then a thought crossed his mind. "But, some of the mineshafts are a long ways from here. Um . . . what do you do if you can't make it back here to use the Crapola?"

Gaully said, "Dig a hole with yer pick and do yer thing. Just make sure ya bury it! A smart miner will always grab a few cobs to take along, just in case."

Thorgrim, grimacing, replied, "Oh, okay. I'll try to remember that."

Gesturing with his index finger towards a few of the shaft openings, Luthor said, "Son, here in the hub, there are four shafts and each has a number posted above its entrance. We have shafts seven, eight, and nine in here. That shaft over there takes you directly to Hub One. Got that?"

"Yes."

Luthor said, "The Main Shaft is the original shaft and the biggest. Most of these other shafts continue up into the belly of the mountain, while the Main Shaft gradually continues downward, deeper underground. The area we will work in is down the Main Shaft about a quarter mile or so. Are ya sure yer getting all of this?"

Slightly dizzy, though doing his best to shrug off the claustrophobia, Thorgrim replied with a sigh, "Yes. I think so."

Luthor continued, "Yudelak mentioned something called 'the point.' Including the Main, there are thirteen working shafts cut into the mountain and each shaft has an end, or 'point', which is its deepest penetration in the mine system. There are also some maintenance tunnels and some temporary shafts. Those are off-limits and dangerous. Stay out of them."

Thorgrim nodded, his claustrophobia raging.

Luthor pointed towards the hub's main door. "Okay, let's get out of here and head down to our area. We'll be back here for lunch, but first, grab a pair of eye goggles and a helmet . . . they're in those big boxes over by the table. Ya don't want to bang yer noggin or lose an eye down here do ya? And everyone, don't forget to grab some water and some cobs on the way outta here too!"

All of them complied and then followed Luthor out of the hub and into the Main Shaft.

Once everyone was back in the Main Shaft, Luthor started to walk towards their designated work area, which was still about twelve hundred feet further into the system. The clinking sounds of the many pickaxes striking the shaft walls could be heard.

Luthor said, "Hear that? That's the sound of miners working! Something we should be doin', right now."

He gestured ahead and said, "Our work area is probably a bit less than a quarter-mile further, and the point is down at the very end, probably another half-mile mile beyond our area! Although there has never been a cave-in accident in the history of the Vog Silver Mine, the Main Shaft is the deepest and by far the most dangerous place to be, especially at the point, because you're furthest from the exit."

Thorgrim, nauseous and extremely nervous, tripped and stumbled into his father's back. "Then I don't want to work at the Main Shaft point, or any point for that matter," he complained, wild-eyed with fear.

Luthor glanced back, "Son, watch yer step in here! Thorgrim, everyone has to eventually work at the point. We take turns. Once a month, each crew is rotated.

"And we're assigned to the Main Shaft?" stammered Thorgrim, trembling. "It's the deepest and most dangerous shaft, is it?"

"Yes, the Main Shaft," replied his father.

"Then, when is it our turn to go to the point?" asked Thorgrim, now battling serious vertigo while bug-eyed with apprehension.

His father replied, "Funny you should ask. We go up there at the end of this month."

Thorgrim fainted straightaway, though Yudelak caught him before he hit the ground.

The next thing Thorgrim knew was that his father was slapping him on his cheeks, while a couple of the others splashed water on his face, as they tried to help him to his feet.

Luthor exclaimed, "Moridon's beard! Son, you fainted. What happened? Are ya feelin' sick again?"

Thorgrim, queasy, was unable to admit the truth. White as a sheet, he replied, "No, I uh, I don't know what happened to me! Maybe it's the stale air down here."

"Ya think the air's stale?" asked Luthor. "The shafts are fully ventilated with fresh air. Are ya sure yer okay?"

Out of excuses, Thorgrim replied, "Yes, I . . . I'm okay now. Sorry! I don't know why I fainted!"

Luthor leaned in close to his son and whispered, "Are ya **sure** yer okay?"

Thorgrim, with embarrassment written all over his face, nodded. His mind spun in circles trying to figure out how he was going to overcome his claustrophobia and get any work done.

Not wanting to let his father down, though knowing he was going to hate the job, he tried to appear excited and said, "Yes, I'm feeling great now. Okay, let's get in there! I can't wait to learn how to use the pickaxe!"

His father smiled. "Okay, that's my boy! Hear that, lads? He's feelin' great and is ready to start work, so let's do it! Follow me!"

***

Luthor motioned to his crew. "Ok, get yer goggles and helmets on!"

After everyone followed his order, he pointed towards the mineshaft wall. "Thorgrim, see the black and silver streaks here and there in those grey-colored rocks? Those are veins of silver! We need to break chunks of that outta the shaft wall and load it into the carts. The rock is extremely dense, so you won't get much with each swing. Sometimes, you have to whack it a few times first with one of the heavy sledgehammers. Yudelak has one if you need it, but watch how I do it with the pick."

Luthor then took his own pickaxe, gripped it with both hands and swung the pointed head into the cavern wall, causing a 'plink' sound. A few small pieces of rock fell away and onto the floor.

"Okay, Son, did ya see how I did that? It will take some time, but do that until ya get a nice pile of rock at yer feet, and then toss 'em into one of the carts with one of those shovels over there."

He pointed to several, large-mouth shovels leaning against the shaft wall nearby.

"Now the trick is to choke up on the handle, like this," continued Luthor, demonstrating how to hold and swing a pickaxe. "There's no need to overdo the swing either. Keep a firm grip so the head don't spin on ya. Take a deep breath, bring it back over yer shoulder, and with a nice, smooth swing, strike the wall. It's important to let the weight of the axe do most of the work. And, take yer time in-between swings, or you'll be exhausted before ya know it!" Got that so far?"

"Yes, I think so, Papa."

"Oh, almost forgot, make sure no one is standing behind ya when you pull it back over yer shoulder! Hah! If ya accidentally hit someone in the face, it wouldn't be pretty, would it!"

Luthor noticed his son was shivering. "Hey, why are yer teeth a chatterin'?"

"It's cold in here."

Most of the others snickered.

Jarv said, "It's cold in here, that's fer damn sure! But after about an hour swingin' and loadin' rock, you'll be sweatin' to beat hell!"

Luthor nodded and said, "He's right, Son. It'll get warm in here soon enough. Now I want ya to try using yer pickaxe a few times. Hold it un swing it just like I did."

Thorgrim grabbed his pickaxe, held it exactly as his father told him and swung it a few times. 'Plink!' 'Plink! Chink, plunk!' The blows only managed to send sparks flying off the incredibly strong rock, but eventually, several small pieces fell to the ground. When one of the larger fragments landed, it broke apart on impact, exposing a raw silver nugget twice the size of Thorgrim's thumb.

"Wow! What a lucky devil you are, boy!" exclaimed Molky. "A silver nugget is rare as rare can be, and that has to be one of the largest I've ever seen!"

The rest of the crew approached to look at the nugget lying at Thorgrim's feet. With everyone standing so close to him, Thorgrim now felt trapped, and his claustrophobia screamed at him. About to faint, his father swatted him on the back, surprising him.

"Yes, the company will pay a bonus for any nuggets found! Put it in yer pocket, but don't forget to report it when you leave at the end of yer shift! Hey, will you boys step back a few feet? Ya greedy bastages are standing so close, that I can smell wut ya had for dinner two weeks ago!"

Grumbling, the crew retreated.

"And get to work swinging yer picks. We've got carts to fill, and we're behind schedule. I'll work with muh son, and get him up to speed, meanwhile, the eight of you split up into two groups of four."

Now feeling that he had some space to breathe, Thorgrim picked up the heavy nugget, then placed it in his pocket.

"Son, the company wants each team to fill two carts in a shift," said Luthor, pointing to several wheeled carts nearby. "The carts hold about five hundred pounds of rock each. That's a half a ton of ore per crew every day. On average, each miner will extract about eighty pounds a day. That doesn't sound like much, but this rock is as hard as iron!"

Thorgrim's eyes widened. "We have to mine a half-ton a day? That's a lot of silver!"

His father chuckled. "Nah, it's mostly just rock. After it's sent to the smelter and processed, they get very little silver out of it. I heard in a whole year, they'll end up with maybe a ton of actual silver."

"I can hear a lot of pickaxes chipping away," said Thorgrim. "How many miners are working in this place?"

"During the eight-hour day shift, when we're fully staffed, there's twelve crews totaling one hundred and sixty-eight dwarves! At night, there's four, twelve-man teams of forty-eight dwarves. Each crew has at least one supervisor. Normally, supervisors don't swing a pick, but I'm an exception!"

Molky stopped working and grinned. "Ya, yer papa was born with a pickaxe in his hand, and he'll prolly die with one in it, too!"

"Probably right, Molky," replied Luthor with a laugh.

"Son, anyway, when we get a cart filled, we'll pull it out of here and out to the front. Once you're out there, you'll unload the stuff in a big ore wagon."

Bloop said, "Thorgrim, you're working with the most experienced crew in the entire mine! When everyone's here, we can usually fill a cart in only three hours! We only need to fill two, so if we get done early, we can leave if we want for the day."

Gaully laughed and said, "Or we can take plenty of breaks if we want! Good time for nappin', smokin' yer pipe, drinkin' some ale, maybe telling a few ghost stories and stuff."

Thorgrim dropped his pick. "Ghost stories?"

Everyone stopped working and grinned.

Thorgrim was numb. Battling his claustrophobia and now worried about spooks again, he glanced around nervously, looking carefully at any dark areas in the mineshaft.

Gaully lowered his brow and gave Thorgrim a sinister look. Slowly nodding, he replied, "Ya, and I've got me some good ones, and they're all true! Some real hair-raisers! The walking dead, vampires and stuff. Yer beard will be standin' straight up by the time I'm—"

Luthor gave Gaully a nudge, interrupting him. "Hmmmph! Shut it! Uh, Gaully's only kiddin', Son. New rule everyone! No ghost stories in the mine. Muh son's a bit nervous down here anyway, we don't need to make it worse. He's already heard some B.S. about a few dead miners wandering around in the mine from some troublemaking kids."

Gaully grabbed his pick and went back to work. While swinging his axe, he said, "I'm sorry Thorgrim. They're just made up stories for fun. None of dem are true."

Thorgrim waved, "It's okay."

Luthor yelled, "The rest of you, get yer arses to swingin' those picks! Damn yer rotten hides and yer mommas', too!"

The group hurriedly started chipping away at the walls.

Luthor turned back to his son and whispered, "No spooks in here, okay? I promise."

Thorgrim forced a half-smile.

"Okay, Son, it's you and me today! Let's get at it and start fillin' a cart. Maybe we can go home early!"

***

For the next several hours, despite missing a few dwarves, the group managed to fill one of the ore carts. Despite his battle with claustrophobia, Thorgrim learned quickly, easily extracting his share of the ore. Although he desperately hated the work, he still hoped it would grow on him, because he wanted to please his father.

But it was not growing on him. In fact, he found mining to be very boring. However, Thorgrim was a creative person with a vivid imagination. In an effort to make the work more fun, while using his pick, he pretended he was digging for a buried treasure chest, or battling a monstrous dragon, a creature that ironically, he did not believe existed.

Sometimes, his pretending got the better of him. During his imaginary quests or battles, he swung his pick too hard and fast causing him to become exhausted. His father, proud and impressed by his son's eagerness, had to tell him to slow down.

***

On Thorgrim Longbeard's first day working as a miner, the lunch whistle shrieked precisely at noon as it always did.

When it blew, despite company rules against running in the mines, and as they always did, the daytime crew of approximately one hundred and sixty hungry dwarves, on their way to eat lunch, would stampede through the tunnels and shafts like an army of starving mice racing to get to the last piece of cheese in the entire realm.

Instantly, over the sound of the whistle, you could hear almost every pickaxe in the mine system simultaneously hit the ground followed by cascading roars of 'Hurrah!' Loud choruses of happy singing would then ensue as well as plenty of swearing by some of the faster dwarves who were blocked by the slower ones . . . often leading to heated arguments or violent fistfights.

The company was not overly strict regarding the so-called 'lunch hour', after all, it took several minutes for the miners to reach their assigned hubs and over ten minutes for those on the Main Shaft point. Usually, the lunch hour would turn into two or more hours, but it did not matter as long as each team's ore quota of one thousand pounds was met by the end of the day.

While most preferred eating in the Hubs, several other of the more seriously introverted types instead headed for the exits. Once outside, they could eat, smoke and enjoy some sunshine by themselves, or maybe sneak some ale that they had concealed in various hiding places.

It was now lunchtime on Thorgrim's first day working in the mines.

It would also be his last day, as well.

During lunch, a traumatic event would occur that would change his life forever.

IV. Of Claustrophobia and Spooks

Hub Three was full to the brim with hungry dwarves who were eating their lunch and heavily engaged in conversation with fellow workers. Thorgrim was seated with his father and the rest of his crew at the end of a long table near the middle of the room.

Gaully, sitting across from Thorgrim, tapped the table with his knuckles to get the young dwarf's attention.

"What ya got to eat there, Thorgrim?" he said loudly, trying to talk above the bedlam caused by over forty yapping dwarves.

Opening his lunchbox, Thorgrim looked in it and replied, "Looks like my momma made me a turtle belly sandwich with black cheese and a side of fried mouse heads! Mmmm!" He was surprised that he had any appetite at all, considering the nausea and fatigue he felt due to his claustrophobia.

Gaully smiled. "Oh, that sounds incredibly delicious!" Looking into his own box, he suddenly scowled. "Well, I sure loves me wifey, but she cooks almost as bad as I do, and I'm the worst cook in the realm!"

Frowning, he pulled out his lunch. It was a cold, bison lip sandwich, topped with moldy, green cheese and seasoned with chicken-bone powder. When he started to unwrap it, a note dropped onto the table. It had a pink-colored, lipstick-kiss stain on it.

Molky teasingly said, "Awww! Gaully! Yer wife sent along a love note! That's so nice!"

Gaully, turning red with embarrassment, quickly grabbed the note and tossed it back into his lunchbox.

"Ain't ya gonna read it?" asked Yudelak. "Muh wife hasn't sent me a love note since we were married fifty years ago!" he complained, with a sigh.

Polis snickered. "So, yer girlfriends make up for that, don't they, Yoody?"

Yudelak exploded. "Shut it, Polis. Shut yer trap! In fact, shove that pathetic beard you have inside yer mouth, so you can't talk!"

"I'm just jokin'," replied Polis with a frown. "Jeez, Yoody, you need to take an anger management class or somethin'."

Yudelak was still ticked. Shaking a big index finger towards Polis, he bellowed, "I don't have any girlfriends! I'm devoted to muh wife."

"Alright, alright," hollered Luthor. "You all shut it and get to eatin.'"

Opening his own lunchbox, Luthor found the same lunch that Thorgrim had, except, like Gaully, he also found a love note. It was a small piece of paper with a big, red lipstick-kiss stain on the front.

Gaully noticed Luthor's note and smiled, "See, even the boss got a love note! If you idiots haven't noticed yet, two of us got love notes from our missus and the rest of you didn't get any! Hmmmm, let's see, I have eight kids, and Luthor's working on number thirteen! You all have how many? None or maybe one? What does that tell ya? Hahahaho!"

Bloop said, "Gaully, you have eight kids, and the boss is working on thirteen? It tells me why you and the boss are always broke!"

Gaully shook his head. "That's not quite what I was lookin' for."

Yudelak smiled. "Hmmm. Tells me that the rest of us better start payin' more attention to our wives!" The comment caused the entire crew to roar with laughter.

Everyone, except Thorgrim.

He was puzzled. "I'm sorry, but I don't get the joke."

"Someday you'll get it, kid!" replied Gaully. "But if you play yer cards right with yer future missus, you'll never have to worry about it!" he said, before taking a big bite out of his sandwich.

After about a half-hour, Thorgrim had finished his lunch first. Worried about going back into the Main Shaft, he tried not to think about it, instead focusing on all of the ruckus in the hub. However, he became bored watching the others eat and chatter.

Luthor noticed that Thorgrim was a bit restless and said, "Son, we'll be a while yet, so if yer done, feel free to explore the room and maybe introduce yerself to some of the other miners here. They're all a friendly bunch."

"Oh, okay," replied Thorgrim as he stood from his chair.

"Don't go wandering off into one of the service shafts, 'cuz it's easy to get lost, or worse," added Luthor, while several of the others grunted and nodded in agreement.

"Okay, Papa."

Thorgrim, ever the shy one, decided he would avoid the other dwarves and keep to himself. Curious, he walked over to a map of the mine system that was on one of the walls. A quick glance at the map revealed how big and intricate the silver mine was. While he was studying the layout, he heard a strange noise coming from somewhere in the room.

"Pssst, pssst!"

Thorgrim glanced around, unable to locate the source of the weird sound due to the loud bantering of the dwarves in the hub.

"Hey, Beardby! Over here!"

Looking all the way to his left, he saw two heads, both with scruffy brown beards, sticking into Hub Three's entrance from the Main Shaft. It was two of his former high school classmates, the troublemakers Zippy Borknoi and Rumbler McGeever.

Gesturing and grinning, they signaled for Thorgrim to come to them.

Glancing back at his father, who was still eating and in the middle of a deep conversation with some of his crew, Thorgrim hesitated. Looking back at Zippy and Rumbler, he saw that they were still gesturing.

Zippy said, "Come on, Beardby! We want to show you something really cool!"

Unable to resist the temptation, though he knew better, Thorgrim approached Zippy and Rumbler.

Zippy, the leader of the two, said, "Hey, Beardby, so you finally made it into the mine! We've been lookin' for ya since we graduated! Rumbler and me are workin' with my pops in Shaft Twelve off of Hub Four. Where ya been?"

"Ya, where ya been?" asked Rumbler.

Thorgrim shrugged. "Been sick, that's all. I'm fine now."

"Good! Hey, ya want to see something really amazin'?" asked Zippy, excitedly. "We found something special a few days ago down in a tunnel! It's cool, and we didn't tell anyone about it! You're gonna want to see this, I'm tellin' ya!"

"Ya, you're gonna want to see this!" said Rumbler.

"What did ya find?" asked Thorgrim, curious.

Zippy leaned over and whispered into Thorgrim's ear, "Diamonds!"

Rumbler leaned in and repeated what Zippy said, "Ya, diamonds!"

"Diamonds in a silver mine?" asked Thorgrim, scratching his beard.

Zippy placed a finger up to his lips. "Shhhhh! Not so loud! Yes, right in this silver mine! They are extremely rare, red diamonds! Worth a fortune!"

"Ya, worth a fortune!" repeated Rumbler.

Zippy turned and scowled at Rumbler.

"Hey, Rumbler, will ya shut yer hole? Why do you always have to repeat everything I say? Besides, yer breath smells like a banana peel that was used to scrub an outhouse floor! Get back away from me, will ya?"

Rumbler pouted. "Sorry, Zippy! I always told ya I got yer back. I'm only repeating what ya say, cuz yer right 'bout everything, just like ya say you always are!"

Zippy smirked and said, "Fine, but would ya mind watching my back from about ten feet away?"

Rumbler, still pouting, nodded and retreated a few steps.

Turning back to Thorgrim, Zippy sighed and continued, "Okay, so we still have some time before this mountain full of bearded boozers all decide to go back to work! Want to see these diamonds or not? I'll split 'em with ya, cuz yer a good pal an all!"

"Uh, I don't know."

"What, are ya kiddin'? Just think. One of the diamonds could pay for a full tuition at the university!"

Thorgrim eyes widened with excitement. "Really? A full tuition?"

Zippy smiled. "Ya! All three of us could afford to go, and think about how much fun we'd have partying all the time! I mean, don't ya want to get out of this dreadful place, or would you rather spend the next twenty years in this dirty hole?"

Glancing back at his father, Thorgrim said, "I would love to see the diamonds! But, my papa—"

Zippy frowned. "Forget yer pops! Hey, think of how happy he'll be when you show him a couple of those valuable red diamonds! He could retire a wealthy man!"

Ten feet behind Zippy, Rumbler said, "Ya, think of how happy he'll be when you show him a—"

Interrupting Rumbler, Zippy turned, glared at him, put an index finger up to his lips and said, "Shhhhhhhh!" he finished with a flap of his red beard.

Zippy grasped Thorgrim by his sleeve. "Come on! We may not have much time! Follow us!"

Thorgrim surrendered and agreed to go.

With Zippy leading the way, Thorgrim followed directly behind him with Rumbler taking the rear.

The trio exited Hub Three, crossed the Main Shaft and entered into Hub Four. Thorgrim noticed the room was identical to Hub Three and it was also full of hungry dwarves who were busy eating their lunch. Unnoticed by everyone, Zippy led everyone across the room and into the entrance of a hundred-foot shaft that led to Hub Two.

"So, where are these diamonds?" asked Thorgrim.

"They are off of this short shaft between Hub Two and Four! We were exploring a few days ago and found the diamonds in another tunnel in here!"

About halfway to Hub Two, Zippy stopped and pointed to a wooden panel that was blocking the entrance to a maintenance shaft.

"The diamonds are in here a ways! Follow me!"

Thorgrim's claustrophobia reared its ugly head. Frightened, he said, "But the sign says no admittance. It's a tunnel? I don't think I want to go in there."

"Why do you think they posted that sign?" asked Zippy with a scowl. "They want to keep all of the diamonds to themselves!"

"Oh, okay, but I was told to stay out of those places."

"Now ya know why! No worries! It's not much further!"

Zippy slid the panel out of the way and stepped into the shaft.

"Hurry, follow me," he said, in a whisper.

With only a couple lanterns mounted on the walls, it was much darker in the hardly used service shaft.

Despite his claustrophobia and the warnings by his father to stay out of the service shafts, Thorgrim could not overcome the temptation to see the diamonds, so he followed Zippy with Rumbler pushing him from behind.

About a hundred feet into the winding shaft, Zippy suddenly grabbed Thorgrim and abruptly pulled him into the entrance of another, much older, abandoned exploration tunnel. It was pitch dark.

Thorgrim, surprised, resisted and said, "Zippy, what are ya doing? It's dark. I can't see a thing in here!"

Zippy lit his lantern and said, "Better light yer lantern if you want to see anything inside this place. Hey, Rumbler, light yer lantern."

Thorgrim, trying to hide his fear from his friends, grabbed the lantern that was hooked to his waist belt and lit it. Rumbler lit his lantern, as well.

Zippy said, "Come on and stay with me. The diamonds are down this tunnel just a little further!"

Rumbler, following right behind Thorgrim, gave him a little push and said, "Ya, follow him! The diamonds are down this tunnel just a little further!"

Thorgrim's inner voice told him 'no' and warned him to turn back, but the voice of greed was louder. Even louder than the voice of his claustrophobia.

On they went, meandering back and forth, for what seemed like forever.

Thorgrim started to panic. "Hey, I thought you said it wasn't much further? We must be out of time on our lunch break! Besides, I'm afraid we might get lost in here."

Zippy replied, "The lunchbreak doesn't end at a specific time. It's up to the supes to decide when it's time to go back to work. They could be in there for hours. Don't worry about it. Hey! We're almost there!"

Zippy stopped to slide a large piece of wood out of the way, exposing the entrance to yet another abandoned and long-forgotten exploration tunnel.

Thorgrim's claustrophobia was winning. Now frightened, he pleaded to go back.

"Why are these tunnels so dark and narrow? I don't like to be enclosed in small areas. Please, I want to go back now. I'm really afraid, guys. I can't go any further!"

Zippy stepped into the tunnel entrance and said, "Are ya kiddin' me? You don't want to turn back now, do you? The diamonds are just a few more feet ahead, I promise! These are exploration tunnels and haven't been used in probably over a hundred years. These were dug out while probing for silver but none was found. Rumbler and me were exploring these, and that's how we found the diamonds."

"Ya, that's how we found the diamonds!" said Rumbler.

Zippy bellowed, "Rumbler, for the love of girls with long beards, stop repeating what I say!"

"Okay, but it's true, that's how we found the diamonds, right?" said Rumbler.

"Yes! Now for the last time, shut it!" yelled Zippy.

"Okay, I'm sorry."

"Let's move! Now, you guys stay with me, or ya might get lost and fall down into a vertical maintenance shaft and die!"

Thorgrim froze in place. "Huh? A vertical shaft? You mean one that goes straight down?"

"Don't worry about it. Just stay close and follow right behind me Beardby, and there won't be any problems. Come on, let's keep movin', we're almost there! We'll grab the diamonds and get out of here."

After several more minutes of following the narrow, meandering tunnel, the three finally exited into a roughly cut, circular area about twenty feet in diameter. It was the end of the exploration shaft.

A very old lamp lay in the corner next to the head of a broken, heavy pickaxe. The light from their three lanterns flickered against the walls of the area, casting weird shadows all around them.

"We're here," said Zippy cheerfully.

"The diamonds are in here?" asked Thorgrim, glancing around.

Zippy nodded. "Yes, right over there on the ground behind that old lamp.

"Where? I don't see anything," replied Thorgrim, squinting.

"I hid the diamonds behind that lamp over there," said Zippy, while gesturing to Rumbler. "Ya gotta move the lamp outta the way to see them."

Thorgrim took a few steps towards the area where Zippy claimed the diamonds were located.

"That's it. What are ya waitin' for? Get over there, move that lamp outta the way, and grab a handful of 'em! Yer gonna be rich, my friend! We all are!"

When Thorgrim reached the wall, he bent over, grabbed the lamp and moved it out of the way.

"I don't see any diam—"

Before he could finish his sentence, Rumbler stepped up and pulled a heavy bag over Thorgrim's head, while Zippy shoved him hard into the wall, causing him to strike the top of his skull against the rock.

Thorgrim, now semi-conscious, collapsed to the ground, moaning.

Zippy grabbed Thorgrim's still burning lantern.

"You won't be needin' yer lantern, Beardby, you fool!" he said, scornfully, finishing with a laugh.

Thorgrim lay on his back, drifting in and out of consciousness.

As they fled, Zippy yelled, "Baby with a beard! Baby with a beard! Good luck, you dumbass! Just so ya know, this is the area where those miners died a ton of years ago! Ya better hope those spooks don't get ya! They'll eat yer soul!"

Both Zippy and Rumbler added a howling, ghostly wail in order to instill more fear in Thorgrim.

Thorgrim, still flat on his back, quickly managed to recover. Sitting up, he pulled the bag off his head and watched as the lights of the hoodlum's lanterns faded away into the black void beyond.

Though woozy from the blow on his head, his adrenalin kicked in. He yelled, "What are you guys doing? Come back! Don't leave me in here!"

He only heard faint laughter.

Thorgrim was slightly injured, lost, alone in the dark and frightened. Quickly sapping his strength, his claustrophobia pressed down on him like a wooly elephant. Add to that, his fear of the spooks that he still believed haunted the mines. His head aching from the impact with the wall, unsure what to do next, he sat still, terrified, trembling, and hardly able to breathe.

***

Gradually, the crews began to return to work after their lunch break, though they always grumbled loudly (a favorite hobby of dwarves) and moved much slower compared to earlier when they were racing through the shafts on their way to lunch. Luthor once said that 'A hungry dwarf on his way to eat, moves faster than an elf with his arse on fire. But after he's eaten and is heading back to work? He moves slower than a dead elf with his arse on fire.'

"Hey, Yudelak, or any of you up there . . . have you seen muh son?" asked Luthor, who was the last of his team to leave Hub Three and enter the opening to the Main Shaft.

Yudelak was already too far ahead and could not hear Luthor, but Polis, who was nearby, replied, "Yes, I think I seen him go up with Yoody."

Luthor was happy. "Really? Thorgrim must be eager to get back to work! That's good news!"

Polis smiled. "Yes, you should be proud of that boy! Ya know, my boy will be graduating next year and he will be wanting to join our crew!"

Luthor replied, "I'm sure I can find a place for him, Polis. It will be good to have someone close to Thorgrim's age working alongside him."

By the time Luthor and the crew reached their work area, they realized that Thorgrim was missing.

Glancing around, Luthor yelled, "What the hell! Where the devil is muh son? Polis, I thought you said he was with Yudelak?"

Polis, embarrassed, replied, "I'm sorry boss, but I swear I thought it was him."

Luthor, now nervous, said, "Yoody, did you see Thorgrim?"

Yudelak returned, "Nope, I never seen him, Luthor. He wasn't with me. I haven't seen yer son since he got up from the table at lunch."

"Well, have any of you seen Thorgrim since he got up from the table?" asked Luthor, anxiously.

Everyone shook their heads no.

Bloop had an idea. "Hey, maybe he went in ahead of all of us. He might have accidentally walked past here and is on his way to the point. Easy to do if yer not payin' attention. Done it muhself a couple times."

Luthor nodded. "I can't believe Thorgrim would come down here without us, but good idea. It's worth a shot. Bloop, I want you and Thorn to run up to the point and see if the kid is there. I just hope he didn't get lost and wander into a maintenance tunnel somewhere. Holy hell, if he did"

Bloop and Thorn dropped their picks and started running down the Main Shaft to the point, a half-mile away. "Don't worry, we'll find yer son if he's down here," shouted Bloop as they went.

Luthor said, "Polis, you and Molky come with me. The rest of you get to work fillin' the cart. We'll be back as soon as we can."

Luthor took off running back towards Hub Three. "Come on you guys, we've gotta find muh boy. Damn his hide anyway!"

***

Thorgrim quickly realized that he needed to gain control of his emotions. "I need to act," he said aloud. "Or I may die in here."

Blind in the dark, he wished for a burning torch or lantern.

"I can't see a dang thing in here. Those punks took my lantern, but maybe that old lamp has some oil."

Searching for the lamp, he instead found the heavy head of the pickaxe.

He thought, *That lamp was near the pickaxe. Gotta be close by.*

Crawling around, Thorgrim continued to probe but was unable to locate the old lamp. He considered that it was possible that it had been kicked away and now lay somewhere else in the room. Or, God forbid, Zippy and Rumbler took it with them.

Frustrated and dizzy, after several minutes, he gave up the search and sat back against the wall. He tried to focus on a solution, but it was difficult to concentrate because his head was still throbbing. The outlook was grim. Without some kind of light, he knew it would be impossible to find a way back through the labyrinthine tunnels in the dark.

He shivered from the chill of the mountain. Hungry, he had no food, thirsty, there was no water.

Then, adding to his troubles, he remembered Zippy's warning that this was the place where the miners died and that their ghosts might get him.

Scared and depressed, he slumped forward and began to sob. After a few moments, wiping his tears, searching for hope, he mumbled, "Maybe they're just messin' with me, and they'll come back in a few minutes."

Then, his mind teased him. *But . . . what if they don't come back? Yer gonna die! No one knows yer here except Zippy and Rumbler, and they won't say a word to anyone! Yer gonna smother in here . . . unless the spooks get ya first! I can hear the voices of the spooks calling yer name now! Thorgrim . . . Thorgrim, we're coming for you! We're gonna getcha!*

67

He slid down to his back. Panic set in. Now frightened to death, he froze, unable to move, barely able to breathe or think clearly.

"Papa! Papa!" His throat dry, he screamed in a raspy voice. "Somebody, anybody please help me!"

Silence.

No one could hear him because he was far away from anyone else, deep inside a long-forgotten exploration tunnel.

***

"And what in the hell do we have here, hmmm?" asked Marvik, the supervisor of Shaft Six in Hub Two. He had just snagged Zippy and Rumbler by their collars after they ran out of the maintenance shaft and into the connecting shaft, that joins Hub Two with Hub Four.

The two teens struggled in his grip, but Marvik was probably the strongest dwarf that ever took a step inside the Vog Silver Mine.

"Let us go, let us go!" pleaded Zippy. "We'll be late getting back from lunch."

"The last crew ended lunch a half-hour ago, my boy," said Marvik as he shook both of them, their feet barely touching the ground. "Yer gonna be late alright. What are yer names and what shaft are you delinquents assigned to?"

"Six! Shaft Six in Hub Two!" lied Zippy, hoping to get out of this mess. "My name's Dutch and that's Greggor. Now can you let us go, please?"

Marvik scowled. Bellowing heavily, he said, "That's interesting because I'm the supervisor in Shaft Six! I don't recall having you two losers on my crew! Now, I'm a-gonna ask ya once more, and ya better tell me the truth this time, or I'll gut ya both and throw ya'll down the latrine!"

"Okay, okay! I'm—"

Rumbler, peeing his pants and panicking, interrupted with the truth. "He's Zippy and I'm Rumbler! We work out of Hub Four in Shaft Twelve! Shaft Twelve! Please don't hurt us."

"Both of you work in Twelve?" growled Marvik, shaking them.

"Yes!" they both replied simultaneously.

"Well, I'm gonna take ya into Twelve! Ya better hope yer not lying to me, and we're gonna find out soon enough."

Zippy yelled, "Shut yer hole, Rumbler. Stop repeating everything I say!" Marvik turned and dragged the squirming teens into Hub Four, with ease. The room was now empty of the lunch crowd, so it was just the three of them.

"Hmmm, Zippy . . . aren't you Claus Borknoi's kid?" asked Marvik, leaning in close to Zippy's face while tightening his grip on both boys' collars.

"Yes!" replied Zippy, red-faced and teary-eyed. "I'm Claus' kid."

"Yes, yes, he's Claus' kid!" cried Rumbler.

Marvik shook Zippy. "Never mind him. What in the hell were you two doing in that maintenance shaft?" he asked angrily, shaking them both again. "Trying to git yerself kilt?"

"We weren't doing nuthin'," exclaimed Zippy with another lie. "We just had to go pee!"

Marvik sneered. "Oh, really! You couldn't use the Crapola in yer assigned hub?"

"No, it was full of workers and we really had to go!"

"You lying little ass. I'm gonna take you to see yer father, and I might plant a boot in both yer butts on the way. I believe he's clear up on point in Shaft Twelve, right?"

"Yes! Yes!" cried Zippy, still squirming.

Marvik grinned sinisterly. "Well, that shaft's at least four hundred feet long. Think of how many times my boot can meet yer butts on the way! When we get there, you can explain to him what you were doin' inside that maintenance tunnel long after everyone else had returned from lunch. Next time, read the damn sign. It says, 'No Admittance.' Can't you read plain Dwarvish?"

"We didn't see the sign!" moaned Zippy.

"Yes, we did, Zippy. Remember, I told ya a week ago that maybe we shouldn't go—"

Zippy glared at Rumbler, "Shut yer flappin' trap!"

Trying to look over his shoulder at Marvik, Zippy whined, "That's not true, Mister!"

"You must get paid to tell lies," bellowed Marvik. "True or not, we'll let yer father decide! Frankly, I can't imagine why he isn't lookin' for you now! Maybe he's happy yer missin'! Come on, I've got to get back to my own crew, but first, we're going for a little walk!"

Marvik then noticed that Zippy had two lanterns. "Why do you have two lanterns? And don't lie to me, or I'll slap yer teeth right outta yer head!"

"I found it, that's all!"

"Found it, did ya? Where exactly? It looks brand new, so I think yer lying again! If ya stole it from someone, we'll find out sooner or later, and then yer hide won't be worth an ale mug with a hole in the bottom! Come on, let's get movin'."

Still gripping their collars, Marvik shoved them towards the entrance to Shaft Twelve. At that moment, coming out of Shaft Twelve, Zippy's father, Claus, appeared with another dwarf from his crew.

Claus yelled, "What in a fistful of moldy bellybutton lint is goin' on in here? Zippy and Rumbler, where have you two fools been hidin'?"

Both teens started to ramble and lie, but Marvik released his grip and spoke over the top of them. "I just caught these liars running out of that maintenance shaft between here and Two. They claim they were taking a leak, but I think they were messin' around in there. They also have an extra lantern with them and it seems brand new."

Claus' bushy monobrow furrowed deep, partially obscuring his burning red eyes.

Marching over to them, his voice boomed. "You're both in for it, I'm tellin' ya! I told ya to stay out of those tunnels, didn't I? Are you two tryin' to get me fired? Where did ya get that lamp, Zippy?"

"I found it in one of the tunnels," his son replied, using his best expression of innocence.

His father growled and hissed. "Sure ya did, ya little thief! You're so stupid, you'd steal the plug out of the bottom of the boat you were floatin' in. Put the lamp down on that table and come with me. Time to get yer butts to work! Yer both gonna get a yellow slip and yer pay docked for this."

Zippy hastily put Thorgrim's lantern down as his father had asked.

Claus continued his rant. "Yer both almost twenty years old, but ya act like little kids."

Claus reached out and grabbed both boys by their front collars. With a big pull, he sent the two stumbling towards the entrance to Shaft Twelve, aided by a swift kick in their rears from both of his boots.

Claus turned to Marvik. "Marvik, I'm sorry about this . . . please don't report 'em," he begged. "I'll teach 'em a lesson they won't forget, and I promise this won't happen again."

Marvik nodded. "I understand. I had the same trouble with my boy when he started here ten years ago! Better get a handle on that kid of yers and his friend, cuz they've been causing lots of trouble in here. I think they were the ones that put hot pepper juice on some of the corncobs last week."

"Ya, sounds like somethin' they'd do. Thanks again."

Pointing to the entrance to Shaft Twelve, Claus yelled at Zippy and Rumbler. "Git in there, now!"

Without hesitation and not a word mentioned about Thorgrim, both of the troublemakers entered the shaft.

Claus and the crewmember followed behind them. Once inside, they started shoving Zippy and Rumbler forward, towards the point.

Marvik could hear loud yelling echoing from deep within Shaft Twelve even after he entered the connecting shaft on his way to Hub Two.

***

Luthor opened the door and entered Hub Three from the Main Shaft with Polis and Molky right behind him, unaware that Zippy and Rumbler were getting their butts chewed out over in Hub Four. Also, at this time, several dwarves from Shaft Eight were exiting Hub Three, pulling a cart full of ore into the Main Shaft.

"Hold the door, please," one of them said to Luthor.

"Hey, have any of you seen my son, Thorgrim Longbeard? He's about twenty years old and wears a really long beard."

The tired dwarves chuckled. One of them said, "Don't all dwarves wear beards?

Luthor frowned and pursed his lips. "Yes, but his beard hangs past his knees! Thanks a lot, you idiot!"

After they left, Luthor pointed to the door and said to Polis, "Go across and check out Hub Four and then Two. If ya see anyone, tell them to ask about Thorgrim when they get back to their areas."

Polis nodded.

"Don't forget to check the latrines! Maybe he fell asleep in one of 'em. God help him if he did! Get goin'."

Polis replied, "Sure thing, boss."

Instantly, Polis left the room and headed over to Hub Four. Arriving, he had missed the commotion with Zippy, Rumbler, and Marvik by only ten minutes.

Luthor said to Molky, "It's obvious, he's not in this hub. Let's check the latrine first, and then we'll go try Hub One. If we don't find him, we'll head up front and report him missin'."

Pointing to the table they were sitting at during lunch, Luthor exclaimed, "There's Thorgrim's lunchbox and helmet on the floor!" Looking over at the Crapola door, he somberly said, "Do ya really think he could have fallen into the latrine?" Shuddering at the thought, he continued, "If he did, he's a goner."

71

Tears rolled down Luthor's cheeks.

Molky patted Luthor on the back. "It's okay, boss. We'll find him. Hey, maybe he really did walk all the way to the point! If he did, Bloop and Thorn will find him."

"I hope yer right. Well, let's go check the latrine, but I don't know what good it will do if he fell in 'cuz he'll be long gone."

Molky nodded.

Luthor yelled, "What will I tell his mother? This is all my fault."

Molky said, "You know, I was thinkin', is there any chance the kid just took off and went home? Maybe he wasn't feelin' good."

Luthor sighed. "I suppose that's possible. But I think he would have told me. We'll check the area out first, and if we can't find him, I'll pray yer right."

Both of them started to walk towards the door to the Crapola when a member of the management team, Beck McWug ran into the room.

"Luthor! I thought I heard your voice in here. I was just on my way down the Main Shaft to get you. There's an emergency at yer home. Yer boy, Thurston is here looking for you. He's up front at the entrance!"

"Mr. McWug, what in all hell?" said Luthor, now visibly shaken by the added trouble. "What's going on? What kind of emergency?"

"Yer boy says' it's yer wife. Something about the baby coming and that yer wife is not doing well. You need to get home right away, so don't even worry about clocking out."

Wild-eyed, Luthor looked at Molky and said, "Find muh boy, Molky! I've got to get to muh misses. When you find him, and I pray you do, tell him I said to clock out and to get his butt home right away."

Luthor looked white as a sheet. He ran towards the exit of the hub and as he passed by the manager, he said, "Mr. McWug, my boy Thorgrim has been missin' since lunch. Please get a search party together and find him!"

Mr. McWug nodded, "No worries, Luthor, I'll send out search crews right away. We'll find yer boy. Get home and the best of luck to yer wife."

***

Thorgrim had drifted off to sleep. While waking from his slumber a few hours later, he hoped that he had only been dreaming about being lost in a dark tunnel.

When he opened his eyes, reality quickly set in.

He had not been dreaming. He was alone, in the dark and lost in a tunnel system somewhere inside a mountain.

His mind tried to entertain hopeful ideas, but the claustrophobia blocked any clear thoughts. Desperate, hoping someone might hear him; he let out a loud scream.

Listening, he heard nothing.

Frustrated, he rolled over and tried to get up to his feet. When he did, he felt an object. It was the old lantern.

Now elated, forgetting his concerns about smothering in a cave-in or being attacked by spooks, he thought, *If I could light this lamp, I might be able to see well enough to find a way out of this place.*

Reaching into a side pocket, he grabbed his flint box. Despite fumbling with it for a moment, he was able to pull out an oil wick and a flint stick. Holding the three-inch-long wick near the box, he struck the flint several times. Sparks flew, and after a dozen tries, the wick finally ignited.

The tiny wick provided a small flame and would only burn for a minute. He quickly brought the lamp up and looked inside. It was an old candle lamp minus the candle. The lamp likely had not been used in over a hundred years.

The small flame on the wick, his only source of light, gradually grew fainter and fainter.

Darkness.

Thorgrim sobbed again. Thirsty and scared, it was also cold and he trembled from both the chill and fear.

The blackness became like an enveloping shroud, smothering him. Thorgrim, struggling to breathe, tried his best to scream again.

"Help me!"

He listened.

No sound.

"Somebody, please help me!"

Again, he listened but heard nothing.

"Papa!" he cried out. "Help me!"

Unknown to Thorgrim, it was now well past midnight and his father had left the mine hours ago to be with his wife who was fighting for her life trying to deliver a baby.

Thorgrim was also not aware that search crews were scouring the mine trying to find him. The searchers of the day shift had gone home and now several teams of two and three from the night shift looked for any sign of him.

73

Virtually every area of the mine system had been searched more than once. Every area except some forgotten tunnels like the one Thorgrim was in. Some of the older exploration tunnels were not even marked on the system map.

Two searchers narrowly missed finding him once, but they did not see the covered entrance of the tunnel that he was in. They called his name, and although Thorgrim was close enough to hear them, he could not. He had been asleep.

Many believed that perhaps Thorgrim had walked out of the mine to play hooky, while others had darker ideas. Some dwarves believed that he had fallen into one of the latrines or down a deep, vertical shaft to his death.

Frantic, he screamed again. "Will somebody please help me?"

He laid down on his back and decided to pray.

"Moridon, great Father God of the dwarves. Please save me. Protect me from spooks, protect me from a cave-in. Help me find a way out…"

He repeated the prayer several times until he again fell asleep. An hour later, while he slept, he entered into a dream-state. During the dream, he heard what sounded like his father and a couple of others calling his name.

"Thorgrim, can you hear me?"

"Thorgrim! We'll get you out of here. You're going to be fine."

"This will all be over soon. We're coming, Thorgrim."

The voices were so vivid that he awoke and sat straight up. Peering ahead in the dark, he heard footfalls and saw the pinpoint of a lantern's light.

Thorgrim cried out. "Hello! I'm in here!"

"We hear you. We're coming."

The light came closer, and now Thorgrim noticed a second light and then a third.

Someone called out, "Thorgrim."

"I'm here! I'm in here!" He pulled himself up against the wall and stood. He wanted to run towards the light, but his feet would not respond.

The tunnel in front of him was aglow with the light from the rescuers' lamps. Soon, three dwarves appeared and shined their beams in on Thorgrim.

"Thorgrim, are you okay?" one of them asked.

"Yes, I think so. I'm cold and thirsty, though."

"We're here to rescue you. Follow us and we'll take you out of here. Walk slowly, and watch where you step, it's very dangerous in here."

Thorgrim approached the three smiling miners. One of them handed Thorgrim an extra lamp, then they turned and carefully led the way out through the tunnel.

"Thorgrim, when we get you out of here, you need to get home because yer parents need you now."

"Why do my parents need me? What's wrong?"

One of them answered, "Yer mother is having her baby, but there are serious complications. Yer father was looking for you, but he had to leave to be by her side."

"Okay, please get me out of here so I can get home! I can't thank you enough! Those two idiots Zippy and Rumbler tricked me. They said they found diamonds in here."

One of them said, "There are no diamonds in this mine. That, I'm sure of. I've been mining here for a very long time, so I should know."

Another said, "Yes, he's right. Just silver in here."

The third rescuer turned and nodded in agreement.

Slowly, the miners continued to lead Thorgrim through the winding tunnels.

"My father will be very happy that you saved me! You see, I'm claustrophobic and afraid of being inside enclosed places! I'm also afraid of spooks!"

They all turned and looked at Thorgrim. One of them said, "There are no spooks in this mine, and there has never been a cave-in. You know, you won't be able to be a miner if you're claustrophobic. That can be a problem for a dwarf. I'm afraid you'll have a decision to make soon."

Thorgrim replied in a glum tone, "I know."

"Stay with us, we're almost there."

Finally, after almost a half-hour, they made it back to the connecting shaft between Hubs Two and Four."

"There you go, young one. Now get home to yer family. They need you."

"Thankee, thankee! I can't thank you enough!"

All three of them returned a warm smile.

Thorgrim said, "Hey, what are yer names?"

"My name is Kleet, this is Joop and Angus."

"Pleasure to meet you all!" replied Thorgrim with a big smile.

He reached out to shake their hands, but they had already started to walk back into the depths of the maintenance tunnel.

"Are you guys part of the night crew?"

All three stopped and turned back towards Thorgrim. "Yes, and we have to get back to work; lots to do in here," replied Angus. "Lucky for you, we were working deep in the maintenance tunnel tonight and heard you calling for help."

"Thank Moridon. I thought I was a goner!"

"Be sure to let them know up front that you are okay before you go home," said Joop.

"Okay, thanks again! I won't' forget you!"

"Bye, young one, and good luck," said Kleet. "We won't forget you, either."

"Bye!" yelled Thorgrim as he ran into Hub Two.

Now in the light of the Hub, Thorgrim, still holding the lamp Kleet had given him, looked down at himself and realized that he was covered in dirt. Even his beard was full of it.

Shaking off the dirt, he grabbed a small jug of water from a table, gulped it down and then ran out into the Main Shaft. From there, he made his way to the front and found two members of the management team standing near the big entrance.

"Excuse me, I'm Thorgrim Longbeard. I got lost in the mine, but three workers found and rescued me!"

One of the managers, Mr. Thesenga said with a frown, "Thank the gods, you're okay, kid! I want to know what you were doing and how you got lost because this has caused quite an uproar around here."

"I'm sorry, but I was tricked by—"

The second manager, Mr. Burkhalter, interrupted him. "We can talk about this some other time, but for now, you need to get home. I don't want to scare you but your mother is having some problems delivering her baby, and your father left soon after lunch to be with her. He's also very worried about you."

Thorgrim nodded. "Thankee, and I am sorry about this. I didn't mean to get lost, and I know about my mother because the three miners who rescued me, told me."

"Who were they?"

"They said that their names were Kleet, Joop and Angus."

The two managers looked at each other and shrugged.

Mr. Thesenga said, "Thorgrim, where did you get that old lamp? It's a candle lamp. Gotta be well over a hundred years old."

"Kleet gave it to me."

Thorgrim handed the manager the lamp and began to run towards the exit. As he went, he tossed them the big silver nugget he had found in the mine earlier. "I guess that's yers."

Later, the managers checked the rosters and confirmed what they had suspected. There was nobody named Kleet, Joop, or Angus currently employed by the Vog Silver Mine Company.

V.   The Only Way

The instant Thorgrim stepped out of the Vog Silver Mine entrance, he had already made up his mind that he would never return. Running as fast as he could, he made it home by four in the morning.

As he approached the house, he noticed two mules tied to a post out front. Unknown to him, one belonged to Dr. Thacker and the other to his nurse. The rest of the neighborhood was dark, but every window in the Longbeard home gleamed with burning candles or lamps.

Exhausted and deeply worried, Thorgrim burst through the front door, stopping in the living room to yell, "Mama, Papa, I'm here!"

After a few seconds, Luthor appeared in the adjoining hallway, ran to his son and gave him a great bear-hug.

Tears welled in Luthor's eyes. He looked pale and exhausted. "Keep yer voice down, Son," he whispered. "Yer mama is resting. But, thank Moridon! I didn't know if I'd ever see ya again!"

"I'm sorry, Papa," Thorgrim whispered. "I can explain."

"That can wait! I want to know where ya been, but first, you need to know that you have a new baby brother, and Mama's not doin' very well."

"A new brother . . . where's Mama? What's wrong with her . . . take me to her."

"She's in our bedroom with Dr. Thacker and a nurse. There were serious problems during the delivery. The baby is fine, but . . ."

"Is Mama gonna be alright?"

"I don't know, son."

"But, why isn't she at the doctor's clinic?"

"Dr. Thacker felt it was unwise to move her."

"Can I see her?"

"I think so. I'll see if it's okay. Follow me, but be very quiet."

Luthor led his son down the hallway to the bedroom.

"Where's everyone else?" whispered Thorgrim, glancing around looking for his siblings.

"They're with yer grandma. I figured there would be less commotion with them outta here."

Reaching the door, Luthor gently rapped.

After a moment, the door slowly opened and on the other side, stood Dr. Thacker's nurse, holding the new addition to the Longbeard family.

78

Luthor whispered, "This is my oldest. His name's Thorgrim. Can he see his mother?"

The nurse replied, "She's sleeping. But you can approach the bed if you like. Just don't wake her."

Lookin' at the new baby, Luthor, despite the concern for his wife, smiled and said, "How's my new boy?"

"Considering the ordeal, he's doing well," the nurse replied. "Here, you can hold him, but if he starts to cry, you need to move out of the room so he doesn't wake your wife."

Luthor carefully took the blanket-swaddled baby into his arms and gently rocked him.

Thorgrim took a quick glance at his baby brother and trying to lighten the mood said, "What, no beard?"

Although very tired, Luthor managed a grin. "Go see yer mother. Oh, Son, she's not aware that you went missing in the mine today. If she wakes up, don't tell her. We don't want to upset her."

Thorgrim nodded. Turning, he looked over to the bed and saw his mother under a pile of blankets. Dark circles were under her eyes, and her complexion was white as snow.

Dr. Thacker was sitting next to the bed, checking her pulse. He motioned for Thorgrim to approach.

Slowly, Thorgrim walked up to his mother, and Luthor followed him with the baby in his arms.

When they reached her side, like magic, she opened her eyes. When she saw Thorgrim, color returned to her face, and she smiled.

"Son?" she said with a raspy voice.

"Yes, Mama. I'm here now."

"I . . . had the strangest dream that you were in trouble. It scared me. I'm glad to see that it was only a dream."

Thorgrim reached for her hand and gently grasped it. Despite the blankets, his mother seemed very cold.

"It was only a dream, Mama. Don't worry about me. I'm okay. How are you feeling?"

"I'm fine, I think," she replied, still raspy. Coughing, she giggled and said, "But I don't believe that I'll be running any races in the near future."

"No, Mama, probably not, but you'll be up in no time, you'll see."

Marjorie noticed that her husband held their new son. When she saw her baby, her eyes sparkled. She said, "Thorgrim, have you met yer new brother, Tadder?"

"I haven't held him yet, but I will later. I just wanted to check on you, first."

"He's feisty like you," she said quietly.

Thorgrim was about to reply but noticed she had suddenly drifted off to sleep.

Dr. Thacker stood. "I'm sorry, but everyone needs to quietly step out of here. She needs a lot of rest." Gesturing, he said, "Nurse."

The nurse quickly opened the door. Thorgrim, very worried, reluctantly released his mother's hand, then looked at the doctor.

Dr. Thacker could only shrug his shoulders.

Thorgrim and his father, both deeply concerned about Marjorie, slowly walked towards the bedroom door. Luthor kissed little Tadder on the forehead, handed him back to the nurse and then led Thorgrim out into the hallway.

The bedroom door was quietly closed behind them.

Luthor whispered, "Follow me. Let's go outside to talk."

The two tired dwarves stepped out into the front yard of the little house. It was Wednesday's dawn and both were numb from lack of sleep.

The summer air was cool though humid. Luthor took a deep breath and sighed. "I'm going to head down to the mine in a bit to let them know what's going on here. They'll understand, but will probably expect us back to work soon."

Thorgrim dropped his head. "Papa, will Mama be okay? Tell me she'll be okay."

"I don't know, Son. It was a tough delivery, and it took everything she had to do it. She lost a lot of blood."

Thorgrim choked up. "If she dies . . ."

Luthor grasped his son's shoulder and said, "Don't talk that way, Son. Always try to be positive. It works like magic!"

"But you always told me magic wasn't real."

"Well, believing in something can work like magic. Although, I can't say I've ever seen magic spells and things, what I can say is that the love yer mother has for me . . . and all of us, is truly magical."

A few tears dropped from Thorgrim's eyes.

Luthor said in a heavy voice, "Look, I know this issue with yer mother is very serious, but what happened today in the mine is nothing to laugh about. You had me so worried that I thought my heart was going to stop. What the hell happened to you after lunch?"

"Papa, I'm so sorry! I got up from the table after I ate and was looking at that big map on the wall. Then two of my so-called friends appeared and wanted me to follow them so they could show me some diamonds they'd found."

Luthor frowned. "Diamonds?"

"Ya, red ones. Of course, I became curious and followed them, but it was a set-up. They took me into some narrow tunnels deep into the mine somewhere, knocked me out and left me there alone in the dark."

Luthor closed his eyes and said in a low tone, "Oh, muh God. You've got to be kiddin' me."

"I know, I should've known better, but they convinced me that they were very rare and valuable red diamonds . . . and I thought that . . ."

Luthor's face turned purple with anger, and his monobrow began to twitch uncontrollably.

Thorgrim saw the storm coming.

Luthor, mad as a northern wasp, clipped his words like never before. "Who were da sons' a bitches who did dis to ya? I want to know, 'cuz not only will dey be fired and sent to jail for dis evil deed, but wun I get muh hands on dem, day'l wish dey were elves livin' in da far north of Sherduin!"

"Zippy Borknoi and Rumbler McGeever. But please, let me deal with them, Papa. They know I can kick their butts if I can catch them one at a time."

Luthor shook his head. "No. I'll take care of it. Aren't doze da same two who told you da silly ghost stories about da dead miners?"

"Ya, they're the ones."

Luthor was trembling with fury. "Dat's it. When I go dis mornin' to talk to da management about takin' some time off to be wit yer momma, I'll find doze two and smack der beards right off der pimply faces. Den, I'll report doze bastards to da authorities.

"Papa, please calm down before you blow a pipe!"

Luthor sighed. "Okay, okay, I'll calm down, at least until I get a hold of their lice-filled beards! So, just doze two, no one else? I think dare were what, about thirty boys in yer graduating class dat ended up in da mine? Nobody else but doze two idiots did dis?"

"Ya, just Zippy and Rumbler."

Looking to the east, Luthor noticed that the sun was rising.

"Son, you stay here with yer mother. Maybe try to get some sleep. I need to go to the mine and talk to dem."

"Okay, Papa, but shouldn't you get some sleep first?"

"I'm fine. I don't know how long I'll be gone, but send for me if there is the slightest change in yer momma."

"Okay, Papa."

"If I don't show up later, check the jailhouse. I might end up in there after I kick Zippy and Rumbler's butts. No one lays a hand on my boy without paying a heavy price."

81

"Please, don't get into any trouble."

"I'll do my best," Luthor said, finishing with a wink.

Before leaving, Luthor leaned over and gave his son another bear hug. "Thank Moridon yer okay. I've been prayin' hard for yer safe return. Counting yer mama, I've actually been prayin' a lot today. Still mad at ya though for what happened. You should have known better. I told ya not to wander off."

"I know and I'm sorry."

"I love you, Son."

After delivering a quick kiss to his son's cheek, Luthor turned and began his walk to the Vog Silver Mine.

Thorgrim watched his father until he disappeared into the haze. He then went back into the house and into his bedroom that was just up the hall from his mother.

Standing in front of his door, he paused and listened to Dr. Thacker and the nurse whispering in his mother's room, but he could not hear them clearly enough to know what they were saying.

The baby began to cry. Instantly, the nurse exited his mother's bedroom with the blanketed newborn in her arms. She approached Thorgrim and said, "He's hungry. I'm going to take him into the kitchen and feed him."

"How is my mother?" Thorgrim asked while staring at his new baby brother.

"She's out of it and very weak. I'm sorry; I wish I knew more, but only time will tell."

"My father went to work to let them know what's going on. I'm going to try to get some sleep. Please wake me if there is any change, okay?"

"Of course," she replied, before continuing on to the kitchen with baby Tadder.

Thorgrim entered his bedroom and collapsed on the bed, completely exhausted. Lying there, his mind spun in circles.

Mama, please, I pray that you pull through this! I can't be without you! And Papa, how am I ever going to tell you that I'll never step foot inside the mine again? Oh, Moridon, what will become of me? They will declare me an outcast! I will be a shame to my entire family. Oh . . . I'm so tired, I must . . .

Thorgrim drifted off, but his sleep was restless.

Silence . . .

Crying and whispering.

A door opens and closes.

Crying. "Nurse, the baby . . ."

Silence . . .

The front door. Hurried footfalls.

A soft, rapping sound. A door opening.

Whispering.

"Mr. Longbeard . . . she seems . . ."

Mumbling, the sound of pacing.

Crying.

Silence . . .

Thorgrim continued to toss and turn, drifting in and out of sleep, until exhaustion finally pushed him into a deep slumber.

His mother entered his room and silently approached his bedside.

Thorgrim, though asleep and dreaming, sensed her.

Peeking out from his blankets, he was stunned though happy to see her standing next to him.

"Mama, you're in muh dream."

At first, she was smiling, but her expression suddenly changed to one of concern.

"Thorgrim," she whispered.

"Mama?"

"Are you okay?" she asked.

"Mama, I'm worried about you. I—"

"Do not worry about me, for I am safe in the hands of God. But I am worried about you, my firstborn . . . something troubles you. Please, tell me about it."

"Mama, I can't work in the mine, and I'll never go back in there. I've been lyin' all of this time about being sick. The truth is that I'm claustrophobic. When I'm in enclosed places, like the mineshafts, I feel dizzy and can't breathe."

"I had suspected there were reasons that you didn't want to go to work in the mine. I wish you would have come to us and told us the truth."

"I'm sorry that I lied. I was just afraid to tell anyone about muh problem. I didn't think anyone would believe me."

"I understand, Thorgrim."

"Mama, I shouldn't tell you this, because you're sick and I'm worried it might upset you, but yesterday, I had a terrible thing happen to me in the mine. I was tricked by a couple of so-called friends and got lost in there. It was dark, and I couldn't find muh way out! It felt like everything was closin' in on me. I could barely breathe, and I thought I was goin' to die!"

"Oh, Thorgrim, I'm so sorry."

"I won't go back! I'm sure Papa will be upset when I tell him. I don't know what I'll do when the authorities find out, but I'm sure that I'll be in big trouble!"

"When the authorities find out, they'll declare you an outcast. If they catch you, you'll be arrested. Thorgrim, you know what you must do and it is the only way."

"What must I do?"

"You know what you have to do."

He thought for a moment. "You mean, leave my home and my country? Leave you, Papa, and my brothers and sisters?"

She nodded slowly. "My heart aches for you, but it is truly the only way.

"But, I don't want to do that! I have no other choice?"

"No. You must leave and start a new life somewhere else."

"When, Mama?"

"Soon. You will know when. And when the time comes, you must not hesitate."

"But, I'll miss you and everyone."

"And we will miss you."

"I'll hate it."

"I know. But, my firstborn, you're an adult now. You must go out into the world and create your own destiny. You're a very special dwarf. In fact, you're extraordinary! I know you'll do well."

"Mama, I'm afraid."

"Son, I'm sorry, but it's time for me to go."

"Do you have to?"

She nodded, whispering, "Remember, when the time comes for you to leave, do not hesitate."

"Okay, Mama."

Smiling, she leaned down and kissed his cheek.

Thorgrim felt an odd, tingling sensation on the spot where his mother kissed him.

Then, there was a long silence.

Thorgrim opened his eyes and noticed the late afternoon sun shining through the window. Groggy, he thought that the dream about his mother seemed very real but also mysterious. Still exhausted, both emotionally and physically, soon he was asleep again, but as before; it was a restless sleep full of sounds and voices.

A weird, humming silence.

"We need to . . . as soon as . . ."

Silence . . .

Whispering, footfalls, then more silence.

Crying, coughing.

"I didn't think that she would . . . I just can't believe it."

Then, Thorgrim heard his father.

"Oh, Margie, I just . . ."

Crying, sobbing and mumbling.

His father whispering, "No, let's not wake him . . . I'll wake him later and tell . . ."

Silence . . .

Thorgrim fell back into a deep sleep, but after a few moments, the strange, tingling sensation on his cheek where his mother had kissed him in the dream, fully woke him.

It was pitch-black in the bedroom. It was Wednesday evening, almost 9:30 p.m.

Lying in bed, Thorgrim clearly heard his father and Dr. Thacker conversing.

Thorgrim heard crying.

It was his baby brother.

Soon, he heard someone else crying.

It was his father.

Thorgrim sat straight up, jumped to the floor and raced to his mother's bedroom and the source of the crying.

Her door was closed.

He stopped. Shaking like a leaf, hardly able to breathe, he listened through the door.

He heard the sound of a female. It was the nurse, but he could not understand her. Then he heard mumbling and more crying. His ears rang from the elevated blood pressure brought on by the stress of what he feared he would find when he opened the door.

Taking a deep breath, trembling, Thorgrim slowly pushed the door open.

Inside, the room was brightly lit with candles. Through blurry eyes, he gazed towards the bed. He saw the shapes of three people standing next to it.

However, the bed was empty; his mother was gone.

Thorgrim's heart cracked. For a moment, he existed in nothingness. He heard voices calling to him, but he could not understand them.

Painfully, his ears rang and buzzed. Wanting to collapse, unable to bear the loss of something as precious as his mother, he caught himself but still staggered back into the wall.

Voices called Thorgrim's name. He looked, but could only see the three hazy shapes of the doctor, the nurse, and his father.

The nurse seemed to be hugging and comforting Luthor.

Again, several voices called his name. "Thorgrim."

He looked at the empty bed.

Thorgrim's bleary eyes could not focus, but he watched as a fuzzy shape approached him.

Luthor reached out and grasped Thorgrim's arm. "Son. Are you okay?"

"Papa!" replied Thorgrim, weeping.

The nurse then approached and placed her arms around him.

"Son!" she said.

Thorgrim's heart jumped into his throat, and he quickly rubbed his eyes. When they finally focused, he looked. It was not the nurse who had placed her arms around him. Instead, it was his mother. Amazingly, she was out of bed and standing directly in front of him.

She was smiling.

Thorgrim could not believe his eyes. "Mama!"

She nodded and kissed Thorgrim's cheek on the exact spot where she did in his dream.

Dr. Thacker, his brow low, said firmly, "Mrs. Longbeard, I must insist that you get back into that bed."

Marjorie was oblivious to everything around her except Thorgrim. Ignoring, or not hearing the doctor, she continued to beam a huge smile.

Thorgrim, choking back tears, said, "When I came in here I thought you were . . ." Unable to say the word, he instead embraced her.

Dr. Thacker said, "Careful there, Thorgrim! Gently! Your mother just experienced a remarkable recovery, but she still has a long road ahead of her. I've never seen anything like it before, and I would have never guessed it could've happened! It's a miracle!"

"The power of prayer," said Luthor. "And of course, the skillful hand of a good doctor."

Dr. Thacker smiled and said, "I would wager that your prayers . . . uh, shall we say, our prayers played a much bigger part in this. To be honest, I can't imagine how she can even stand after what she went through."

Marjorie turned to Dr. Thacker and said, "Thank you. I was praying too. I was truly safe in the hands of God."

Thorgrim recalled the dream he had of her walking into his room. For a moment, he forgot to breathe, and his heart skipped a beat.

Marjorie looked at Thorgrim and gave him an ever so subtle wink.

"Mrs. Longbeard, you had lost so much blood, that even with the transfusion, I didn't think you would last the night. Look, I know you're feeling better, but you need to lay back down, now!"

She surrendered. "Okay, I'll lay down. But, I do feel very good."

"Lay down!" growled the doctor. "You're worse than my wife, and she never does anything I say!"

She giggled. "Okay, okay."

Luthor helped his wife get back into bed, then after giving her a kiss, he said, "I love you, get some sleep. Don't worry about the baby."

She smiled warmly and said, "Can I see Tadder again . . . just for a moment?"

"The baby is sleeping, Mrs. Longbeard," replied the nurse who had just stepped into the room. "He had a rough day, too. I'll be here all night to take care of him while you rest. Get some sleep. You need it!"

"Yes, please remain in bed," said Dr. Thacker. "You don't want to overdo it. I'll be back in the morning to check on you. Promise me that you'll stay in bed unless it's absolutely necessary."

"Okay, I promise, I'll get some sleep."

"Good."

Giving her another look as he packed up his bag, Dr. Thacker said, "Amazin', absolutely amazin'."

Marjorie said, "Thank you all, for everything."

Dr. Thacker replied, "You're welcome Mrs. Longbeard. Luthor, send for me at any time if there is a problem. My nurse will be lookin' in on her until I return in the morning."

Luthor shook Dr. Thacker's hand. "Okay, thanks again, doc."

"Sure," the doctor replied with a smile. "Luthor, you look exhausted. You should probably try to get some sleep."

Luthor nodded. "Ya, I could use some."

Dr. Thacker turned towards the bed. "Oh, Mrs. Longbeard, one more thing . . ." He stopped talking. She was already sound asleep.

For the first time in a couple of days, everyone in the little house was smiling.

So was baby Tadder.

VI. On Destiny's Road

Marjorie slept well and seemed to feel much better the next day, though she would become exhausted easily. Dr. Thacker prescribed another full day of bed rest and warned that her full recovery could take several days or even weeks.

On that Thursday morning, Thorgrim offered to stay home and help his mother until she was feeling well enough to resume her normal routine of taking care of a houseful of children, including a newborn.

Although he would also be taking time off to help out, Luthor wholeheartedly agreed with Thorgrim's proposal. However, he suspected that there were other ulterior motives behind his son's desire to stay home instead of going to work.

On the same day, Luthor asked the mine's company management to grant a temporary leave for himself and Thorgrim so they could tend to Marjorie until she fully recovered. Because of Luthor's years of service and stature, the company allowed it without hesitation.

The company informed Luthor that he could return to work at his own discretion, however, due to his poor work attendance, Thorgrim must report to work within two weeks. Failure to comply would result in serious repercussions including being reported to the civil authorities in Bur Dhulgren.

After Luthor had his meeting with the company management, he went up to Shaft Twelve and beat the pulp out of Zippy Borknoi and Rumbler McGeever. Also beaten were Zippy's father, and several others who tried to intervene. When Zippy and Rumbler later admitted the trouble they caused Thorgrim, they were promptly fired from their jobs while still lying in their hospital beds.

The company considered dismissing Luthor, but instead, let him off with a written warning.

Luthor spent the night in jail but was released the next day with all charges dropped after the judge heard what had happened to Thorgrim at the hands of Zippy and Rumbler.

As the days went by, Marjorie continued to improve. Thorgrim realized that the hour was fast approaching when he must tell his father that he does not plan to return to the silver mine.

Luthor would be disappointed, probably angry, and would likely warn him of the consequences. Thorgrim knew that because of his claustrophobia, joining the Army or Navy was not an option. He also knew that simply leaving the country would automatically make him an outlaw, because he would be leaving without an official release from his duties as a miner.

Thorgrim often cursed the government and the seemingly unreasonable laws, believing them to be unfair and controlling.

'Is this freedom?' He would often ask himself. He understood why the enforced mining laws were in place because the mining of ore generated the vast majority of the Dwarven Clans' gross national product. Without it, the kingdom would become bankrupt. Many thousands of dwarves worked in the kingdom's mining industry. Fortunately, most dwarves loved to mine ore; they were naturals at it, and the best in the world.

Thorgrim knew that he would hate mining even if he did not have to battle claustrophobia. His dream was to work with books, not pickaxes. He understood that if he left his homeland to chase his dreams, the road would be tough. Without a formal education at the university, he would likely never land a job in a school or library. He hoped that there would be another way to achieve his dream, and he vowed to himself that he would somehow find a way.

Within a week, Marjorie had fully recovered. Because his wife was back to her normal self, Luthor decided to return to work.

Despite prodding by his father to also return to work, Thorgrim found excuses to stay around the house in an effort to avoid the inevitable.

On Wednesday, July 17, the company's mandated deadline for Thorgrim to return to work was only one day away. The night before the deadline, during supper, the entire family enjoyed a delicious meal of rat tail marinara lovingly created by Marjorie. Everyone seemed to be having a good time, except Thorgrim. He was deeply depressed, though he hid it well.

He was out of time.

"Son, are you feeling okay?" asked his father.

"Yes, I'm just tired."

His mother replied, "Tired? You've been sleeping all day!"

It was true. Thorgrim had been sleeping on and off all day, preparing for what was to come.

Luthor took a final bite of food and said, "I still want you to get to bed as soon as we're finished here. I don't want you oversleeping tomorrow, because if yer late, I don't know what they will say since you've been gone two weeks. I'm afraid they've run out of patience, and you've run out of excuses."

Thorgrim felt pinned against a wall, and his face wore a blank expression. He did not intend to return to the mine, but he did not have the courage to face his father with the truth.

"Son? Did you hear what I said?"

Lying, Thorgrim replied, "Okay, Papa, I'll go to bed right after I'm done, and I won't be late tomorrow."

"In fact, everyone is going to bed early. I don't want any disturbances. Hear me, kids? It's seven-thirty. Everyone's in bed by nine."

The rest of the kids uttered a collective, "Awwww!"

Trying to change the subject, Thorgrim took a big, chomping bite of rat tails and exclaimed, "Wow, Mama, this dinner is fantastic! Yer best meal, ever!"

"Mama, Thorgrim's smacking his lips again when he's eating!" complained Hannah.

Thirteen year old, Crabby, the third-oldest child, said, "He does it on purpose." The young boy then stuck his tongue out at Thorgrim.

Thorgrim shook his head. "Shut it, Crabby. I do not. I just like it, that's all, and my lips smack together when I eat something I like."

Thurston said, "I think he does do it on purpose because he knows it's annoyin'."

Thorgrim grinned. "No, I don't"

Marjorie said with a slight frown, "Thorgrim, it is annoying, so please, try to chew with yer mouth closed.

"Okay, Mama."

She smiled. "But thank you for the compliment about the dinner. It takes a lot of work to make rat tail marinara. Why, do you have any idea how difficult it is to remove the hair from all of those tails?"

Trying to hide his anxiety, Thorgrim smiled, "It's one of my favorites, and you cooked the tails al dente, just the way I like 'em! The red sauce is perfect, too!"

His mother beamed.

"Yes, my dear, you've outdone yerself again!" said Luthor, before uttering a loud belch.

Everyone laughed except Marjorie.

***

After finishing dinner, Thorgrim spent a few minutes with his siblings, eagerly chasing them through the house (much to his parent's chagrin), followed by a short game of hide and seek.

A half-hour later, Luthor again reminded Thorgrim that he needed to get to bed. Thorgrim understood but asked if he could hold baby Tadder for a couple of minutes, first.

His little brother, now barely two weeks old, always smiled whenever Thorgrim held him. Even when the baby was upset, whenever Thorgrim picked him up, Tadder would calm down and smile a wide, toothless grin. Of course, Thurston and the rest of the kids teased Thorgrim saying that Tadder is only smiling because he thinks Thorgrim looks funny.

After a few minutes, Thorgrim kissed Tadder's cheek. His beard tickled his tiny brother's plump face, causing the baby to giggle. Then he gave his parents a big hug before going to his bedroom. Tonight, he hugged them extra tight.

It was dusk, just after 9:00 p.m., and he had to be up at 6:00 a.m. in order to prepare and get to work by seven. Although dwarves typically only require five hours of sleep each day, this meant Thorgrim could get nine hours of rest, however, tonight, there would be no time to sleep.

Not that he was sleepy, anyway. He sat on the edge of his bed, his mind, racing in circles, was full of worry.

For the past week, he had been working out a plan, though now that the moment had arrived, he did not know if he could bring himself to follow through with it.

Around 9:30 p.m., lightning flashed, announcing the arrival of a thunderstorm.

Full of worry, concern, and fear of the unknown, he thought, *Do I really want to do this? I have no choice, I guess . . . what else can I do?*

The thunderstorm roared and rumbled. Soon, a soft rain began to fall.

Thorgrim parted the curtains of his window and reconsidered all of his options.

Around 9:45 p.m., while watching the storm's light show, he finally made up his mind.

He sighed, put his hand up to the windowpane, and studied the rivulets of rainwater as they flowed down the glass.

As tears do.

∗∗∗

The crowing of several roosters signaled dawn, and as they always did, Luthor Longbeard and his wife rose from their bed to begin the new day.

91

Marjorie would start breakfast and prepare the lunchboxes for her husband and Thorgrim. Luthor would sometimes manage a quick bath before dressing, followed by an equally quick morning breakfast.

Luthor was excited. Though he was poor, life could not be better. Finally, things were normal for him and his family. Thorgrim would be coming back to work in the mine, his newborn son and the rest of the children were healthy, and his beloved wife had fully recovered from her extremely difficult, life-threatening labor.

While dressing, Luthor could hear his children chatting with their mother in the kitchen while eagerly awaiting their breakfast of hot sausages, cakes, and eggs. On his way to join them, He popped his head into Thorgrim's bedroom to make sure his son was awake and getting ready.

"Son, it's almost six . . . are you up?"

With only the glow of the dawn coming through the lone window's curtains, Luthor could barely see anything. He spoke again. "Thorgrim?"

Nothing.

"Thorgrim? Are you awake?"

Stepping into the room, Luthor approached the bed. Reaching the bedside, he nudged it.

"Thorgrim, time to get up, Son."

No response.

Slightly puzzled, Luthor looked closer and discovered Thorgrim's bed had been made.

He actually made his bed? That's a first. Hmmm, maybe he's up already.

Leaving the room, he called down the hallway. "Margie, is Thorgrim in the kitchen?"

"No, he's probably still in bed."

"Nope. In fact, he made his bed. Can ya believe it?"

She offered a brief chuckle. "No, I can't! Well, I haven't seen him. I've been in the kitchen cooking. Maybe he's taking a bath or using the outhouse. Did you check?"

"No."

Luthor looked in the bathroom but found it was empty. Then, he went to the back door and called for Thorgrim.

Watching the outhouse for any sign of him, he said, "Son, you in the outhouse?"

No reply.

"Hmmm." As he turned, he ran straight into his wife, who was coming up from behind him. Her eyes were full of sadness, and she held a piece of paper in her hand.

92

Luthor was baffled. "What's the matter? What's this?" he asked, pointing to the paper.

"A letter from Thorgrim," she replied, teary-eyed. "I just found it in the kitchen."

"A letter?" asked her husband. He took the letter from her. "What does it say?"

"He's gone, Luthor," she replied, her tears flowing. "He left in the middle of the night."

"What? But, why?"

Luthor, his hand shaking, looked at the hastily written letter and read it aloud.

Dear Mama and Papa,

When you find this letter, I will be traveling on destiny's road. I don't know where the road will take me, but I will never forget where it started. Thank you for everything that you taught me and for all of your kindness and love.

Papa, I am claustrophobic and because of this problem, I can't work in the mine. Although I would have loved to work by your side, I cannot.

My true love is books. Maybe one day I'll become a researcher or a writer. I would really enjoy getting a job in a library somewhere though it probably won't be in the Dwarven Clans, for obvious reasons.

I'm sure that soon I'll be outcast for my decision to leave without an official release from my obligations in the mine. I'll be wanted by the law and may never be able to return home.

Mama, I believe that somehow you already knew that I was going to leave, but Papa, I'm sure this is a surprise and that you are disappointed in me. The last thing I wanted to see was the look in your eyes after I told you that I would not be returning to work. This is why I left in the middle of the night. I know when you go to work tomorrow; you'll be asked many questions about me. I'm sorry to put you through this, but I have no choice.

I can't tell my brothers and sisters goodbye. Tell them for me, and please forgive me.

Someone once told me that I must go out into the world and create my own destiny. It is my time to do so.

But maybe one day I can return home.

I love you all . . . Mama, Papa, my brothers, and sisters. I will miss you.

Thorgrim

PS: I will write as often as I can.

Luthor paused and looked up. With a blank stare, he handed the letter back to his wife.

"You knew of this?" he asked.

Between sobs, she replied, "I sensed it."

"You sensed it?" Luthor said as he slowly walked towards Thorgrim's bedroom. "I can't believe it. He's really gone."

Marjorie, still crying, followed.

Entering the bedroom, they both glanced around. With the light of the rising sun helping, they could see that Thorgrim's room was spotless.

Luthor pointed. "When did he have time to pick this place up? See, he made his bed! The books ... there had to be over thirty of them from the library and all probably past due. Where are they?"

They both noticed a small note and two books sitting on top of Thorgrim's nightstand. Picking the note up, Luthor read it aloud.

I returned the books to the library yesterday and paid the late fees. While I was there, I bought the two books that are here on my nightstand. They're for my little brother, Tadder. I won't get to see him grow up, but please, one day, make sure you let him know that the books were two of my favorites, and I wanted him to have them.

Luthor and Marjorie, tears flowing, looked down at the books. They were entitled, 'The Adventures of Huckleberry Dwarf' by Mark Caboose, and 'The Dwarf and the Ring, by J.R.R. Baggins.

Luthor looked at his wife. "My God. When I go to work this morning, what do I say?"

Speechless, she could only shake her head.

94

Luthor said, "Should I try to find him? He can't be far. Maybe we can fix this claustrophobia thing."

Marjorie, wiping her tears, said, "I asked Dr. Thacker about it a few days ago. He said there is no known cure for claustrophobia."

"So, you have known about Thorgrim's problem?"

"Yes."

"When did he tell you?"

"The day after Tadder was born. When I was very ill."

Luthor's brow furrowed deep over his misty eyes. "I wish you would have said something to me."

Unable to look at her husband, ashamed, she looked down at the floor.

"I'm sorry," she whimpered.

"Well, it's too late for that. Thorgrim should have been the one to tell me, anyway. Now, we need to buy our son some time so he can get out of the country. Moridon, help me, I'll think of something."

***

Map of the southern Dwarven Clans.

By the time his parents had found his goodbye letter, Thorgrim was already about fourteen miles out of Vog, walking along the wet, metalized highway, southwest towards the small farming town of Stug. He had been traveling since 10:30 p.m. and was very tired from lack of sleep.

He had walked over seven hours in the dark of night and at least an hour of that time in the rain. His clothes were wet, and his boots were soaked with water. Lacking a torch, it was difficult to see and then avoid stepping in the myriad of puddles that were on the road.

Thorgrim believed spooks and darkness went hand in hand. While he walked down the road in the middle of the night, whenever the thought of encountering a ghost crossed his mind, he would try to think about other issues. Important things such as wondering if he was making the right decision, how he might acquire more food and water when he needed it, and how much time he had before the authorities began looking for him.

Fortunately, the technique worked, although a couple of times he almost filled his pants when he was startled by the ghostly call of a haunt owl and when a giant opossum suddenly ran across the road in front of him.

Initially, because the rain had brought cooler temperatures, he made good time, but that would soon change. Now, with the sun coming up, it was getting hot and humid as it usually does after a summer storm. The weather, and his heavy backpack, overly stuffed with supplies, would slow his pace, forcing him to stop and rest every few miles.

The fear of getting caught tormented him as it had since he first began working on his plan to leave, so he wanted to get out of the country fast. His destination was the Great Kingdom, where he hoped to find a job and start a new life. His first problem was to figure out the safest and fastest way to get there.

During the previous week, while planning his departure, using a small map, he had studied his options.

Heading north was not a good choice because he had heard that the Darum River was severely flooded and currently impassible. The only other option, and a shorter distance to the border, was south. He would travel around the tip of the Brimger Mountains, through the capital city of Bur Dhulgren, then east into Brimger Province and eventually the Alacarjian border.

Because he, like most dwarves, disliked elves, Thorgrim would have preferred to avoid the elven Republic of Alacarj, instead, traveling southeast towards the Great Kingdom. Unfortunately, that idea presented its own problems. In the wilderness and outlands of the southern parts of the Mharrak and Brimger Provinces, travelers risked encountering groups of bandits and thieves who enjoyed hunting unwary victims at night.

The area was also peppered with military outposts. Everyone coming through any security checkpoint must present identification papers, but Thorgrim had none (he had forgotten his) and that usually meant an interrogation, which in his case could lead to imprisonment.

Something else was also luring Thorgrim south. Recommended by Dr. Thacker, two locations inside Bur Dhulgren called to him. The Supreme Library and the Grand Hall of the Dwarves.

It would take several days to travel to the capital on foot, and every day he remained in the country increased the risk of capture, but regrettably, he had no other options.

Griping about having to walk, he wearily trudged along the road towards the unknown and his destiny. His only companion was his big, high school backpack full of food, water, some clothes, a small map, a few bars of soap, a toothbrush, some other hygienic items, and what remained of his life savings (a silver piece and fourteen coppers).

While reading his favorite books, Thorgrim had imagined traveling all over the known world many times, though in reality, with the exception of a field trip to Lake Vog, he had never been this far away from his hometown in his entire life.

He had heard many exciting stories about Bur Dhulgren and could not wait to get there. Of concern to him was the fact that the city had a large police force. Bur Dhulgren was the seat of the monarchy and the headquarters of the kingdom's civil authority. The very people who would be looking for him.

So far, the number of travelers on the road had been few, but occasionally, Thorgrim would encounter someone on a horse or mule. In addition, some locals were seen on foot near their small huts or farms and they always offered a friendly wave.

Everything Thorgrim saw or heard caused him anxiety, and even an occasional dog or cat crossing his path, put him on edge. Paranoid, he imagined that anyone who saw him recognized who he was and would soon contact the authorities. He feared that everyone who approached on horseback, coming from the direction of Vog, was going to arrest him.

***

Thorgrim checked his small timepiece (a beloved gift given to him by his parents on the day he graduated from high school). The time was 12:30 p.m. Counting rest breaks, Thorgrim had been traveling for approximately fourteen hours, averaging slightly less than two miles per hour. Not bad for a four and a half foot tall, two hundred and twenty-pound dwarf, who was hauling a backpack that weighed over fifty pounds.

Although he carried a small map that he had 'borrowed' from one of the library books, he had no way of knowing exactly how many miles he had walked since he left home. In reality, he was about twenty-five miles from Vog, and it was still about twenty-two miles to the next town. A farming community called 'Stug.'

Thorgrim was very tired from lack of sleep, the heat, and the heavy load of his pack. The paranoia of getting caught and arrested also sapped his energy. He knew that soon he would have to stop and get some sleep somewhere before continuing, but his fear of capture drove him onward.

In truth, no one other than his parents knew that he was illegally avoiding his obligation, but it would only be a matter of days before this would change. That morning, his father had bought him some time by telling a series of lies to the Vog Silver Mine Company management, most specifically, the time clock manager, Biff Knickers.

***

"What do you mean Thorgrim is sick again?" yelled Biff Knickers. "And damn yer hide Luthor, yer late again! Now look, I don't care who you are, but if yer going to continue to be late, I'll—"

Interrupting Biff, another official from the company approached the front of the clock shack. It was Marko Krumwiede, the day-shift manager. He was holding a little brown dog.

Marko said, "What's this, Luthor? Yer son's ill again?"

Biff interjected with a screech, "Yes! And this particular dwarf is late again like he is every day!"

Mr. Krumwiede glared at Biff through the window. "I wasn't asking you, Biff. Are you forgetting that this particular dwarf, as you call him, has been with us for over fifty years? You've been with the company for how long?"

"Almost two years, Mr. Krumwiede. In fact, it will be two years next month! You know, I'm only doing muh job."

"Hmmm. And I appreciate you doing yer job, but are you forgetting that Luthor Longbeard's ancestor founded this mine? Not to mention the fact that Luthor and his crew have never, ever missed their ore quota?"

Biff was speechless and could only nod his head.

"Good then! You need to learn when to cut some slack."

More nodding from Biff.

Mr. Krumwiede smiled. "Anyway, Luthor, there are a few dwarves standing behind you waiting to clock in. Why don't you step over here for a moment, so we can discuss yer son."

Placing his dog on the ground, Marko said, "Don't go running off too far, Baron."

The little dog stopped to sniff Luthor's pant leg, then scampered to the back of the shack to do dog stuff.

Though nervous, Luthor smiled. "Dat's a cute dog ya got there, Mr. Krumwiede."

"Thank you. Baron's the first dog I've ever owned. I had a pet mouse once that I called Swissy, but my neighbor's cat ate him."

"Sorry to hear that, sir."

"That's okay, thank you. Uh, as far as yer son. I'm sorry, but what's his name again?"

"Thorgrim, sir. Thorgrim Longbeard."

"Yes, that's it. Yer son was the one born with the beard, right?"

"Yes, dat's him."

Marko tugged on his long, black beard. "Yer boy's been ill a lot, and then there was the health issue with yer wife, so Thorgrim's missed a lot of work. By the way, how is yer wife doing and that new baby?"

"Uh, she and my new son are doing very well, sir."

"Good! Well, maybe one day I can meet yer family and yer new boy. A future miner I'm sure!"

"Yes sir, of course."

Marko lifted the right side of his big, furry brow. "And uh, of course, Thorgrim had that terrible incident with those two troublemaking hoodlums. Again, I am very sorry for that, and I hope he'll be able to put that episode behind him."

"I believe he can, sir."

"Of course, those two idiots, uh, what were their names . . . oh, yes, Rupples and Vinny . . . uh . . . ."

"Rumbler and Zippy, sir."

"Yes, yes, yes, That's it. Rumbler and Zippy. Well, you can assure your son that those two clowns won't be working here anymore. Once they get their teeth fixed, and after their broken legs and noses mend, I heard they'll be sent off to the Army, but of course, they'll probably be kicked out of there in no time. Personally, I'd like to see them sent off to the Navy. I have a good friend by the name of Admiral Heinrich Koenig who would teach them a lesson or two. If they didn't learn, they'd be walkin' the plank."

Luthor could not resist a smirk.

Marko presented a serious look and said, "Luthor, I hate to tell you this but regulations require a doctor's slip for Thorgrim. We've been able to look the other way so far, but going forward, I uh . . . well, can you get one and bring it the next time you come to work?"

Luthor, sweating profusely from both the hot summer weather and anxiety, nodded. "I will have the missus contact Dr. Thacker tomorrow."

Marko patted Luthor on the back. "I can give you until this coming Monday, okay? So, you have today, tomorrow and the weekend to deal with it. Luthor, your boy isn't the only one who's not showing up for work, and I've come down hard on all of them. I'm sure you realize that I can't set a precedent with yer boy. The law is the law. You have to understand that the company is required to file a monthly employment report."

"I understand, sir."

"Let me be clear. Monday is the deadline, okay? Unless Thorgrim shows up for work, I must have a doctor's examination slip on that morning, or I'm afraid I'll have to file a report with the authorities in Bur Dhulgren. At this point, I have no choice in the matter."

Luthor could only purse his lips and look down.

Turning to leave, Marko said, "Uh, muh best to yer wife and that new son . . . an uh, of course, I'm hopin' Thorgrim feels better soon."

"Thank you, sir."

"Baron, where are ya, boy?"

Baron barked a few times and ran towards Marko, jumping into his arms. Marko gave his dog a hug and then began walking towards his office inside the mine entrance.

Luthor turned, then walked slowly towards the entrance of the mine to join his crew. As he went, he glanced towards Biff Knickers who was finishing with the last, tardy dwarves. When they made eye contact, Luthor winked and offered Biff a quick flap of the end of his beard.

"I saw that!" yelled Biff.

But Mr. Krumwiede saw it, too, and his belly laugh ended any more yelling from the irate, time clock manager.

∗∗∗

It was after 2:30 p.m. Now sixteen hours into his journey, about twenty-eight miles out of Vog, hungry, and exhausted, Thorgrim began to search for a place off the road where he could hide, eat a quick lunch, and take a nap.

Looking to his right, just past a small farming cottage, about fifty yards away, he spied a stand of oaks that were growing out of a shallow depression.

Thorgrim smiled. "Hmmm, that looks invitin'! Some food, a couple hours of shut-eye, and I'll be as good as new!"

Glancing around to make sure no one would see him, he hastily ran through a muddy ditch and over to the oak trees, plopping down on the other side of them.

There, safely out of sight from anyone, he slipped off the heavy backpack and opened it. Thirsty, he quickly drank some water from one of his flasks, then rummaged through his pack looking for a couple of biscuits and a few pieces of the bison jerky he had brought with him.

Sitting against one of the trees, Thorgrim enjoyed his lunch. Ten minutes later, with his hunger satisfied, he slowly became drowsy.

Deciding that it was time to take his nap, he slid onto his back beneath the shade of the oak trees and dozed off.

***

"I'll be damned if I know wut that sound is, Julia!" exclaimed the old dwarf farmer to his wife. "Whatever it is, it's louder than a sick river moose, un it woke me up from a sound sleep!"

"Well, damn yer lazy hide, Gustav, go have a look-see!" replied his wife while cowering under the covers. "I'm frightened!"

Gustav flinched. "Are ya jokin'? It's after ten un pitch black out there. I won't be able to see a thing."

"You can't see a thing in broad daylight either, husband! Take yer lantern un go have a look. It's your duty to protect yer wife un home! Whatever that thing is out there, get rid of it!"

"Protect muh wife un home? Well, that thing ain't hurtin' nothin', Julia. Jus' makin' a bunch of racket, is all."

Julia scowled. "How do you know it ain't some kinda horrible monster? Besides, how can we sleep with that terrible noise? Go!"

"Alrighty, alrighty!" he replied, crawling out of bed. "I'll go! Hang on to yer beard, I'll be right back. Monsters, pffft!"

Dressed in a pair of pajamas, with the back flap hanging open, Gustav picked up the lantern from his nightstand and lit it. Walking out to the back porch, he grabbed a rusty pitchfork. Exiting the house, he paused to listen. Sure enough, coming from a nearby grove of oak trees was a loud, rattling, moaning sound that permeated the night.

With goosebumps on his arms, his long grey beard tossed over his shoulder, lantern held high, and the sharp points of the pitchfork protruding straight out in front of him, the old farmer carefully approached the source of the creepy sound. Within a half-minute, he had reached the trees and looked closely.

In the light of his lantern, Gustav noticed a young dwarf with a very long beard, lying on his back, sound asleep and snoring loudly.

"Wut in dee hell?" hollered Gustav, while gently prodding the sleeping dwarf with his pitchfork. "Wake up, young 'un. Wut in Moridon's name are ya doin' sleepin' on muh property? By God, yer snoring is louder than muh wife, her sister, un muh mother in law when they're all yappin' at the same time!"

Thorgrim had fallen asleep for a short nap around 2:30 p.m., but because of his fatigue, he failed to wake up and had now been slumbering for almost eight hours. Oblivious to the world, he remained in his deep, snoring sleep, despite the fact that an old farmer was yelling and poking him with the pointy tips of a pitchfork.

Also unknown to Thorgrim was that he had fallen asleep next to a nest of large, poisonous field snakes, and they were crawling all over him.

When Gustav brought his lantern closer, he finally noticed the deadly snakes. Alarmed, he jumped back.

Yelling loudly, Gustav shrieked, "I said, boy, wake up!" This time, he gave Thorgrim a firm poke with the fork.

"Owww!" complained Thorgrim, waking from his sleepy stupor. "Go away, I'm sleepin'."

"Boy, git off of muh property un do it quick or you'll be permanently sleepin'! Yer lyin' in a nest full of—"

"Huh?" said Thorgrim. Opening his eyes, he realized it was nighttime. He quickly sat up and looked around.

Gustav brought his lantern over again. "Boy . . . yer covered in—"

"I'm sorry, sir. I just fell asleep un . . . I'll go, I'll go."

Gustav shined his lantern down near the ground. "Boy, yer covered in poisonous field snakes. I'd be careful when—"

Before Gustav could finish, Thorgrim Longbeard, backpack in hand, was up, screaming wildly, and running down the road as fast as his stumpy legs could carry him.

A couple of minutes later, when Gustav returned to the bedroom, his wife asked, "Well, what was that thing out there? Did ya kill it? I heard it screamin' for its life!"

"Well, I think it was a young dwarf . . . maybe a teen-ager who fell asleep out there. That strange noise we heard was his snorin'. Uh, at least I think it was a dwarf, but it could've been a bearded elf!"

"A bearded elf?"

"Julia, I ain't ever seen any dwarf run that fast before, nor have I ever seen a beard that long!"

"Thank you for being my hero, husband. Douse the lantern, un get in here close un snuggle with yer wifey."

"Snuggle? Well, Julia, I ain't heard you use that word for quite a few years!" exclaimed the excited old farmer as he extinguished the lantern and climbed into bed next to her.

"Uh, husband, the pitchfork."

"Oh, sorry 'bout that!" replied Gustav with a chuckle. Lifting the covers, he tossed the pitchfork out of the bed and onto the floor.

***

Thorgrim ran as fast as he could until he was sure every snake had fallen off him. He hated snakes almost as much as spooks, and while running down the strange, darkened road, he soon forgot about the snakes and began worrying about spooks. He knew that spooks haunted the night, and now he found himself far from home, alone and in the dark.

It was very dark. The overcast sky hid the stars and there was no moon, making it difficult to see anything, even for humanoids like dwarves or elves, who are known for their excellent night vision. To make matters worse, Thorgrim had no idea what time it was because it was too dark to see his timepiece.

Unknown to him, it was almost 10:45 p.m.

Tired from running, he slowed to a walk. He was about eighteen miles from Stug.

Frightened by the surprise encounter with the old farmer, then the snakes, and now worried about running into spooks, he became homesick and wished he was tucked safely in his old, comfy bed.

He began to cry but caught himself. "I'm an adult now," he mumbled and grumbled. "This was my choice, un I have to see it through."

Although Thorgrim was concerned about spooks and monsters, he also began to worry about brigands and other criminals that he heard liked to ply their evil trade on roads such as this. He had no weapon and vowed to fix that problem as soon as possible.

However, Thorgrim had no training in the use of any weapon such as a hammer or an axe. Regardless, he still wished he had either one in his hands now, though he did not know how much good any weapon would do him if he ran into a seasoned highwayman.

Nervous about the possibility of meeting an unsavory character, or worse, a bunch of them, he picked up his pace to a hurried walk.

Although it was late into the evening, Thorgrim wondered why there were no other people on the road with him. Hoping someone might come by on a horse and give him a ride, he said to himself, "If I could only get lucky enough to get a ride, but then, only a foolish idiot would be out here in the middle of the night! Ha! Uh, well, I probably should rephrase that."

For several hours, despite the heat of the night and weight of his pack, with annoying gnats and mosquitoes pursuing him, he continued to walk at a fast pace down the empty road towards Stug. With no one else around, his only friends were the sounds of his own footfalls, a random barking dog, or the screech of a haunt owl.

Then an eerie sound caught his attention. It was a new, unwanted friend.

Though it seemed far off in the distance, he heard the cry of a wolf. In an instant, there was another howl, only this one was much closer. Now fearful of an attack by the Brotherhood of wolves, he tried to convince himself that the howling was from farm dogs.

But he knew better and needless to say, driven by fear, he hurried his pace.

Occasionally, the faster pace and heat forced him to stop to rest. Sometimes, he would find a suitable log or large rock to use as a makeshift chair, other times, he simply sat down in the middle of the road for a few minutes. However, it seemed that whenever he stopped, the mosquitoes swarmed him, and worse, the wolves always chose that moment to howl. Their eerie cries, sending chills down his spine, had him up and rapidly moving again.

Anxious to get to Stug, afraid that spooks or the wolves were closing in, though very tired and low on water, he pushed himself forward down the road. Soon, off to his left, Friday's dawn highlighted the outline of the Brimger Mountains.

After another mile, up ahead, Thorgrim heard the murmur of men's voices in conversation, along with the whinnies of several horses. Soon, in the dim light, he saw the outlines of three dwarves on horseback.

Oh, oh. Police or farmers?

When he got closer, he recognized that they were farmers, and hoping to hitch a ride to Stug, he hailed them.

"Good morning!" shouted Thorgrim.

One of them replied, "Morning."

"Hey, I was wonderin' . . . I'm on my way to Stug. Could any of you give me a ride into town? I have a few coppers that I could pay ya."

Another one of them pointed and said, "Well, Stug is just right down the road a bit. Hardly a quarter-mile. Yer almost there."

Thorgrim waved. "Thankee! I think I can handle that."

When Thorgrim came closer, the three farmers tipped their hats and nodded. Despite the dim light, Thorgrim looked away, hoping they would not get a good look at him in case the police would come through later, asking questions.

Hustling past them, Thorgrim rounded a bend, and then encountered a bridge that spanned a narrow river. Beyond it, lay a small town.

Looking to his right, posted at an intersection, he noticed two wooden signs. One sign pointed down a narrow connecting road that went west towards the coastal fishing town of Grekk, some ninety miles away. The other sign, much to Thorgrim's glee, displayed the name of the town that lay directly ahead. Painted in big black letters, it read: STUG.

VII.   Welcome to Stug

The small farming town of Stug was situated about halfway between Vog and Bur Dhulgren. It had a population of about two hundred dwarves, most of them living on their farms in little cottages around the edge of town.

Stug was about the same size as Vog, also having a quarter-mile long main street, as well. As in Vog, the main street contained several businesses for locals or visitors, including a bank, doctor's clinic, general store, bar, cafe, and a two-story inn. To meet the needs of the area farmers, the town also featured a blacksmith, horse stable, and a veterinarian.

Thorgrim would later discover, to his disappointment, that unlike his hometown, Stug lacked a library. He would shrug it off, telling himself that he did not have the time to stop and read, anyway.

***

Around 6:10 a.m., on Friday morning, in the dawn's early light, tired, thirsty, and hungry, he crossed the bridge and stopped to inspect the sleepy town from a distance. The street's torches were still burning. Everything was quiet and peaceful.

As Thorgrim had suspected, much to his regret, Stug's main street had a sheriff's office. Although he realized that he was probably not yet wanted by the authorities, his worry increased when he saw the sheriff's office, giving him an instant headache.

Thorgrim understood that he was paranoid about being identified and getting caught because it had only been one day. Besides that, the police had more to worry about than hunting down and capturing a nineteen-year-old kid who was refusing to work in the mines. Still, he had to be cautious until he was out of the country.

After several minutes, he spotted a few merchants entering their respective establishments. He also noticed smoke wafting from the cottage chimneys that dotted the area around the town. When the breeze shifted and blew towards him, his nose caught the delicious aroma of breakfast, lovingly prepared by the wives for their farming husbands and children. The smell reminded him of his mama's cooking.

Thorgrim wished for a hot meal, not having one since his last dinner at home two nights ago, and the smell of the food enraged his hunger.

107

Surveying the town, he decided to stroll down the main street in hopes of finding a café.

A couple of minutes later, up ahead and on his left, he saw what appeared to be a café. Instantly, obeying direct orders from his stomach, his feet hurriedly marched straight for it.

Soon, he was standing in front of what seemed to be a restaurant of some kind. He hoped the place was open for business, but unfortunately, it looked worn out and abandoned. The building had a single door flanked on both sides by large windows. The window on the left had a heavily faded image of a cup of coffee painted on it. The one on the right had an image of flapjacks with eggs and sausages.

He scratched his head while looking up at the sign over the single door entrance. It was written in a language that he was not familiar with.

Studying the front of the place, he did not see an 'Open' or 'Closed' sign, though Thorgrim swore he saw someone enter the one-story, whitewashed building ten minutes ago. Unsure about the name of the place, or if they were even still in business, he peered through one of the windows.

It was too dark inside to see anything.

He checked the time. It was 6:31 a.m. Sunrise was imminent.

Disappointed and famished, he decided to explore the rest of the town in hopes of finding another café' or even purchasing food at the general store.

After looking up and down the street, not sure where he was going next, he took another look through the window. Thorgrim now noticed a few sources of light inside. There was a torch burning on a wall sconce as well as a couple of lanterns sitting on a countertop. He was startled when a shadowy figure walked up and rapped on the glass.

It was a middle-aged, female dwarf. She said in a friendly voice, "I'm not open for about another half-hour, but the door's open. Come on in if yer hungry! I've got fresh eggs and smoked bison sausages!"

Pushed by his growling, empty stomach, Thorgrim shot like a bolt to the door and swung it open.

She said, "If ya want a table, ya better hurry, 'cuz soon this place will be crawling with some hungry boys! I only have room for twenty-four!"

Standing in the doorway, he looked inside and saw the middle-aged female dwarf walk behind a counter full of homemade pies. Her graying, shoulder-length hair was meticulously braided with beautiful strands of silver and brunette locks, each ending with a jeweled, platinum decoration. Her beard, perhaps the longest Thorgrim had ever seen on a female dwarf, hung nearly to her waist and was curled to perfection. Her eyes twinkled like a pair of stars, and she had the smile of his mother.

"Hi. I wasn't sure if you were open or not," said Thorgrim timidly, as he stepped into the café. "Heh, I wasn't even sure if this was a café, 'cuz I can't read the sign over the door."

She swiftly walked around the counter and towards the door. "Oh, those Zarkov kids. They flipped my sign upside down again, didn't they!"

She paused before going outside and said, "Yes, this is a café! Welcome to Mackel-Murkel's Café! The best place to eat in Stug! Well, it's the only place to eat in Stug, and that means it's the best one! I'm the owner! My name is Maybelline, but please call me May. I'll be right back. I need to take a look at my sign."

He smiled and waited while May walked outside.

"Oh, I just knew it!" she said with a scowl and a shake of her head. "They're either stealin' it or flippin' it upside down! I guess I didn't notice it when I arrived this morning, but it was pretty dark out then, ya know."

Walking back into her café, still scowling, she said, "Wait 'til I see their father later! I can guarantee you that those two boys will be wearing a reddened rear-end sometime today! But what good it will do, I'll never know. Well, I don't have time to mess with that sign now. I've got food to prepare."

She closed the door and said, "Well, ya better grab a table before my regulars get here at seven. Seating is limited!"

Thorgrim chose the nearest table to the door. As he turned to walk towards the table, she noticed the backpack he was wearing.

After studying his backpack for a second, she said, "Hey, hold up for just a moment."

Thorgrim, having only taken two steps, stopped, looked over his shoulder at her and said, "What is it?"

Without asking, she rapidly stepped forward, reached into an open side pouch of the backpack and grabbed something. Frowning, she fiddled with whatever it was for a moment.

Flabbergasted by her actions. He scrunched his brow and said, "Excuse me, but what are you doing?"

In one swift motion, she pulled a two-foot-long, very pissed off, field snake out of Thorgrim's backpack. While it struggled in her grip, she snapped its neck. Walking over to the front door, she opened it and tossed the dead serpent outside onto the street.

Thorgrim turned white as a sheet.

Closing the door, she said, "Oh, Moridon help me, but I hope that wasn't a pet of yers?" she said, her eyes wide and cheeks pink with embarrassment.

"No, I umm."

"Well, I didn't think so, 'cuz those field snakes are deadly!" she said, as she went back to the counter to grab a menu. "I saw his nasty head and beady eyes pokin' out of yer backpack, and I was worried he might slither out and get loose in here. I don't want any poisonous snakes pestering some of the customers!"

Thorgrim's world began to spin.

"Yer lucky he didn't bite ya, young 'un! Usually, yer dead in a matter of minutes, and it's a horrible, painful death! I think that's the only one in yer backpack, but we should make sure. Wherever did you acquire that snake?"

Thorgrim fainted, collapsing into a heap on the floor.

***

Thorgrim felt a splash of cold water on his face. Opening his eyes, he found himself still on his back next to a tipped-over chair. May was hovering above him.

"Are ya okay there, young 'un?"

He moaned, "I think so . . . what happened?"

"You fainted! Here, let me help you up. Quick now, before my regulars show up!"

Grabbing an arm, she sat him up. "How ya feelin'?"

He sighed. "Okay, I guess. Why'd I faint?"

"I think ya fainted because I found a poisonous snake in yer backpack. No worries, I snapped his neck and tossed him out front. You know, I'd probably faint, too, if I realized I'd been haulin' one of those nasty things around."

His head whipped around as he surveyed the area. "Snakes!" he yelled, panicked and red-faced. "Are there any more? I hate snakes!"

"You hate snakes? Well, I think they kinda like you, though. No worries, while you were sleepin', I checked yer backpack and didn't find any more. I took it off you and set it on a table. Hope ya don't mind."

"No, no, that's quite okay! Thanks for checking!"

"Do you feel like getting up?"

"I think so. How long was I out?"

"Oh, twenty minutes, maybe."

"Twenty minutes? Yer kiddin'!"

"Ya, you were snorin' to beat hell! Thought I'd let ya sleep a bit."

"Okay, I'm ready to get up, now."

With her assistance, he got to his feet.

"There ya go! Why don't we try this again." Gesturing towards the nearest chair, she said, "Please, have a seat. I put a menu on the table next to yer backpack."

Thorgrim's face and beard were wet from the water she had splashed on him, so she tossed him a towel from the counter.

"Ya might want to wipe yer face. Sorry 'bout that, but I tried everything to rouse ya. You must really hate snakes, huh? I even slapped yer face a few times, but you didn't move. Had to use cold water, 'cuz it always does the trick!"

Wiping his face and beard with the towel, he said, "Thanks again."

"Are ya still hungry?"

"Oh, yes," he replied, looking at the menu, his stomach howling for food. "I'm starvin'! I've been walkin' all night, and I've worked up a huge appetite. Been a while since I had a hot meal."

"Walkin' all night? From where?"

Still a bit woozy, Thorgrim let it slip before he realized what he was saying.

"Vog. Uh, well sort of."

Oh, no. Why'd I say that?

"You walked all the way from Vog? Welcome to Stug! Uh, don't ya have a horse?"

Thinking quickly, he said, "Well, I had a horse, but uh, I lost him up around Vog yesterday morning. He just ran off, somewhere. Been walkin' ever since. I stopped along the way in the afternoon and took a nap. I guess I kinda overslept. I woke up and spent all night walkin' and arrived here just before the sun came up."

"Do you live in Vog? What brings ya down here?"

Again, he had to think fast. He remembered the name of a city that Dr. Thacker had mentioned.

"Uh, No. I don't live in Vog. I'm from Dartag Bur and on muh way to Bur Dhulgren. I have a scholarship."

More stupidity! Why did I tell her where I was headin'? I don't want anyone to know that!

Thorgrim was not a good liar, yet.

She exclaimed, "That's a heck of a walk, so I bet you are hungry!"

"Yes, that's an understatement."

"Well, take a look at the menu, and let me know what ya want. You know, I don't think I caught yer name, young 'un.'"

He started to say his name but stopped. Not wanting to reveal his true identity, he had to come up with an alias, soon.

"Oh, yes, muh name, it's . . . uh, it's, mmmm."

"Still feelin' a bit groggy, young 'un? Well, maybe yer name will come back to ya after ya get some hot grub in yer tummy."

He nodded, "I hope so."

"I think I already told ya my name, but in case I didn't, it's Maybelline Mackel-Murkel. Now, that's a mouthful, ain't it! Just try to say that three times really fast! Hohahahaho! Anyway, the pleasure's all mine, and please call me May."

Thorgrim grinned. "Yes, you introduced yerself when I walked in. By the way, that's a very pretty name."

She laughed. "Mackel-Murkel? Yer either kiddin' or yer still out of it!"

He chuckled. "No, I mean Maybelline is a pretty name."

Catching himself, he turned red and continued, "Well, uh, of course, Mackel-Murkel is a pretty name too, I didn't mean to imply that it wasn't . . . ummm, I—"

It's okay," she said, interrupting. "That's what I get for getting married a second time and hyphenating my previous last name with the new one!"

She started to ask more questions, but luckily for Thorgrim, the front door flew open with a bang as several dwarves stampeded into the little café to grab some tables. It was 7:00 a.m.

Running to the kitchen, she yelled, "Mornin' boys! Right on time, I see! Hungry I presume?"

"Yes, yes, that's an understatement!" one of them replied. "Bring us our usual, May. Oh, and yer sign's upside down again."

Another yelled, "Ya, yer sign's upside down, and there's a dead field snake lying out in front, too."

"I'll get yer food ready in a bit! Help yerselves to the coffee. It should be ready. And I know about the sign. It's those Zarkov boys again. The dead snake's another story."

Two of them walked past Thorgrim's table towards the counter. There, they each took a pot of coffee off a pair of small oil burners. Returning, one of them stopped and offered Thorgrim some.

"Care for some coffee, boy?" asked the dwarf farmer, his burning pipe hanging from his bottom lip.

Thorgrim moved his backpack off the table and flipped over a cup. Nodding he replied, "Why, thankee, I sure would like some."

The farmer tipped the pot and filled Thorgrim's cup to the brim. "Careful there, boy. That coffee's hotter than a fire giant's fart!"

"Okay, thanks again."

As the farmer started back towards his own table and friends, he suddenly stopped next to Thorgrim. Dropping his brow, he said, "Skuse me, but you look awful familiar. Do I know ya?"

Thorgrim looked up. Panicking, he still managed to answer in a calm voice, "No, I'm not from around here. Just passing through."

The farmer leaned in close, ashes falling from his pipe on to the table. "Are you a farm boy or a miner, perhaps?"

Thorgrim had to think quickly. "Neither, I'm, uh, I'm on my way to the university in Bur Dhulgren. I have a scholarship." He cringed when he realized that he again revealed his destination to someone.

He thought, *How stupid of me. If I keep this up, I might as well turn muhself in now!*

"Oh, a brain! Well, good for you, boy! Why break yer back on a farm or in one of the mines when you can instead work with yer noggin!"

"Thankee, sir."

As Thorgrim was about to take a sip of the hot coffee, the farmer patted him on the back.

"Good luck to ya!" the farmer said.

The slap on the back caused some of the coffee to spill out and burn Thorgrim's lips. "Oww!" he cried, rubbing his mouth.

"I tole ya the coffee was hotter than a fire giant's fart, didn't I!" the farmer said with a chuckle, as he headed back to his own table.

A moment later, the door burst open and the rest of May's regulars flooded inside. Everyone scrambled for the remaining chairs and tables. Those that did not get one, complained loudly.

Thorgrim was alone at his table with three empty chairs. Three dwarves approached and one of them asked, "Hey, kid, do ya mind if we join ya?"

Hesitating for a moment, he was concerned they would ask a bunch of personal questions. But he knew that he had no choice and gestured towards the chairs, nodding. Each said 'Thank you' and took a chair.

As they were sitting down, Thorgrim heard a commotion outside the café's windows. Looking, he saw several more dwarves peeking through the glass. All of them were irate that the café was full, and a few select curse words could be heard. After a minute, they gave up and wandered off, some flapping the ends of their beards as they went.

A few of the dwarves chuckled at the misfortune of those who didn't make it into the café in time to get a table.

The dwarf that was seated directly across from Thorgrim, said, "Serves 'em right! That's what they get for stayin' up all night and pounding their ale! Hahohaho!"

Reaching out his hand towards Thorgrim, he continued, "Nice to meet ya, kid. Brogal is muh name."

Thorgrim shook his hand, then carefully took another sip of coffee and said, "Why don't they just eat at home?"

The dwarf seated off to Thorgrim's right replied, "Sonny, anyone eating breakfast in this café is either divorced or don't know how to cook their own food. And, uh, nice to meet ya, too. You can call me, Puck."

The dwarf on Thorgrim's left said, "Puck's ain't kiddin'. I shore miss muh wife's cookin' but alas she's passed on! Oh, un Schultzy is muh name. Nice to meet ya."

"Yer wife hasn't passed on, as in dead passed on!" commented Brogal. "The only thing she's passed on is you, Schultzy! She left ya for that banker!"

"She's passed on dead as far as I'm concerned," replied Schultzy with a low brow.

May came over to the table with a fresh pot of coffee. "Coffee, boys?"

They all flipped their cups over. Everyone said, "Sure!"

"I know ya won't be needin' menus, so what will it be today? Yer usual?"

Each of them nodded, smacking their lips.

Looking at Thorgrim, she asked, "How about you, young 'un? What would you like?"

Thorgrim took another glance at the menu she had given him earlier. He only had a silver piece and fourteen coppers, so he had to be careful that he didn't order something he couldn't pay for.

Brogal said, "Bring him the works! I'm buying today!" The others in the café overheard him, and they all cheered.

"The works it is!" May said, turning towards her kitchen.

Thorgrim was speechless.

While everyone cheered, Brogal stood up halfway from his chair, waving his hand. He said, "Not you guys, I'm buying breakfast for my new friend. Now shut yer holes, and get back to drinkin' yer coffee!"

A few chuckled and others booed or hissed.

Brogal laughed. "Listen to those beggars! Ha! They'll get over it. I hope ya don't mind me payin' for yer breakfast, kid. It's the friendly thing to do for a stranger. Uh, we didn't get yer name, I don't think, did we?"

Thorgrim was astounded and embarrassed. Despite not wanting any attention, it seemed that everyone in the café had stopped talking to listen for his response. He stammered as he tried to make up a believable name. "Uh, muh name? It's, uh . . ."

Unable to quickly come up with a name, he tried to relax by taking a couple of deep breaths.

"You okay, kid?" asked Brogal.

About to enter the kitchen, May said, "He wasn't feelin' so well when he came in here earlier, so don't expect much outta him."

They all eyed him, still silent, waiting for his name.

You could hear a pin drop.

Perspiring, Thorgrim was aware that he had no choice. He had to give them a name, and he had to make one up now, or it would be obvious that he was lying. He finally chose a name that had been stuck in his head since he first heard it.

"Shem."

"Shem?" several asked.

"Uh, yes, muh name's Shem."

May hollered from the kitchen, "Ah, yer head's cleared up! You remembered yer name!"

Brogal slapped the table, rattling the coffee mugs. "Oh, so Shem it is! Shem . . . hmmm, I've heard that name before, somewhere, I think. Hmmmm, oh well, uh, what's yer last name?"

Now Thorgrim was really caught in a trap. *What kind of believable last name can I invent?* he thought, panicking.

He thought of the name Shem. *What goes with Shem?* The only name that came into his mind was . . .

"Library," mumbled Thorgrim.

Puck chuckled while scrunching his brow. "Did you say yer last name was Library?"

Thorgrim realized how stupid that sounded. Embarrassed, thinking fast, he said, "Uh, no . . . not Library. Hahahahohaho . . . I said, Lybree. Ya, that's muh name, Shem Lybree."

At that moment, May approached from the kitchen with several plates full of fried potatoes, honey flapjacks, and a pile of sizzling hot, bison sausages.

"Got hot syrup and fresh butter comin' up in just a second."

"Oh, that looks so good!" said Thorgrim, his hunger screaming for mercy. He was the first to help himself to a few cakes and sausages.

"May, can you make me a couple of tree ostrich eggs, over easy?" asked Schultzy.

"Sorry, I'm outta tree ostrich eggs, but I do have some snake eggs. Will those do?"

Schultzy nodded.

Thorgrim, his mouth stuffed with a sausage, grimaced and almost choked. "Snake eggs?"

"No worries, Shem . . . not field snake eggs," she replied with a giggle. "They're carpenter snake eggs. Shem hates snakes and he had an incident with a field snake this morning. That dead one that's lying out front."

Puck's brow shot up to the moon. "Oh, a field snake! Yer lucky that ya didn't get bit! You'd be climbing Moridon's golden beard right now if ya had!"

Thorgrim turned white and stopped eating.

"He knows," May said, patting Thorgrim on the back. "Don't talk about it, or he might faint again. You okay, Shem?"

Thorgrim, apparently now going by the alias, Shem Lybree, nodded.

"Alright, I'll get those eggs going," she said, as she was heading back to her kitchen. "Now, enjoy yer food."

After she entered the kitchen, someone off to the left, complained. "Hey, May! We ordered our food first! Why did they get theirs before we did?"

"Shut it! Yer food's a comin' I wanted to be polite and serve our new visitor first."

A snake egg came flying out of the kitchen, hitting the complaining dwarf in the middle of his beard. The explosion of eggshell and yolk caused a huge roar of laughter from everyone else in the room.

Scooping what egg he could off his beard, the dwarf put it in his mouth, eating it, shell and all. "Ya know, I kinda prefer em raw, anyway!"

Back at Thorgrim's table, everyone was rapidly eating their breakfast.

Wiping syrup from his mouth, Brogal grinned and said, "Shem, sorry that we're bolting our food, but we have to get to our fields. It rained yesterday morning. It's going to do it again later tonight, and that will make it muddier than hell. Big storm a comin'."

"Sure, I understand," replied Thorgrim.

Schultzy said, "Hey, Shem, not to be nosey, but, where ya from and where ya headed? Seems to me that a kid yer age must be fresh out of high school. I mean, shouldn't ya be in the mines, or are ya farming or in the military?"

Though he deeply regretted his stupidity for revealing his true destination earlier, Thorgrim had no choice but to stay consistent with his story. "No, I, um, I'm headin' to Bur Dhulgren. I've got a scholarship to attend the university there."

116

"A scholarship!" exclaimed Schultzy while taking a big bite of pancake. "Congratulations! I dropped out of school in the ninth grade because my parents needed help on our farm."

Puck laughed. "You dropped out of school, 'cuz you kept flunking yer classes."

"That's not all true! My parents did need help on the farm. My flunking only encouraged me to quit!"

Both Puck and Brogal laughed, sausage juice rolling down and onto their beards.

Brogal took a last bite of the spicy meat and said, "Anyway, Shem, you said you were heading to Bur Dhulgren to attend the university?"

"Uh, yes."

Brogal smiled. "Congratulations. Where ya from? I hope we're not being too nosey, just curious, trying to make conversation."

May, pushing a cart full of hot food on her way to a table, paused to listen.

Remembering the lie that he had told May, he replied, "No, that's okay. I'm from Dartag Bur."

"Dartag Bur!" replied Puck, surprised. "You're a long way from home! That's practically two hundred miles. You must be tired of ridin'!"

May said, "Shem only rode as far as Vog. He lost his horse up around there the other day and has been on foot ever since. He walked all the way here."

In a corner, someone at a table full of hungry dwarves, hollered, "May, can we please get our food?"

"Sorry, coming now," she replied as she pushed the cart over to their table.

Brogal said, "I've been to Vog before, and Dartag Bur. Shem, there's a university in Dartag Bur. I'm surprised that yer high school would award a scholarship for a university outside the province."

More lies were needed.

"Uh, well my scholarship is transferable. My interest is in history, and the great university in Bur Dhulgren is the best choice for such studies."

Schultzy said, "I heard that the Darum is flooded. How in the hell did ya get past that? Did ya rent a dragon and fly over the river? Hahahaahoha!"

The questioning caused sweat to pour down Thorgrim's back. Having no choice, the lying continued, though he was getting better at it.

"No, uh . . . well, I took a boat across the river."

"With yer horse?"

"It was a big boat," explained Thorgrim, firmly.

After taking a last drink from his mug of coffee, Brogal smiled. "I see! Well, congratulations on yer scholarship! I wish you well in Bur Dhulgren! You know, the capital is over fifty miles down the road, so unless you want to pay someone to give you a ride, you might want to stop down at the stables here in town and purchase another horse!"

Thorgrim knew he could not afford a horse, but played along. Nodding, he said, "Buy a new horse? That's a good idea."

Brogal placed his empty coffee cup on the table and said, "Come on boys, swallow that last bit of coffee. The sun's high in the sky, and we have to get to the fields."

Rubbing his belly, Brogal put on his hat and stood up from his chair. He pulled out a coin bag. Looking towards the opening next to the kitchen door, he hollered, "May, how much today?"

May replied, "Um, let's see. Four silver should cover it."

Brogal reached in his bag and dropped four silver pieces for the food and a few coppers for a tip.

A few of the other dwarves who were finishing their meals yelled, "Don't forget that Brogal's paying for ours too!"

"No, I'm not," replied Brogal with a smirk. "Nice to meet you, Shem! See ya around!"

"Thanks for the breakfast," said Thorgrim.

Brogal tipped his big hat. "Welcome."

The rest of the dwarves began to rise from their tables and after paying what they owed May for their food, departed the little café.

Only Thorgrim remained behind, numbed by all of the lies he told. He thought, *I've probably told more lies today than I've ever told in my entire life combined.*

Plopping a last piece of sausage in his mouth, Thorgrim chased it down with some cold coffee.

"Finished?" May asked as she came out of the kitchen.

"I dunno, I guess so."

Picking up the plates, she said, "Take yer time. No hurry to leave if you'd like to stay. I'll keep yer coffee mug filled."

Checking the wall clock, it read 8:30 a.m. "Thank you," he replied. "I can stay for a while. It's still early, where are your customers?"

"Oh, a few will sometimes trickle in, but Stug is a small, farm town. For a farmer, eight o'clock in the morning is not early. Practically everyone is out in their fields. I won't see anyone 'till noon for lunch."

As May wandered over to fill his cup again, Thorgrim drifted into deep thought. For another hour, twice, almost falling asleep, he sat at the table thinking about his decision to leave home. His past, present, and future flashed before him as he sipped on the coffee, (sometimes burning his lips during a drink because he had been oblivious to May's refills). Occasionally, Thorgrim thought he could hear May talking, but he was not sure if it was her or someone in his daydream.

Soon, he nodded off in his chair, snoring loudly.

May let him sleep, while she quietly cleaned up after the breakfast crowd.

***

Finally finished with her cleaning, glancing at the wall clock, May saw that it was almost 9:30 a.m.

Thorgrim was still snoring.

She let him sleep for another ten minutes, then roused him.

"Shem, are you awake?" she asked, gently nudging him.

"Huh?" he said, his eyes half-open.

"Ya better wake up. It's after nine-thirty."

He sat up and rubbed his face. "Nine-thirty? Wow. Have I really been here for three hours? Doesn't seem like it's been that long."

May chuckled and replied, "Yes, I guess so. Of course, you've been sleeping for about an hour of it!"

"Ya, I suppose. Just tired from the walk last night. Sorry to be a bother. I better get goin'."

"Not a problem, Shem. It was a joy to meet you."

As Thorgrim rose to leave, he smiled, grabbed his backpack and waved to May, who was busy setting the tables for lunch. Pointing to his pack he said, "No snakes?"

"No snakes! I triple-checked."

"Thankee, Maybelline. The food was delicious. I'm so full, I can barely move. And uh, I really could use a garderobe. All of that coffee, it's uh—"

She laughed softly. "You'll find an outhouse behind the café."

"Oh, great. Thanks again!"

"Yer welcome, Shem . . . or is it Thorgrim Longbeard?"

Thorgrim was stunned and about dropped his pack. He stammered, "Thorgrim Longbeard? Who's he? Muh name's Shem Lybree."

"Well, the name written on the top of your backpack says Thorgrim Longbeard, so I assumed that was your real name."

Caught like a ratfish in a net, Thorgrim immediately thought of another lie.

"Oh, hahahoha, how stupid of me! Of course, Thorgrim Longbeard was a friend of mine. He gave me this backpack a while ago un —"

May interrupted. "Thorgrim . . . I mean . . . Shem, you be careful out there, okay? Be safe, and watch out for field snakes . . . or any kind of snakes, if ya get my drift," she said, finishing with a serious look, her manicured brow held high.

He stepped towards the door and opened it. "I will. By the way, yer food was almost as good as muh mama's. Prolly, the second-best breakfast I ever ate. Oh, un yer name . . . Maybelline Mackel-Murkel . . . it's as beautiful as you are, both inside un out. Ya know, you remind me a lot of muh mama."

She beamed a huge smile and blushed. "Why thanks, Shem!"

Thorgrim took one last look at her and stepped through the door. "Bye, bye," he said, with a tear forming in his eye.

After closing the front door to the little café, and not knowing when or where he would get his next hot meal, he looked down the street towards the building that appeared to be the horse stables.

The thought of walking over fifty miles to Bur Dhulgren in the heat of summer nauseated his full stomach. He would somehow have to acquire a horse (or catch a ride with someone). Before continuing his trek, he would also have to purchase some food and refill his water flasks at the general store across the street.

While thinking about his plans, his full, coffee laden bladder reminded him that he had to use the outhouse. Walking around behind the café, he found it and hurried inside.

Once he was finished, he tore off the name tag from the top of his backpack. Looking at it, he mumbled, "Well, at least for now, Thorgrim Longbeard will not exist. From now on, I guess I'm Shem Lybree." Dropping the tag into the hole of the garderobe, he exited and immediately began to walk towards the horse stables.

How can I afford a horse? he wondered.

As he walked down the street towards the stables, he said to himself, "How much does a horse cost anyway?"

Arriving at the stables, a large barn-like structure, he looked up and read the crudely written sign. Oddly, it was written in Avalonian, a human language he barely understood. The sign read, 'Tuckerheim Equine and Shoeing.'

He checked the time. It was almost 10:00 a.m.

VIII.   An Elven Horse Named Nugget

L istening, Thorgrim could hear the sound of a blacksmith working on metal (likely making horseshoes), as well as the whinnying of several horses. He also heard the murmuring of a couple of people talking from somewhere inside the building.

Opening the main door, Thorgrim stepped in and approached an empty counter. Looking around for someone to help him, he noticed the walls were covered with horse collars, ropes, and other equine-related items. He also noticed a door behind the counter, and he could clearly hear the sounds of voices coming from the room beyond. Off to his right was another door that probably led to the stables or to the blacksmith's shop. The sound of the banging metal seemed to be coming from that direction.

"Hello?" Thorgrim called out.

He waited for a few moments and tried again, only louder.

"Hello!"

Instantly, the door from behind the counter popped open, and a pretty, middle-aged female dwarf, wearing a pair of dirty bib overalls, walked out. Approaching the counter, she nodded to Thorgrim, then took a huge drink from the ale mug she was holding. It was obvious to Thorgrim that she had probably been doing the morning chores in the stables and like most dwarves, likely drinking her share of whatever ale might exist on the property.

Placing her half-empty mug down on the counter, she said, 'I'm sorry, I didn't know you were here. Charla's muh name. How can I help you, sir?"

"Uh, do you deal in horses? I mean, can I buy one here?"

"Do we deal in horses?" laughed Charla. "Are ya jokin'? What does this place look like, a flower shop? Look around, how many flower shops sell horse collars, saddles, and the like?"

Realizing that Charla was probably drunk or close to it, Thorgrim was still surprised by her rudeness. He tried to respond but was speechless and only able to return a shrug of his shoulders.

"Ha! I'm only messin' with ya! Sure you can buy a horse here." Charla said, with a big belly laugh followed by a swig from her mug. "Just havin' some fun. Ya know, it's almost the weekend un I'm just primin' up for the big celebration."

He shrugged again. "Celebration?"

121

Charla appeared puzzled. "Yes. Were ya born yesterday or somethin'?"

"Well, no, I wasn't born yesterday. I'm not from here. See, I'm just passing through, and I'm—"

She blushed. "Oh, my apologies! You don't look like anyone that I've seen before! I should have guessed! Well, startin' tomorrow on the weekend, our town is celebratin' its five hundredth anniversary! It'll be the biggest party ever! We have a huge shipment of ale comin' in from the brewery in Pretzel. Not to mention, we'll be cookin' up a ton of food, too! Music, dancin', eatin', and my favorite thing . . . drinkin' ale . . . ah, I just can't wait!"

He smiled. "Five hundred years! That's amazin'. "What are the odds that I would be coming through here on yer town's five hundredth anniversary?"

"Well, technically, our five hundredth anniversary isn't for another forty-two years. We're just practicin', so when it finally gets here, we'll be ready."

He raised his brow and said, "Oh, I see. Well, congratulations, anyway."

Charla belched, giggled, and said, "Thanks! Uh, now, friend, what can we do for ya? Oh yes, you're in need of some ale? Well, we don't have any extra to give away, and we don't sell it, neither, so I'm sorry. You could try the bar next to the store across the street, but you know it's not good to be drinkin' this early in the morn."

Thorgrim watched as Charla tipped her mug back and emptied it.

He shook his head. "No, I don't want any ale . . . I don't really drink the stuff much. I'm in need of a horse."

"Huh? You don't drink ale much?" Charla asked, leaning closer, over the counter. "What kind of dwarf are you, anyway?"

Baffled, he replied, "I don't know. I didn't know there were different kinds of dwarves."

Charla squinted. "Oh, I can see yer a young 'un!" Reaching below the counter, she pulled up a decanter full of ice-cold ale and refilled her mug to the brim.

Charla took a big slurp of foamy brew and continued, "Well, trust me; you'll eventually develop a taste for the golden elixir! When the time comes, don't forget I told ya that!"

Thorgrim sighed. "Okay, I won't forget, but can I buy a horse? How much are they?"

"You want to buy a horse? What do ya need a horse for?"

He sighed again. "Uh, to ride."

Charla took another swig and beamed. "Oh, you be wantin' a ridin' horse, is it? Well, ya came to the right place! We have the best and lowest cost horses in town! Ya hear me? The best and lowest cost horses in town!"

He lifted his monobrow. "You mean there are other places in this town that sell horses? I didn't notice any other—"

Interrupting him, she said, "Ha! Just messin' with ya again! No, me and the husband started this place over forty years ago, and we were then, and still are, the only place in town that sells horses. And we have the best ones, too. Oh, and the lowest prices of any in town! Bet ya didn't know that, did ya?"

Thorgrim's face went blank.

She continued to ramble. "Purebred dwarven horses. None of those junk horses that are a blend of a bunch of breeds! No sir, you won't find a better selection of horses anywhere in this town!"

Frustrated, he replied, "Okay, but you just said that you were the only place in town that sold horses."

"That's correct, sir. That's why you won't find a better selection at such low prices!"

He rolled his eyes. "Can I take a look at what you have? You see, I'm in a big hurry."

"Sure, follow me!"

The inebriated female dwarf led Thorgrim through the back of the building, up to the blacksmith, who had just finished making a set of horseshoes.

Taking another drink, Charla wiped the froth from her mouth and beard, and said, "Husband, this dwarf is interested in purchasing one of our horses! Uh, I didn't get yer name, sir."

"It's Shem. Shem Lybree."

Charla's husband laid his hammer down and made his way over to Thorgrim. Standing over six feet tall with a full build, it was obvious that he was a human. Reaching down, he took Thorgrim's hand and shook it.

"Sorry, I'm a bit dirty," said the man, in broken Dwarvish.

"It's okay," replied Thorgrim, his eyes wide.

"You seem a bit surprised to find a human in the middle of the Dwarven Clans!" said the man. "Allow me to introduce myself, Mr. Lybree. My name is Gary of Tuckerheim, and in case she didn't introduce herself, this is my lovely wife, Char."

Thorgrim offered a quick, half-grin and said, "Yes, believe me, she introduced herself when I arrived. Uh, pleased to meet you, Gary. And uh, yes, I guess I am surprised to find a human here in the Dwarven Clans. In truth, I've never met a human before."

Gary replied, "Ah, well you're young. I'm originally from the town of Tuckerheim in the Great Kingdom. I had my equine business there, but then I met Char. After we were married forty years ago, she talked me into coming here to Stug, because this is her hometown. How could I refuse? I would do anything for her."

"That was nice of you." Thorgrim smiled, remembering the love his father and mother had for each other.

Gary said, "So, you want to purchase a horse? And please, forgive my poor Dwarvish. You don't happen to speak Avalonian do you?"

Thorgrim shook his head. "Yer Dwarvish is fine, but no, I only know a little Avalonian. I would like to learn more one day, though."

"Yes, Avalonian is spoken about everywhere in the realm, and of course, it's my native language," said Gary. "You should learn it! I hear even the trolls are speaking Avalonian. You never know when it might come in handy."

Thorgrim grinned. "Trolls are speaking Avalonian? Never seen a troll, so I don't believe in them."

Gary replied, "I've never seen one either, but—"

Charla interrupted with a screech. "Husband! This dwarf came here to buy a horse, not chitchat all day! He says he's in a big hurry."

"Sure, honey. Uh, Mr. Lybree, I'm sorry, I get to talking and well, you know. I didn't realize you were in a hurry. Please, follow my wife. She'll show you what horses are available."

"Okay, thankee."

Gary said, "Uh, Char, I'll take that."

He reached out and grabbed his wife's half-empty ale mug. She pouted and then shrugged.

Gesturing and still pouting, Charla said, "This way, please."

Thorgrim followed Charla out the back and into a large building that contained about a dozen stalls. Stacks of hay were everywhere. He counted six horses inside and noticed that two stablemen were giving a couple of them a brushing.

Charla beamed a big, toothy smile. "As you can see, Mr. Lybree, we take good care of our horses." Pointing to the two stablemen, she added, "Those two grooms have been with us for as long as we've been in business."

Thorgrim was in way over his head and he knew it. Not only could he not afford to buy a horse, he had never ridden one before, either. The only thing he knew about horses was what he had read in a couple of books. Naïve as naïve can be, he hoped that they might rent him one for the day, or in the least, provide him with a ride to Bur Dhulgren.

Praying for a miracle, and building on his new alias, Thorgrim pretended to be an experienced equestrian.

"Yes, I can see that they are well cared for," he said with a nod. "Whenever I purchase a horse, I always choose a reputable dealer."

Charla chuckled for a moment, then stepped up and took a close look at Thorgrim.

"What is it?" he asked, retreating a step.

She scowled slightly. "Whenever you purchase a horse? You look very young to me. Exactly how old are you, and how many horses have you purchased?"

To reinforce the fable that he was an experienced equestrian, he added twenty years to his actual age.

"Uh, I'm thirty-nine. Turning the big 'four-oh' in about five months. Uh, I've purchased so many horses, I've lost count."

Charla giggled. "Yer almost forty years old? Now, I know we dwarves look very young, even at forty, but you still look like a kid! I'm serious! With the exception of that beard that's hangin' past yer knees, you don't look a day over fifteen, if ya ask me! As a matter of fact, I've seen babies barely out of diapers that look older than you!"

Taking another step back, Thorgrim said, "Thankee! I try to take care of my complexion."

"Oh, well, whatever yer doin' don't stop, 'cuz it's sure workin'!"

"Well, thankee very much, but about a horse. I really need one."

Pointing into the stables, Charla said, "Take yer pick! With the exception of the breedin' mare and that stud stallion down there at the end, we have two females and two males for sale. But the two females are fillies and one of the males is still a colt. I don't think they would be a good option for ya."

Thorgrim, hardly understanding what she had just told him, shook his head. "Hmmm. Yer probably right."

Charla pointed towards a big brown horse. "I think the best choice for you is that gelding over there. He's ready to ride! A purchase will come with shoes, if you like, at no extra charge, but saddles aren't freebies, I'm afraid."

"Oh, of course," replied Thorgrim, not sure what he was getting himself into. Having little money, now he had to ask a dreaded question. "Uh, can I ask how much for the gelding?"

Charla frowned and said, "You can ask, but I ain't tellin' ya!"

Perplexed, he raised his monobrow. "But, I thought—"

She slapped her knee, "Hahaohoahaha! Just kiddin'! Uh, the purebred gelding comes with papers and is a hundred gold pieces. Now, that includes shoes! Our saddles are made from premium cow leather and they run from ten to fifteen gold."

Although he had expected the prices to be far beyond what money he had, Thorgrim slumped his shoulders. "A hundred gold?" he muttered, depressed.

"Yes, think that's too much? Can you tell me where you can find a purebred dwarven gelding for a cheaper price, especially in this town?"

He shook his head. "No, I don't know of any place cheaper. Look, I just need something to ride. I don't need a purebred horse. I didn't bring that kind of money with me . . . don't you have anything cheaper?"

"No, we don't, I'm sorry."

Walking into the stables, Gary had overheard the last part of Thorgrim and Charla's conversation.

"Char, what about that elven cremello out back? No one wants him. Maybe Mr. Lybree would consider purchasing him."

Char said, "Nugget? Uh, sure. Want to take a look, Mr. Lybree?"

Thorgrim tugged on his beard and said, "An elven cremello? Exactly what is that?"

Gary replied, "Well, it's native to the elven lands of Alacarj and Sherduin. A few years ago, it just wandered in here one day from God only knows where, but likely from the Alacarj. I'm guessing that it crossed the border and made its way down here. We've had other strays find their way here, so I've seen it happen before. Poor thing was pretty beat up and full of demon ticks."

Thorgrim shuddered. "Demon ticks. Ohhh, those are terrible. One of my brothers got some of those in his hair once. My papa had to shave him bald and pour turpentine on his head to get rid of 'em."

Gary nodded. "Yes, they're nasty, but we cleaned him up and nursed him back to good health. Didn't take much to break him, and in fact, he's fully trained and very calm. It would be great if you would take him. He needs a good master and home."

"But it's an elf horse?" asked Thorgrim, wearing a slight frown.

"An elf horse? Well, technically, yes. We call him Nugget. Come on back behind the stables, he's already out running around."

Gary and Charla led Thorgrim around back to a gated, fenced-in area. Over a hundred yards away in the field, a tall, beautiful, creme-colored horse roamed around.

Gary whistled and Nugget responded with a long neigh. Another whistle and the horse began running towards Gary, arriving within a matter of seconds.

"Mr. Lybree, I'd like you to meet Nugget."

Thorgrim looked up at Nugget. The horse, towering over him, brought his dark brown muzzle down and licked the surprised dwarf across his forehead.

"I think he likes you, Mr. Lybree!" said Gary.

Charla nodded in agreement.

Wiping his brow with a sleeve, Thorgrim responded, "Yes, I can see that he likes me, I guess."

"What do you think?" asked Gary.

Thorgrim looked the horse over, up and down. "Well, I can't possibly get on that horse! He's made for tall, skinny elves, not short, fat . . . ugh, I mean short, stout dwarves!"

"We have portable mounting blocks," said Gary. "We'll throw one in if you buy Nugget. Also, he's already shoed, and I might be able to toss in a used saddle for little or nothing."

Thorgrim seemed a bit puzzled. "Can I ask why you want to get rid of this horse? I mean, you seem very eager to sell him."

"In truth, as you know, most dwarves wouldn't go near anything elven," replied Gary. "Because of the war and all. Dwarves still hate elves, as I'm sure you know. So, chances are we'll never be able to sell him, and we can't just release him into the wild. He wouldn't last a day with the wolves and other horrors that are out there."

Charla nodded. "Yes, and the expense to keep this horse here. We would really like to sell him, but I know we'll miss him and all, but we want him to go to a good home. What do you think?"

"Errr . . . how much?" asked Thorgrim, meekly.

"How much do you want to pay?" asked Gary. "Make us an offer."

"Well, I only have a silver piece and a few coppers with me, so I—"

"Sold!" exclaimed Gary.

"Huh?" replied Thorgrim, his eyes bigger than pies.

"Sold! For one silver and a few coppers!" said Gary excitedly. "Heck, keep the coppers, the silver piece will do! Congratulations Mr. Lybree, you are now the owner of a beautiful, elven cremello!"

"I am?" asked Thorgrim, unable to believe his own ears.

"Yes! Follow me and we'll get everything ready for you. Honey, will you tell one of the grooms to get Nugget ready for Mr. Lybree?"

"Okay, husband."

Thorgrim, still numb, followed Gary into the front office.

After attaching a lead rope to Nugget's halter, Charla unlatched the gate and brought the horse into the stables, handing him off to one of the grooms.

She said, "We sold Nugget! Say yer goodbyes, but no sobbing and crying and stuff, okay?"

Both stablemen nodded, but tears formed anyway, as did some in Charla's eyes.

She said, "Get him ready. Grab that used saddle over there and one of those portable mounting blocks. When yer done, bring him around front."

They nodded.

Thorgrim pulled out his lone silver piece. Raising his single brow in disbelief, he said, "Gary, you've got to be kiddin', just a silver piece for an entire horse?"

"Just a silver!" replied Gary, from the other side of the counter.

Leaning over, he gestured to Thorgrim to come closer. Whispering, Gary said, "Look, Mr. Lybree, or whatever your name is. I know yer just a kid, and it looks like you might need a little help."

Thorgrim was shocked and now wore the expression of a child caught with his hands in the cookie jar.

Gary continued, "I've been living here for some time now, and I'm not as naïve as you might think. You do know why we never see young dwarves like you running around lose, don't you?"

Thorgrim knew, but he shrugged anyway.

Gary frowned slightly, "You know why. Because they are usually supposed to be either in the mines, in the military, or working on a farm. Now, no offense, but you don't look like you would know your way around an ore mine, a battlefield or a farm. So, unless you own a business or are on your way to the university, well . . ."

Thorgrim dropped his head and said the first thing that came to his mind, "Yes, I have a scholarship and—"

Interrupting, continuing to whisper, Gary said, "It's okay . . . no need to lie to me. I don't know who you are or where you're from, but I would advise you to jump on this horse and get on down the road to where it is you're going. Understood?"

Thorgrim, with his lips pursed, slowly nodded and handed him the silver piece.

Gary refused it. "No, you'll probably be needing that. In fact, take this."

Gary reached in a pocket and flipped Thorgrim a gold piece.

128

Staring at the shiny coin in his hand, Thorgrim could not believe it. Puzzled, he said, "But why?"

"Someday, I want you to do the same for someone in need, okay? Just be careful out there when you leave. I sure hope you know what you're doing, kid."

"I hope I know what I'm doing too, and thankee," replied Thorgrim.

"Nugget should be ready soon. Take good care of him and he'll take good care of you."

Thorgrim smiled and nodded.

Gary said, "Where are you heading, if I may ask? And no worries, I won't tell a soul."

Thorgrim hesitated but felt he could trust Gary. "Bur Dhulgren first. I want to visit the Supreme Library and also see the Grand Hall of the Dwarves."

"The capital? Oh, yes. Been there myself a couple of times. Bur Dhulgren is a beautiful city and huge. Probably the cleanest city I've ever seen. Shem, have you ever been there before?"

"No."

"You'll love it. Lots to see and do there. You said you were stopping there, first? Where are you going after that?"

Thorgrim dropped his brow and turned his head away.

Gary reached out over the counter and patted Thorgrim on his shoulder. "Shem, it's okay. I'm just making conversation. You can trust me."

"Okay. I'm leavin' the country, but to exactly where, I'm not sure. I guess I really just want to go the Great Kingdom and find a job or somethin'."

"A job? Do you have to leave the country? We could use an extra hand around here. Might be able to teach you something."

Thorgrim offered a quick headshake. "Work here in Stug? No, it's too close to . . . Uh, yes, I have to leave the Dwarven Clans, but I don't want to talk about why, if that's okay."

"Not a problem."

Thorgrim continued, "Thanks for the job offer, but I'm hopin' to work with books somewhere. That's what I love . . . books. Who knows, maybe I'll become a writer or researcher."

"Shem, you'll likely need a degree from a university to do those things well enough to earn an income."

"I know. But, I'm hopin' anyway."

***

Outside of the building, the clomping sound of a horse walking could be heard as well as some voices.

"That must be Nugget," said Gary, pointing towards the front window.

Thorgrim turned and watched as his new horse came around the corner to the front, led by Charla and one of the grooms.

"Shem, are ya ready for your horse?" asked Gary. "He's out front waiting for you! Look at how shiny his coat is!"

"He's beautiful. And I guess I'm ready."

"Great. Here's your certificate of ownership. Don't lose it. You may need it to prove you own Nugget."

Thorgrim took the paper, folded it, and slipped it into his pocket.

Gary said, "Okay then, follow me."

Gary walked towards the front door and opened it. Expecting that Thorgrim had followed him, he noticed that the young dwarf had not moved and seemed upset about something.

Thorgrim was very nervous. He had never been on a horse in his entire life and had no understanding of how to ride or communicate with one.

"Shem, what's the matter?"

"I don't know how to ride a horse," he replied, embarrassed.

"This horse is fully trained and gentle. I'll show you how to mount him and then how to control him. You'll be able to steer him and command him to stop. Everything!"

Thorgrim uttered a long sigh. "Okay, I need to do this, so let's try."

It was 11:55 a.m.

Gary led Thorgrim out to the front of the building. It was getting hot, but the cloudy sky helped keep the summer temperature lower than normal.

Gary pointed to the west. "Looks like more rain, Char."

"Yes," she replied. "I heard a storm's coming, but not 'til tonight. I hope it won't spoil the celebration tomorrow! Shem, I know you said you were in a hurry, but you might want to stay and have some fun."

Gary spoke on Thorgrim's behalf. "No, Shem has an appointment somewhere else. He has to get going."

Charla pouted. "I know, and that's too bad. You would have a blast!"

"I'm sure I would," replied Thorgrim.

"Maybe you could come the next time we have a celebration."

"I would like that. Yes, maybe next time." Thorgrim knew that likely for him, there would not be a next time.

"So, here's Nugget!" said Charla. "He's all yours! Hop on and try him out!"

The groom stepped up and placed the portable mounting block and rope on the ground next to Nugget.

Fearful and not knowing what to do, Thorgrim stood several feet away, unable to move.

Charla put a hand on her hip and cocked her head. "What are ya waitin' for? Come on over and try him out!"

Nervous, Thorgrim slowly walked over and looked up at Nugget. The horse was probably the most beautiful animal he had ever laid his eyes on. Nugget's coat shimmered like velvet, and his dark, brownish-black snout, ears, and mane gave him the appearance of a show horse.

Nugget then licked Thorgrim's face again.

"Yes, he certainly likes you!" said Charla with a big smile.

Gary stepped forward. "Char, I'll take it from here. Why don't you let the other horses out so they can run?"

"Are ya sure, husband? I'd like to wait around and see Shem ride—"

Gary gave Charla a peck on her cheek. "Char, I've got this. Did you say your goodbyes? I know how attached you get to these animals."

"Yes, I guess so," she replied with a sigh. Her saddened expression was typical each time they sold a horse.

Gary said, "Char, say your goodbyes so Shem can get going."

Charla took a shuddering breath, her eyes, laden with tears. She replied, "Okay."

Reaching up, Charla rubbed Nugget's face and neck for a moment and whispered, "Bye, my sweet boy. I'll never forget you." Then, with tears falling, she turned and walked with the stableman towards the barn.

Always the tender-heart, Thorgrim's eyes were misty.

Gary said, "Shem, she'll get over it. Believe me; I'm used to it by now. She falls in love with every animal she meets. You should see how she gets when one of the cats turns up missing."

"I can see she loves animals," replied Thorgrim. "I love them, too. I never had pets growing up. Never even had a dog or a kitty cat. We didn't have room inside the house." Looking up at Nugget, he said, "You know, this horse is so big that he kinda scares me."

"There is nothing to be afraid of. You will find that horses are amazing animals. He'll become your best friend."

"Okay, I hope so. Are ya sure you can teach me how to ride this thing? I mean, he's so tall, I'll probably look like a two-year-old sittin' on his back!"

"Sure, I can teach you everything in an hour, maybe less. First, step up on this block. Make sure you take the rope because you are going to want to keep the block with you. After you get on the horse, pull the block up, and tie it to the back of the saddle."

Thorgrim's brows jumped. "Sounds easy enough. What about my backpack?"

"Most riders use saddlebags to store things. You can just keep wearing it on your back. It would be better to use a saddlebag, though."

"Sure, if you say so."

"Alright, now go ahead and grab the block's rope, then step up."

With Gary's assistance, Thorgrim cautiously complied.

"Shem, you seem nervous. I can feel you shaking . . . relax."

"I am nervous. This animal frightens me. What if he tosses me off?"

"Nugget can sense if you're scared, and it will only make him nervous, too. Take a couple of deep breaths and try to calm down."

Thorgrim fretted. "He's so tall . . . did I mention I was afraid of heights?"

Gary offered an eye-roll. "It's not that high up there."

"Easy for you to say, you're a six-foot tall human."

"Just trust me. Take the reins with your left hand, then put your left foot up into the stirrup. It's already been adjusted for your height. Then grab the back of the seat with your right hand, and pull yourself up. Swing your right leg over the saddle. When you're comfortable, pull the block up and tie it behind you."

Thorgrim was turning white.

Gary said, "Go on the count of three, ready? I'll help you, just try to relax."

Thorgrim was not sure if he was ready. "Uh . . ."

Gary began the count. "One . . . two . . . three!"

Thorgrim, frozen like a statue, didn't move.

"Shem! Come on now. At least try. There's nothing to fear. I'll count again. Go on three, ready?"

"Ummmm."

"Come on, Shem. I don't have all day. I still want to get in a round of golf."

Thorgrim scrunched his monobrow. "Golf? What's that?"

"It's a game I made up. You take a stick and try to hit rocks into a hole. Lots of fun."

Thorgrim shrugged. "If ya say so."

"Okay, let's do this. Ready?"

Thorgrim took a deep breath and sighed. "Okay, okay, I'm ready . . . so all I do is jump up, right?"

"Yes!"

Thorgrim took another deep breath and said, "Alright then, count it."

Gary sighed. "Good, here we go then. One . . . two . . . three, up!"

Thorgrim pulled with all of his might, and assisted by Gary pushing from below, went up and over the saddle . . . headfirst into the ground on the other side, making a loud 'ka-plomp' sound. A large cloud of dust rose over the spot where he landed. Thorgrim also brought the mounting block with him as he went over, and it flew through the air, landing thirty feet away.

Rolling onto his side, Thorgrim uttered a long moan. "Oh, muh head."

Nugget offered a playful whinny.

Gary ran over to Thorgrim. "Holy crap, Shem, are you okay?"

"Ugh, I think so . . . what happened?" asked the stunned and exasperated dwarf.

"Well, you went up and over a little bit too hard and fast. We need to practice a few times. You'll get it. Just lie there until you feel like trying again. You sure you're okay?"

"Ya. I'm alive, I think."

Thorgrim opened his eyes and partially sat up. Glancing around, he said, "Wow, that was a trip, let me tell you! My head feels like it's going to explode, but I'll be fine. Hey, hey, did anyone see that? It was embarrassing."

"No, I don't think so. At this time of day, hardly anyone is in town." Gary glanced to his right. "Well, except maybe the sheriff. Here he comes now."

Still sitting halfway up, Thorgrim looked across the street and saw the sheriff coming over from his office. The sheriff was a rotund dwarf with a greying beard, who wore a wide-brimmed, black hat, and a freshly pressed, tan uniform. A huge, diamond-studded star decorated his shirt.

Filled with anxiety that the sheriff was coming, Thorgrim slowly stood up. Trying to appear nonchalant, he began chuckling while slapping the dirt and dust off his clothes and out of his hair.

When the sheriff reached them, he tipped his hat and said, "Morning, Gary."

"Morning, Sheriff Buckler."

Looking at Thorgrim, the sheriff said, "And whom do we have here?"

Before Thorgrim could answer, the sheriff continued, "Hey, that was quite a show, although I have to admit, I had to chuckle a bit when I saw you trying to mount this beautiful horse. Ain't seen nothing quite like that since I and the missus went to the circus down in Pretzel last year."

Gary, trying not to laugh, said, "Sheriff, this is a customer of mine. His name is Shem Lybree, and he just bought this horse from us."

Sheriff Buckler tugged on his beard and said, "Mr. Lybree, a pleasure to meet you, sir. Uh, you just bought this horse?"

Thorgrim's face was beet-red with embarrassment. Smiling, while trying to hide the pain in his head, he said, "Yes, I did. Gary was just showing me how to get on this really, really, tall elf horse! Never been on such a tall horse before. You know, these types of horses are made for elves and taller people."

"Yes, it's an elven horse and a pretty one at that," replied the sheriff, patting the side of Nugget.

Nugget brought his head down and gave Thorgrim a big lick on his face.

"Ah, and I see that he likes you, Mr. Lybree," commented Sheriff Buckler. "It's kind of rare to see an elven anything take to a dwarf and visa-versa. Wouldn't you agree, Gary?"

Gary replied, "Yes, highly unusual. But Nugget's a sweet horse, and I think he could get along with anything! Maybe even a troll!"

Thorgrim offered a half-grin. "A troll? Do trolls ride horses?"

Sheriff Buckler chuckled, "Uh, I think Gary was only jokin' there, Mr. Lybree. You know, humans and their odd sense of humor . . . never understood them much, really! No offense, Gary. Uh, and no, trolls don't ride horses. They would more likely eat a horse if they could catch it."

"I told Gary that I've never seen a troll before," said Thorgrim, still dusting himself off. "I've heard plenty of crazy stories about trolls . . . and dragons, too. Never seen either, so I find it hard to believe such things exist."

The sheriff laughed. "I can't speak for dragons. But, trolls? Oh, they're around alright . . . and if you ever see one, you'll never forget it. Rare in these parts though. Find 'em in caves but more often in forests."

Thorgrim nervously took a glance towards the woods to the southwest.

Both Gary and Sheriff Buckler grinned.

The sheriff continued, "No trolls around here my friend. They tend to like the thicker woods, anyway, where they can hide and sneak up on ya! But hey, if ya don't believe in 'em, what are ya worried about?"

Thorgrim replied, "Umm, I'm not worried, but thanks for the advice."

Sheriff Buckler cocked his head. "You're not from around here, are you, Mr. Lybree? I pretty much know everyone in a twenty-mile radius of Stug. Don't recall seeing you before."

Thorgrim's anxiety peaked. His paranoia of getting caught bit at him like a wolf. He had no choice but to continue masquerading as Shem Lybree from Dartag Bur.

"No, I'm from Dartag Bur. Just passing through."

"I see," said the sheriff. "I've got some kin up there in—"

Gary interrupted before Sheriff Buckler was able to ask too many questions. "Sheriff, Mr. Lybree has an appointment in Grekk, and I have to finish working with him and Nugget. The wife has some fresh coffee brewing, why don't you go on in and have some. I'll be in when we're done . . . shouldn't be much longer."

Sheriff Buckler nodded. "Grekk! Gonna do some fishin'? Watch out for those junk charter tubs they use there. Half of 'em sink while they're still tied up at the docks!"

Thorgrim nodded and said, "Oh, okay, I appreciate that, sir. I'll stick to fishin' off the pier then."

"Gary, I'll head inside and chat with your wife. Uh, Mr. Lybree, good luck, and watch out for trolls!" the sheriff laughed softly, and began walking towards the front door.

Gary smiled and waited for the sheriff to enter and close the door. Then he turned to Thorgrim and said, "My wife will keep him tied up for hours! So, now that he's gone, let's finish here.

"Thank you, Gary, for lying for me. You didn't have to do that, but I appreciate it."

"I don't like to lie, ever. But sometimes you have to bend the rules, right kid? I thought telling him that you were heading to Grekk might throw him off your trail, if you know what I mean."

Thorgrim dropped his head and muttered, "Ya."

"Okay, let's get this done. We don't have much time because although Sheriff Buckler is a good dwarf, he's very nosey. I don't want him coming back out here asking more questions."

Thorgrim could not have agreed more.

***

135

It took over an hour, but amazingly, Gary was able to get Thorgrim up and into the saddle, and he also taught him how to dismount. Not falling while doing either was another story and something Thorgrim would struggle with for some time.

In addition, the inexperienced dwarf learned how to control Nugget using the riding methods and commands that Gary and his wife had used to train the elven gelding. Soon, Thorgrim was able to ride Nugget out and around the area comfortably. Gary even managed to talk the young dwarf into running the horse up and down the road. Thorgrim was wild-eyed at first, but on the third run back, he arrived with a big-toothy grin.

Gary was impressed. "I must say, Shem, you really picked that up fast! Are you sure you've never ridden before?"

"Nope! Not unless you count when I was a wee dwarf. I used to ride on my papa's back, and we would play cowboy."

"Well, that doesn't really count, but I guess you could say it's a start. Just one word of advice though. When you come to a sudden halt, your beard is flying forward and covering Nuggets head. I don't think he's used to that, uh, that might cause you some problems one day, especially if you're riding near a cliff! Shem, your beard has to be the longest I've ever seen. Perhaps you should walk across the street to the barber and have it trimmed."

Thorgrim looked down and sure enough, his beard completely covered the top of Nugget's head and eyes. Reeling it back in, Thorgrim flashed a big grin and said, "Trim this? Not until it's so long that I step on it!"

Gary laughed and said, "Think you've got the riding figured out?"

"Ya, I think so! I still don't like to look down though. It's a long drop from way up here."

"You'll get used to it. Just don't lose that mounting block or you'll have a heck of a time getting into that saddle."

"No kiddin'! I'd have to jump off the roof of a house to get into this saddle without the block."

"I'm not kidding, don't lose it! Now, I showed you how to control his speed, but don't run him too hard. When it's hot like this, walk or bring him up to a trot, but give him plenty of breaks and fresh water.

"How fast can he run?"

"Horses move at various speeds that are called gaits. Normal walking is the slowest at around four miles an hour. The next gait is faster and is called the trot. While trotting, your horse will travel about eight to ten miles per hour. The next gait is faster than a trot and we call it the canter. You can cover about twelve to fifteen miles an hour but only for short distances when it's hot. The fastest speed is called the gallop. Nugget can gallop about twenty-five to thirty miles an hour, but don't do this for over a mile or so. Everything depends on the terrain, his conditioning, how much weight he's carrying, and the weather. Understand?"

"Yes, I think so."

"Shem, listen carefully. Because you're inexperienced, running him at top speed will tire him out in no time, and it's also very dangerous, not only for him but for you, too. Got that?"

Thorgrim nodded again.

"Before I forget, make sure that you remove his saddle and blanket each night, especially in the summer when it's hot."

"Blanket?"

"Yes, it's under his saddle. Here, let me show you how to do it."

Gary proceeded to show Thorgrim how to remove the saddle and blanket, as well as the bridle. He then explained how important it is to brush the horse to remove any dirt or other debris before putting the saddle back on. He also demonstrated how to properly fasten the girth.

Next, Gary let Thorgrim try it a couple of times. Thorgrim, being only four and a half feet tall, needed to use the mounting block to put the saddle on his big horse. Fortunately, he learned quickly and was confident he would have no problem doing it in the future.

Gary continued with his instructions. "Now, horses need to eat constantly. Don't go more than a few hours without feeding him and when he does, you'll need to remove the bridle first because it will be easier for him to graze. Nugget loves alfalfa, but it's expensive unless you find a field of it somewhere. Long wild grass, oats, or fresh hay will do, too. His favorite treat is carrots if you can find any. Oh, and remember, plenty of water, especially on hot days like this."

"Gonna be costly caring for a horse, isn't it?" asked Thorgrim with a worried look in his eyes.

"Yes, and you'll have to find a veterinarian where ever you end up. Nugget will need medical care from time to time, just like people do."

Thorgrim was reminded of his mother and the medical care she recently needed. The image of her face flashed in his mind's eye. He missed her and wondered if he would ever see her again.

"Shem, you'll need to land a job somewhere to care for yourself and your new friend here. You understand this, don't you?"

"Ya, I guess I haven't thought that far ahead."

"Good luck with that," replied Gary.

Nervous about the future, Thorgrim tightened his lips, patted Nugget on his neck while staring down the road towards the southwest.

Gary walked up to get closer to Thorgrim so he could whisper something. "Shem, bend down here. I want to tell you something, but I don't want to say it too loudly."

Thorgrim leaned over in the saddle toward Gary.

"Shem, you told me that you're stopping in Bur Dhulgren on your way out of the country, right? If that's where you're really going, go to a pub called the Iron Golem, and ask for a one-eyed dwarf by the name of Uuno Kanto. He's the owner and an old friend of mine. He can help you. Make sure you tell him I sent you."

"He can help me?"

Gary replied, "Yes, he will. So, get to the pub as soon as possible. Just don't forget, when you find Uuno, tell him I sent you and he'll take it from there."

Thorgrim became excited. "Okay, I'll do that."

"The Iron Golem Pub is in the southeastern part of the city. The pub looks intimidating, and it's a rough-looking neighborhood, so be careful when you go there."

"I'll try to be careful."

"Shem, you should try to time your arrival at the city during the day because if you arrive after sunset, you might not be able to get in without presenting proper identification. Now, I'm guessing that your name isn't Shem, and you don't want anyone to know who you really are. Am I correct?"

Thorgrim started to answer but looked away instead.

Gary noticed Thorgrim's apprehension. "Kid, no worries. Like I told you earlier, I won't say a word to anyone."

After thinking for a moment, Thorgrim nodded. "Okay, I trust you and you're right. I don't want anyone to find out who I really am."

"Well, that's why I want you to see Uuno right away. He'll take care of you regarding your ID papers, but you have to get into the city first. As I said, get to the city before sunset or you'll have to wait until morning. Keep in mind that even during the day there's always the chance someone will ask to see your papers. Especially someone as young-looking as you."

"I understand."

"So, who did I tell you to ask for at the Iron Golem Pub?"

"Uuno Kanto."

"That's right, Shem. Any questions?"

Thorgrim, deep in thought, his eyes staring off into space, slowly shook his head.

Glancing at his timepiece, Gary said, "Kid, it's pushing on towards two o'clock. You won't make Bur Dhulgren before sunset. It's too far away. You'll have to stop in a town called Pretzel and spend the night. It's a ride of thirty miles or so."

"Okay."

"Then tomorrow, you can easily reach the capital during the day."

Thorgrim nodded.

"You better get movin' before ol' nosey comes out and starts asking questions again. No worries, I'll cover for you."

"Thank you. But before I leave town, I need to go across the street and get some food and water from the general store."

"Hurry it up. I'll head on in and keep Buckler busy. Make sure you stock up on plenty of water. It's going to be a hot ride for you."

Thorgrim yawned. "Ya know, I don't know if I can make it all the way to Pretzel. I'm feelin' a bit drowsy now. I wish I could get some shut-eye somewhere before I go. I fell asleep yesterday around two in the afternoon and didn't wake up until after dark. I was up all night, walking to get to this town."

"I'll bet you're tired. You could stay the night at the inn across the street, but I would advise against it. If Buckler sees you, he'll be asking questions."

Thorgrim yawned again. "Dang. I don't need that. I guess I'll have to wait 'til I get to Pretzel."

"It's only a few hours. You can make it! If you have to, pull off somewhere and take a nap."

"The last time I tried that, I ended up sleepin' all day, in a nest of field snakes. I'm used to goin' without sleep. I'm sure I can make it."

"Best of luck to you on your adventure. You watch your back, okay?"

"I will."

With a wave and another yawn, Thorgrim turned Nugget around and rode him across the street towards the general store. Arriving, he began to dismount.

Gary nervously watched as Thorgrim carefully dismounted the horse. Happily, the young dwarf managed to do it without a mishap.

"Shem," hollered Gary.

Thorgrim looked back and saw Gary gesture with a thumbs-up sign.

Thorgrim, ever naïve, looked up into the sky. Seeing nothing but clouds, he looked back at Gary and shrugged his shoulders.

"A thumb up in the air, means 'you did good'!"

"Oh!" Thorgrim shrugged again, then returned a thumbs-up signal.

139

Hoping that Thorgrim was going to be okay, Gary turned and entered the front door of his business to talk with the sheriff in order to keep him busy long enough for the young dwarf to get out of town.

Back across the street, Thorgrim tied Nugget to a nearby hitch and gave him a pat on his cheek. As the horse began to drink from a water trough, Thorgrim entered the 'Stug General Store.'

The store was a ramshackle old building where all kinds of things were available for purchase, such as tools, building materials, clothes, medicines, and other common items. Most importantly, they had food supplies.

"Good afternoon, sir," said the elderly store owner.

Standing in the doorway, Thorgrim replied, "Thanks. And good afternoon to you, too."

The old dwarf pulled on his frazzled white beard. "Muh name's Bartholomew Quint. I'm the owner of this place, and I'll be pleased to help you today."

"Nice to meet you, Mr. Quint. Muh name's Shem Lybree."

Cupping an ear, Mr. Quint tipped his head. "Shem, you say?"

"Yes. Shem Lybree."

"Pleasure to meet you. Is there anything I can help you find? You won't find nicer things from here to Bur Dhulgren and beyond!"

Thorgrim approached the counter. "Well, I'm traveling on horseback, and I need some food and fresh water to take with me."

Mr. Quint cupped an ear again and said, "Huh? What was that? You'll have to speak up cuz my hearin' ain't what it used to be."

Thorgrim raised his volume and repeated himself. "I'm sorry, sir. I said that I'm traveling on horseback, and I need some food and fresh water to take with me."

"Oh ya?" said Mr. Quint, peeking over the top of his thick spectacles. "Is it a long ride? We've got hardtack, jerky and other foods that will last forever. Uh, where might ya be headin' if ya don't mind me askin'."

Thorgrim used Gary's idea. "Uh, I'm headin' to Grekk to do some fishin'."

Cupping his ear again, Mr. Quint said, "Huh? Ya said that yer headin' to Grekk to do some what?"

"Fishin'," yelled Thorgrim.

"Oh, ya? Fishin' is it? Well, watch out for those charter boats! They'll sink the moment you step foot—"

"Ya, I know," Thorgrim said loudly. "The sheriff already told me."

"Oh, ya? Well, just thought I would warn ya! I should know cuz, I'm from Grekk, and I used to run a big fish charter out of there years ago!

140

Ya know, the fishin' might be better down at Lake Mharrak. But yer prolly after those big-toothed ocean fishes and not interested in goin' down the pond chasin' blue gills and tommycod. No sir, those big uns out there in the ocean? Twenty-five feet and two tons on 'em and that's some of the smaller ones! When they getcha in their jaws, they'll swallow ya whole and then—"

"Uh, that's okay, sir. Ya know, I'm kind of in a hurry, so can I buy a few things, real quick?"

"Real what?"

Thorgrim shouted, "Quick. Real quick. I want to buy some—"

Mr. Quint interrupted with a slight scowl. "I heard ya. You know you don't have to yell at me."

Thorgrim sighed. "Please sir, I'm in a hurry."

"Oh ya? Yer in a hurry, is it? Well, you've come to the right place, friend! No quicker service from here to Bur Dhulgren and beyond!"

Thorgrim dropped his brow. Pointing to the shelves behind the old owner, he said, "That's great. Uh, I will take three packs of that jerky and maybe an extra water flask."

"Maybe? Well, do you want one or not?"

Thorgrim rolled his eyes. "Yes, please."

Mr. Quint peered over his specs again and bombarded Thorgrim with a bunch of comments and questions.

"Oh ya? Is that it? You want nothing more? Uh, Do I know you? You don't look familiar. Are you a farmer from around here? . . . or a hired hand? You look kinda young to be running around fishin' and not workin'! Shouldn't you be in the military, or workin' a farm, or maybe workin' in the mines? Where ya from, friend?"

Thorgrim grimaced, gritting his teeth. *So many questions! Will this guy ever shut up? He's so deaf, I wonder if he can even hear himself talk?*

"Uh, I'm not from around here . . . I'm from the north. From nowhere special. Just passin' through. Uh, how much do I owe you?"

"Huh?"

Thorgrim shook his head slightly, uttering another sigh. "I said,—"

Mr. Quint started to chuckle. "I heard ya! Just jokin' this time. My ears sometimes take a bit to warm up but they're running jus' fine now! But I'll admit, I didn't quite catch where ya said you were from."

"From up north."

"Oh, ya? You say yer from up north, and I think ya also said that yer just passin' through? You know, we're celebratin' our five hundredth anniversary tomorrow."

"Yes, yes, yes," replied Thorgrim, irritated and out of patience. "You know, sir, I would love to stay and celebrate the anniversary, but as I said, I'm in a hurry, so can we get on with this?"

"Oh ya? Yer in a hurry?"

"For the sake of beastly beards, and for the final time, yes!"

"Okay, okay. Just tryin' to make conversation. Ya know, we don't see many new faces in this town. Just the same ol' folks running ore wagons from Vog or some of the other mines. Same dwarves every time. It's good to see a new face and—"

The mention of ore wagons from Vog caused Thorgrim to become nervous.

"Mr. Quint, how much do I owe you?" asked Thorgrim, now exasperated.

"Um, let me see."

Mr. Quint added everything up in his head and replied, "Uh, three bags of jerky, and a water flask . . . will be a silver."

"A silver! That seems like a lot, but well, okay, I guess I need em."

Thorgrim reached into his pocket and pulled out his lone silver piece, which left him with fourteen copper pieces, and the single gold piece given to him by Gary. As he handed the silver coin to the old dwarf, Thorgrim thought of his new horse, Nugget.

"Uh, do you happen to have any carrots? Muh horse likes 'em."

"Oh ya—"

Thorgrim interrupted with a growl, "Please, will you stop sayin' 'oh ya' every time you begin a sentence? It's really annoyin' in case you didn't know."

Mr. Quint raised his grey brow. "Oh, I was just sayin' oh ya, I've got some carrots. I wasn't just starting a sentence with 'oh ya', I was answering your question."

Thorgrim smiled. "Oh ya? I'm sorry then. Well, in that case, I'll take a few carrots. How much are they?"

"See, you said 'oh ya', yerself! Kinda catches on, don't it!"

"The carrots, please."

"Uh, tell ya what, you take yerself a handful of those for that horsey of yers. On the house!"

"Well, thank you! You are very kind, sir. Please forgive me if I seemed irritated a while ago, I'm just in a hurry and probably could use some sleep. I'm kinda crabby."

"Not a problem, young 'un."

Thorgrim reached in his backpack and grabbed his water flasks. "Would you mind filling my flasks and the new one with some fresh water while I gather up these carrots?"

"Not at all! Uh, I've got some cold ale I could throw in one of those for ya if ya like!"

While gathering up a dozen carrots, Thorgrim said, "Ale? Hmmmm . . . don't think so. I've never taken a real liken to it, though I'm told that might change one day."

"Huh? A little louder, please," replied Mr. Quint, cupping his ear again.

"I thought you said that you could hear better now because yer ears were warmed up?"

Mr. Quint grinned. "Well, they sometimes cool down again."

Thorgrim raised his voice and repeated what he had said about ale, "I said, I've never really taken a likin' to ale, but I was told that might change one day."

"True! All dwarves love ale. Well, Beer of some kind, anyway. You probably will when you get older. Uh, how old are you, if you don't mind me askin'?"

Thorgrim, now a master liar, replied, "Forty. Uh, I just served my time in one of the mines, and now I'm out seeking new adventures."

The old dwarf about dropped the flasks as he was filling them. "Forty!" he exclaimed. "Did I hear that correctly? Yer forty years old?"

"Well, technically, not 'til the first of the year."

"Here's yer full flasks of water."

Pausing first to make sure there were no snakes inside, Thorgrim took the flasks, three bags of jerky and the carrots and shoved them into his backpack.

Staring through his book-thick specs, the old dwarf studied Thorgrim for a few moments and then said, "Incredible! Even with that beard, ya don't look a day over fifteen, to be honest!"

"So I've heard. I've tried to live a clean life."

Mr. Quint smiled and replied, "Well, it's working! Betcha' can't guess how old I am!"

Thorgrim looked at the bespectacled, balding, old dwarf with the white beard. Trying to be polite, he replied, "Well, I'm not a good judge of age, but I would guess . . . maybe ninety?"

Mr. Quint's jaw dropped. "Ninety? Well, thanks, but are ya blind!" he said with a chuckle. "I'm a hundred and seventy-six!"

Thorgrim turned to leave and when he reached the door, he cupped an ear and jokingly said, "A hundred and seventy-six! Did I hear that correctly? No, really, you don't look a day over ninety! You must be livin' a clean life, like me."

Opening the door, he stopped and offered Mr. Quint a big grin.

Mr. Quint replied, "Well, thank you, but I've not really lived the cleanest of lives, I guess, but I have me a good missus! My true love for her keeps me going! Make sure you find a good missus!

Exiting the building, from beyond the door, he could hear Mr. Quint shouting something about watching out for man-eating, killer fish.

Now outside, Thorgrim froze. He watched as two wagons full of silver ore were pulled through town by teams of four horses each. The sides clearly marked with the Vog Silver Mine Company logo. Concerned that someone might recognize him, he quickly stepped back inside the store.

Surprised, Mr. Quint said, "Oh, yer back. Did ya forget something, Mr. Lybree?"

"Well, I'm thinking. I want to make sure I have everything before I go," replied Thorgrim, trying to buy some time.

As Mr. Quint began rambling from behind the counter, Thorgrim watched through the storefront window as the two wagons slowly rolled down the main highway towards their destination: the smelting facility at Vumfumik, a short distance north of Bur Dhulgren.

Thorgrim stalled around for fifteen minutes while Mr. Quint yapped on about monstrous, dwarf-eating fish, gold dragons, giant squid, and other terrors that he claimed inhabited the ocean.

Thorgrim glanced at his timepiece and saw that it was 2:50 p.m. Anxious to get on the road, he decided to once again leave. Not wanting to be rude, he offered the old dwarf a big smile and a wave goodbye before closing the door.

When Nugget saw Thorgrim, the horse offered an 'I'm happy to see you' whinny.

Looking across the street at the Tuckerheim Equine and Shoeing building, he saw no sign of the sheriff. But up the street, having finished their late lunches, a few dwarves were seen scrambling out of May's little café on their way back to the fields.

Checking, Thorgrim saw no one else around, except for a little stray dog who happened by. The hungry pooch stopped and offered Thorgrim a brief 'bark' or two along with a whimper. Thorgrim loved animals and his heart ached for the little dog. Knowing what the starving dog wanted, he gave it a piece of jerky. The happy dog licked Thorgrim's hand, took the jerky and scampered off into the unknown to face its own destiny.

Thorgrim was hungry again and thought about grabbing a quick bite to eat at the café. He would have loved to see May once more, but fear of running into the sheriff ruined the idea. Instead of May's homemade food, he settled for a piece of bison jerky.

Tired, he glanced at the inn next door and considered it, but thought it best to follow Gary's advice and head for Pretzel. It was time to leave town and with the coast clear, there was no time like the present.

Thorgrim untied Nugget from the post, then slipped the happy horse a fresh carrot. While Nugget munched on his treat, Thorgrim then stepped up onto the mounting block and with a jump, easily swung up and into the saddle. Pulling the block up, just like Gary had taught him, he latched it behind the cantle. "Wow, that was easy! I've already mastered getting on this giant horse!"

He would later discover that he had been lucky that time.

"Are ya ready to take me for a ride, elf horse . . . errr . . . sorry, I mean Nugget? Let's do this and please, don't toss me! I don't know about elves, but dwarves don't like to be tossed!"

Nervously glancing around, still hoping that the sheriff would not see him, he steered Nugget out onto the main road.

As Thorgrim left the town of Stug behind him, he looked back and wondered if he would ever be able to return and see his new friends again.

Then he thought of his parents, his siblings, and especially his new baby brother. A tear . . . then several tears formed in his eyes as he trotted down the road. Ahead, was his destiny and the unknown.

Brogal and Char both mentioned a storm was coming later. Concerned, Thorgrim looked to the west and could see a dark line of clouds spread across the distant horizon. Though the storm was still hours away, it brought him some worry. But for now, more concerning were the slow-moving Vog Silver Mine ore wagons that he would have to pass. He feared that someone from the company might recognize him.

It was still over fifty-five miles to Bur Dhulgren and as Gary had said, he would never reach the city before sunset. That meant at least one night spent somewhere. The only option, as Gary had suggested, was the small mining town of Pretzel, over thirty miles away. If all went well, Thorgrim would arrive before dark.

***

[Author's Note:]

Luckily, for Thorgrim, Nugget was an elven horse. For a common horse, carrying a passenger, eight hours of riding time or thirty to forty miles distance traveled per day was typical. This depended on the weather, fatigue, how many stops for rest and grazing, the grade and condition of the road, average speed, and other factors.

Like unicorns, the abilities of elven horses exceeded most other breeds. On Nugget, at a normal walking speed of four miles per hour, not including time for rest or other stops, Thorgrim could ride nine or ten hours, even twelve or more during cooler weather, and travel forty to eighty miles a day. Because the stamina of an elven horse was greater, it could trot (eight to ten miles per hour) longer and further in between rest periods. Because of the hot weather, this would mean that he could cover the thirty miles to Pretzel in four to five hours.

***

Sitting in a wide chair, Sheriff Buckler finished another mug of ale. "Thank ya, ma'am, but that about does it for me. I'm on duty and twelve mugs of ale, no matter how good and cold . . . is about my limit. Besides, except for using yer garderobe a half dozen times, I've been sittin' here doin' nothing for a few hours now."

Charla replied, "You said there was not much going on in town, and the ale sounded good, so I kept fillin' yer mug."

Gary, glancing out the front window watched Thorgrim ride away. Smiling, he said, "Yes, you've only had twelve, I'll have my wife fill that thirteenth for you."

Sheriff Buckler frowned. "Only twelve? Muh head feels like I drank an entire keg! Well, I guess fill 'er up then!"

Gary looked at his wife and gestured towards the ale decanter. His plan to keep the sheriff busy had worked.

The sheriff was over the top. His slurred speech confirmed it.

"Hey, about dat young kid . . . da one dat bought yer elf horse. Uh, how old is he again?"

As Charla topped off the sheriff's mug with her special recipe of extra-strong ale, Gary replied, "I've told you five times that he's almost forty years old. I know he looks like a young teen, but he's an adult. His identification papers confirm it."

The sheriff shook his head. "Forty! I can't get over it. He looks like a kid with a beard! Well, no offense, but it's muh duty to check for illegals.

146

If he can show me his official release papers, uh, or if he's in da military, etcetera, den fine. Otherwise, well, you know what happens. When I'm done with dis ale, I'm going out there to check his papers muhself."

Gary nodded. "Sure, I understand."

Gary knew that the Thorgrim had left town and was on his way to the capital. Of course, he would try to steer the sheriff the other way.

He opened the door and glanced around to make sure that Thorgrim was indeed gone. Sticking his head back in, he said, "Welp, it looks like Shem's already left town, heading for Grekk. If yer gonna catch him, you better get going. Why he might already be five miles up the road. It's hot, really hot out there, so you might want to finish that ice-cold ale first, sheriff."

Sheriff Buckler's brow furrowed. "He's gone? I need to see doze papers!"

Tipping his mug, he downed the last of the ale, belched, and said, "You know, it is hot out dare . . . ugh, mmm, maybe hit me with another fill of dat icy ale, will ya, ma'am? Burp!"

With a long sigh, Sheriff Buckler passed out before Charla had a chance to lift the decanter.

IX. One Night in the Town of Pretzel

Riding steadily down the road, perspiring from the unbearable summer heat, Thorgrim drifted off in thought, thinking of his home and family back in Vog. He mumbled, "What did my father say to the managers when he went into work yesterday? What does my family think of me? Do they hate me? I wouldn't blame them if they did."

He was not aware that his father was trying to buy him as much time as possible to aide him in his escape from the country. Regarding his family, everyone loved and missed him. Although they were deeply saddened that he was gone, they also accepted his choice and understood.

Thorgrim knew that the Vog Silver Mine Company ore wagons were on the road, not far ahead, and he feared the wagoneers might recognize him because his face was well known in Vog. They certainly would report him.

Finally, about a mile outside of Stug, after rounding a curve, he spotted both wagons a quarter-mile ahead of him.

"Well, Nugget, there they are. Those fat-ass transports are so wide that they practically take up the whole road. We've got to get around them, and quick." He slowed Nugget down to a slow walk, while he tried to figure out how to get around the behemoths.

***

[Author's Note:]
The massive ore transports were thirty feet long and nearly half as wide. The main highway, designed for the express purpose of moving ore, was wide enough to allow an approaching wagon to pass another one coming from the other direction.

Though rare, breakdowns usually resulted in a roadblock that could delay traffic for hours. Sometimes, damaged wagons were unloaded, then pushed into a nearby ditch where they might be salvaged later.

Empty wagons coming from the smelter would carefully turn around at the closest open area and return to the site of the breakdown where the unhappy dwarves would recover as much ore as possible, and then transport it to the smelter.

Watching, Thorgrim could see that both wagons had a driver and two backups who took turns controlling a team of four powerful draft horses. Usually, averaging about five miles an hour, the slow-moving wagons each hauled about twelve tons of mined ore.

Typically, the company always had several filled wagons on the road on their way to the smelter. Thorgrim knew this and fully expected to encounter more wagons, filled or empty, during his journey to the capital.

He carefully scanned the area and seeing no other traffic nearby, said to his horse, "Nugget, are ya ready to show me what you can do? I'm not gonna lie to ya, I'm a short dwarf riding on a very tall horse, and I hate heights. I'm scared to death, but I need ya to run as fast as you can past these wagons."

Nugget, as if he fully understood, replied with a couple neighs.

Thorgrim offered a brief prayer to Moridon, then leaned forward and using his knees as Gary had instructed, popped them into the side of the saddle.

Nugget responded with a loud whinny and bolted at high speed down the road towards the slow-moving transports.

"I've got this, I've got this!" repeated Thorgrim aloud, his beard flailing behind him as Nugget raced ahead. In a few moments, they overtook the first wagon, blowing by the surprised crew and team of horses. Without looking, Thorgrim waved at the cursing crewmembers who were yelling at him to slow down.

Thorgrim, though frightened to death while riding on the speeding horse, was pleased that passing the first wagon went so well. However, the next wagon, about a couple hundred feet ahead, would be another story.

Closing fast, he was about to overtake and pass the last wagon, when its horses were startled by Nugget's stampeding approach. Alarmed and confused, the wagon's team of horses abruptly turned to their left and crossed to the other side of the road, pulling the transport with them, completely blocking the highway.

The unexpected turn tossed two of the crew overboard and into the ditch, both of them cursing as they went. Additionally, hundreds of pounds of ore jostled loose, falling out of the wagon and then onto the road.

Shocked, with little time to think, Thorgrim looked straight ahead into a nightmare. There was no safe path for him. Going into the ditch at high speed would be suicide, but the road was completely blocked by four horses and an ore wagon. Although it was too late to stop, he had to try.

Shutting his eyes tight, he screamed as loud as he could while pulling back hard on the reins.

Nugget had other ideas.

To the shock of everyone, including the wagon's huge draft horses, Nugget gracefully jumped up and over the wagon, landing perfectly on the other side without losing a stride.

With his eyes still closed, Thorgrim finally stopped screaming, but only because he ran out of breath.

Now, safely on the other side of the wagon, Nugget finally obeyed the hard pull on the reins, slowing to a complete stop.

Thorgrim opened his eyes and looked around, not believing what just happened. Exultant, he started to laugh.

"I can't believe it! Nugget, you did it! I thought we were doomed fer sure! Good boy, good boy!"

At that moment, Thorgrim heard a commotion behind him. Turning in his saddle, he saw several pissed off, cursing dwarves approaching. Shaking their fists, the angry wagoneers began to run towards him.

"You goofy idjit! Ya about got us kilt! When we catch ya, we'll tie ya to the wagon by yer beard and drag ya all the way to the smelter and then back again!"

Another one yelled, "Let's get that clown!"

Alarmed, Thorgrim quickly said, "Nugget, I need you to run again. Sorry, but we've got to git outta here now!"

With the furious crew only a few feet behind him, Thorgrim popped Nugget again with his knees, surprising the horse.

Nugget reared back on his hind legs and whinnied loudly, almost unhorsing Thorgrim, before taking off down the road in a blaze.

Thorgrim glanced back and saw that the three dwarves were holding up middle fingers. If they were ever going to catch him, they would have to wait for another day.

After a few minutes of galloping, they were completely out of view of the irate dwarves, who were now a couple of miles behind them. Deciding he was now safe from the pissed-off wagoneers, he tugged on the reins of Nugget, slowing his horse down to a walk.

Having not eaten a decent meal since breakfast, Thorgrim reached into his pack and grabbed another piece of jerky. Chewing on it, he wondered when he would see another hot plate of food. Then he remembered Gary telling him that horses eat a lot and need to be fed often. He wondered if Nugget might be hungry, too.

"I'm sorry, my friend, are ya hungry?" Taking a carrot, he stretched and managed to get the attention of his horse, who became excited at the sight of his favorite treat. Thorgrim had an idea and pulled on the reins until Nugget stopped.

"I could stop, climb down and then feed the carrot to ya," Thorgrim said, looking behind him in the direction of the angry dwarves. "But there's no time for that because it might take me forever to get back in this saddle. Besides that, if I get down, I'm so tired, I may want to take a nap! Instead, I'll throw it on the ground in front of you and then you can pick it up and eat it, okay? Here goes!"

With a gentle toss, the carrot went tumbling over Nugget's head towards the ground. Much to Thorgrim's surprise, the elven horse caught the carrot in midair and started munching.

"You're unbelievable!" chuckled Thorgrim. "Even for an elf horse!"

Nugget, still enjoying the carrot, shook his head and neighed happily.

"Hopefully that carrot will tide you over until we can get far ahead of those guys. They want my head, I'm sure. Maybe there's a field full of wild grass up ahead somewhere. We'll stop at the first one we see, okay, buddy?"

After a nudge from Thorgrim's knee, Nugget was trotting down the road again.

As they traveled, the hot sun began to wear on them. Somewhat woozy, Thorgrim wiped the sweat from his brow, then grabbed a water flask, almost emptying it with one big gulp.

Realizing his horse probably needed water, Thorgrim said aloud, "Nugget, I'm so stupid. I've been running you in this heat and didn't stop to think that you might be thirsty. I'm new at owning a horse, so please forgive me. I'll get better, I promise. I'm sure you're thirsty. I have a few flasks of water but they won't last us long."

Concerned about finding water, Thorgrim glanced around and noticed off to his left that the ditch held a narrow stream that carried water from the mountains to the Mharrak River.

"Hey, Nugget, that solves our problem! There's plenty of water around here. We'll be fine!"

Looking off to his right, he could clearly see a line of storm clouds.

"Well, it looks like I didn't have to search for any water. There's some comin' our way, that's fer sure."

He dropped the block and dismounted without falling. Leading his horse over to the stream, there, he refilled any empty flasks while Nugget enjoyed big drinks of the cool, mountain water. Twice, Thorgrim jumped in and completely immersed himself in the stream. The water, surprisingly chilly, revitalized him and had the added benefit of chasing away the drowsy, groggy feeling he was experiencing from lack of sleep.

After the short break for water, Thorgrim, soaking wet from head to toe, struggled a few times trying to get up in the saddle, but finally managed it without a mishap.

Again, looking to the menacing line of purple clouds on the western horizon, he said, "Nugget, we've got to pick up the pace and get to the next town before that storm hits us."

A quick check of his timepiece showed that it was after 4:30 p.m. He guessed he was about twenty miles away from Pretzel.

"We've got some travelin' ahead of us, Nugget. Let's get movin'.

For the next few hours, with the heat beating on them again, Thorgrim alternated between walking and trotting, occasionally slowing for a break and stopping twice, each for a half-hour, so Nugget could graze in the fields of alfalfa and clover.

Both times, he managed a quick catnap, which helped to energize him. He could have slept for hours, which would have left him exposed to the storm without shelter. Luckily, the rumble of the distant thunder woke him.

Along the way, he encountered many locals, as well as an empty ore wagon that was returning to Vog. As he passed it, Thorgrim simply pointed to the advancing storm clouds in the west to keep the crew's attention off him.

Finally, around 8:30 p.m., he halted and gazed at the town of Pretzel. Although Thorgrim needed sleep and was hungry, his first task was to find some type of protection from the rapidly approaching storm.

***

At the same time that Thorgrim had reached the town of Pretzel, back in Vog, sitting at the kitchen table in the Longbeard's home, Dr. Thacker shook his head and said, "I'm sorry, Luthor, but I can't make up a false note for your son. I want to help, but I'm afraid that lying on a report is beyond what I'm willing to do."

The look on the doctor's face was one of regret. Although he loved and deeply cared about the Longbeard family, he was unable to fulfill Luthor's request.

Deeply furrowing his brow, Luthor sat back in his chair and nodded. Glancing over at his wife, he could see that she was equally disappointed.

Luthor wore an expression of shame. "I'm truly sorry, doctor. I hope you know that we're not dishonest people, but we're desperate to help and protect our son. But you're right. It was wrong of me to ask in the first place. Forgive me for putting you on the spot. It's not of my character to deceive, and I—"

Dr. Thacker smiled gently. "No need to apologize, Luthor. Believe me, I fully understand and probably would be doing the same thing if I were in your situation. Besides, even if I could write a note on his behalf, they will send the company physician in to confirm my findings . . . and they'll probably do that in a matter of days."

Luthor's weary eyes revealed his frustration and concern. He said, "What can I do? The company is demanding a doctor's note explaining why Thorgrim can't come to work. As I told you, they need it by the first of the week, or they'll have to report him absent without cause."

Dr. Thacker sighed heavily. "I understand. Truly a serious matter."

"Serious, yes," replied the distraught father. Emotional, he raised his voice. "The company will file a report with the authorities in Bur Dhulgren and also contact the sheriff's department here in Vog. They'll look for Thorgrim immediately, and he'll be placed on a wanted list. If they find him, he'll be sent to prison or in the least, be made an outcast."

Marjorie, trying her best not to cry, said in a broken voice, "Luthor, not so loud, the children are sleeping."

The doctor cleared his throat. Doing his best to calm them, he said, "Please, listen to me. There's a good chance he can make it out of the country before getting caught. Do you have any idea how busy the authorities are? The chances of them finding and catching your son are slight, in my opinion. However, Thorgrim has to be smart and make the right choices until he gets out."

Luthor reached over to his wife and put his arm around her. Looking at the doctor, he said, "But I hear they're very aggressive in hunting down people who skip out on their service obligations. I mean, you don't see many young dwarves running around the countryside, do you? Seems to me that he'll be easy to spot . . . especially with that extra-long beard he has."

"That's true. Again, if Thorgrim plays this smart . . . and depending on which way he goes, he could be out of the country in two to three weeks if he's on foot. Did he take a horse by chance?"

Luthor shook his head. "A horse? No, he's never been on one in his life and is likely afraid of 'em".

"How far could he be?" asked Marjorie. "Maybe we can go get him and—"

Luthor interrupted. "No, I wish we could and believe me, I've thought about it. But Thorgrim is basically an adult now. Bringing him back won't change a thing. Doctor, is it true that there is no cure for his claustrophobia?"

"Well, there's no medication that I'm aware of for the treatment of claustrophobia. There's psychotherapy, but that could take years to cure him."

Luthor pleaded, "But isn't claustrophobia an illness? Why can't that be used as an excuse for Thorgrim?"

"It's considered a medical condition but not an illness, like a cold or some other disease. There are no visible symptoms like you would get, for example, when you have the flu. The problem is, there's no way to determine if the person is telling the truth when they claim to be claustrophobic."

More frustration was painted on the faces of Thorgrim's parents.

Dr. Thacker said, "Look, we all know that the mandatory employment law is archaic, at best. But mining is a beloved and natural line of work for all dwarves. The law is in place to ensure that the mining industry remains strong."

"We understand that," replied Luthor.

Deeply depressed, Marjorie said, "What's going to become of our son? It's my fault. I knew, deep down inside, that he would be leaving, and I didn't say a word to anyone about it. I wonder where he is, right this minute. I mean, I don't know if he's dead or alive . . . how can he survive out there without food, water . . . no job and soon to be hunted like a common criminal."

Luthor rapped the table with his knuckles. "Don't talk like dat, Margie! Thorgrim will be fine. And it's not your fault, nothing could have stopped him from leaving. I'm as worried as you are, but I believe he'll be able to take care of himself. Still, we must pray to Moridon to help him. We must have confidence and faith that everything will be okay."

The doctor nodded. "He's right."

"But where could he be going?" Marjorie asked, broken-hearted.

Dr. Thacker stared across the room as if in a trance. Lost in thought, he hesitated and then said, "I believe I know where Thorgrim is heading."

"Where?" both parents asked.

"You can bet he's on his way to the capital."

"The capital?" exclaimed Luthor. "But, that's the last place he should be. That's the seat of the government! The King and Queen live there, and the city is crawling with security!"

The doctor replied, "Yes, but Bur Dhulgren is physically a very large city. Lots of places to hide there. Besides that, I'm not aware of any city having a larger population. There's probably two hundred thousand dwarves running around inside those walls, maybe three hundred thousand or more during the week, so being young and wearing an extremely long beard or not, he won't be easy to spot."

Puzzled, Luthor said, "But, how do you know he's going to Bur Dhulgren?"

"Because I once told him to visit a couple of places there. I'll bet my beard that's exactly what he is doing . . . he is going to stop to see those places on his way out of the country."

Luthor wrinkled his brow. "What places?"

"The Supreme Library and the Grand Hall of the Dwarves. Yes, Mr. and Mrs. Longbeard, I'm sure your son is on the road to Bur Dhulgren. Besides, he can't go north because the Darum River's flooded. He can't go east over the mountains nor would it be a good idea to try to escape by sea. Without proper papers, the port authorities would seize him the moment he tried to board a boat."

He continued, "Either way, I don't believe anything would stop him from visiting the Supreme Library or the Grand Hall. Because of his love of books, I don't see how he could resist. I'm sure he knows that he'll probably never get another chance to do it."

Dr. Thacker stood up from his chair and grabbed his bag.

"You're leaving?" asked Luthor, also standing up from his chair.

"Yes."

Dr. Thacker opened up his medical bag and pulled out a small sheet of paper, along with his inkwell and pen. Scribbling quickly, he handed the note to Luthor and said, "I don't know what good it will do, but give this to the company officials when you go to work."

Before Luthor had a chance to read the note, the doctor said, "Try not to worry about it and I know, it's easy to say that, right? Well, everything is in Thorgrim's hands now. Hopefully, some common sense will guide him. You know, your son is unique in many ways. I believe that he'll be successful and do many great things in his life. I can't explain how I know this. It's just something I feel inside."

Luthor and Marjorie forced a smile.

Dr. Thacker sighed and said, "It's been a long day. I'm tired and I've got to get home to my missus. Good luck my friends. Please, keep me informed if you hear anything from Thorgrim. And relay my best wishes to him if the opportunity arises."

Luthor shook the doctor's hand. "We certainly will. Thank you for stopping by this evening."

"Absolutely, and thank you for that delicious supper. I'll let myself out. Goodnight."

Both Luthor and his wife watched as the doctor went out the front door, then gently closed it behind him.

Marjorie looked at her husband and then at the note.

"What did he write?" she asked.

Luthor turned the paper over and read it to himself.

To whom it may concern:

I recently examined Thorgrim Longbeard and have determined that he suffers from an unusual, possibly untreatable malady. The symptoms are serious. They include nausea and frequent fainting spells.

Such symptoms could be dangerous for Thorgrim and others while working in the mines, and thus I request that he be temporarily released from mandatory duty until a satisfactory treatment can be prescribed and made effective.

Please feel free to contact me if you have any questions regarding this matter.

(Signed)

Dr. R.E. Thacker, M.D.
July 19, 2248

"Honey," Marjorie asked with concern, "What does it say?"
Luthor smiled while carefully folding the note.
He replied, "The truth."

156

Thorgrim and Nugget jumped, as loud crashes of thunder exploded overhead in between bright flashes of lightning. Hurriedly riding into the little town, he glanced around, praying he would be able to find a place to stay for the night. Both he and Nugget were hungry, thirsty and exhausted.

Upon entering the torch-lit, main street of Pretzel, Thorgrim gently tugged on the reins to slow Nugget down, while anxiously searching for an inn and stable. The blowing wind battered the flames of the tall pole torches, snuffing out several of them.

Famous for its ale brewery, Pretzel was a very small town, about half the size of Stug and Vog. Thorgrim knew little about the place, but he hoped it might have an inn for the weary traveler.

A loud crack of thunder almost caused Nugget to bolt. The jittery horse reared up for a moment, but Thorgrim managed to gain control. Patting the horse's neck in an effort to calm him, he said, "Nugget, we'll be fine, but we've got to find shelter, soon. The storm's upon us!"

Thorgrim had ridden the entire three blocks of the town's main street, but unfortunately, no inn was found. Along the way, he thought about stopping to ask for help, but all of the businesses had closed for the evening. The town seemed abandoned.

He was about to give up and ride for a large clump of oak trees ahead which he hoped would provide some kind of shelter. However, at the edge of town, during flashes of lightning, off to his left, he spotted the shape of a large building about a quarter-mile away.

He noticed a wooden signpost stuck in the ground across the road, but even with his excellent night vision, it was impossible to read what it said.

With the brunt of the storm only minutes away and his horse crying in fear from the crashing of thunder, Thorgrim rode closer to the sign and squinted. During another flash, he was able to read it. It said: 'Welcome to the Pretzel Brewing Company & Inn.'

"Why not!" he said aloud. "What better place to have an inn for dwarves, then next to the largest brewery in the realm! I hope there's a spare room. The place is probably packed with alcoholics. Either way, I'm so sleepy, I'll take a spot on the floor."

All around, uncountable streaks of forked lightning lit up the night sky, followed by frightening explosions of thunder. A steady wind blew from the west with occasional, powerful gusts shaking him and Nugget. As if dancing to the music of an ethereal orchestra, the tops of trees rhythmically swayed back and forth, while leaves and other debris flew in all directions.

Terrified, Thorgrim turned Nugget, sending his horse forward, galloping down a narrow side-road towards the brewery.

Halfway to the brewery, a few heavy raindrops began to pelt them, some of them stinging on impact. He looked and noticed a few white shapes, about a fourth the size of a copper piece, striking the ground.

It was hail.

Running fast, it took Nugget less than two minutes to cover the distance to the brewery.

Upon arrival, Thorgrim's first concern was finding shelter for Nugget. Luckily, there was a sign that pointed to a barn and stable behind the brewery's massive building.

Peppered with small hail, Thorgrim followed the sign and hastily rode for the barn.

Near the barn, two dwarves, both of them employed by the inn to care for the stable, were working hard gathering items that would otherwise be blown away or damaged by the storm.

The two stablemen watched as Thorgrim rode up to them, his long beard waving in the wind.

With the howling tempest blowing hard, Thorgrim held on to his beard and said, "Can you help me? I'm in need of shelter for my horse and myself."

One of the stablemen laughed and responded, "Certainly, but you can't stay in the stable with yer horse! You'll have to check-in at the front and get a room."

Larger hailstones began to batter the area. "Ya better hurry or yer gonna get hammered," warned the stableman. "This storm's about to bring a lot of trouble down on us!"

Unsure how he was going to pay for the lodging, Thorgrim yelled over the roar of the storm, "Will you take my horse? His name's Nugget, and he's likely very hungry and thirsty."

One of them quickly ran up and took Nugget's reins. Gazing up at the elven horse, he said, "Wow, he's a tall one, ain't he? Hop down and I'll get him into the barn."

Thorgrim, embarrassed that he had to use a mounting block, decided that he would try to dismount without it. Stepping off the stirrup, he fell right on his butt.

Both stablemen laughed. The one holding the reins said, "Are you okay, sir? Your horse is so tall that ya almost need a ladder!"

Now beyond embarrassed, Thorgrim jumped up and started to make excuses, but before he could speak, he was struck with a walnut-sized hailstone. "Owww!" he yelled, rubbing his head.

The stablemen hurriedly pulled Nugget towards the open barn door. When they reached it, one of them said, "You fool! Go around to the front and get inside before a really big one hits ya! Hurry, we've got yer horse."

Another big chunk of hail hit Thorgrim, again on the top of his head. Cursing, he began running towards the front of the building, and as a loud crack of thunder sounded, he yelled, "Thankee, I'll see you in the mornin'. Please, take good care of Nugget!"

Reaching the front, he saw a pair of large, oak doors. Looking up, he counted five stories, most of them glowing with many torch-lit windows. It was the biggest building he had ever seen.

Now raining, with the hail mercilessly beating him, Thorgrim prayed that the doors were not locked for the night. He gave one of them a pull, and luckily, it opened easily. Quickly stepping inside, he closed the door behind him.

Looking around, he found himself standing in a forty by forty foot, richly carpeted, oak-paneled Reception Room. Three arched windows, with curtains drawn, graced the front wall. Despite its obvious age, the interior looked and smelled clean, although an occasional odor of brewing hops met his nose.

On the right, at the far end, a grand staircase went up to the next floor. To the right of the staircase, beneath a sign that read 'Brewery', another set of stairs went down to a lower level.

Several hand-carved, floral motifs decorated the grand staircase as well as the edges of the room's flat ceiling. In the middle of the ceiling hung several candle chandeliers, half of which were burning.

The Reception Room, despite the summer humidity, was surprisingly cool and comfortable. It offered a selection of cozy looking furniture, a large counter, and a door behind it, which Thorgrim assumed led to an office. With the exception of the storm raging outside, it was quiet, and no one seemed to be around.

He glanced at the wall clock. It was 9:10 p.m.

Thorgrim approached the counter and examined it. On top, was a registry book, an ink well, quill, and a heavy wooden mallet sitting on a of a block of oak. A small sign read 'Strike mallet on block for service.'

Shrugging, he grabbed the mallet.

"Bang – bang – bang!"

Thorgrim waited a full minute, but no one came.

Groggy, hungry and impatient, he banged the mallet again, only this time, harder and longer.

Bang-boom-bang-bang-bang-boom-whack-smack-boom-boom-bang-bang-bang-boom-wham-smack-boom-boom!'

Suddenly the door thrust open, and a strange-looking, very short, older fellow approached and jumped up on a chair, so he could see over the counter. He proceeded to wipe his mouth with a towel while chewing on something. His heavily drooped, grey brow signaled that he was irritated.

Thorgrim was shocked because he had never seen anyone quite like this before. The older fellow was beardless and stood about three-foot tall. Thorgrim's first thought was that the man was an extremely short elf but without the pointed ears. Whoever this was, he was certainly not a dwarf.

Still chewing on some food, the old fellow angrily cried out, using a language Thorgrim had never heard before.

Thorgrim was flabbergasted. *Who or what is this character?* Raising his monobrow, he said, "I'm sorry, sir. Uh, I can't understand a word yer sayin'."

In a slightly calmer tone, the old fellow interrupted and said in perfect Dwarvish, "Oh, that's right, you're a dwarf . . . sorry. I was speaking in Togglish." Smiling, he said, "Would you mind if I tried that again using your language?"

Thorgrim, smiling, nodded.

The old fellow, now angry again, leaned far over the counter and shouted in perfect Dwarvish, "I said, good God, do you have to beat that mallet to death? Can't a guy eat his dinner around here in peace, without being interrupted all of the time? I'm asking you! What's your answer, sonny-boy? Hmmmmm? I say, hmmmmm?"

Thorgrim was virtually speechless. "Uh—"

"That's not an answer! Give me that mallet!" The old fellow swiped the mallet from Thorgrim's grip, dropping it on the countertop with a loud bang.

Leaning further over, his nose touching Thorgrim's, he yelled, "Couldn't you see that I'm eating my dinner? Couldn't you see that?"

Thorgrim shook his head. "Well, no. Yer door was closed."

The old fellow growled, "Oh, is that right?"

Thorgrim did a quick shrug. "Yes, it was closed."

The old fellow gave his office door a brief glance, and then he looked back at Thorgrim. With a softer voice, he said, "Well, uh, okay I guess I'll give ya that one, but you still interrupted my dinner! What do you want?"

Thorgrim was embarrassed but did not understand why. He tried to explain and said, "Look, I haven't had much sleep in the past twenty-four hours. I was riding through town when this storm hit. I was looking for a place for my horse and muhself to stay, and I found this inn. I'm sorry I interrupted yer dinner."

The old fellow became angry again. "That's what they all say!"

Thorgrim was surprised. "Really? Everyone always says, 'Look, I haven't had much sleep in the past twenty-four hours, I was riding through town when this storm hit, I was looking for a place for my horse and muhself to stay, I found this inn, and I'm sorry I interrupted yer dinner?"

"No! Just the last part. They always say that they're sorry for interrupting my dinner!"

Thorgrim meekly replied, "Oh. Well, I'm truly, truly sorry, and I feel really bad I interrupted yer meal. Ya know, I'm starving myself, so I understand."

The old fellow sighed. Jumping down from the counter, he softly said, "You are? You're really sorry?"

"Yes!"

"Oh, in that case, what can I do for you? You said that you need a room for the night, and you also want to stable your horse?"

Thorgrim, relieved, smiled. "Yes, that would be great. And maybe a hot meal if that's possible. I really need to get to bed, but I can't sleep on an empty stomach."

"Sure! My wife just whipped up a hot batch of ear wax stew!"

Thorgrim turned a shade of green. "Ear wax stew? Uh, I don't think I've heard of that, so—"

"Oh, I know it probably sounds horrible to a dwarf, but it's really delicious. It has potatoes, onions and devil's garlic in a deer meat broth."

Thorgrim frowned while his stomach rumbled. "But, why is it called ear wax stew? May the gods forbid it, but does it have real ear wax in it or somethin'? That doesn't sound very appealing; even though I'm so hungry I would eat about anything."

"Well, yes, it has swamp skunk ear wax in it, as a seasoning. It's a famous Togglin dish!"

Now a darker shade of green, Thorgrim mumbled, "Swamp skunk?"

161

"Yep! Hey, it's not so bad! What are ya afraid of? You dwarves eat rat tails and other horrible things like the heads of birds, mice, rabbits. Talk about disgusting! At least we togglins take pride in our cooking!"

Thorgrim had heard of togglins but had never met one before. "You're a togglin?"

Scowling, the old fellow replied, "Yes. You're not a racist, are ya?"

"Oh no, it's just that I've never met a togglin before."

"Well, ya can't say that anymore, cuz I am a togglin! My name's, Pooper McNoogle, but you can call me, Noog."

Thorgrim tried to withhold a grin. "Pooper?"

"I said, call me, Noog! Uh, what's your name?"

"Shem. Shem Lybree."

"Okay, Shem. Nice to meet you. So, do ya want some ear wax stew or not? I'll tell the wife if you do. Speaking of which, my stew's getting cold, so we need to hurry this up, or she'll start yelling at me."

Thorgrim's stomach growled. "Sure, I guess I'll take some. Can I get it without the ear wax?"

Noog opened his registry book. "Don't be choosy. First, let me check you and yer horse in for one night, then we'll eat. Are ya going to be taking a tour of the brewery? That costs extra."

"Uh, how much will it cost for me to spend the night?"

"For both you and your horse?"

"Yes."

"Well, it will cost a gold piece for you and a silver for your horse. If you want a hot bath, well, that's another two coppers. The tour of the brewery is five coppers. How does that sound?"

"Well, no offense, but that sounds expensive," replied Thorgrim trying to talk above the banging of the avalanche of hailstones as they pounded the building.

Noog glanced up towards the ceiling. "Wow! That is a very nasty storm out there! Those hailstones must be as big as ogre heads! I hope they don't knock out any windows, or worse, go through the roof!"

Thorgrim also looked up at the ceiling and cringed. "I'm worried about my horse, Nugget. He's out in the barn."

"Listen, don't worry 'bout yer horse. My stablemen will take good care of him."

Thorgrim sighed. "So, it's a gold and a silver?"

Another crash of thunder exploded overhead. Rain fell in sheets, sounding as if someone had poured a giant bucket of water over the top of the inn.

Noog replied with a grin. "So would you rather stay in here or out there? Your choice!"

The booming sound of a couple of extra-large hailstones smacking the side of the building caused Thorgrim to almost jump out of his boots.

The adrenaline rush caused by the storm gave Thorgrim a second wind, clearing some of the cobwebs from his groggy mind. For now, he could forget about sleeping, but his stomach continued to pester him.

Rubbing his nose and eyes to clear more cobwebs, he asked, "How much extra for the stew?"

"I'll throw that in."

"Thankee!"

Thorgrim did the math. He only had the gold piece Gary gave him and fourteen copper pieces. After paying for his room and the boarding of his horse, he would only have four coppers remaining. He realized that he would soon need some type of income to survive. He tried not to dwell on it, though the thought of not having any money sickened him.

More thunder crashed directly overhead.

"Well?" said Noog.

Shrugging, Thorgrim replied, "Okay, I guess I don't have a choice."

"Good. Please, sign your name here. You can pay tomorrow morning."

Thorgrim took the quill out of the inkwell. He started to write his real name, getting as far as 'Thorgr' when he caught himself. Scribbling it out, it out, he took a deep breath and signed: 'Shem Lybree.'

Placing the pen back in the well, Thorgrim asked, "Hey, I'm curious. How do you keep it so cool in here?"

"We ship dry ice in and ventilate it throughout the building. My idea and it works well, don't you think? Your room will be cool, and you'll be able to sleep comfortably."

"I was expectin' it to be hot and humid in here, but it's very nice. Um, so are you the owner of this place?"

"Yes. Myself, my wife and a staff of locals take care of the inn and stable. There's another group that does all of the brewing. Of course, most everyone has already gone home for the day."

"So this building is both the inn and the ale brewery?"

"Yes. Well, the place started out as an inn. The brewery is down in the basement. Takes up the entire space down there. They claim it's the biggest in the world! We ship a ton of ale out of here to every province in the Clans."

Thorgrim scratched his head. "Seems kind of odd to have a brewery in the basement of an inn, but—"

"Well, if you think having a brewery in the basement of an inn is odd, there's a town, on the coast, called Karnival. It has an inn with a funeral parlor in the basement. How weird is that? How would you like to spend a night in that place?"

Thorgrim visualized an inn crawling with spooks, and the walking dead. Shuddering, he replied, "Uh, no thank you! I'll stick to inns with breweries in the basement."

"Good choice! You have no idea how many dwarves stay here just so they can sample the ale. Look, I know it seems odd but hey, it keeps bread on the table and ale in the mug, so to speak!"

"And ear wax stew on the table, too?" replied Thorgrim, wrinkling his nose.

"Yes, exactly!"

Between flashes of lightning, from beyond the door, Mrs. McNoogle yelled, "Pooper, your supper is going to be cold as ice! I'm not going to reheat it again."

Noog crinkled his brow. "Look, Shem, my supper is probably cold and . . . my wife has conniption fits when she has to warm up my food. I need to get in there and eat, besides, I'm sure you want to get to your room."

Grabbing a key from a drawer, he continued, "You'll be staying in room number one. Here's your key. If you need anything, just whack the mallet. Just don't beat it to death, and if it's after midnight, it better be for a good reason!"

Thorgrim grabbed the skeleton key and said, "Room number one? How many rooms are in this place?"

"Fifty. Ten on a floor."

"How many others are staying here, tonight?"

"Just you."

"But, it's Friday night, shouldn't you be filled up?" asked Thorgrim, puzzled.

Several flashes of lightning flickered through the long curtains of the inn's windows, followed quickly by another furious crash of thunder.

"Are you kidding? Only a fool would be out traveling with this storm raging!"

Thorgrim smirked and said, "Ya, only a fool would do that. Uh, I'll check into my room first and then be back to eat in a few minutes. Is that okay?"

"Sure. I'll have the wife prepare some stew for you. When you're ready, feel free to come right in." Pointing to the door behind him, Noog said, "That' my office and beyond that is the kitchen. Uh, can I help you with your bags?"

Thorgrim pointed to his backpack. "I only have this one."

"Traveling kind of light, aren't we? If you don't mind me asking, where ya heading?"

Thorgrim, now a professional lying machine, answered quickly. "I'm headin' north towards Stug and then on to the coast for some fishin'."

Noog's eyes widened. "Fishing! Well, be careful. You know there's some fish in that ocean that are bigger than mammoths and they can sw—"

"Swallow you whole?" interrupted Thorgrim with a raised monobrow.

"Yes!"

"I'm aware, but thanks, anyway."

Noog said, "Speaking of Stug, did you know this weekend, they're celebrating the five hundredth anniversary of the founding of the town?"

"Ya, so I hear."

Noog continued, "They ordered a wagon full of ale just for the occasion. Should've arrived tonight unless this storm delayed them. You know, if you leave early in the morning, you could make tomorrow festivities! Should be a wild ale-drinkin' party. Any dwarf would think he'd died and went to heaven."

"Sounds like fun, Noog. Maybe you should go."

Noog frowned. "I can't stand ale. Don't know why you dwarves drink so much of it."

"I don't know, either."

Wanting to avoid any further personal questions, Thorgrim looked around, unsure where room number one was. "Uh, where's my room at?"

"I'm sorry. it's the first one down that hall on your right. There are plenty of candles inside, as well as a fireplace, though you won't be using that in the middle of July. You'll find a box flint-strikers next to the bed. Oh, and there's a public garderobe at the end of the hallway."

"Thankee, Noog."

A brief, though massive blast of wind shook the entire building, rattling windows and blowing off a few shutters.

Noog's eyes widened. "Whoooo! That storm's getting diabolical!"

Before Thorgrim could reply, Noog's wife yelled, "Damn it, Pooper, your supper's cold again!"

Noog shuddered. "Coming, dearest one!"

"Uh, you'll be needing this."

Noog reached down and grabbed a small, portable candle lantern. He lit it, handed it to Thorgrim and then opened the door to his office. "It'll be dark in your room. Like I said, plenty of candles in there though. If you need more, let me know."

"Pooper!"

Noog hurriedly entered his office and closed the door behind him.

Thorgrim could overhear Noog and his wife arguing.

"I'm sorry, I'm sorry! I had to take care of that customer."

"Oh, you're always saying that. I slave in the kitchen, and you let it get cold every time."

Leaving them to fight with themselves, Thorgrim, with his backpack and burning lantern, began walking towards the hallway on the way to his room. He thought, *Moridon, help me if I ever get married!*

A strange, monster-like roar interrupted his thoughts. Concerned, he paused for a moment and listened. Although it seemed the hail had finally stopped, he could still hear a continuous blast of howling wind battering the building, while torrential rains flooded the ground, turning it into a muddy swamp. But another sound now accompanied that of the wind as it swept across the area. It was a sound that seemed familiar to Thorgrim, but oddly, at the same time, unlike anything he had ever heard before.

That's a strange sound. Like the big waterfall in the mountains near Vog.

Unknown to Thorgrim or anyone else in the town of Pretzel, a mile-wide tornado was bearing down on them.

He reached the hallway and using the key, immediately entered the room marked with a big number '1' on the door. Inside, due to the ventilated dry ice, it was cool and comfortable. Using the light of his lantern, he found a small bed, a table with several candles, a dresser, and a storage chest.

The bed called to him, but his stomach's voice was louder.

Setting the lantern on the dresser, he studied the room. In an instant, amidst the fury of the storm, another sound caught his attention. It was a tapping noise coming from the direction of the lone, curtain-drawn window.

'Tap, scratch, tap, tap, tap.'

He frowned and looked towards the window.

More tapping. This time harder and faster, and now he also heard a crunching sound.

It was as if someone was outside of the window, tapping on the glass. Thorgrim's hair stood on the back of his neck. With goosebumps, the size of peas, he slowly approached the curtains.

'Tap, tap, tap, tap, scratch, tap.'

Lightning flashed across the night sky, and during that brief moment, through the curtain, Thorgrim could see the outline of a large, dark shape standing outside in the rain.

Again, the lightning flashed and this time he got a better look. The dark shape looked like a large creature, far bigger than a bear. A body, arm, and hand could be clearly seen during the brief moment of flash.

Thorgrim shuddered and dropped his backpack to the floor.

He thought, *It's raining rats outside. Who or what is this and what do they want?* Panicking, he raised his voice, "Who's out there?"

'Scratch, scratch, tap, tap, tap.'

A crack of thunder jolted him. Now horrified, he thought of only one thing. *Maybe it's a spook out there!*

Thorgrim froze, unable to move. He waited and listened while the violent storm pummeled the area. The wind blew steadily, now gusting so hard that it sometimes pushed the downpour almost horizontally.

He also noticed that the waterfall sound seemed louder.

'Tap, scratch, scratch, tap, tap, tap.'

Whoever or whatever it was, seemed to be trying to get his attention.

'Tap-tap! Tap, tap, tap, scratch, tap!'

Thorgrim's stomach, though flip-flopping from fear, was also screaming at him for food. Knowing that his hunger always ruled the day, he took a deep breath. Trying to convince himself that there are no such things as spooks, in a quick motion, he pulled the curtain back to see who or what was on the other side.

It was a large tree.

Protruding from a thick trunk, a lone branch, shaped like a long, twisted arm with a hand at the end of it, hung down close to the window.

Relieved, Thorgrim watched as the crooked, wind-driven branch repeatedly brushed against the window, tapping and scraping almost in a beckoning manner.

Thorgrim laughed briefly, pulled the curtain closed and said to himself, "I knew that was a tree the whole time! Ha! Even a spook is smart enough not to stand outside in the middle of a storm!"

The moving branch continued to brush against the window.

'Tap, tap, tap, rap, rap, scratch, scratch.'

Lighting a few candles, he said to himself, "I won't be able to sleep a wink tonight with that branch hitting the window. I'll have to see if Noog can trim it for me."

With the tempestuous storm still raging outside and his hungry stomach rumbling nearly as loud, he decided he would head down to Noog's office to sample some of the so-called ear wax stew.

Although the thought of such a revolting sounding meal nauseated him, going all night without eating was simply not an option. Thorgrim considered staying in his room to eat some of the food in his backpack, but he was tired of eating bison jerky. His hunger demanded a hot meal.

"How bad can this stew be?" he muttered.

Still laughing to himself about being terrified by a tree, leaving his lantern behind and a few candles burning, he exited his room while the tree's branch continued its rapid tapping and scratching against the glass.

As Thorgrim closed the door, outside in the rain, the huge, window tapping, tree-shaped monster chomped its fangs, laughed sinisterly, before wandering off into the stormy night.

On the way to the office, Thorgrim checked his timepiece. It was 10:20 p.m.

Now the fury of the storm's onslaught intensified, shaking the building down to its foundation. As he reached the office door, it thrust open and a terrified Mr. and Mrs. McNoogle scrambled out.

Handing a lit lantern to his wife, Noog ran for the front entrance doors. "Holy hell, listen to that!" he yelled. "Do you know what that is, Shem?"

Thorgrim shrugged and shook his head. He listened and heard the sound of what again reminded him of the noise of the Vog waterfall, only now it sounded like a hundred of them.

When Noog opened one of the doors, the strong wind ripped it out of the little togglin's hand, breaking the iron hinges and cracking the heavy, three-inch-thick oak door down the middle.

Noog's wife screamed, almost dropping her lantern.

Standing in the entryway of the broken door, Noog watched as wind-driven sheets of rain relentlessly blasted the hail covered fields around the area. The hailstones looked like little white-colored boats that were floating aimlessly in a vast, stormy sea.

The low-pitched sound that a short time ago seemed like a hundred waterfalls to Thorgrim, now increased its pitch to that of ten thousand screaming horses.

"Shem, do you hear that sound? Hurry, come over here and see this!"

Thorgrim ran to the doorway and looked outside.

Noog pointed into the black sky towards the west. "Look!" he yelled, trying to shout above the sound of the vicious turbulence.

Thorgrim, trying to shield his face from the pelting rain, peered into the dark sky but saw nothing.

"I don't see anything," shouted Thorgrim. "What am I lookin' at?"

Noog yelled, "Wait for the lightning."

Noog's wife hollered, "What are you doing? Are you two crazy? We have to—"

Then the lightning flashed, and Thorgrim saw something. A gigantic, black, cone-shaped object that was silhouetted against a grey-black sky.

"What is that?" he yelled.

Noog's eyes were bugged out with fear. "Are you kidding? That's a tornado, and it's a big one! It's heading this way! Come on, we've got to get down to the basement!"

Having never seen a tornado before, Thorgrim was transfixed by the sight of it. He exclaimed, "It's incredible! It sounds like a—"

Noog grabbed Thorgrim by the hand and tried to run to join his wife, who was waiting for him by the basement stairs. Though he ran hard, the poor little togglin was not going anywhere.

With his feet running in place, he looked back at Thorgrim and shouted, "I can't budge ya . . . you weigh a ton! Would you mind helping me out here? I don't want to get killed by that thing!"

Thorgrim reached down, and in one motion picked up the still running Noog under an arm, then swiftly hauled him towards the stairs.

Noog's wife, holding the burning lantern and covering her face with her other hand, was sobbing from fright. She stood frozen in place at the top of the stairwell.

Thorgrim grabbed her without missing a step and carried them both down the stairs to the safety of the dark basement.

At the bottom of the steps, he released the two frightened togglins, setting them carefully on the floor. Looking around, with only the light of Mrs. McNoogle's small lantern available, Thorgrim could barely see a thing, other than the shapes of several fermenting vats and some brewing equipment.

The demonic roar of the approaching tornado grew louder. Adding to the terrifying chaos, the sounds of breaking glass, the cracking of wood, heavy thuds, and other destruction could be heard above them.

Noog took the burning lantern from his wife and pointed to a corner of the basement, shouting, "We've got to get over there and hunker down until this thing passes! Come on!"

All three of them ran for the corner and quickly sat down, cowering next to several boxes filled with ale yeast.

The entire basement seemed to shake and Noog shouted, "My God, it might take the building and us with it!"

"Pooper, don't say that!" cried his wife. "I'm already scared to death!" No one heard a word she said. The powerful roar of the monster tornado was deafening.

Thorgrim could feel its suction. He gritted his teeth, closed his eyes, and while holding on to the two togglins, waited for fate to take its course. Unsure how massive the storm system was, although believing he might perish, he unselfishly thought of his family. *Is Vog safe? My family. God help them if they're somehow caught in this. What about my friends in Stug?*

Then he remembered Nugget. He was deeply worried about his horse and sadly assumed that he and the barn had already been swept away.

Pulled by the tornado's suction, Thorgrim's beard was drawn out, horizontally.

Noog saw Thorgrim's beard and joked. Shouting he said, "That beard of yours is so big that if it gets sucked up, it will probably plug the tornado and stop it!"

The angry voice of the wind monster reached an ear-shattering crescendo, numbing their ears. Terrified, knowing death could arrive at any moment; they held their breath, waiting for the inevitable.

Except for Noog.

Noog was yelling something about needing to use the garderobe because he could not hold it anymore . . . but now, there was no need to yell.

The murderous storm had become silent. Now, only the rhythmic sound of raindrops drumming above them could be heard.

"Listen," whispered Noog.

"It's pretty quiet up there," said Thorgrim, also whispering. He opened his eyes. "It's pitch-black. I can't see a thing . . . are we dead?"

Noog laughed but continued whispering. "No, Shem, we're not dead . . . at least not yet. It's dark because the wind blew our lantern out."

Thorgrim was elated. "You mean it's over? The storm's over? Why are we whispering?"

Noog shrugged, squeezed his wife and chuckled.

"Oh, Pooper, we made it!" said his wife, returning the tight hug. "Do you think our inn is gone?"

Noog gave his wife another squeeze. Standing up, he looked around the yeast boxes towards the stairwell.

"Hey, I can see a faint glow of light coming from the top of the stairwell. Could be the torches upstairs, so that's a good sign. We'll find out in a minute. Let's head up there and see how bad it is."

Walking in the dark, all three of them managed to make it to the stairs without tripping over anything. Everyone looked up the stairwell towards the main floor. Surprisingly, the torch hanging on the wall sconce directly overhead still burned. Anxiously, they slowly ascended the steps.

When they reached the main floor, they looked around and were astonished.

Unbelievably, the structure was intact. With the exception of the ruined front door and a couple of broken windows, there was no other visible damage.

"My God, I can't believe it," exclaimed Noog. "I figured that twister would have carried this place away. I thought we were finished!"

His wife happily said, "We would have been finished had it not been for this heroic dwarf! Thank you for saving my husband! He always has to run outside during the middle of a storm and watch it."

"Yes, thank you for that, Shem," said Noog. "And thank you for saving my wife, too. Uh, I guess you've sort of already met, but this is my wife, Jezzabelle."

Thorgrim smiled. "Ma'am, nice to meet you. I hope you didn't mind me grabbing you, but you looked as stiff as a statue, and I was afraid that—"

Jezzabelle, smiling, interrupted, "I didn't mind. I was more concerned about my foolish husband. I don't mind these summer storms . . . but tornados? Thankfully, we don't get them very often."

"Never seen one before, until now," commented Thorgrim.

Noog looked up at Thorgrim who stood a foot and a half taller. "And until today, you'd never seen a togglin before, either!"

Thorgrim grinned. "That's right! But you were as angry as that tornado when I first met ya."

Noog returned the grin. "Oh, yes. The mallet banger! Hey, are you still hungry?"

"I was so scared, I forgot I was hungry. Uh, yes, is it too late to try some of that ear wax stew?" Checking his timepiece, Thorgrim saw that it was almost midnight.

Jezzabelle smirked. "Ear wax stew? Is that what he's been calling it? Look, Shem. My husband is a practical joker. There's no such thing as ear wax stew. It's deer stew, and I'll be happy to heat up a big bowl for you."

Thorgrim raised the corner of his brow. "Practical joker, is he? Well, he had me convinced. Sure, I'll take some. I haven't had a decent meal since early this morning. I'm so hungry, I think I could eat a horse!"

Thorgrim's face turned white. "My horse!"

With his heart lumped in his throat, Thorgrim dashed out the entrance, his massive beard flailing behind him. Moving as fast as his chubby legs could carry him, he headed around towards the barn, running through the pooled waters of the rain-soaked ground.

The worst was over. A light, chilly breeze, and a soft rain replaced the heavy winds and torrential downpour delivered earlier by the wicked tempest. What remained of the storm had moved east over the mountains. As he ran, Thorgrim glanced and witnessed wild forks of lightning illuminating the peaks, accompanied by delayed rumbles of thunder.

Halfway to the back of the inn, he slowed to a walk.

"I don't want to see that the barn is missing," mumbled the worried dwarf. "Moridon . . . please, let it be there. Please, let Nugget be okay."

Once he reached the back, he stopped and looked.

The overcast night was black as coal and even with his excellent vision, it was difficult to see anything. He peered into the dark void. When his eyes focused, his heart sank.

The barn was gone.

Debris was littered everywhere, and most of the siding from the inn was missing, exposing the underlying, heavy oak framework.

Thorgrim started to weep. Although he had only known Nugget for one day, he loved him, as he did all animals.

What am I going to do now? I'm so sorry Nugget. This was my fault!

Thorgrim turned around. With a heavy heart, he began to walk back to the front but stopped when he heard voices coming from behind him.

Looking in the direction of where the barn used to be, he saw a pair of torches approaching out of the darkness.

It was the two stablemen.

Thorgrim shouted and ran to them. "My horse! The barn, it's—"

"No worries, we have a reinforced shelter back yonder. We wouldn't leave any animal out here during that kind of storm."

"Is my horse okay?"

"Yes, he's fine."

"Thankee, thankee!" cried Thorgrim. "He's about the only friend I have!"

"You're welcome," they both replied.

One of them said, "Do you want your horse right now? He's sleeping like a baby."

"Uh, no, let him rest. I'm still stayin' the night here. I'll be back sometime in the mornin'. Thankee again! How can I ever repay you?"

"Not a problem, friend. Go get some sleep."

Now happy and content, Thorgrim turned around and ran back to the inn. Once inside, starving and anxious to get some sleep, he bolted down a piping hot bowl of deer stew and then went straight to his room. Crashing onto the bed like a zombie, he was out the moment his head hit the pillow.

***

Waking at Saturday's sunrise, after managing over five hours of sleep, he rose, refreshed.

Bur Dhulgren was on his mind. Excited, he hurriedly gathered his belongings and left the room.

In the lobby, at the counter, he gently smacked the mallet a few times.

Within a minute, Noog came out of the office door. "Ah, Shem. I hope you were able to get some sleep."

"Yes, the bed was a bit lumpy, but I managed. I could have slept all day, but I've got to get goin'."

Noog frowned. "The bed was lumpy? Oh, I'm so sorry. I should have told you that possums like to crawl under the mattress pad and make a nest."

Thorgrim's mouth plopped open.

At that moment, Jezzabelle walked out of the office with some warm honey rolls and offered a couple to Thorgrim, who gratefully accepted them.

She said, "Pooper's only joking, Shem. The only problem with the beds is that they're old, and I have been telling him for months to replace them."

Noog laughed.

Thorgrim chomped on one of the rolls and said, "Nice one there Noog. Got me again. First, ear wax stew and now possums in my bed."

While her husband continued to laugh, Jezzabelle poured everyone a fresh cup of coffee.

Thorgrim carefully took a sip of the hot java. "Ah, this coffee is great! Wasn't expectin' breakfast this morning! I'm very grateful, indeed! Thank you! Uh, Mrs. McNoogle, would you mind filling up muh water flasks before I head out?"

"Certainly," she replied.

Thorgrim handed her the bag that contained his half-dozen flasks, and she took them back through the door, towards the kitchen.

Noog took a sip of his own coffee and said, "Well, everything turned out okay, I guess. Your horse is okay, you got some sleep, the inn and brewery are intact, though the upper works is damaged, siding's ripped to hell and back but nothing major. Of course, we lost the barn."

Thorgrim dropped his head. "The barn. My poor horse. I was really worried when I saw that the barn had been blown away."

Noog smiled. "Your horse was safe the whole time. I should have told you about the storm bunker out there. Built as strong as a fort."

"Thank Moridon, you had that shelter out there. The stablemen took good care of Nugget."

"Thank you, Shem. They're a good crew. Hard to find anyone that want's to work these days, you know."

"Hey, Noog, what about Pretzel?" said Thorgrim as he finished the first roll. "Any idea how bad the town is?"

"At dawn, I went down there and took a peek. Plenty of trash everywhere, but I couldn't see any major damage. I ran into the sheriff, and he said we had been lucky."

Thorgrim choked on a swallow of coffee. "The sheriff?"

"Yes, Sheriff Snord and his deputies. They were out inspecting the damage. He said some of the farms west of here were hit pretty hard."

"I don't ever want to experience another storm like that again," replied Thorgrim, wearing a grim expression.

Noog said, "If you think that storm was bad, I heard the weather in the Alacarj is much worse."

"The elf land? I don't think I would ever have a reason to go there."

Then Thorgrim remembered that the Library of Shem, the largest library in the realm, was in the Alacarjian city of Calibut.

His mind teased him. *Books. Untold thousands of books.*

"At least I don't think I'd ever go up there." Bolting the second roll, Thorgrim chased it with a big sip of coffee.

Jezzabelle returned with the small bag, now full of refilled water flasks. "Here you are. All filled with ice-cold water."

"Thank you, ma'am."

Noog said, "Ya know Shem, I've been talking with the missus about your stay here and the fact that you helped out and all. No charge for you this time. How does that sound?"

174

"No charge?"

"No charge," replied Noog, smiling.

"Oh, thankee! I can't tell you how much that means to me."

"No problem."

"I won't forget this kindness."

"We won't forget you, Shem. You have friends here in Pretzel, so the next time you come through, stop and see us! I'll throw in a free tour of the brewery and that includes plenty of free ale samplings!"

"That's very nice of you to offer. Thankee again for the breakfast, too!" Thorgrim reached over the counter and shook the hands of both Mr. and Mrs. McNoogle.

Jezzabelle handed Thorgrim a cloth bag with a few, extra honey rolls.

"In case you get hungry on your journey," she said with a big smile.

"Oh, wow! I'm sure that I'll appreciate those later!"

When Thorgrim reached the front pair of doors, one still hung off its hinges. Stepping up to the opening, he turned and waved goodbye.

Noog said, "When you get up to Stug, tell everyone hello. Be sure to try the ale! And be careful, it's going to be a hot ride for you, today."

Thorgrim felt ashamed lying to his new friends, but he could not divulge his true destination.

"It's summer and it's hot. I'll be careful!"

Noog waved and said, "Shem, watch out for the old dwarf who runs the Stug General Store. He'll talk your ears off!"

"Okay. I'll try to remember that."

Jezzabelle, also waving, said, "Have a safe journey. And where ever you end up sleeping tonight, I hope it's a restful one."

Thorgrim remembered something. "Oh, that reminds me. Noog, you should trim the tree that's right outside the window of the room I stayed in. When the wind blows, one of the branches slaps against the glass. I was out of it, but all night long I thought I heard it tapping and scratching."

Noog looked puzzled. "Can't be a tree branch. There's no tree outside that room."

"Are ya sure?"

"Yes. In fact, there isn't a single tree in front of the whole building. Not even a bush."

Thorgrim scratched his head. "Okay, very strange! Maybe I was dreamin'. Well, I'm off on another adventure! Hopefully, I won't run into any more tornados! Thanks again for everything, especially the extra honey rolls."

"Goodbye, Shem!" replied Noog. "Take care on your journey."

Thorgrim stepped outside to meet a clear sky and a bright morning sun. The storm had left behind a parting gift of heat and high humidity, making it difficult to breathe.

He began walking towards the barn to get Nugget, but he stopped after taking only two steps.

Curious, he had to see for himself. Turning around, he walked towards the window of room one.

As Noog had told him, there was not a tree or bush anywhere near the window. The entire front of the inn was devoid of any foliage, with the closest tree over a hundred feet away.

Shrugging, he muttered, "Hmmm, must have been a branch or something that had blown up against the window."

Eager to see his horse, he went around back and found Nugget eating some fresh alfalfa, near where the barn once stood. The two stablemen from the night before were gone. Two new faces had replaced them for the weekend, day shift.

Thorgrim ran to his horse and hugged him. Nugget stopped eating long enough to give his master a big, wet lick on his face.

"You must be the fella that owns this elf horse?" one of the stablemen said. "The night guys told us that someone with the longest beard they'd ever seen owned this horse."

Proudly tugging on his extra-long beard, Thorgrim replied, "Yes, that's me."

Envious, both of the stablemen stared at Thorgrim's beard. "You're horse is ready. You can take him whenever you want, sir. We had to use a ladder, but we managed to get yer mounting block from the saddle."

"Thankee."

One of them said, "Sir, I have to say, you're in beast mode with that beard of yours. You should be the envy of every dwarf in the land! How do you keep it so long? It hangs past yer knees!"

Thorgrim blushed and shrugged.

The other stableman, tugging on his own beard, chuckled. "Ya, your huge beard makes me feel inadequate. And how can you ride a horse with your giant beard flying everywhere? Do ya tie it up?"

Thorgrim stuck out his chest and bragged, "My friends, when you've been riding horses as long as I have, you'll find that yer beard will sail behind you like a flag. Let it wave proudly!"

Nugget could not resist a quick whinny.

Both of the stablemen smiled. One said, "If I can ever get my beard to grow that long, I'll remember that! Thank you, sir!"

"Yes, riding with a beard like mine is just a matter of practice. You'll get used to it!"

Wearing his backpack, Thorgrim reached around and grabbed a piece of jerky for himself, sticking it into his mouth like a pipe. Then he pulled out a carrot for Nugget. While the horse munched on his treat, Thorgrim grabbed the reins and rope, then stepped up on the mounting block.

Preparing to mount, looking back at the two stablemen, Thorgrim nodded, winked and said, "Farewell and thankee again." Then, with the grace and confidence of a master rider, he jumped and went up and over the saddle . . . face-first into a huge puddle of thick mud on the other side of his horse, while the block went sailing high overhead, landing fifty feet away into another puddle of mud.

The two stablemen scrambled and helped Thorgrim to his feet. "Are you okay, sir?" they both asked simultaneously.

Thorgrim was covered in sticky mud from top to bottom. Wiping the muck out of his eyes, embarrassed, he said, "Whoops! I guess I missed that one!"

After gathering up his mounting block, the two attendants helped the very wet and muddy dwarf up into the saddle. After attaching the block, still embarrassed, he rode away from them, waving.

They waved back, but Thorgrim thought he could hear them laughing. Looking down, his entire front side, beard and all, was caked with mud.

"Nugget, thank God you're okay, but I don't blame them for laughing. I'm going to have to get this mounting thing mastered, or I'm going to be in trouble."

Steering Nugget down the half-flooded, quarter-mile road en route to the main highway, Thorgrim was shocked by what he saw. The monster storm had delivered torrential rains that had soaked the countryside leaving behind lakes of water. Dozens of trees uprooted by the tornado lay scattered around the area like toys. Even the brewery's sign was missing.

Stopping at the intersection, Thorgrim wiped the sweat and more mud from his brow, then looked to his right at the town of Pretzel. As Noog mentioned, there was debris and trash everywhere.

To his left, the grove of trees that he originally had considered using for shelter, were gone. Unknown to him, the oaks had been uprooted and tossed like sticks, landing several miles away.

The lucky dwarf paused for a minute to reflect on his good fortune. Then he wondered about everything up north. *Did the storm go through Vog and Stug?* For the time being, there was no way to know and it bothered him.

Then he remembered that the Pretzel sheriff and his deputies were out inspecting the damage. Although he reminded himself that it was only the start of the third day since he left Vog, he still wanted to avoid contact with anyone who might ask for his identification papers.

Thorgrim shook the reins and popped the saddle with his knee, sending Nugget cantering down the road towards his next destination: the great, capital city of Bur Dhulgren, some twenty-five miles away to the southwest. It was almost 7:45 a.m., and if all went well, he hoped to arrive at the city's outer walls in the early afternoon.

Thorgrim's heart pumped with excitement. Having only read about it, he tried to imagine what the city looked like. *How big is it? How tall are the walls? What does the Grand Hall look like and even more exciting, what wonders await me in the Supreme Library?*

Then dread struck him. *What if they ask for my identification? I don't have any.*

"I'll find a way. We'll find a way . . . right, Nugget?"

Nugget replied with a neigh.

The young dwarf had experienced a lot in only three days.

However, it was only the beginning.

X. The City of the Dwarves

Bur Dhulgren, the capital city of the Dwarven Clans, was the third-largest city in the world. Only the ancient, elven city of Calibut, in the Republic of Alacarj, or the splendid, human capital city of Eastfair, in the Great Kingdom, surpassed its size, though not by much.

Though eager to get to Bur Dhulgren, because of the intense heat, Thorgrim took his time that Saturday morning. Wanting to spare his horse, he alternated between a walk and trot. Including stops for breaks, he guessed it would take four to five hours to reach the city.

Along the way, as expected, he encountered a few empty ore wagons and other wayfarers. To avoid being recognized, he furled his beard and looked straight ahead, greeting them with a friendly 'Good morning' as he passed by.

An hour and a half into the journey, needing a break from the heat and humidity, he steered Nugget off the road and stopped near a field of blue-flowered alfalfa. There, after removing Nugget's bridle, he let his horse graze and rest.

Slipping off his backpack, Thorgrim looked down and noticed that he was still covered in grey mud from his mounting mishap earlier. Though most of it had dried, his face, beard, and clothes were caked with it. Daydreaming about taking a refreshing bath to clean up, he found a large piece of wood nearby and propped it up against a cherry tree for shade. Sliding beneath it, he watched, while his horse happily foraged a short distance away.

A comforting, cool breeze blew in, and though he was anxious to get on with it, he wanted to let Nugget enjoy his break. Thorgrim ate one of the honey rolls and continued to watch his horse graze, still unable to believe that he actually owned the elven gelding.

After an hour, checking his timepiece, he noticed that it was 10:20 a.m. There was no hurry. With only fifteen miles to go, he contemplated waiting awhile before continuing. Nugget was still grazing, and the refreshing cool breeze continued to blow. The moment was serene, especially compared to the terrible storm he had experienced the night before.

While relaxing, Thorgrim, only managing about six hours of sleep in the past thirty-six hours, became drowsy and soon fell into a deep slumber.

***

The cawing of a squadron of mountain crows flying overhead woke him. Flat on his back, Thorgrim looked up and saw the underside of his makeshift, wooden sunshade. Squinting, he realized it was a sign. It read: 'Welcome to the Pretzel Brewing Company & Inn.'

Astounded, he shook his head and chuckled. Then he heard the cawing of the crows, again. Pushing the broken sign away, he gazed into the bright sky and watched the giant birds circle overhead.

Shielding his eyes from the sun, he mumbled, "Those are the biggest birds I've ever seen." Still in a groggy daze, he began to look around for Nugget and found him fast asleep on the other side of the cherry tree.

Then Thorgrim realized that there was something odd about the sun. Instead of climbing in the east, the sun was now well into its downward arc in the west. Stunned, he checked his timepiece and sure enough, it was almost 6:45 p.m.

He sat up and roared, "Damn it all to hell! I fell asleep and slept the whole day away!"

Nugget, startled by the yelling, woke and rose to his feet.

Jumping up, Thorgrim hurriedly put on his backpack, installed Nugget's bridle and then set the mounting block down next to his horse.

"Nugget, we fell asleep! We've got to get to the capital before the sun sets because if we don't, Gary said I can't get in without identification papers! If we can't get in tonight, we'll be stuck outside without shelter."

What Gary had told Thorgrim was correct. During times of peace, unlike other walled cities in countries like the Alacarj or the Great Kingdom, those in the Dwarven Clans remained open all night to any citizen who could show proper identification.

Angry, Thorgrim grabbed the reins, gave himself a big pull and of course, went over the saddle, landing hard on his rear. Cursing and shaking off the pain, the dwarf tried again and repeated the mishap. Finally, on the third attempt, he mounted perfectly, pulled the block up by the rope and tied it to the saddle.

With his back aching, he applied a big nudge with his knee that sent Nugget flying down the main road towards Bur Dhulgren.

With fifteen miles to travel, but less than two hours remaining before sunset, Thorgrim now had no choice but to test the limits of his elven horse. Alternating between trotting and cantering, there would be little time to rest. Unfortunately, it was hilly near the southwestern tip of the

Brimger Mountains. This meant he would have to slow his horse while ascending any hills to avoid exhausting him.

He encountered many more people on the highway the closer he got to the capital, including farmers, traders and empty ore wagons returning to Vog or other mines. He also met common folk who lived in huts along the way, or in some of the scattered villages that dotted the land.

Initially, Thorgrim made good time, though twice, he found himself stopped by a traffic jam of slow-moving travelers. Already in time trouble, the delays did not make things better for him.

During the stops, he used this time to fill his flasks and to let his horse catch a drink from the stream. Still covered in caked mud, he thought about jumping in to wash off, however, there was little time to spare, and the long shadows cast by the low sun confirmed it.

It was now almost 7:45 p.m. and the sun would set around 8:30 p.m. He had forty-five minutes to ride ten miles. Despite the oven heat, it was possible, but only if he rode at a canter and without further delays.

What Thorgrim did not realize, was that even if he arrived before sunset, he would have to wait his turn in line to get into the city. In all likelihood, it would be well after dark by the time it was his turn to enter the gates. This, of course, would mean trouble.

After refilling his flasks, he mounted up. Looking ahead, he saw hundreds of people, mostly farmers, trudging down the highway, likely on their way to Bur Dhulgren to sell their goods. Filling both sides of the road, all of them were weary and roasting in the intense summer heat. Some were taking turns jumping into the nearby, cool mountain stream, while others yelled at them to get back on the road or they would be left behind to deal with the wolves after the sun went down.

Regrettably, Thorgrim would have to force his way through the mass of people and their wagons full of personal effects and farm goods. Much to their displeasure, those on foot had no choice but to get out of the way or be trampled by Nugget.

Some of the travelers ignored Thorgrim as he rode his horse through at a trot, while others barked a few select curse words along with tossing an occasional rock or tomato his way.

After he had passed the rowdy ruck, he signaled Nugget to speed onward. After a few minutes of riding at a canter, the shorter peaks of the southwestern tip of the Brimgers were now clearly in sight. Thorgrim became excited because his little map showed that the capital city lay just beyond the end of the mountain range.

Stopping to rest his horse, Thorgrim scanned the southern horizon hoping to catch a glimpse of Bur Dhulgren, but the mountains thwarted any hopes of viewing the city. He also searched but was unable to see any signs of smoke that might be coming from the enormous smelting facility at Vumfumik, which sat a quarter mile north of the capital.

Soon, Thorgrim had Nugget running again. Rounding a bend at a canter, unfortunately, he had to slow down in order to safely work his way through a traffic jam caused by an overturned cart. After he was clear of the area he urged his tired horse, back up to speed.

Worried that he was about out of time, he glanced towards the west. Disappointed, he saw that the bottom of the sun's disk was rapidly approaching the horizon.

Slowing to a trot, once again, he looked for the city. Straining his eyes, he scanned along the horizon, and much to his dismay, he saw nothing except a dusty haze that seemed to be drifting away to the southeast.

Thorgrim knew that Bur Dhulgren had to be close by. With a firm nudge from his knee, he sent Nugget charging ahead. After riding hard for several minutes, he reached a crest in the highway and stopped.

His mouth hung open in disbelief.

Before him, at a lower elevation, perhaps five miles away, off to the left of the highway, were several large buildings surrounded by many smaller structures. Constructed in the small town of Vumfumik, it was the biggest smelting facility in the realm.

Expecting to see several big smokestacks, he noticed, much to his surprise, there were only a half-dozen, very small stacks, and only a few of them seemed to be venting smoke.

***

[Author's Note:]
Thorgrim did not know that almost all of the black smoke traveled through a twenty-five mile long, underground pipeline, away from Bur Dhulgren. The exhaust gases eventually vented out of a ninety-foot tall smokestack that had been constructed in an unpopulated, swampy area, upwind and east of the city.

***

The incredible sight of what lay just beyond the smelter stunned Thorgrim Longbeard to the core. Forgetting to breathe, he gazed in awe.

Having only dreamed of it, he had never seen anything like it before. A beautiful, massive, walled city, decorated in white, silver, and gold, lay just beyond the end of the Brimger Mountain range.

It was Bur Dhulgren.

East of the city, a wide river flowed from the mountains, continuing south, then southwest, where it finally emptied into the Great Sea of Atlas, over ninety miles away.

The main source of the capital's water supply, Lake Mharrak, stretching nearly twenty miles, lay nearby, west of the city.

Like a giant spider's web, an intricate network of roads and highways connected Bur Dhulgren to the rest of the realm.

Mesmerized, forgetting that he had little time available, Thorgrim watched as seemingly thousands of people, horses, and other animals, some pulling wagons or carts, were moving steadily along the roads, in and out of the city.

Although he was too far away to observe much detail, Thorgrim had read in a book that Bur Dhulgren's fifty-foot high walls were made of gigantic blocks of thick white granite. The tops of the walls were adorned with torches and royal flags of the Dwarven Clans. The walls also had dozens of deadly, scorpion artillery pieces, all nestled inside a series of battlements, for added defense against any outside threat.

He had also read that many of the major buildings inside Bur Dhulgren were made of solid white granite and iron, then decorated with motifs of silver, gold, and platinum.

Though he could barely see them, spaced five hundred feet apart, all the way around the city, the thirty-foot wide, white trimmed, gold and silver-checkered flags proudly waved in the breeze. Because he was at a high elevation in the foothills of the Brimgers, he could clearly see many buildings, homes and other structures scattered throughout Bur Dhulgren. Standing in the central part of the capital, were several large structures, some, over twelve stories tall. He also did not fail to notice the gigantic, seventy-five-foot torch that was mounted on top of what seemed to be the tallest building. Unknown to him, it was the Royal Castle. The home of the King and Queen.

Like a giant piece of jewelry, the entire city seemed to shimmer in the late afternoon sun.

Thorgrim wondered which of the buildings belonged to the Supreme Library and the Grand Hall. As he gazed, Nugget whinnied, waking him from his trance-like state.

Cursing himself for wasting valuable time, he checked his timepiece and saw that it read 8:13 p.m.

With fifteen to twenty minutes before sunset, he still had five to six miles to go. This meant that Nugget would have to alternate between a canter and gallop for the remaining distance in order to have any chance of making it on time. In the heat, it would be a difficult task, even for an elven horse.

Thorgrim understood that the highway was full of activity and the congestion would certainly slow him down, though he still had to try his best. Unfortunately, he was still unaware that he would have to wait his turn in line to get in, which likely meant that he would be turned away into the night by the city guards.

"Sorry, my friend . . . we're late," he said, patting his horse on the neck.

He gripped the reins tightly and then applied a sharp push with both knees, causing the horse to bolt. Rearing up on his back legs, Nugget whinnied loudly then leaped forward while Thorgrim held on for his life. Running at top speed, Nugget galloped down the highway towards the City of the Dwarves.

The high-speed ride was a harrowing experience for Thorgrim. Galloping hard, he flew by many travelers, and several times, almost thrown from the saddle, when he was forced to go off-road to get around the traffic. As Thorgrim thundered down the highway, almost everyone he encountered, fearful of being trampled by the huge, elven horse, offered their usual cursing, middle fingers, and threats.

Thorgrim glanced to his left as he approached the buildings of the Vumfumik smelting facility.

The noise coming from the facility was a discordance of almost every sound imaginable, all blended together and repeating continuously in the same pattern. Added to the sound of Nugget's hooves pounding on the highway, Thorgrim heard a combination of whinnying, snorting, and the crying of many dozens of horses. He also heard men cursing, laughing, and arguing, as well as wagon wheels rolling on the gravely surface of the main lot. Mixed in with all of that, was the sound of ore falling off wagons and onto the ground, which in turn, elicited more cursing.

Off the main highway, in a huge receiving area, dozens of ore wagons waited in line to be unloaded onto wide, steam-powered conveyor belts, which then, carried the ore, deep into the complex. Other wagons, now empty, waited their turn to pull out onto the highway and then go back to their respective mines. Even on the weekends, the place was full of activity. Like ants milling around an anthill, an army of dwarves could be seen going in and out of the many buildings as they went about their work.

Speeding into the busy area, Thorgrim had no choice but to slow down to avoid an accident, something his nearly exhausted horse appreciated. Ore transports, both full and empty, were everywhere, and there was no easy way to get around them. Cursing the delay, he wondered which of the wagons belonged to the Vog Silver Mine Company.

When Thorgrim finally made it through the mayhem, he was less than a quarter-mile from Bur Dhulgren's northern entrance gates. However, as he approached, the deafening sound of an extremely loud horn, blasting from the city, startled him.

Thorgrim dreaded that the horn was heralding the end of the day. Checking his timepiece, it read exactly 8:31 p.m. The sun had set, and he was too late.

Cursing loudly, continuing on, he watched the traffic flowing into the city suddenly slow to a stop when the city militia closed the gates. Extremely disappointed, he now realized that he would have to get in line and wait for his turn to enter.

It had been a hot, humid day, and despite a swift breeze, it was to be an equally miserable night. Sweating heavily, Thorgrim faced a bigger problem. Glancing around, there was no sign of a nearby inn. As he had feared, because he lacked proper identification, this meant that he would be spending the night camping in the wilderness, outside the city's walls. Additionally, he was nearly out of food and water. His hunger and thirst raged, and he knew that Nugget was probably worse off.

Grumbling while wondering if this whole adventure had been a big mistake, he rode as far as he could towards the northern, city gates. There, he was stopped several hundred feet short due to the mass of people who were now waiting in line for their turn to get into the capital.

Up ahead, Thorgrim noticed that rows of torches had been lit and were now burning on the parapets. Near the gates, several torch poles were now in the process of being ignited by the city militia.

Over fifty feet above him, still visible in the twilight, he could hear the snapping and flapping of the royal flags that decorated the top of the city's wall.

Looking around at the mass of people, he saw some riding in horse-drawn wagons, on horses or donkeys, while a vast majority were on foot. The crowd, all of them, hot and sweaty, on this balmy, summer night, offered plenty of chatter and laughter but also shouting and occasional, rambunctious, shoving matches.

The militia repeatedly shouted out warnings to the crowd, to calm down or they would lock the gates for the night. Many ignoring the threats, mocked the guards, while others risked arrest or beatings due to fist fighting over who was next in line.

Most of the people standing in line near Thorgrim, gazed up at him as he sat atop his tall elven horse. They were in awe of the spectacle of a dwarf riding such a big horse, and Thorgrim could clearly hear their comments, some of them rude, about himself and Nugget.

While the crowd gossiped about him and his horse, Thorgrim reached for a flask to take a quick sip of what little water he had left. Then he realized that Nugget was likely very thirsty after such a hard ride. Deciding to give his horse some water, praying there would be no mishap during the dismount, he carefully stepped down from the saddle without the block.

Fortunately, it went well.

When he landed, his gigantic beard unfurled, the tip of it hanging well past his knees. Of course, the appearance of such a magnificent beard caught the attention of everyone around, some of them even gasping at the sight of it. Much to Thorgrim's displeasure, more talking and mumbling about him could be heard. He ignored them, and eventually, the gawkers moved on to other gossip and chitchat.

Checking his flasks, he still had a full one and half of another. Tipping the full flask into his thirty horse's mouth, he said, "Thankee my friend. You worked hard today. I'll get ya some food and more water, soon."

Unsure how he was going to gain entrance to the city, his mind spun in circles. He needed to figure out what he would say to the guards when it was his turn to enter.

Hungry, he reached into his pack and grabbed the last honey roll and the few remaining carrots. While he ate, he fed the carrots to his grateful, though very tired horse.

Perspiring in the hot summer night, his thirst was as fierce as his hunger. Taking his last, half-empty flask, he chased the pastry with a couple of gulps and then tipped the rest into Nugget's maw. The horse happily drank every drop.

Looking around at everyone, he now realized he might have to ask someone for water, but they all looked equally thirsty.

While the bantering of the anxious crowd continued, from behind him, someone tapped Thorgrim on the shoulder.

Not wanting anyone to get a good look at him, he froze and ignored whoever it was.

Another tap on the shoulder, but this time someone spoke.

"Hey, old-timer. Ya got a light for muh pipe? I lost muh flint."

Old-timer? thought Thorgrim. *Why would he call me that?*

Then he remembered that he had fallen face-first in the mud when trying to mount Nugget in the morning at the Pretzel Inn. Looking down at his beard and clothes, he was still covered head to boot in dry mud and dirt.

In the twilight, the dried mud gave the illusion of grey hair and old skin. Excited that his appearance was disguised, he decided to take full advantage of it.

Turning to the person behind him, Thorgrim was greeted by the nod of a middle-aged dwarf probably in his eighties.

Thorgrim tried to sound like an older dwarf.

"Yes, young 'un. I've got a flint right here in muh backpack."

Reaching in the side pouch, he hesitated because he remembered May had pulled a field snake out of it back in Stug. Realizing he was being paranoid, he chuckled and grabbed his flint box. Striking it, he lit the stranger's pipe.

"Thank'n you, old-timer," replied the stranger. "Grateful for dat, very grateful, indeed."

After taking a long draw from his burning pipe, the stranger blew out a cloud of grey smoke and commented, "Must have been one hell of a storm up north last night. I heard there was a big tornado out dare, somewhere." Pointing towards the Brimgers, he continued, "Could see the lightning a flash'n all night long."

Thorgrim turned and looked north towards the mountains. He could barely see them, their shapes, slightly darker than the night sky. Still using his old dwarf's voice, he replied, "Ya, I got caught in the middle of some of that last night."

Taking another drag from his pipe, the stranger expelled the smoke and said, "What's yer name, old-timer? Mine's, Mooky."

"Uh, nice to meet ya, Mooky. Muh name is Shem."

Mooky reached out and shook Thorgrim's hand.

"Nice to meet ya, too," replied Mooky.

Looking at Nugget and then Thorgrim's beard, he continued, "I have to say dat in my almost ninety years a livin', I don't think I've seen a taller horse den dat, or a longer beard den da one yer wearin'."

Pretending to be partially deaf, Thorgrim said, "Huh, would ya mind repeatin' that, youngster? Muh hearin' ain't what it used to be."

"Oh sure. I said, I have to say dat in my almost ninety years a livin', I don't think I've seen a taller horse den dat, or a longer beard den da one yer wearin."

"Oh, thankee!"

Mooky nodded and puffed on his pipe. "If ya don't mind me askin'. How old are ya?"

Thorgrim had no idea how old the dried mud made him appear. *How old is an old-timer?* he wondered. Guessing, he replied, "Uh, I'm a hundred and sixty."

Removing his pipe, Mooky took a big draw of ale from a golden flask and said, "Well, dat's not so old now a-days! Uh, excuse me, but da line's a-movin'. Would ya mind scootin' up a bit? Otherwise, we'll be standing out here 'til mornin'."

Thorgrim turned and saw that the line had been moving at a slow but steady pace. He took Nugget's reins and walked his horse ahead until they caught up with the back of the line.

Then, he noticed that Mooky held a silver card in his hand.

"Youngster, what is that? That silver thing yer holdin' in yer hand."

Mooky replied, "It's muh City Resident Identification Card. Everyone who lives in Bur Dhulgren gets one. Obviously, ya don't live here. Where ya from? If'n ya don't mind me askin'."

Cupping an ear, Thorgrim replied, "Huh?"

After taking a quick sip of ale, Mooky repeated himself, only louder, "Shem, I said it's muh City Resident Identification Card. Everyone who lives in Bur Dhulgren gets one. Obviously, ya don't live here. Where ya from? If'n ya don't mind me askin'."

Thorgrim raised his monobrow and nodded. "Oh, it's an ID card! No, I'm not from here. I'm from Dartag Bur and just visiting some friends in the capital."

"I'm sure ya know dey'll be askin' for yer ID papers . . . ya did remember to bring yers, didn't ya, Shem?"

Thorgrim grinned. "Oh, yes, I remembered!"

Mooky took another drink from the ale flask and then offered it to Thorgrim.

"Is that ale?"

Mooky nodded, "Ya, from da Pretzel Brewery! Take a sip. Best stuff around."

"Thankee, I am kinda thirsty."

Despite not caring for ale, his thirst badgered him, so Thorgrim took the flask and tipped it back into his mouth. Smacking his fat lips, he said, "Hmmm. Not bad, and cold, too." He swallowed another gulp and said, "It's good, but I never really took much of a liken' to ale."

Mooky appeared flabbergasted. "Yer kiddin'! Ya don't care for ale? A rare dwarf, indeed ya are!"

Thorgrim was slightly embarrassed. "Uh, Thankee, I guess."

Though the fire was out, Mooky put his pipe back in his mouth and gestured towards the gates, still over a hundred feet and several dozens of anxious people away.

"Uh, Shem. Da line moved again,"

Thorgrim glanced and said, "Oh, sorry." He then walked Nugget a dozen feet forward, catching up with the back of the line.

Sweat was rolling off everyone. "How long will this take?" asked Thorgrim, wiping his brow. "The heat and humidity are killin' me, not to mention muh horse and I are starvin' and thirsty."

"Oh, not real long . . . unless a big fight breaks out. If dat happens, we'll be here for a while. In da meantime, I hope dey hurry. Da damn vampire 'skeetos will be arriving soon and da only thing dat keeps dem away is a good torch."

When Mooky mentioned the vampire mosquitoes, Thorgrim shuddered. He was aware of the annoying bloodsuckers. Swarms of them had invaded Vog every summer for as long as he could remember.

Around him, others were aware of the pests, too, because he saw many in the crowd lighting torches followed by shouts of 'hurry up there, damn ya! The 'skeetos are comin'.

Thorgrim knew Nugget desperately needed water. "Muh flasks are empty. Ya don't happen to have any water, do ya? I'd sure like to get some into muh horse if possible."

"Yes, I've got some water. Give dis to yer horse and take a drink yerself if ya like. I have another, so drink all ya want."

Mooky pulled out a big flask of water out of his bag and handed it to Thorgrim.

"Why, thankee very much." Thorgrim took a couple sips, then unselfishly gave the remainder of the water to Nugget.

Returning Mooky's empty flask, Thorgrim studied the silver, metalized City Resident Card that his new friend carried in his hand.

"Mooky, do you mind if I take a look at yer card? Never seen one before."

"Sure!" Mooky replied, handing his card to Thorgrim.

Thorgrim looked at the card, but the darkness made it extremely difficult to see anything. He squinted. "It's too dark out here. I can't see a thing. What's on the card?"

"Not a damn thing, really. Just da symbol of da Dwarven Clans etched on dare and da name, Bur Dhulgren."

"That's all?"

"Yep"

189

Thorgrim was puzzled. "But, how do the guards really know you didn't steal that card. You know, if anyone found one, couldn't they use it to get into the city even though they're not a resident?"

"Exactly. Anyone could use it and get into da city. No problem. Dat's unless dey get caught illegally using one of deez ID cards. It does mention dat on da back in fine print."

Flipping the card over, Mooky looked at the back. "Uh, I can't read it either, but I got it memorized. It says somethin' like, "Attention. Dis card for use by Bur Dhulgren residents only. Non-residents, who are found in possession of dis card will be prosecuted to da fullest extent of da law. You have been warned."

Thorgrim frowned. "Sounds like they mean business. What's the fullest extent of the law?"

"Ya mean, what will happen' if ya get caught usin' one of deez and ya really don't live in da city?"

"Yes."

Mooky smiled and finally put his pipe back in his pocket. "Don't know for sure, but I heard you could get a year in da crowbar motel . . . also known as the Kronk Prison! If ya get muh drift! Ouch! Looks like da damn 'skeetos have arrived."

Thorgrim saw the dreaded bugs buzzing around. Trying his best to wave them away, he said, "A year in prison! That seems a bit severe."

"One year, plus hard labor! Not as bad as gettin' caught with fake ID papers. Dat'll get ya three to five years! I imagine dey just want to keep out troublemakers. After all, da city is da seat of the government and center of learning. I don't think the King wants riff-raff hanging around outside of his castle door."

"Riff-raff?"

Mooky grinned. "Same as troublemakers." Gesturing, he said, "Uh, da line moved, again"

Thorgrim looked. "Oops, Sorry, guess it did."

With Nugget in tow, he soon caught up with the back of the line. Now closer, the pressure on him increased. He still had no idea how he was going to get past the guards, and he was running out of time.

"Mooky, how do you become an official resident here?"

"Well, if yer born inside da city, dat'll do it. Other den dat, you have to apply, and if dey accept you, den you can buy or rent a place to live inside. Business owners have da best shot at it. You can technically live or work in da city and not be an official resident. But, I would advise against it, because you could end up stuck outside after sunset and unable

190

to get home! Yep, get one of deez silver cards, and you'll never have a problem gettin' in.' "

Thorgrim glanced at the multitude of people around him. Many were holding their silver cards, waiting to present them to the guards.

"So, if you forget or lose yer card, can you still get inside?"

Before he answered, Mooky swatted, killing a couple of vampire mosquitoes that had lit on his cheek. "Damn, shoulda' brought a torch with me tonight. Uh, if ya forget yer card, you can still get in if ya have yer regular identification papers. Dey will check da registry for yer name and description. If it matches, you get in. If it don't match or dey don't have you on file, you are stuck out here or in some cases, arrested on suspicion of possessin' forged papers. I've seen it happen."

Up ahead, Thorgrim could hear the guards urging everyone to be prepared to show their City Resident Cards. Panicking, he knew that he would have to somehow acquire one. If he and Nugget could not get in tonight, he feared they would be eaten alive by the aggressive and always hungry vampire mosquitos. To make matters worse, he had no weapon to defend himself, no shelter, and no food or water.

Thorgrim looked around on the ground nearby, hoping someone had dropped their card.

No luck.

Behind him, a commotion broke out between several, heavily inebriated dwarves. They were fighting over who could drink the most ale in an evening. As they argued and shoved each other, Thorgrim, crafting a plan, saw an opportunity and intervened.

Stepping in between the belligerents, he said, "Okay, you idiots. Do you want the guards to arrest you? I would suggest that —"

One of the drunk's fists landed hard on Thorgrim's jaw, interrupting him.

Although his jaw hurt like hell, Thorgrim grinned. Following his scheme, he said, "Is that the best you've got?" At, which point, two sweaty drunks rushed in and tackled him to the ground. Mooky and a few others came to Thorgrim's rescue, pulling off the drunkards and shoving them away.

"Are ya okay, Shem?" asked Mooky, helping Thorgrim to his feet.

Thorgrim wiggled his jaw. "Ya, I think so."

Turning to the drunks, Mooky yelled, "What's da matta wit you idiots! Can't you see dat dis old guy is probably tree or four times yer age? Where's yer respect for da elderly?"

Thorgrim was fine. Although he was a bit bruised and now wore a slightly fattened lip, fortunately, his ruse worked, and he got what he wanted. Using a trick his younger brother Thurston had taught him, he pilfered the City Resident Card from the front pocket of one of the drunks who had tackled him.

After thanking Mooky and the others for helping, with the stolen card in hand, he stepped back into line to await his turn to enter the city.

Now, all he had to worry about was getting caught with an illegally obtained City Resident Card. There would be little risk because he planned to leave the country and did not intend to stay in the city for more than one or two days. He knew that he probably would never have to use the card again.

"Are ya sure yer okay, old fella?" asked Mooky.

"I'm fine, thank you, youngster," replied Thorgrim, once again using his old dwarf voice. Smiling, he said, "I'm tougher than I look."

"No offense, but when I helped ya to yer feet back dare, I noticed dat you also smell riper than you look," commented Mooky. "And you look pretty ripe. My advice would be to use one of da public baths as soon as you get inside."

Thorgrim grinned. "Ya, I suppose I don't smell the best. Been a rough few days getting here."

"I'm surprised the 'skeetos would want to go anywhere near ya," said Mooky with a big laugh, swatting at a squadron of them.

Now closer, within the light of the many burning pole-torches, Thorgrim could clearly see what was happening up ahead. There were four sets of large, double-door gates. Six of the gates were used for those trying to enter the city, while two were wide open for those trying to leave. A squad of burly, city militia guards enforced the rules.

Occasionally, someone would be turned away for lacking the proper credentials, and although they would try pleading, cursing, arguing, and sometimes using threats, the guards would always win any debate.

Thorgrim, still somewhat naïve about the city's ordinances, was confused.

"Mooky, I don't understand. You don't have to show identification to enter the city during the day . . . just at night?"

"Yes, dat's true," replied Mooky, swatting at a couple more mosquitos. "Sometimes, dey will ask during the day, too, but always do at night."

"Why always at night?"

"Riff-raff. Da best time for a troublemaker to sneak into the city is at night. We don't need any more of doze types. Dare are enough of dem dat already live in da city, 'specially in the southern districts. We call doze districts the unsavory south. Best to avoid doze areas."

"So, if non-residents come into the city, they don't have to leave?"

"If dey want to stay with friends or at one of da inns, dat's fine. Otherwise, dare eventually rounded up, kicked out or sent to da city jail for a few days. Repeat offenders or bad criminal types are sent way down south to da Kronk Prison on Flounder Island. After dey spend a few weeks in prison, dey usually don't come back here. All in all, da system is far from perfect, but it's better den nuttin'."

"Hey, you," barked a gruff voice. "Do you want in or not?"

Startled, Thorgrim turned and saw a muscle-bound militia guard glaring at him.

"Oh sure, sorry."

The line had cleared, so he scooted up to meet the guard. Nugget, guided by his reins, followed.

"Hey, that's a tall horse you got there, sir," commented the guard.

Thorgrim smiled and proudly looked at Nugget. "Yes, he's tall, and also very faithful."

"That's nice. Now, let's see yer ID."

As Thorgrim nodded his head, a fight broke out in the line next to him. Two guards planted a pair of boots in the rear of an extremely drunk dwarf and rolled him down the hill towards the Mharrak River.

The guard scowled. "Come on, old-timer. I need yer ID. Yer holdin' up the line."

Thorgrim panicked and hesitated. *Does he mean my identification papers or the silver card?*

Mooky leaned in and whispered, "Just show him da City Resident Card dat you pilfered from dat drunk back dare a while ago. Dat was really a slick move, I've got to admit!"

Thorgrim turned red with embarrassment.

"It's okay, show him," whispered Mooky.

Thorgrim presented the stolen card to the impatient guard.

The guard looked at the card twice, then gave Thorgrim a quick once-over. Nodding, the guard growled, "Okay, come on in. Next!"

Breathing a sigh of relief, Thorgrim stepped through the main gate and into the city, stopping in the middle of a wide street. Thrilled, he had finally made it.

He quickly checked his timepiece. It was after 10:30 p.m.

"My God," he mumbled. "It took over an hour and a half to get through that line."

When Thorgrim looked up from his timepiece, he got his first good view of the city's interior. Having never seen anything like it before, he was astounded. The fact that he was actually standing in the capital city of the Dwarven Clans, overwhelmed his emotions.

Tears formed in his eyes. Though he deeply missed his home and family back in Vog, he knew he had made the right decision and promised himself no matter what happened, he would never regret his choice to strike out on his own.

Inside, a dozen feet past the gate, he noticed a sign that pointed south, down the street that he was standing on. It read: 'Central Avenue.' Gazing down the long avenue, which ran towards the center of the city, Thorgrim could not believe his eyes.

On both sides of Central Avenue, as far as the eye could see, was a seemingly endless chain of hundreds of flaming pole torches and lanterns. In the distance, atop the Royal Castle, the tallest building in the Bur Dhulgren, he could easily see the giant torch and its massive flame burning in the night.

Torches were ablaze everywhere he looked. On poles, on the sides of buildings, or in the hands of some of the residents who were going about their business. Thorgrim remembered his father talking about the special torches used in the mines. Dwarven engineers had developed a low-soot, indoor/outdoor torch that could burn five or more hours, making them ideal for use in the mines, or even in homes.

Central Avenue and the flanking sidewalks were packed with milling throngs of Saturday night revelers. Most of them, already half-drunk, were doing their best to drink the last drop out of every beer keg in the city. As a cheap form of entertainment, as if at a circus, some of the others were there to watch the rollicking spectacle as it unfolded.

Nearby, fresh militia troops stood outside their barracks waiting to relieve the current squad and then start their shift to check in any wayfarers arriving late to the city. Sometimes, it was an all-night job, and tonight would be no exception. Outside, hundreds of dwarves still stood in line, complaining about how slow the line was moving and cursing the vampire mosquitos.

Mooky stepped up and stood beside Thorgrim. "Would ya look at dat! Da great city! It's so full of excitement!"

Thorgrim was still in awe. "It's amazin'! I've never seen anything like it."

"So, Shem, you say yer here to see some friends? Where might dey be? Maybe I can direct ya. Da city is very big, and you can easily get lost in here."

194

Nearby, outside the gates, an intense argument broke out. Apparently, one of the dwarves had lost his City Resident Card. He also lacked his identification papers and was denied entrance.

Mooky grinned and elbowed Thorgrim. "Oopsie! Looks like someone lost dare card."

Thorgrim sheepishly said, "About that, I uh—"

"No need to explain. Look, I know yer not an old-timer, and I don't care. No worries, I won't say a word. Either way, you look like you could use a little help."

"Thankee," replied Thorgrim, relieved. Swallowing a bit of pride, he continued, "Ya, I guess I could use a little help."

"You need a place to stay?"

"Yes, lots of water and a hot meal. Oh, and fresh hay for my horse."

"And probably a hot bath, along with a change of clothes, too," commented Mooky.

"Yes, that too. Problem is that I don't have much money. Where can I stable my horse and get all of those things tonight, cheaply?"

Mooky smiled. "I know just da place," he said, pointing due south down the street they were standing on. "I have a good friend who runs an inn about a mile away, straight down here on Central Avenue. I'll see to it that he gives you a good deal on a room."

Thorgrim beamed a big smile. "That would be great!"

Looking down the expanse of Central Avenue, his expression changed to a frown. "This city is so big. I'll get lost in here. Where can I get a map?"

"Sorry, no maps are available dat I know of, but let me explain how da city is laid out. Bur Dhulgren is huge. It runs ten miles north to south, seven miles east to west and is surrounded by a circular wall. Dis big road we're on is called Central Avenue. It's called Central because it runs right down da center of da city, north and south. A similar road, called Middle Street, runs across da middle of the city, east and west. So, Central Avenue and Middle Street form a big plus sign at da very center of da city. We call dat place Da Heart of da City!"

Thorgrim nodded his head. Doing the math, he said, "Like ya said, this city is huge. Seventy square miles?"

"Dat's right. Da city's a big un!"

"Uh, no offense, Mooky, but you have an unusual accent. Where are you from?"

"Oh, dat's my northeast Ulm Barim accent sneakin' in. Dey say ya never lose it, but I'm workin' on it. I'm from a town called Cluj."

Thorgrim grinned slightly. "You pronounce words a lot like muh papa does when he gets upset."

"Oh, dat's funny," chuckled Mooky.

In his mind's eye, Thorgrim pictured his father. He loved and missed him. The thought causing him a brief moment of depression.

Mooky noticed. "Hey, Shem, you okay?"

"Ya, I'm okay. Ya said you were from a town called Cluj? Never heard of it."

"Oh, believe me, you're not missing much. Tiny town, but there's a nice lake nearby, dat's about it. I should know . . . I lived dare for over forty years helping to pull gold outta da lake. Ya see, gold comes down da river from an old mine—"

Thorgrim felt tingles run up and down his body. Trying to get off the subject of mines, he cut Mooky off. "Anyway, sorry to interrupt, you were telling me about the layout of Bur Dhulgren."

"Oh, yes, let's see where was I? Uh, all roads dat run north and south are called avenues, and all of da roads that run east and west are called streets. Every road in da city has a number."

Pointing to a street sign, Mooky continued, "We're now standing at da intersection of North Sixtieth Street and Central Avenue. If we walk one block south, we'll be at North Fifty-Ninth Street and Central Avenue. Da next one is North Fifty-Eighth Street and so on. Eventually, you'll reach da City Center where most of da big buildings are. Da Royal Castle, administrative buildings, police and Army Headquarters and da like."

"The Supreme Library, and the Grand Hall of the Dwarves, too?" asked Thorgrim, wild-eyed with excitement. "A friend of mine told me they were in the City Center."

"Yes. When you get to da intersection of Middle Street and Central Avenue, like I said, dat's da place we call da Heart of da City. All of da buildings on dose four corners make up what we call da City Center. Da library and Grand Hall sit right at the intersection. Ya can't miss 'em. Got dat?"

Thorgrim, picturing it all in his mind's eye, nodded in excitement.

"Keep goin' south and you'll come to South First Street and Central Avenue. Den, South Second, South Third and so on. If ya go a block east of Central Avenue, you would be at East First Avenue, den East Second, etcetera. Don't forget, roads dat run north and south are called avenues. Roads dat run east and west are called streets. Remember dat and you'll never get lost. Ya sure ya got all of dat?"

"Ya, sounds pretty easy, I guess."

"But, avoid going beyond South Fiftieth Street."

"Riff-raff?"

"Ya, Riff-raff. Dat area is part of da unsavory south dat I mentioned earlier."

"I need to go to a place called the 'Iron Golem Pub'," said Thorgrim, concerned. "Do ya know where I can find it?"

Mooky's eyes widened, and the whites of his bulging eyes could be clearly seen in the torchlight.

"Did ya just say dat ya need to go to da Iron Golem Pub?"

"Ya."

"Now dat's a dangerous place. It's in da unsavory south! Is dat where yer friends are?"

"Uh, yes."

"But, you've never been dare before?"

"No."

Mooky frowned. "Well, I've been dare before . . . a couple of times, but dat was many years ago, back when I was young and dumb. Now, I don't know if I would brag much 'bout havin' friends who hang 'round da Iron Golem Pub! You watch yer back if ya go dare. Even da police avoid dat area. Da pub is down on da corner of East Forty-Second Avenue and South Fifty-Fifth Street. Kind of in da southeastern corner of da city."

Thorgrim raised his monobrow. "East Forty-Second Avenue and South Fifty-Fifth Street?"

"Ya, dat's it."

"The police won't go there? Is it really that dangerous in the southern part of the city?"

"Dey don't call it da unsavory south for nuttin'. Da police seem to ignore what's goin' on down dare, but I would suspect dare's some corruption goin' on. I would think dat da police could just go down dare and clean up da riff-raff, but dey never do."

"Uh, I see. Okay, I'll try to be careful," promised Thorgrim, now deeply concerned after hearing Mooky's dire warnings about both the pub and the area he would have to ride through to get to it. Gary had told him that the pub was in a rough-looking neighborhood, but Mooky made it sound much worse.

Next to him, Nugget whinnied.

"Mooky, muh horse is very thirsty and hungry. Would it be a bother if you took me to the inn you mentioned? To be honest, I'm parched and starvin', muhself."

197

"Sure, it's not far out of muh way. My house is on da corner of East Ninth Avenue and North Forty-Ninth Street. I'd feed ya and put ya up for da night, but muh missus would have muh head if I brought a guest over before she had a chance to tidy up da place."

"I understand, but thankee."

Mooky pointed down the avenue. "Da inn is called 'Da Scalded Dwarf' and it's straight down Central Avenue on da corner of North Forty-Ninth Street. 'Bout a mile away."

Thorgrim frowned. "The Scalded Dwarf? I don't think I like the sound of that."

"Oh, it's nuttin'. It's called dat 'cuz da inn has da hottest baths in da city. It's a sales gimmick of sorts, really."

"Ah, a hot bath, yes, I want that. You sure you can get me a good deal? I think I told you that I don't have much money."

"Like I said, I know da owner really well . . . he's muh best friend, so I can pull a few strings for ya. No worries. Ya ready to get movin'? We've been standin' around since we got inside the city."

"Yes, I am, and I can't thank you enough."

"Thank God it's finally cooling down, but the 'skeetos are eatin' me alive," complained Mooky. "Alright then, follow me, dey won't bother us much if we keep movin' and stay near da pole torches!"

With Mooky leading the way, Thorgrim followed with Nugget in tow.

As they walked down Central Avenue towards the inn, Thorgrim was still astounded by the multitudes of torches that lined the streets, as well as the vast number of dwarves who were hanging around or going in and out of buildings.

"I can't imagine how many torches the city goes through in a year!" he exclaimed. "There are ten on each side of the street and a few on every corner."

Pointing down Central Avenue, Thorgrim continued, "Look at the giant one way down there on top of that big building. I hate heights, so I wouldn't want to be the one who has to climb that thing to light it."

Mooky laughed. "Only Central Avenue and Middle Street are lit up like dis. Da rest have one on each corner and a few on each side of da street. Dat giant tower torch? It's sitting atop da Royal Castle, and it's lit every night by a flamin' arrow. It's not a real torch anyway. It's a mockup. It has some kind of gas dat burns inside it."

Thorgrim noticed the many businesses that flanked them as they walked. Approaching North Fifty-Eighth Street and Central Avenue, they had walked two blocks towards their destination.

"Mooky, I've never seen so many businesses in all my life."

Pointing, Mooky replied, "On almost every block dare's at least one pub, an inn, tattoo parlor, public bath, or some kind of joint where most dwarves love to hang out. And it can be a wild circus down here after 'nuff ale gets a flowin'."

At that moment, off to their right, a loud ruckus erupted inside a pub. Both Thorgrim and Mooky stopped to watch the action.

Yelling, cursing and crashing sounds could be heard coming from the inside of a small pub called 'The Clown House.' Then without warning, the main door of the pub swung open with a bang. A few dwarves, who were standing nearby, scattered, when a drunken dwarf was kicked in the rear and then rolled out into the avenue, coming to rest on his back, next to Nugget's front hooves.

"And stay out!" yelled the irate owner of The Clown House. "That'll teach ya to keep yer dirty mitts off of the bar maidens!" The owner swiftly turned and went inside. A few seconds later, a scruffy hat flew out the front door and landed next to the semiconscious soak.

The owner then stuck his head out the door and continued his castigation of the drunk. "The next time you try that, Jasper, when I toss yer hat out, yer head will still be in it!"

Everyone still standing around outside jumped when the pub's door slammed closed.

Jasper remained flat on his back, and when the half-beaten, heavily inebriated dwarf opened his eyes, he found himself looking straight into the face of Nugget, who was licking his cheek.

Jasper belched, then puckered his fat lips. "Oh, yer a beauty aren't ya, honey? Thanks for the kisses. Would ya like to dance, dearie?"

Thorgrim grimaced. "Come on, Nugget. That drunk thinks you're a pretty bar maiden."

Mooky and Thorgrim continued on their way to the inn, leaving the lovesick drunkard lying in the avenue where he landed, crying for Nugget's return.

Upon reaching North Fifty-Sixth Street, Thorgrim said, "Wow, that was something back there, wasn't it? Listen to all of the commotion around us. Does this city always get this rowdy?" As he spoke, a couple of police officers, clubs in hand, ran by them on their way to some disturbance.

Mooky chuckled. "What do ya expect from a city full of dwarves on da weekend? As you can see, da police are out in force and dey'll be busy all night. Typical weekend, really. Da city jailhouse will be overloaded as usual, but dey'll let most of dem go in da morn."

199

When they reached the next intersection, Thorgrim checked his timepiece. It was almost midnight. His stomach, rumbling and complaining, felt like it was stuck to his backbone.

"Mooky, do you hear that dog growling? That's my stomach! I haven't eaten a hot meal since late last night! I've been livin' on bison jerky and honey rolls. I can't wait to find somethin' good to eat, and I'm sure my horse feels the same way. How much further to this inn you mentioned?"

Thorgrim rubbed Nugget's cheek and the horse responded with a big lick to his master's face.

"Won't be long, Shem. Da Scalded Dwarf has a great selection of food. You'll see!"

Wiping his cheek, Thorgrim replied, "Thank Moridon. I'll eat everything they have in the place."

Mooky pointed to the left. "If you want to thank Moridon, you can do just that! There's a church right across da street over dare."

Thorgrim looked and shook his head. "A church sitting in-between two pubs? Kind of an odd place for a church, don't ya think?"

"I guess, but dat church used to be a pub. You know, some dwarves have to go home to face da missus after a night of drinkin', and it's probably not a bad idea to stop in a church and say a prayer or two before ya go home, if ya know what I mean!"

"No, never been married, but I guess I can imagine."

"Oh, you'll get married one day. Yer still young. Like I said earlier, I know yer not an old-timer. That muddy face and beard won't fool many people for long."

Thorgrim was embarrassed. He turned his face away as they walked.

Mooky patted him on the back. "No worries. I don't know why yer here or what yer doin'. Don't care, but I'll help ya out."

"Thankee. I really appreciate anything you can do, Mooky."

***

After having walked nearly a mile from the northern gates, Mooky and Thorgrim, with Nugget in tow, finally reached the corner of North Forty-Ninth Street and Central Avenue.

Pointing to a brightly lit, two-story building on the corner, Mooky said, "Well, dare's da place you'll be stayin' tonight. Da Scalded Dwarf."

The experience of getting to the inn was one not soon to be forgotten by Thorgrim. The mile walk from the gate had been full of action. He had observed the crème de la crème of the finest boozehounds that Bur Dhulgren had to offer, practicing what they do best.

He saw and heard almost everything imaginable. Fighting, arguing, cursing and yelling. Teams of 'ladies of the night' calling out for business. Paddy Wagons arriving empty from the jailhouse only to return to it fully laden with angry or passed out partiers. He even witnessed an ambulance wagon arriving at a public bath where two alcohol-saturated dwarves had accidentally fallen in the pool and drowned.

Mooky pointed towards several posts. "Tie yer horse up to one of da posts, and let's go inside so we can get ya checked in. Dare's a stable out back, so we'll put yer horse inside for da night and he'll be groomed and fed. Dat's if he'll fit in dare. Never seen such a tall horse, before."

Thorgrim secured Nugget to a post and the thirsty horse immediately began drinking from the water trough. As Nugget drank, Thorgrim kissed him on the cheek and rubbed his ears for a moment.

Mooky went to the front door and gestured. Thorgrim followed.

Thorgrim said, "You mentioned that yer friend runs this place?"

"Yes, I know him very well. He's muh oldest and greatest friend. And, no worries about da money. Da guy owes me some favors, so I'll see to it dat he takes good care of ya."

"Yer kiddin'," exclaimed Thorgrim as Mooky opened the door. "You'd do that for me. You hardly know me."

Mooky stepped through the door and said, "No, not kiddin'. I like to help people out when dey are in need. I can see you are exactly dat. By the way, how long do ya plan on stayin' in da city?"

Thorgrim shrugged a shoulder. "Not long. I'll probably leave in a couple of days. Most likely, Monday."

Mooky smiled. "Okay. You'll be staying here for free for a couple of days. Dat includes food and everything."

Thorgrim was stunned. "Food, too? I just can't believe it. Are you sure yer friend will be okay with this?"

Mooky grinned. "If he argues with me about it, I'll set him straight, real quick! Let's go in and get it taken care of. Ya want to eat, don't ya?"

"Well, I don't want to cause anyone any problems, and yes, I'm starvin'!"

"Not a problem, Shem."

Thorgrim entered and Mooky closed the door.

"Shem, wait right here."

Mooky walked to the check-in counter and rang a small bell.

While Mooky waited for service, Thorgrim looked around.

201

The place was spotless, reminding him of his own home back in Vog. His mother was meticulous about cleaning her house. Everyone always said that you could eat off the floor, and it would be cleaner than most of the plates found in some of the best cafés.

The Reception Room, at twenty by twelve feet, was rather small, though still comfortable and adequate. There was a door behind the counter just like at the inn back in Pretzel.

On the right side of the modestly decorated room, stood a staircase that led up to the second floor of the inn. Adjacent to the staircase was a set of double doors that he assumed belonged to the inn's café. His stomach growled at the thought of the delicious food that awaited him on the other side of the doors.

After another ring of the bell, a dwarf wearing a short, neatly trimmed, bright-red beard, probably in his sixties, entered from the office and approached the counter. He smiled and greeted Mooky with a firm handshake. Mooky then leaned over the counter and began whispering into his ear.

While he whispered, twice, Mooky pointed towards Thorgrim, and both times the red-bearded dwarf nodded.

Mooky looked at Thorgrim and said, "Shem, ya think you'll be headin' out Monday, is dat right?"

"Uh, yes."

Mooky whispered a few more words into the red-bearded dwarf's ear, shook his hand, then turned and walked back to where Thorgrim was standing.

"Dat's it, I've got everything worked out. Yer all set for two nights. Dat includes a hot breakfast and dinner for both days and two hot baths, which by da way, I suggest you take advantage of before you go into dat café back dare."

Thorgrim half-grinned.

"Norton will take good care of ya," said Mooky, pointing to the red-bearded dwarf. "And yer horse is also included, of course. He'll be well-treated and happy back dare in da stable. Now, if things change and you decide you need to stay a bit longer, let Norton know."

"Thankee! I can't thank you enough!" said Thorgrim excitedly, reaching out to shake Mooky's hand.

"Yer welcome, Shem. Now get some rest. Perhaps one day we'll meet again! Good luck to ya! Oh, and if ya head down to da Iron Golem Pub, it could change yer life, and I don't know if it would be for da better! Beware down dare!"

"I'll be careful."

"I've gotta git home. My missus will not be happy, 'cuz I'm very late."

Curious, Thorgrim said, "Mooky, I never asked, what were you doin' outside the walls tonight?"

Mooky shrugged. "I don't know. Strange you should ask. When I get off work, I sometimes like to go for walks. Well, I went out for a walk, and I found myself outside da wall, walking along da stream towards da tip of the Brimgers. Must've walked three or four miles. Odd, I hadn't done dat since I was a kid. Anyway, we would've never met hadn't I taken dat walk!"

"I'm grateful you did and thanks again."

Mooky winked, then exited the inn, whistling a song as he went.

Norton smiled and gestured. "Sir, come on over here, and we'll get you signed in!"

Thorgrim excitedly strolled up to the counter.

Opening up the registry, Norton said, "Just take that quill and sign yer name, please."

Thorgrim obliged, signing his name 'Shem Lybree.'

Norton glanced at the signature. "Mr. Lybree, everything has been taken care of. As Mooky said, my name is Norton, and I will be at your service."

Pointing towards the door in the back, he continued, "The café is through that door, and it's open from five-thirty in the morning 'til two-thirty the next morning, every day. You're in room one and it's on the other side of the stairs over there."

Thorgrim brought his brow down. "Room one? There doesn't happen to be a tree outside the window in room number one, is there?"

"No. Why do you ask?"

Thorgrim chuckled. "Oh . . . never mind."

"There's a hallway that leads to the hot baths on the other side of the stairs, too. We even have a laundry service available. Inside your room, you'll find a basket. Put your dirty clothes in it, and set it outside your door. We'll take care of it."

Having only three sets of clothes, Thorgrim was pleased with the idea of having them washed.

"Oh, Mr. Lybree, I almost forgot. Each room has its own private garderobe and sink."

Thorgrim seemed surprised. "Every room has its own garderobe? What about the rooms on the upper floor? I mean, where does everything—"

"Well, we have everything piped out into the back alley. The kitchen keeps a garden back there, so we use the stuff as fertilizer."

Thorgrim raised his brow and said, "Oh, I like that! Excellent idea! My Grandpa Pistachio always said that everything should serve a purpose."

Norton gave a quick nod and said, "Yes, I agree. Why waste it?"

"Um, what about muh horse? He's parked out front."

Norton smiled. "I'll have a stableman come 'round and get him, shortly."

"Oh, thankee. He's pretty hungry and loves carrots."

"Not a problem. We have fresh hay, carrots, apples . . . you name it. Horses who stay here are treated like royalty."

Thorgrim nervously said, "Good . . . uh, I need to ask ya . . . uh, are ya sure this won't cost me anything?"

"Not a copper! Mooky explained everything to me, and it's all taken care of."

"Wow. I don't know what to say, but thank you. Mooky said his best friend owned this place, and I can see that yer friendship with Mooky must run very deep."

Norton shook his head. "I'm not the owner."

"You're not? I assumed you were the owner because Mooky spoke to you."

"No. I assumed you knew that Mooky was the owner of The Scalded Dwarf."

Thorgrim's mouth hung agape. "Mooky? But he said his best friend was the owner."

Norton smiled softly. "Well, he was telling the truth. He always says that you are your own best friend."

Thorgrim became lost in thought, as he tried to comprehend Mooky's wisdom.

Norton closed the registry book and said, "I hope you'll enjoy the stay, and if you need anything, I'll be right here 'til my shift ends at five a.m. A dwarf by the name of Goober will be at yer service all day tomorrow."

"I'll likely be gone most of the day, but thankee again, Norton."

"Very welcome, sir. Oh, and one more thing, please watch the noise after ten at night. Most of the rooms are booked, and everyone is probably trying to sleep."

"I understand. No problem." Thorgrim yawned, then glanced at his timepiece. It was almost 1:15 a.m. "Well, I suppose I better get to muh room and then to the café. I'm starvin'! But first, I should probably take a bath!"

Quickly dressing after his hot bath, Thorgrim raced to the café for an equally hot meal. He was famished, having not eaten anything but bison jerky and honey rolls since he left Pretzel the previous morning.

After enjoying an appetizer of turtlehead soup, he bolted a huge plate of rabbit ear goulash, followed by an entire chocolate cake for dessert. With his gluttonous feast finished, barely able to move, he stumbled out of the café and went to his room.

Once inside his candle-lit room, he filled the laundry basket with virtually every piece of clothing he owned before placing it outside his door as instructed. Finally, he brushed his teeth for a full five minutes, just as his mother always taught him to do.

Exhausted, his belly stuffed with food, he eagerly wanted to collapse on the comfy-looking bed, but first, he checked it for any hidden mattress possums. Satisfied there were none, he was about to crawl under the covers but realized there was still one more task to do.

He listened but thankfully did not hear any tapping sounds coming from the bedroom window. Despite Norton telling him that there were no trees nearby, he had to be sure. He parted the curtain and looked out.

Peering through the glass, he noticed a pair of big, pumpkin-orange eyes staring back at him from the other side.

At first, Thorgrim thought he was seeing his own reflection. However, it was not long before he became aware that someone or something was on the other side of the window watching him, closely.

Unsure what he was dealing with, a tingling sensation went down his spine.

Patiently, the mysterious set of eyes continued to stare through the window at Thorgrim. Studying him. Watching, waiting. Then the eyes tilted to the left and blinked a couple of times. Then they tilted to the right and blinked again. Every two or three seconds the orange eyes blinked while tilting back and forth.

Now concerned that the orange eyes belonged to a monster or a spook, Thorgrim became frozen with fear. He wanted to run or call out but could only stand unmoving like a statue.

He then realized that whoever was watching him, spook, or not, could see that he was standing in his bedroom, completely naked. The warmth of embarrassment flooded his face.

Though he had most of his front-side covered by his great beard, he quickly moved his hands to cover himself in an attempt to restore some dignity.

Unsure what to do next, Thorgrim stared through the glass, and the haunting, blinking orange eyes stared back.

Then he heard, "Meow."

"Huh? A cat?"

"Meow, purrrrrrrrrrrr."

Thorgrim breathed a huge sigh of relief, then laughed. He leaned in close to the window and saw that it was a tiny black kitten. It had big, orange eyes and long, fluffy fur.

"Awww, yer a muplet!" (The Dwarven slang word for 'cutie.')

The kitten rubbed up against the window and continued to purr.

"Are you hungry, little one?"

"Meow."

Thorgrim, loving all animals, could not resist. Carefully, doing his best not to frighten the kitten, he opened the window.

Without hesitating, the kitten jumped into the room and swirled around Thorgrim's feet.

"Oh, if yer hungry, I don't know if I have any food in muh backpack. Let me check for ya, little one."

As Thorgrim moved to reach his pack by the side of the bed, the little kitten, though very weak from starvation, grabbed hold of his beard, climbing all the way up to lick his nose.

It tickled, causing Thorgrim to utter a huge belly laugh.

"Purrrrrrrrrrr."

Digging through his backpack, Thorgrim said, "Okay, let's see what I have here. Gee, I hope I have something you can eat. Hmmmm."

He found a small end from a piece of jerky.

Carefully placing the kitten on his bed, Thorgrim tried to feed the jerky to him.

The kitten sniffed the dried bison a few times and licked it once before rolling on his back for a belly rub.

Thorgrim studied his new friend. He was a rack of bones and probably only a few days from starvation.

"You poor little thing. You probably can't eat that hard jerky. Where can I find you some food?"

He thought for a moment. Then he remembered the café.

"The café! They've got a ton of food! Hopefully, they're still open!"

"Meow, purrrrrrrrrrrrr."

"Wait right here, little muplet! I'll be back with some milk and stuff for ya."

The time was now 2:25 a.m. Although completely exhausted from the wild adventure of the past few days, with only five minutes before the café closed, he hurriedly went down to ask if he could get some river rabbit meat and a saucer of goat's milk.

A few guests of the inn, who were seated at a table and finishing a late meal, became loud and boisterous when Thorgrim walked through the door of the café.

The diners, two male dwarves and a female, upon seeing Thorgrim, laughed loudly and pounded their fists on the table.

Thorgrim thought, *Those Stupid drunks . . . I'll never drink ale, again!*

He ignored them and approached a tired and nervous-looking, café host. Several employees of the café stuck their heads out from the kitchen area, curious about all of the commotion.

The host, a balding older dwarf who wore a curled mustache scowled and said, "Sir, uh . . ."

"Sorry to bother you. I know you're about ready to close for the night, but I need a saucer of milk and a few pieces of river rabbit for my kitten if you have any."

The host quickly barked an order for the food, asking his staff to hurry up.

There was more laughing and ruckus from the three diners.

Thorgrim frowned. "Drunks," he mumbled, shaking his head.

The host, wearing an alarmed expression, said, "Sir, you need—"

Thorgrim interrupted. "Wow, here comes the food now. That was fast!" He was stunned by the speed of the kitchen staff. They had quickly gathered up the food and brought it out in under a minute.

The diners, as rowdy as ever, continued to snicker, whoop and chuckle. As Thorgrim walked towards the door with the food, they called to him.

One of them said in a boisterous tone, "Hey, fool. Whatcha doin' with that saucer of milk?"

Thorgrim stopped and tried to remain cordial despite the drunk's arrogance.

"It's for muh kitty."

The tableful of dwarves laughed, all of them almost tipping over in their chairs.

Thorgrim sneered. "And, why is that so funny? Tell me, do you drunks always laugh at everything?"

The dwarves looked at each other and shook their heads. "We're not drunk, friend."

"Then, what's so funny?"

"Uh, you're not wearing any clothes."

Looking down at himself, Thorgrim turned bright red with embarrassment. "Oh, I guess I am not! Sorry!" he replied, as he fled out of the café and down the hall. Running into his room, he tripped over his laundry basket, almost spilling the milk.

He found the kitten on his bed, but it appeared motionless. Fearing the worst, Thorgrim approached, his heart aching.

The little kitten opened its big, orange eyes. Smelling the food, it immediately began to purr. It looked up at Thorgrim and blinked its eyes several times while tilting his head back and forth.

"You really are a muplet!" he said happily. "Oh, I thought you were a goner! Thank God, yer okay! I never had a pet before! I'll call you 'Blinky Eyes' cuz yer always blinkin' yers. We'll be friends forever!"

Thorgrim had no idea how he was going to care for himself, a horse and now a tiny kitten, but he immediately fell in love with his new friend.

Blinky Eyes purred while he enjoyed his first meal since he and his siblings were dumped into the street a few days ago by some uncaring jerk.

***

[Author's Note:]

Although illegal, the dumping of cats and dogs was a common occurrence, not only in the Dwarven Clans but also across the entire realm. Tragically, most of the animals will never find a loving home and eventually perish from starvation or abuse. On his coronation day, twenty years ago, devoted animal lover, and the current King of all Dwarves, Kris Muechenberg, issued a royal decree to protect all animals from abuse. The penalties were stiff (including prison time or even capital punishment, in severe cases) for anyone caught abandoning or abusing any animal in the Dwarven Clans.

The King ordered that any stray animal was to be carefully rounded up, then moved to a special shelter southwest of Bur Dhulgren, along the Mharrak River. There, the animals would receive love and care for the rest of their lives. The massive, animal sanctuary was called 'Teddy's Retreat' named after an abandoned, starving puppy the King had found and rescued when he was a young boy.

***

It was 2:50 a.m. Both Thorgrim and his new friend had full bellies. Thorgrim had slept all afternoon during the previous day, but the hot temperature and hurried ride had worn him out again. With a big day ahead, he needed more sleep. The temperature had dropped and he was able to leave his window open, allowing the cool, comforting night air to flow in . . . but not wide enough to allow his helpless friend to leave.

Lying on his back in bed, completely exhausted, Thorgrim closed his eyes and tried to fall asleep. He was content. He had made it to the capital, making a few friends along the way. He had a full belly and still had some money in his pocket. He knew that his horse was in good hands at the inn's stable, and also, he had saved the life of a kitten. A kitten who seemed to be making himself right at home.

Although he was extremely worried about the future, for the moment, Thorgrim Longbeard was happy. So was Blinky.

Softly purring, Blinky Eyes, using his paws, made a little bed in the dwarf's grand beard and snuggled in. The purring and pressing motion of the kitten's paws relaxed Thorgrim, and soon he joined his furry friend in dreamland.

XI. The Iron Golem Pub

It was Moridon-alod (Sunday), the day of worship for all dwarves. Many would be spending their mornings at a temple or church service, however, Thorgrim would be spending his morning in bed. Normally up just before sunrise, on this day, he decided to remain in bed to catch up on his sleep, although his new kitten had other ideas.

Cats, like people, need to eat, drink and sleep. Unfortunately, like people, cats need to relieve themselves. People typically use a latrine or a garderobe (or somewhere in the woods, if nothing else is available). Thorgrim remembered reading that cats naturally do their business in flowerbeds, sand, or anywhere they can find loose dirt.

Blinky's persistent whining woke Thorgrim around 8:00 a.m., and at first, the dwarf thought his furry friend might be hungry. Although it was true, the cat was hungry, in reality, Blinky was trying to tell Thorgrim that he needed to go outside and find a nice flowerbed to do his thing.

Sitting up, stretching and yawning, Thorgrim said, "What's the matter, Blinky? You hungry again?"

Blinky stretched and continued to complain. Thorgrim guessed that the kitten could not understand Dwarvish (although it is a known fact that cats do understand everything that is said to them, they just choose to ignore it.) On the other hand, Thorgrim could not understand cat-talk, either.

Finally, the kitten jumped off the bed and went for the gap in the open window, but it was too narrow to squeeze through, even for his tiny body.

"Oh, you're not going to leave me, are you?" asked Thorgrim, jumping out of bed. Already in love with the kitten, he moaned, "I would miss you!"

Going over to the window, he gently picked his cat up and stroked his fur. Blinky was small enough to fit in the palm of Thorgrim's hand.

"Tell you what. Let me get some clothes on, then I'll take you to the café for breakfast."

Placing Blinky back on the bed, Thorgrim was about to get dressed, when he remembered that he had placed all of his dirty clothes in the laundry basket outside his door last night. Opening the door, he happily found that everything had been washed and then neatly folded by the inn's staff.

"I could get used to living like this," he chuckled. After pulling the basket inside, he began to quickly dress.

When he finished, he looked and found that his kitten was again trying to squeeze through the window.

"Hang on Blinky, I need to use the garderobe first, then we'll get something to eat." While using the garderobe, it was then that he realized what might really be troubling his cat.

"Where do cats go when they have to poop?" he mumbled. "Hmmmm. That's probably why he's tryin' to get outside!"

Thorgrim finished and quickly scooped up Blinky before there was a smelly accident in the room. Rushing to the front door of the inn, he fled outside where an overcast sky greeted him. Thankfully, it was cooler than the day before, and it looked like it might rain.

Looking around, Thorgrim found a grassy area next to the inn and an adjacent building. He carefully placed his cat on the ground and waited. Sure enough, Blinky finished what needed to be done, and after burying it, he ran and jumped up into Thorgrim's arms.

"Feelin' better? Great, I'm starvin' . . . let's go eat now!"

With Blinky in his arms, he began walking towards the entrance to the inn.

Then something unusual happened.

After Thorgrim had taken a few steps, the purring kitten climbed from the dwarf's arms and into his massive beard, curling up deep inside.

"Purrrrrrr."

For Blinky, it was like being snuggled next to his mama . . . a mother he hardly knew.

Flabbergasted, Thorgrim stopped walking.

"Now, you can't stay in there during the day. When we're sleepin' I don't mind, but you can't do that now! Come on, you . . ."

Blinky purred louder.

Unable to resist the sweet kitten, he chuckled. "Hahahohaho! Okay then, you can stay in there if you want."

After entering the inn, driven by his insatiable appetite, Thorgrim, with the kitten cradled in his beard, made a beeline straight for the café.

He started to open the café door but stopped to confirm that he had remembered to wear clothes this time.

Entering, he looked around. The place was filled to capacity with yammering, hungry dwarves.

A young, café hostess, wearing pink ribbons in both her bleach-blonde hair and recently permed beard, approached.

"I'm sorry, sir. We're full right now. Would you like to wait for a table?"

"How long?" asked Thorgrim, rubbing his growling stomach.

"Maybe a half-hour."

Thorgrim glanced at his timepiece. It was almost 9:15 a.m.

"I'm really hungry, but I guess I have no choice."

"Are you a guest of the inn?"

"Ya, I'm in room number one."

"You can place an order and take it to your room if you like."

Before he could answer, the hostess raised her manicured eyebrows and whispered, "Sir, I don't know if you're aware, but you seem to have some kind of animal living in your beard."

"Oh! Yes. That's muh cat, and he's hungry, too."

Giggling, the amused hostess nodded and handed Thorgrim a menu.

After a quick look through the menu, he said, "Uh, I guess that I'll go ahead and place an order and then take it with me."

***

An hour later, after consuming enough food for two dwarves (and Blinky, enough for two kittens), Thorgrim decided it was time to get Nugget out of the stable, then ride to the Iron Golem Pub.

With his kitty still nestled in his beard and his backpack full of leftover breakfast food and water flasks, Thorgrim went back to the stable and introduced Blinky to Nugget.

The stablemen installed Nugget's saddle, then held onto the kitten while Thorgrim tried to mount. Stepping on the block, he jumped and then went up and over the saddle to the other side, where he hung upside down with his boot stuck in the stirrup.

"Help, please," he begged. His massive beard, now covering his entire face, hid his embarrassment.

Thorgrim was heavy, so it took both stablemen to help him get on his horse.

While Thorgrim was tying the mounting block to the back of the saddle, still embarrassed, he said firmly, "Thanks for helping me up! Uh, just so ya know, that's never happened before."

One of them replied, "Oh, sure . . . but, that's a tall horse you have there. Wouldn't you be better off with a dwarven horse or a donkey? It'd be easier for you to get into the saddle, you know."

Thorgrim grinned. "Ya, probably. But, why make it easy? There's no excitement in that!"

One of the stablemen handed Thorgrim his kitten. Purring, Blinky promptly crawled up his arm and into his beard.

While the stablemen laughed at him behind his back, Thorgrim signaled and Nugget began walking out of the barn towards Central Avenue.

"Well, Nugget and Blinky, I need to go someplace called the Iron Golem Pub, and you two are coming with me," he said aloud. "Or, maybe I'm going with you. Either way, we'll do it together."

Halting, Thorgrim looked up and down Central Avenue. He noticed that it was unlike the previous night when the sidewalks and businesses were packed with rowdy revelers and other night owls. Now, hardly a soul could be seen. Most people were either home sleeping off a hard night of partying or were in church worshipping Moridon, or some of the other gods.

Thorgrim was never much of a churchgoer, although he had a deep faith in all of the dwarven gods, most especially, Moridon, the King of the Gods and creator of everything.

He checked the time. It was 10:45 a.m. Nervous about riding through the huge city and eventually, the unsavory south, in order to reach the Iron Golem Pub, he thought it would be proper on this Sunday morning to offer a prayer to Moridon for guidance and protection. "Always best to be on the good side of the gods," he said to himself.

Regrettably, today, there would be no time to stop and visit the Supreme Library or the Grand Hall of the Dwarves. Tomorrow, on his last day in the city, he planned to make what would likely be his one and only visit to the library and the Grand Hall. Besides, today was Worship Day, and he was not sure if either location would be open for visitors.

Though the library and Grand Hall tempted him, fortunately, Thorgrim understood his priorities. Considering his dire situation, he thought it best to follow Gary of Tuckerheim's advice. Gary told him to go to the Iron Golem Pub as soon as possible and meet with a one-eyed dwarf by the name of Uuno Kanto.

Gary said Uuno could help him, and Thorgrim knew that he needed a lot of help. He had no income or official ID papers, and he was hoping that somehow Uuno would be able to provide some assistance. The ID papers would help Thorgrim while he still remained in the country and might be of some use in a foreign land such as the Great Kingdom.

Any money would help with food expenses, for himself and his two animal friends, until he was able to get a job. Failing that, he would not

213

let himself or his friends starve, but this meant turning himself in to the authorities. The thought of it nauseated him.

"Uuno Kanto," he mumbled. "Hmmm. That name sounds kinda' intimidatin', if you ask me, Nugget. He's prolly someone you wouldn't want to cross swords with. Then again, I don't even own a sword."

"Meow."

"Oh, I'm talking to you too, Blinky," Thorgrim said with a light chuckle. "Your opinion matters, too."

Purring sounds radiated from his beard.

Mooky had said that the Iron Golem Pub was on the corner of East Forty-Second Avenue and South Fifty-Fifth Street. He warned that the pub was in a dangerous part of the city; calling the area the 'unsavory south.'

Thorgrim realized that there were risks involved entering an area that is likely full of trouble, but now he had a weapon with him . . . just in case. When he ordered breakfast, he had pocketed a butter knife from the café, although he didn't know how effective it would be if he had to defend himself, but it was better than nothing.

Examining the knife, he chuckled and said aloud, "I can at least butter their bread if they have any."

He decided it was best to ride south on Central Avenue to South Fifty-Fifth Street, a distance of almost nine miles, and then travel east, three and half miles to East Forty Second Avenue. According to Mooky, there, he would find the Iron Golem Pub. The total distance of the trip would be about thirteen miles, and at a normal walking speed would take over three hours. The city was truly massive.

There was no hurry to get to the pub, though Nugget could easily trot that distance and arrive in less than half the time. However, the horse had been pushed hard since he left Stug, and Thorgrim assumed that Nugget would probably enjoy a nice, leisurely walk.

Thorgrim inhaled deeply, held his breath for a moment, then exhaled. "Okay, my two friends, we've wasted enough time. Let's ride."

At precisely 11:00 a.m., praying that the pub would be open on Worship Day, he steered Nugget onto the avenue and headed south towards the City Center and the intersection known as the 'Heart of the City.'

Looking down Central Avenue, the topmost part of the giant torch on the Royal Castle was clearly visible, far away in the distance. Oddly, not a soul could be seen anywhere, though he guessed that most were attending a worship service somewhere or sleeping in.

214

While he rode, Thorgrim studied the buildings as he passed them. As expected, he found more pubs, gaming halls, an occasional public latrine and bath, even a barbershop and a general store. Most of the buildings were old, though well maintained. With the exception of the latrines and baths, not one of them seemed to be open for business.

After fifteen minutes of riding, he had reached the corner of North Thirty Sixth Street and Central Avenue, having only encountered a handful of dwarves along the way. The few he met, offered him a friendly smile or wave, and he always returned it.

Ahead, near the intersection of North Thirty-Fifth and Central, he spotted a couple of dwarves, dressed in dirty, worn clothing, hanging out on the steps in front of one of the shops.

Though Thorgrim was not aware, the two were hungry transients, who were busy trying to figure out how they were going to obtain some food.

At the next intersection, North Thirty-Fourth, he saw several more scraggly-looking dwarves. A few of them were sleeping along the sidewalk. One, standing near the edge of the avenue, was holding a crudely written, 'Please help. Hungry and Homeless' sign.

Wearing filthy rags, sadly, some of them were shoeless.

Thorgrim had heard of them, but he had never seen a homeless person before. "Moridon's holy beard. Homelessness even in this city? May the gods bless them, but may all the gods help me, too. I don't want to end up like them."

A few blocks ahead, dozens of transients and beggars lined Central Avenue. Thorgrim was not yet aware of their presence, however, the clomping of Nugget's hooves on the cobblestones caught the attention of some of them . . . and they waited.

Thorgrim understood that he was not far off from becoming a transient himself. True, he was technically homeless, but he hoped Uuno Kanto would be able to offer some solutions to that problem. So far, since he left his home in Vog three days ago, good fortune had provided a roof over his head and food for his belly. He also understood that his luck could run out at any time and if it did, something had to be done in order to survive.

Uuno Kanto. Who is this guy? he wondered. As Thorgrim slowly rode past the homeless, he thought, *My father always said that things happen for a reason. I was on foot until I met Gary of Tuckerheim in Stug. He gave me a horse, some money, and advice about meeting this one-eyed dwarf, who'll supposedly help me. Is all of that fate or destiny?*

215

Curled up inside Thorgrim's beard, Blinky was now snoring, having been rocked to sleep by the motion of Nugget's gentle cadence as he walked.

While deep in thought, the soft snoring sound of his cat, a heavy breakfast, and the slight rocking of the saddle as he rode, caused Thorgrim to become drowsy. Soon, he became oblivious to his surroundings, only knowing that he was moving forward, down the avenue.

Occasionally, as he nodded off to sleep, his head would drop, causing him to slump forward. The sudden motion would wake him for a moment, then the process would repeat.

After almost falling off the saddle, he slapped his own face a few times and rubbed his nose and eyes vigorously in order to clear the sleepy cobwebs.

"Hey, pal, ya got any coinage or food to spare?" said a raspy voice, nearby.

Thorgrim, still trying to wake, was startled and glanced down to his right. There, walking beside Nugget, was a lone transient. Thorgrim was surprised and unable to respond. He could only look at the starving dwarf's weary eyes as they stared back in despair. The unfortunate beggar, a middle-aged dwarf, had grimy skin that had been yellowed by liver disease. He was also full of cuts and bruises. Wearing tattered clothes, he was toothless, shoeless, hungry and homeless.

Caught off guard by the beggar's sudden appearance, Thorgrim instinctively reached into his backpack and tossed the poor soul a leftover breakfast biscuit.

The overjoyed beggar instantly shoved the biscuit into his mouth, almost swallowing it whole.

While watching the happy beggar gum the biscuit, someone else tugged on Thorgrim's left pant leg. Startled again, he looked and saw another transient walking alongside Nugget. All around, Thorgrim noticed that several more of them were slowly coming towards him, hoping to receive some type of handout like the first one did.

Nugget whinnied, fearful of the crowd that was forming and approaching with their hands outstretched.

Thorgrim saw several dozen of them coming; they, with their pale faces and sunken eyes full of desperation. Some held small children and babies or carried bags containing everything they owned in the world. Sadly, most of the adults were uncontrollable, hopeless alcoholics or drug addicts.

216

One of them tried to grab at Thorgrim's backpack. Shoving him away with his left boot, he now became worried that the starving mass of people might pull him down from his mount in order to rob him of what little he had.

Grasping onto tiny Blinky, who was still sleeping soundly in his beard, he took a deep breath, tightened his grip on the reins and drove a knee sharply into the saddle.

Nugget, surprised by the sudden poke in his side, responded with a snort and bolted ahead at a gallop, nearly trampling a few beggars in his path.

Over the sound of Nugget's thundering hooves, Thorgrim heard the crowd yelling, crying and cursing. Although deeply saddened by their desperate situation, he resisted the urge to look back at them.

His mind chastised him. *Must be more careful next time.*

As Nugget raced ahead, with a heavy heart, Thorgrim said aloud, "Nugget and Blinky, I feel for those poor souls back there. I wish I could help them, but I can't. And may the gods forbid, if I'm not careful, I might become one of them someday."

As his horse galloped towards North Twenty Seventh Street, off to his left, much to his concern, he noticed a group of hoods loitering on the corner.

Upon seeing Thorgrim's approach, they yelled and gestured towards him in a menacing way, brandishing knives and clubs.

With his great beard waving behind him, Thorgrim flashed past them at speed, hoping to avoid any trouble.

Having traveled several more blocks, though wary of miscreants, he was forced to slow down due to traffic.

Finally, he thought, with relief, *regular people.*

Passing by him, going the other way, a few dwarves rode their short dwarven horses, some pulling little carriages filled with their families, likely returning from an early church service. Looking up at Thorgrim's tall elven horse, many pointed or made comments. Some laughed at the sight of a dwarf riding on such a big horse, while others were speechless.

Thorgrim was proud of Nugget. His horse was special, and probably, no one else in the city had one like him. Other than the trouble Thorgrim still had mounting and dismounting, his chief concern was all of the attention his big horse was getting.

Obviously, Thorgrim did not want any attention.

Thorgrim rode slowly along, keeping pace with the sparse, though, steady flow of Sunday traffic. Still nervous about the previous encounters, he reached North Eighteenth and Central Avenue. This area, about a mile and a half from the City Center, was packed with all types of shops, cafés, temples, exotic baths, premium inns, and other upscale businesses. Some blocks had brand new apartment complexes and public parks.

Looking around, the area was spotless and free of 'riff-raff', as Mooky would call them.

Why are there no transients or thugs around here? This part of the city would be like heaven for those types of people.

Then he saw the reason why transients and gangs avoided this area. To his right, on the corner of North Seventeenth and Central, was a police station and jail belonging to the headquarters of the Central Bur Dhulgren Police Department.

Outside, several police officers, dressed in their superb, black and red uniforms, stood on the steps in front of the three-story police station. Others, mounted on donkeys or horses, were riding off to patrol their assigned areas.

Highly respected by all citizens, the police, affectionately called 'club-heads,' by most, carried large batons that were often used to whack criminals on the head, prior to their arrest.

As Thorgrim rode by, a few of the policemen hailed him, commenting on his tall horse. Not wanting to reveal his face, he stared straight ahead and waved. Anxious, desiring to get out of the area quickly, he gave Nugget a slight nudge on the saddle, increasing the horse's speed to a trot.

Ahead, less than a mile and a half away, the great torch on the top of the Royal Castle could easily be seen. Thorgrim's heart pounded. He knew that the Supreme Library and the Grand Hall were somewhere near the castle, and soon he would actually get to see them for the first time.

Trotting towards the City Center, he began to encounter many more people. Because of his speed, he was forced to ride around the slower travelers, who sometimes yelled at him to slow down.

As Thorgrim passed each intersection, he became increasingly excited and began to count down the numbers. "North tenth . . . North ninth . . . North eighth . . . North Seventh . . . North Sixth . . ."

He was less than a half-mile from the Heart of the City intersection of Central and Middle when countless bells began to ring announcing the end of public worship services.

It was noon.

After attending worship service, all dwarves were encouraged to spend the rest of the day enjoying time with their families; sadly, this would not include Thorgrim Longbeard. His family was over one hundred miles away in a little town called Vog.

With the services ended, throngs of dwarves surged through the city trying to get home, causing brief, though frustrating traffic jams. Thorgrim became entangled in a couple of them, only three blocks from the Heart of the City.

Though irritated, the delays gave him time to study the giant buildings and other structures that flanked him on both sides of Central Avenue. Now, instead of apartments and shops, he found theaters, museums, monuments, and government administrative buildings. On the corner of North Second and Central, on his right, he found another place to avoid. The massive Army Headquarters building of the Mharrak Provincial Guard.

Ahead on the next block, near the corner of North First and Central, were four fountains that sprayed multi-colored streams of water one hundred feet into the air. In between the fountains, was an enormous, one-hundred-foot tall golden statue honoring the first king of the dwarves: King Authumus Oakenhorn.

He now realized that he was only about a block and a half away from the City Center and the Heart of the City intersection. Though he could not see them yet, both Dr. Thacker and Mooky had told him that the library and Grand Hall were there.

His heart began to pound in anticipation.

Across the avenue on the left was another one-hundred-foot tall statue honoring the backbone of the entire Dwarven Kingdom: The ore miner.

Immediately, the sight of the statue depressed him. Pulling Nugget to the side of the avenue, he stopped to study the beautiful, solid iron effigy.

The statue was of a dwarven miner hard at work, his pickaxe held high over his helmeted head, about to strike a wall of rock. His face, weary though proud.

Thorgrim watched as dozens of dwarves stood around the giant statue looking upon it in admiration. He was stunned when he witnessed a squad of military personnel, in full dress uniform, turn and salute the statue as they passed by it.

At the statue's base, a twenty-foot wide engraved plaque made from pure silver, read:

The Forgotten Miner

'His pick meets the rock, time and again, for twenty years or more, do not pretend . . .

. . . to know the toil and sweat of he, the forgotten hero of the mine; the heart and soul of the Kingdom and we.'

Thorgrim now felt deeply ashamed for avoiding his obligation to work in the mines. As he gazed at the massive iron figure, he realized that, for all he knew, it could have been a statue of his father. For a few minutes, laden with guilt, he fought back tears. Finally, he took a deep breath, straightened up in the saddle and rode on, content in knowing that he could not be a miner even if he wanted to be.

Looking on the right, about a block ahead, near the Heart of the City intersection, he noticed four Royal Guards, dressed in silver and gold uniforms, standing at attention. Flanked by two, colorful flower gardens, they stood, unmoving, in front of a columned passageway that led to the Royal Castle. The giant torch and the upper works of the castle were now easily visible behind the other buildings on the avenue.

Slowly, he approached the 'Heart of the City intersection. Riding past the guards, he halted off to the side of the avenue on the corner. There, he gazed up at the castle.

He had arrived at the four adjacent blocks of the City Center.

From each window hung elegant tapestries of silver and gold. The base of the castle consumed one-third of a city block and the entire area from the outer walls to the sidewalk was blanketed with every type of flower imaginable. Thorgrim thought it looked like someone had poured a rainbow around the building.

It was hard for him to imagine that any dwarven king would want his castle to appear effeminate. However, he remembered that King Muechenberg was married to the Queen. As Thorgrim's father had always told him, 'It's always best to keep the woman of the house happy.'

Directly across Middle Street, south of the castle was the University of Mharrak. The magnificent, ten-story tall, black granite building looked like a fort. The university filled an entire city block, part of another and could accommodate five thousand students. It was a place Thorgrim had dreamt about attending since his high school days. For now, it would have to remain a dream.

Excited, he then slowly turned to his left and looked towards the southeast corner of the City Center. What he saw there, was breathtaking.

It was the Grand Hall of the Dwarves Historical Museum. The sight of it astounded him. The vast complex, filling an entire city block, was stunningly beautiful.

The museum was actually several, interconnected buildings, nestled in-between fields of flowers and trees.

At the northwest corner of the block, beyond an area to tie horses, was a one hundred foot long, marble passageway. Flanking the passageway were rows of sparkling fountains and eighty-foot tall stone columns, all capped with sculptures of golden hammers. The ornate passageway led to a rectangular, single-story building that functioned as a foyer. Connecting the foyer to the main building were three, unique, one hundred foot long, enclosed hallways.

The main structure, called the Grand Hall, originally held the Aurumsmiter Hammer until its theft by grey elves several hundred years ago. The silver and gold-trimmed, star-shaped, white granite building, stood at the southeast corner of the city block.

For a couple of minutes, Thorgrim sat on Nugget's saddle, completely spellbound by the beauty of the Grand Hall of the Dwarves.

However, he could resist no longer. Finally, saving the best for last, he looked south directly across Central Avenue. There, he saw another breathtaking sight.

It was a two-story tall, white granite building, about one-fourth the size of a city block. In front of the structure, a sign read: 'The Supreme Library of Mharrak.'

At first, he beamed a huge smile ear to ear. But, overwhelmed by what he saw, his eyes soon welled with tears. Oblivious to the many people around him, who were going about their day, he relished the moment.

West First Ave. | Mharrak Provincial Guard HQ | Central Avenue | East First Ave.

North Second Street

Monument of King Authumus Oakenhorn

North First Street

Monument of the Forgotten Miner

Royal Castle

Supreme Library

Middle Street

Campus

University Of Mharrak

Grand Hall Of the Dwarves Complex

South First Street

For nineteen-year-old Thorgrim Longbeard, finally getting to see the library and the Grand Hall was a dream come true. At least in part. Seeing the Supreme Library and Grand Hall was an incredible experience, but what he really wanted to do was enter and explore their wonders.

It was Worship Day, and although the Grand Hall appeared open, it was obvious that the library was not.

Though seriously tempted to spend time here, he reminded himself of his priorities.

He needed help. He had no choice but to heed Gary's advice and seek out Uuno Kanto at the Iron Golem Pub, as soon as possible.

An exploration of the Supreme Library and the Grand Hall would have to wait until, hopefully, tomorrow.

He took several deep breaths, trying to shake off a strong desire to ride over and in the very least, actually touch the buildings.

Blinky had his own ideas.

Thorgrim felt his cat stirring inside his beard. Soon, Blinky stuck his head out and meowed. It was a signal that he was hungry or had to do his thing.

"Okay, Blinky. Let's get up here a couple of blocks and we'll figure out what you need."

He took a final look at both structures before nudging his horse forward. In a matter of seconds, he crossed the intersection of Central and Middle and continued south.

Blinky always seemed hungry, but Thorgrim was more concerned that his kitten might need to use a flowerbed soon. There were plenty of flowerbeds a block behind him around the Royal Castle or at the Grand Hall complex, but he knew those were not good choices for obvious reasons.

A short distance ahead, on South Third and Central Avenue, he spied a beautiful park full of flowers and trees. A perfect place for Blinky to eat or do his number. Thorgrim was also excited to find a public latrine across the avenue from the park because he had to go, himself.

There were many dwarves loitering near the park including a couple 'club-heads.' Although he was worried that one of the policemen might ask to see his personal ID, Thorgrim had no choice but to stop, because it was becoming increasingly obvious that Blinky was anxious to relieve himself.

Luckily, no one seemed to pay any attention to him as he rode up and halted in front of the park.

After a rare, successful dismount of his horse, he tied Nugget to a nearby post. At that moment, further down the sidewalk, the two police officers, who had been chatting with some dwarves, noticed him. They stopped talking and offered him a friendly wave.

Thorgrim smiled and waved back.

Still nervous the police might approach and ask questions, Thorgrim quickly ran deep into the flower gardens. Blinky did his business and after cleaning his furry friend up, he stuffed the kitten back inside his beard.

First, making sure the coast was clear, Thorgrim did his own business behind a tree instead of crossing the street to use the latrine and risk an encounter with the police.

Now finished, Thorgrim was shocked by what he saw when he was about to exit the park. Nugget had gained the attention of several dwarves, including the two policemen. After all, it was not every day one would see an elven horse, especially in the middle of the capital city of the Dwarven Clans. Worried, Thorgrim quietly retreated to a nearby bush, then watched and listened.

"Dat thing is as tall as a tree, I say!" exclaimed an older dwarf, looking up at Nugget.

"Who does it belong to?" asked another.

Thorgrim, overhearing all of it, became increasingly worried with each passing moment.

Shasta, a bald, grey-bearded dwarf, complained, "It's one of dem elf horses, I'm tellin' ya. To me, it's a shame upon da city to have anything elf around here."

"Git over it, Shasta," replied McGillicuddy, his equally cantankerous friend. "It ain't the horse's fault he's an elf horse, is it?"

Shasta bellowed, "Gill, dat's not the point, you fool,"

"Don't ya dare call me a fool, you fool!" shouted McGillicuddy.

A few more dwarves stepped up to join the argument.

One of the police officers intervened and said, "Okay, okay, move along . . . all of you, and do it now, before I haul ya in for being a pain in the neck."

Mumbling and grumbling, a few of them flapped their beards towards the police.

One of the officers said, "Go home. Grumble and flap yer scraggly beards at yer missus, then try to have a good day."

After the old dwarves left, the two officers stood around Nugget and chatted, while Thorgrim, anxious to get on with his ride, still watched helplessly from the bushes.

"I wonder who owns this beautiful horse?" the first officer said.

Chuckling, the second officer replied, "Hahahoha, you don't suppose that it really belongs to some elf, do you?"

"If it does belong to an elf, he can count himself lucky for being able to ride this far into the city and not getting kilt by someone in the process."

"Right. I'm just kiddin'. We know it wasn't an elf, because we both saw him dismount. The guy had a beard a mile long."

The first officer laughed. "Yes, maybe even longer. Moridon himself must be jealous of that dwarf's beard."

"Now I'm curious," commented the second officer. "I think he ran off into the flower garden. We might as well stand here and wait 'til he comes back. Then we can see whose horse this is. Technically, we're out walking our beat, and the donut shops are closed, so what else is there to do?"

"Good idea. I want to know how he acquired an elf horse. You know, maybe it's stolen?"

"Who knows? It could be stolen. If it is and we catch the perp, the sergeant might give us the rest of the day off!"

"Yes, another good idea!"

Listening to the police, Thorgrim was flabbergasted and beyond agitated. "Why won't they go away, damn them!" he muttered.

For Thorgrim, it looked hopeless. It appeared that the club-heads were not going to leave anytime soon.

Then Nugget saved the day by offering the club-heads a nice, long, silent fart.

"Holy Moridon, do you smell that?" complained the first officer, looking at the other with a suspicious glare.

Holding on to his nose, the second officer replied, "Yes, unfortunately, I can smell that, but don't look at me, I didn't do that number."

The first officer retched. "That stink's bad enough to make yer beard jump off yer face and run for the mountains! Look, there's a weird, green gas floating around us!"

The second officer turned away, pointed across the street and started to run north down the sidewalk towards the City Center. He shouted, "Let's get out of here! Maybe the latrine's about to blow up!"

The first officer, coughing and gagging, covered his nose and followed close behind.

Unsure about the source of the green gas, Thorgrim was grateful that the police and everyone else had disappeared.

Exiting from behind the bushes, he quickly walked over to Nugget and stepped up on the mounting block. It was then he realized the source of the horrid odor.

"Nugget! Whooowee! That must've been some potent hay you ate this morning back at the stable. Unless you snuck a few of those hardboiled pigeon eggs from muh backpack, I don't know what's giving you that gas! Hopefully, I'll be upwind from yer rear end for the rest of the ride!"

Thorgrim laughed and then with a big push, gracefully launched himself up and over the saddle, landing on the ground, hard on his backside. The mounting block flew into the branches of a waiting tree and hung there by its rope.

His backside and rear were numb. He groaned, but could barely speak, because the wind had been knocked out of him. "Oh! I'll say that landing . . . <cough, cough> . . . on cobblestone is a bit rougher than mud."

Nugget whinnied.

While trying to regain his breath, Thorgrim said, "Nugget, are ya laughin' at me? Uh, I . . . <cough, cough> . . . suppose that looked pretty funny! Can't say that I blame—"

He stopped before finishing his sentence and yelled, "Blinky!" Forgetting the pain in his back and rear, he frantically felt inside his beard, hoping to find that his kitten was safe.

Blinky was not in his beard.

"Meow."

Thorgrim listened. "Blinky?"

"Meow."

Anxious and alarmed, Thorgrim said, "Where are ya, kitty cat? Are ya okay?"

"Meow. Purrrrrrrrrrrr."

Oddly, the kitten's meowing seemed to be coming from Nugget. Looking up, Thorgrim saw Blinky sitting on top of the saddle, unharmed and purring. Evidently, the agile cat had bailed out before Thorgrim had crashed to the ground.

Laughing, he said, "So, Blinky, maybe you can teach me a thing or two about how to get up into that saddle without falling!"

With some difficulty, Thorgrim managed to pull the mounting block down from the tree.

Successfully getting into the saddle on his next attempt, he directed Nugget south on Central Avenue.

***

Along the way, he saw more of the same, although, by South Twenty-Fifth, the business structures gave way to residential homes and hovels. Other than children playing in the streets, very few dwarfs were seen outside. Most were either inside their homes or tending to their vegetable gardens in the back of their residences.

Sometimes, children would timidly approach Thorgrim, entranced by the sight of his tall, creme-colored, elven horse. A few of the kids asked if they could pet the Nugget, and Thorgrim allowed it.

226

By 2:45 p.m., he had reached South Fifty-Fifth Street without difficulty, stopping only to feed and water his horse . . . and Blinky, the kitten with the endless appetite.

Exiting Central Avenue, he turned left on South Fifty-Fifth Street, and slowly rode east towards his destination three and a half miles away on East Forty-Second Avenue. Somewhere in that area, he was told he could find the Iron Golem Pub, and hopefully, Uuno Kanto.

Playfully tugging on his horse's mane, Thorgrim said, "Hey Nugget, only forty-two blocks to go!"

Nugget didn't seem to care, nor did Blinky, who was still tucked away in Thorgrim's massive beard, alternating between snoring and purring.

South Fifty-Fifth Street was purely residential, containing older but well-kept homes and apartments. Few dwarves were encountered, but those that saw him, stopped to stare.

Thorgrim patted his horse's neck. "Nugget, you're an elf horse, and they either like you or they don't like you. I don't care what they think, because I like you and that's all that matters."

Thankfully, the cool weather had been persistent, but it was obvious by the looks of the clouds, far off to the west, that rain might be coming later. Frightened by the prospect of getting caught in a downpour, he gave his horse a slight nudge. Nugget responded by speeding up to a trot.

By 3:10 p.m., he was only five blocks from his destination. Looking around he saw that most of the homes in this area were in a slum-like state of disrepair. Many had missing siding, broken windows, or other physical problems. The sounds of large, barking dogs seemed to come from every house.

Then he noticed, much to his displeasure, several groups of rough-looking hoods and thugs hanging around on porches and doorsteps.

They noticed him, as well.

Having been warned that this area was dangerous, he thought, *The unsavory south. I can see why.*

The denizens suddenly reacted to Thorgrim's presence in a threatening way.

Shouting for Thorgrim to stop, several stepped off their porches and menacingly approached him.

Naturally, Thorgrim picked up the pace to a canter and rode on, looking straight ahead, ignoring the yelling and cursing directed his way.

Although he could not be certain, Thorgrim thought he heard the whistle of an arrow as it flew over his head.

Now terrified, grabbing hold of Blinky, he dug his boots into Nugget's belly, sending the horse galloping ahead at full speed.

A minute later, he glanced behind and saw that no one had followed. Slowing his horse to a walk, still anxious, he carefully examined the area. The houses and other structures were in poor shape, but oddly, unlike the previous few blocks, not a soul was outside anywhere in the neighborhood.

Halting Nugget, Thorgrim looked around again.

Where is everyone?

He checked his location. He had stopped at the intersection of East Forty-Second Avenue and South Fifty-Fifth Street.

"I'm here, but where's the pub?"

Looking to his right, on the corner and tucked away behind a few heavy bushes, was a large, two-story building that looked like an abandoned funeral parlor.

Hanging over an entrance gate at the front of the property, a rickety-looking sign read: 'Welcome to the Iron Golem Pub.'

He agreed that the place looked intimidating, just as Gary had said it would.

An eight-foot-tall, black iron fence surrounded the entire property. Designed to keep unwelcomed individuals out, countless, sharp, spear-like projections adorned the top of the ominous-looking fence. Although the building had a fresh coat of black paint and was in excellent condition overall, it still reminded Thorgrim of a spook house.

He could not believe his eyes. "This is a pub?" he said aloud. "Nugget, I don't like the looks of this place. Be ready to run."

He took a deep, shuddering breath and slowly rode Nugget over to the front of the property, coming to a stop next to several horse posts, and a half-filled water trough.

Nugget eagerly began drinking.

Past the gate, up on the porch, two dwarves carefully studied Thorgrim as he sat on his very tall horse. One had a black beard and the other one was blonde. Both wore a dark-red eyepatch and both seemed to be scowling.

Thorgrim could hear them murmuring about something.

Nervous, he tried to smile at them, but unable to manage even a slight grin, he just waved.

Adding to Thorgrim's apprehension, they did not return the greeting. Instead, the black-bearded dwarf knocked on the front door of the pub, while the other continued to maintain a heavy frown, keeping his lone eye on Thorgrim.

Deciding to approach them in a friendly manner, introduce himself and then ask for Uuno, Thorgrim dropped the mounting block. Luckily, he managed to dismount without incident. Next, he tied Nugget to a post.

In response to the knock, the front door of the pub partially opened, and another dwarf poked his head out and looked around. Thorgrim noticed that the third dwarf also wore a red eyepatch.

"Does everyone around here wear an eyepatch?" muttered Thorgrim.

More mumbling could be heard, and then the third dwarf pulled his head back in and slammed the door. At that moment, a little white dog happened by. It was at least five times the size of Blinky, wore a red eyepatch, and growled while pausing to sniff Nugget's hooves.

Thorgrim chuckled. "I guess everyone around here **does** wear an eyepatch."

From the porch, one of the dwarves whistled then shouted, "Bone Grinder, get up here, boy! Hey, you! Don't get too close to dat dog, or he might take yer leg off."

Thorgrim cringed and stepped back a few feet. *Bone Grinder? Must be a mean dog to have a name like that.*

The dog, his tail wagging, barked once, then ran up to the gate. After squeezing through a gap in the fence, the pooch barked again, scrambled up to the front door and jumped into the arms of the blonde-bearded dwarf.

Unsure if he was welcome, Thorgrim cautiously approached the gate with Blinky still sleeping soundly in his beard.

Noticing that the gate was locked, he performed another quick glance around to make sure there were no evil interlopers nearby. Satisfied that the area was clear, he waved to the dwarves on the porch and said, "Hello, there. I'm—"

The black-bearded dwarf adjusted his eyepatch and interrupted, "What do ya want? The pub is not open on Sundays."

"Oh, sorry. I'm—"

"I asked you a question. What do you want?"

Thorgrim, perplexed by dwarf's insolent behavior, did not know what to say.

The black-bearded dwarf adjusted his eyepatch again and said, "Well?"

"I'm, sorry. I'm here to—"

Continuing to be rude, the black-bearded dwarf interrupted Thorgrim, again.

"Hey, are ya deaf? I'll ask ya a final time. What do ya want?"

Thorgrim was now irritated. In an effort to overcome any further interruptions, he shouted loudly, "You keep interrupting me. I'm here to see Uuno Kanto. Muh name is Shem Lybree."

The black-bearded dwarf smirked. "Oh, you're here to see Uuno Kanto, is it?"

"Yes."

"And yer name is Shem Lybree, is it?"

"Yes."

"And why would Mr. Kanto want to see the likes of you?"

"Well, Gary of Tuckerheim sent me."

The black-bearded dwarf hollered, "What's yer name again?"

"Shem Lybree."

The two dwarves looked at each other and exchanged whispers. Soon, the black-bearded dwarf knocked on the door. After a moment, the door opened and then he went inside.

Within a few minutes, the black-bearded dwarf returned, only this time, he walked down to the gate.

When the dwarf was close enough, Thorgrim took a close look at his red eyepatch. It had two black letters stitched in the middle that read: I A (the abbreviation for Iron Golem in the Dwarven alphabet).

"Da name's Moocher and dat's Booger up dare on da porch. Yer name please," he asked, adjusting his eyepatch.

"Muh name is Th . . . uh' I already told you. Muh name is Shem Lybree."

"Oh, yer name is Shem Lybree, is it?"

"Yes."

"And you said Gary of Tuckerheim sent you to see Mr. Kanto?"

"Yes, he did."

"Listen . . . if yer lying in any way, shape or form and we find out about it? Well, let me tell you somethin'—"

"I'm not lying. Gary of Tuckerheim really did send me here to see Mr. Kanto. Gary told me that Mr. Kanto can help me."

Moocher sneered. "If yer lying, you'll need help, alright."

Thorgrim waited, unsure what was going to happen next.

Moocher studied Thorgrim with his one eye, his brow furrowed deep. After a full minute, tugging on his jet-black beard, Moocher said, "Okay, I believe ya. Come on in."

Thorgrim uttered a sigh of relief when Moocher unlocked the front gate and gestured for him to enter.

"Where did ya get such a tall horse?"

Thorgrim had grown tired of everyone making a big deal about how tall Nugget is. He smirked. "He's not tall. We're just short."

Moocher crumpled his brow. "What are ya, some kinda' comedian or sometin'? Head on up to da door, before I change muh mind."

Nervously, Thorgrim obliged and walked the thirty feet to the porch, followed closely by Moocher.

On the porch, Booger, still holding the little dog named Bone Grinder, pointed to the front door and said, "You can relax."

Booger proceeded to use the secret knock for admittance. 'Knock, knock . . . knock, knock . . . knock.'

A second later, the door unlatched and opened slightly.

Booger said, "Go on in and grab a seat at the bar. When Mr. Kanto is ready to see you, someone will let you know."

Thorgrim nodded. As he opened the big oak door, Bone Grinder began to growl menacingly.

Looking at Thorgrim's beard, Booger immediately knew why the dog was upset. He said, "Hey, I suppose you're aware that a kitten has made a home inside yer beard? I can see his beady eyes looking out, and muh dog knows it's in there, too."

"I'm aware," replied Thorgrim, unconcerned.

"Just a word of warning. If you value the life of that cat, don't let it get near Bone Grinder, or you won't find anything left of it."

Blinky decided to poke his head out of Thorgrim's beard.

"Meow."

The dog instantly turned into a howling, fang-slashing, white-hot ball of canine werewolfness.

At which point, Blinky, hissing, and screeching, flew out of Thorgrim's beard and attacked the surprised dog. Bone Grinder immediately jumped out of Booger's arms, crying, with its feet kicking, as it tried to flee for its life.

Everyone watched in astonishment, as the tiny kitten chased after the terrified dog. The pursuit, lasting for several minutes, went up and down, back and forth and all around the fenced-in area in front of the pub.

Blinky continuously swiped at the routing canine's rear. Each time his sharp claws made contact, fur flew and the poor dog yelped.

Moocher yelled, "Booger, for da love of bearded women! Help me get da dog inside before he gets kilt!"

Panicking, both dwarves jumped off the porch and chased the howling dog around and around in circles but were unable to catch him.

Booger pleaded, "Please, sir, do something about yer cat before it kills our dog!"

"Blinky!" yelled Thorgrim. "Come here, right now!"

Blinky immediately ended the chase and scampered back to Thorgrim. Jumping onto his beard, the kitten climbed straight up to settle into his usual nesting area, deep within.

Once inside the beard, the satisfied cat curled up into a ball and purred.

"Holy sheee-ite!" exclaimed Moocher. "Dat's a wild cat if I've ever seen one!"

A moment later, Booger had the little, whimpering pooch, minus some fur, back in his arms.

"Bone Grinder, are you okay, buddy?" he asked the shaking dog. "Daddy's here now. Dat mean cat is gone."

Booger scowled and said, "Keep that miniature tiger of yers in check and away from Bone Grinder, or you'll be in real trouble. Do you understand?"

Thorgrim was flabbergasted and embarrassed.

"I'm very sorry . . . I uh, I don't know what happened! He's never done anything like that before. He's only a kitten."

"A kitten?" replied Booger angrily. "Dat's a hell-cat if ya ask me!"

Opening the door and entering, he said, "Moocher will keep an eye on yer horse. Go sit at the bar and wait until you're called. Mr. Kanto will see you when he's ready. And keep that crazy cat in check, will ya? Meanwhile, I need to tend to our dog."

Thorgrim, still embarrassed, entered behind Booger, while Moocher remained outside.

Once inside, Thorgrim closed the door and looked around. He was astounded by what he saw.

The place was as magnificent as any royal throne room in the entire realm.

He stood inside a fifty by fifty-foot room. Several jeweled chandeliers full of burning candles hung from the flat ceiling. Straight ahead, on the right side of the room was a grand staircase that led to the upper floor.

To the left of the staircase was a finely polished cherry wood bar, stocked to the brim with every kind of booze imaginable. Two dwarves sat on stools in front of the bar, drinking, chuckling, and conversing with whom Thorgrim assumed was the bartender.

A half-dozen, colorful, leaded windows, all depicting battles from the war with the elves, were arrayed along the pub's walls. Though the afternoon sky was mostly overcast, the summer sun still managed to stream through the colored art glass and onto the floors and furniture, creating beautiful, prismatic paintings of light.

The walls, richly paneled in rare, ancient black oak, held several ornately framed oil paintings. The wood trim along the ceiling was decorated with many exquisitely carved motifs of dragons and other creatures of lore.

The main floor contained twenty round oak tables that were stocked with chairs. Though Thorgrim had been told that the pub was closed on Sunday, in addition to the two dwarves sitting at the bar, a dozen others were sitting at tables, mingling, chatting and consuming their drink of choice.

Thorgrim noticed that all of them, including the bartender, wore an identical dark-red eyepatch that had the initials | A in the center.

He thought, *These guys must be some rough individuals. Everyone here seems to have lost an eye!*

A gruff voice from behind the bar, spoke.

"Have a seat here, friend. Whatcha' drinkin'?"

Thorgrim, still overwhelmed at the sight of the interior of the pub, slowly approached the bar. Behind it, the source of the gruff voice was a redheaded dwarf who wore a beard, almost as long as Thorgrim's.

Thorgrim chose the nearest stool and sat down. Placing his backpack on the floor, he checked to make sure Blinky was okay and then replied, "What am I drinkin'?"

"Yes, what will it be," asked the bartender after he finished topping off the ale mug of one of the dwarves seated at the bar.

Thorgrim looked, and the two dwarves greeted him with a friendly nod, which he returned.

"I'll have a cold water, if that's okay."

"Just plain ol' water?"

"Yes, please."

"Okay. Do you want to use yer ale mug, or would you prefer a house glass?"

"Ale mug? I don't have one."

The bartender was incredulous. Adjusting his eyepatch, he said, "What? You don't have an ale mug? Did ya lose yers?"

Of course, Thorgrim did not care much for ale, but in order to fit in, he lied.

"Uh, yes . . . I lost mine. So, a glass is okay."

The bartender brought over a fresh decanter of chilly water and poured Thorgrim a glass. "Sorry to hear that, friend. Before ya leave the pub, remind me, and I'll see to it that you get a new mug. No dwarf should be caught dead without his ale mug!"

"Thanks. That's very kind of you."

Thorgrim took a big drink of the water. It tasted amazing compared to some of the water he had been drinking since he left home.

The bartender poured himself a shot of pine gin and drank it. Slamming the empty glass on the bar, he said, "Muh names Scootz McDonald. What's yers?"

"Shem Lybree."

"Pleased to meet ya. Ya know, it ain't every day I meet a dwarf with a beard longer than mine. Yer beard hangs past yer knees! Amazin' and congratulations!"

"Thankee," replied Thorgrim with pride.

"And I assume ya already know ya got a cat livin' in yer beard, don't ya?"

"Oh, yes."

"Okay, just checkin' Uh, why are ya here. Normally, we're closed to the public on Sunday. The boss likes a day off once in a while, ya know."

"The boss? Is that Mr. Kanto?"

Scootz nodded. "Yes, do ya know him?"

"No, a friend of Mr. Kanto sent me here to see him."

"Oh, just wait 'til ya meet the boss," said Scootz. "He's a real character."

Thorgrim took another brief look at the dwarves that were lounging in the pub. Curious about the eyepatches, he whispered to the bartender, "Scootz, excuse me but . . . I can't help but notice that everyone I see around here is wearin' a red-colored eyepatch. All of them have, what I assume to be, initials that stand for Iron Golem. Even the dog out front was wearin' one."

Scootz smirked and offered a quick chuckle while drying a couple of freshly washed mugs. "So, what about it?"

"Well, I, um . . . I don't mean any disrespect, but I was just wondering why everyone seems to be wearin' one."

"Why do you think everyone is wearing an eyepatch?"

"I dunno," replied Thorgrim with a shrug.

Scootz offered a sinister grin. "We're pirates!"

Thorgrim shuddered. "Are ya kiddin'?"

"Hahahohaho! Ya, I'm only jokin'."

Thorgrim grinned. "Well, I wondered, uh, 'cuz, we're quite a ways away from the ocean."

"Well, we're retired pirates."

Thorgrim chuckled. "That's funny stuff!"

Scootz laughed. "Ya, in-between killin' people, we try to have a little fun around here."

234

Thorgrim's eyes widened and his mouth hung open a bit.

"Hahahahaho! Gotcha' again, didn't I?"

"Ya, I guess," replied Thorgrim with another grin. "But I'm still curious why everyone wears—"

A tap on Thorgrim's shoulder startled and interrupted him. "Sir, Mr. Kanto will see you now," said another red eyepatch-wearing dwarf. "Muh name's Yarborrow. Follow me, please."

Thorgrim rose from the stool and thanked the bartender for the water. "Do I owe ya anything for the water?"

"On the house."

Scootz offered Thorgrim a wink with his one eye along with a smile.

"This way," said Yarborrow, as he walked towards the stairs.

Thorgrim grabbed his pack and followed the dwarf up the stairs, down a long hallway to a door.

There, Yarborrow knocked. "I have Mr. Lybree here, Mr. Kanto."

From beyond the door, a smooth, baritone voice said, "Mr. Lybree, please come in, and close the door behind you."

Yarborrow opened the door and Thorgrim nervously stared into a large, somewhat stuffy office. Inside, sitting behind a desk was the one and only, Uuno Kanto.

"Well, come on in."

Thorgrim slowly entered and closed the door as asked.

Uuno rose from his desk and gestured towards a chair in front of it. Smiling, he said, "Please, have a seat right there."

Thorgrim hesitantly approached the chair and sat down. Looking up, he was astonished at the physical appearance of his host. Uuno was an extremely muscular, powerful-looking, grey-bearded dwarf, who of course, also wore a dark-red eyepatch over his left eye.

Despite Uuno's intimidating appearance, there was also something very friendly about him. Something fatherly. Thorgrim noticed a warmth in Uuno's smile that contradicted the rest of his tough-looking exterior.

"So, Mr. Lybree, I understand Gary of Tuckerheim sent you to see me?"

"Yes, Mr. Kanto, Gary sent me to see you. He said you were a good friend and that you might be able to help me."

Uuno did not reply. Instead, he continued to smile and stare at Thorgrim.

Extremely nervous and somewhat intimidated by Uuno, he tried again, his voice shaking, "Uh, I, uh, I'm hopin' you can help me. But, if you're too busy, maybe I can come back another day."

235

Thorgrim started to get up from the chair, but Uuno said, "You can relax, friend. Please, sit back down. Any friend of Gary's is a friend of mine. Take a minute and catch yer breath, then we can chat. By the way, that's an incredibly long and thick beard you have. I don't recall ever seeing a better one."

Thorgrim felt instant relief.

"Thankee," he said with a smile.

Feeling relaxed, he looked around the office and noticed several musical instruments and a few framed drawings of a dwarf on the wall. The dwarf in the drawings held a long-necked lute. He was dressed in a black suit and wore a wide black hat.

Thorgrim pointed to one of the drawings and said, "A friend of yers?"

Uuno smiled. "Yes, he's a good friend, who also happens to be my favorite singer."

"Who is he?"

"They call him the Dwarf in Black. His real name is J.R. Moolah."

Thorgrim gave a slight headshake. "Hmmmm. Never heard of him."

Uuno appeared surprised. "You've never heard of J.R. Moolah? Then you've been missing out. He's a famous country singer. I love his music, especially songs like 'The Dwarf Comes Around', 'The legend of Moridon's Hammer', 'Don't Take Yer Axes to Town', and one of my all-time favorites, 'I Walk the Mine.' Now, that's a classic dwarf country song if there ever was one!"

Thorgrim thought for a moment. Tugging on his beard, he accidentally woke his kitten. "Hmmmm, J.R. Moolah. Come to think of it, I remember when I was a small boy, someone by that name came through my hometown and performed at the fair. Long time ago, though."

Uuno lifted his salt and pepper monobrow. "Really? Yer hometown? Where's that?"

Thorgrim looked down and hesitated to answer.

Uuno saw the hesitation and started to speak but was caught by surprise when Blinky stuck his head out of Thorgrim's beard and meowed.

"Mr. Lybree, there's a—"

"Cat in muh beard, I know," replied Thorgrim, stuffing the little kitten back inside. "He's probably hungry."

Uuno leaned back in his chair. "Oh, so that's the man-eating cat that Booger was tellin' me about. He said yer cat kicked the crap out of our dog, Bone Grinder."

236

"His name is Blinky and about that, I'm sorry . . . I don't know what got into him."

Uuno laughed. "Hahahhoahho, not a problem. Our dog is fine . . . jus' missin' a bit of butt fur, that's all."

Then Uuno uttered a huge belly laugh.

"What's so funny?" asked Thorgrim curiously.

"Well, I just realized that a kitten named Blinky beat the hell out of a dog named Bone Grinder. Sounds kinda funny, don't ya think?"

Thorgrim offered one of his toothy grins. "Yeah, I suppose that does sound funny."

"Reminds me of the time when the All-Star Wrestling tour came through the city. My favorite wrestler was a powerful dwarf by the name of Chuck Steak. He lost the championship to a dwarf who wore a pink tutu and went by the name of Cream Cake. Now you tell me that's not funny!"

Thorgrim laughed loudly. "Yeah, that is hilarious!"

"Mr. Lybree, I had asked you about yer hometown. Since you obviously did not want to mention it, I can assume that it is, in part, why yer here to see me?"

Thorgrim looked down and nodded.

"Mr. Lybree . . . or can I call you . . . uh, I'm sorry, they told me yer first name, but I forgot."

"Shem."

"Uh, Shem, we need to get somethin' straight. You have to trust me, and I have to trust you. That's the only way I can help you."

"Okay," replied Thorgrim, still obviously unnerved.

"So relax. If Gary sent you, then I know you need help. Let's see, judging by yer looks I would guess you to be, what— twenty or twenty-one?"

"I'll be twenty in five months on the first of the year."

"Hmmm. I was close. Okay, let me continue to guess. Yer supposed to be workin' in the mines, but you don't want to."

Amazed that Uuno had guessed his plight, Thorgrim looked away, ashamed. Nodding his head, he replied sullenly, "How did ya know that?"

"Lucky guess."

Thorgrim mumbled, "It's true."

Uuno tugged on his grey beard. "I understand. I spent about five of the mandated twenty years in the Krupp coal mines and hated every minute of it. One day, I decided not to go back to work and eventually, they arrested me. I didn't bother to even offer an excuse. I was sentenced

237

to three years in prison. After spending some time behind bars, I worked out a deal with the authorities and joined the military. Have you considered joining the armed forces?"

Thorgrim, still ashamed, shook his head. "Mr. Kanto, I'm severely claustrophobic. I can't work in any ore mine or join the Army."

"Hey, please call me Uuno."

"Okay, Uuno."

"But, what about the Navy?"

"Uuno, I can't go below decks inside of a ship. I'd go crazy in there."

"Okay. I can see that would be a problem for a claustrophobic. Ya can't work in the mines or join the military, so I have to assume yer on the run, is it? Where ya going?"

"Ya, I'm on the run. I graduated from high school at the end of May, and I'm supposed to be workin' in the Vog Silver Mines with my father. But obviously, I can't because of the claustrophobia."

Uuno nodded. "I understand."

"I left my home in Vog last Thursday morning, and I'm on my way out of the county to start a new life somewhere else. Maybe in the Great Kingdom. I just know that I can't stay here, because once the authorities learn that I skipped out, they'll arrest me."

Uuno nodded. "Yes, they will if they can find you. And let me tell you, they're very good at tracking down lawbreakers. Even if you leave the country, you will be a wanted dwarf. I happen to know that sometimes they'll send out bounty hunters into other countries searching for all types of criminals. If they catch them, they bring 'em back to stand trial."

Thorgrim became frightened at the prospect of being arrested no matter what he did. "But it's safer out of the country, far away from here, isn't it?"

"Perhaps, but Shem, do you think that you're the only dwarf who has refused service in the mines? Why, although the government is good at catching deserters, they can't catch everyone. Hell, the prisons couldn't hold 'em all, anyway."

Desperate, Thorgrim said, "What can I do then?"

"Well, that's where I come in. You might say that I've helped several others who were in yer situation."

"You have?"

"Oh, yes. Here's what I can do. I can get you some identification papers that look even better than the official ones. Basically, what I'm sayin' is that I can give you a new identity."

"A new identity?"

238

"Well, you seem pretty smart, so can I assume that you've been going by a different name already, right?"

"Yes, for the last few days."

"Excellent. Then you already have a new identity, but you'll need papers that match. I mean, you can't run around without ID papers. I can get you these papers, but you must do exactly as I say to avoid getting caught. If they catch you with false papers, you'll be in real trouble. And if yer caught, just so you know, I'll deny any involvement. You understand?"

"Yes."

"For you, the good news is that I've helped quite a few dwarves in my time. As I said, many were in the same situation you are in now. Most of them were good eggs, but some, not so good. It's what I do though. I like to help people. What they decide to do after I help is up to them."

"What do I need to do to get ID papers?"

Uuno reached into his desk and pulled out a sheet of paper. Grabbing the quill from the inkwell on his desk, he said, "First off, I need yer real name. You've already told me that yer goin' by an alias, so I know yer name's not really Shem Lybree."

"You're right. Muh real name is Thorgrim Longbeard."

Uuno sat back and scratched his cheek. "Thorgrim Longbeard? I've heard that name before."

Thorgrim bashfully said, "Well, I'm kinda famous, I guess."

"Famous? How?"

Thorgrim pulled up his long beard. "I was born with this."

Uuno snapped his fingers. "That's it! I knew it! You're the dwarf that was born with a beard!"

"Yes. That's me."

"I remember hearing about you, and I always thought it was a made-up story. A baby born with a long beard who happens to have Longbeard as a last name!"

"Yes, that's right."

"Well, that long as hell, auburn beard is certainly going to grab attention. You don't want any attention. You want to blend in, but be intimidating enough where people will tend to ignore or avoid you. Does that make sense?"

"Yes," replied Thorgrim, nodding and smiling.

"We need to change yer appearance and then I'll have ID papers made that will match the new you, name and all."

Thorgrim became nervous again. "Change my appearance? How?"

Leaning over his desk. Uuno replied, "We'll cut yer beard and hair and then color it. I think black would work."

Thorgrim's face turned pale. "I need to cut muh beard and hair, then color everything black?"

"Yes. Relax."

Thorgrim twirled his beard. "But muh beard, too?"

"Yes, yes. You know, now that I think about it, there'll be no reason that you'd have to leave the country if you play this smart."

"Really? You mean I could even stay in this city?"

"Yes. Not only that, if you stay here, you'd still be close to your home in Vog. If you leave the country, you might never see your family again. Of course, any contact with them would be risky, but who knows what the future may bring."

Thorgrim considered Uuno's words and became excited. "That's all true! Tell me what you want me to do."

"So you want to do this?"

"Yes, I do."

"Okay. Of course, we can't use yer real name. I like the name Shem Lybree. But, since you left home, did you tell anyone your real name?"

Thorgrim thought for a few seconds, then shook his head. "No."

"Are you absolutely sure?"

"Yes."

"So no one else, besides me, knows that Shem Lybree is really Thorgrim Longbeard?"

"That's right."

"Good. When I get done with the paperwork, for all practical purposes, yer name will legally be Shem Lybree."

Thorgrim's excitement increased with every word Uuno said.

"But I need a job and a place to live."

"I can take care of that, too," replied Uuno with a smile. "What kind of work do you want to do?"

The library. The thought of working in the Supreme Library of Mharrak overwhelmed Thorgrim. He began to sweat and his pulse pounded.

Is this really happening?

"I would love to work in the Supreme Library if that's possible."

"Oh, yer a bookworm? Good. I can easily make that happen. I have connections in the Supreme Library."

Thorgrim's eyes grew to the size of plates. "You can get me a job in the library?"

Uuno smiled. "Sure, not a problem. Consider it done."

240

"But . . ."

"Trust me."

"Okay. I trust you. I just can't believe all of this!"

"Believe it. As far as a place to stay. You can stay in one of the rooms down the hall here in the pub until you save enough money to get yer own place."

"I can stay here?"

"Sure. You should be able to afford yer own place in a month or two. Uh, I assume you have a horse, don't you? Unless you plan on walking about eight miles to work every day and then back."

"Ya, I've got a great horse. I bought it from yer friend, Gary."

"Nice! Then that's more good news for you. It's a long walk on foot!"

"Believe me, I did enough walking when I first left Vog."

"I'm sure you did. Any questions so far?"

"I can't think of any right at this moment."

"Uh, let's see. Is there anything I'm forgetting? Hmmmmm. Oh, yes. From now on, you'll be wearin' this."

Uuno reached into his pocket and tossed a red eyepatch onto the top of his desk. It was like the others but did not have the letters IA stitched in the middle.

Thorgrim saw it and cringed.

"I have to wear that?"

"Yes. You'll want to appear older and intimidating, so people will leave you alone when you're out in public."

"They'll leave me alone if I wear that?"

"Yes. There's an old saying. Everyone knows that you don't mess with a one-eyed dwarf."

Thorgrim understood. "Is that why everyone around here's wearin' an eyepatch?"

"Of course!" Uuno flipped up his eyepatch to reveal that he had both eyes. "Only a few of the dwarves that frequent the pub have lost an eye in battle or barroom brawls. I thought it looked menacing, so that's why we all wear one around here. Even the gangbangers down the street avoid us!"

Thorgrim said, "When I rode in here, I noticed some of those hoods hanging around up the street. I don't see any near the pub, though."

"That's because they don't want anything to do with us. Ya see, we are an organization and have connections to some, let's say, extreme undesirables elsewhere. Those punks up the street? They know the consequences of messin' around with any of us. I can assure you, if they do anything to any of us, they'd be wiped out overnight. Every last one of them and their families, too."

Thorgrim blinked his eyes rapidly, excited, though startled about what Uuno had just told him.

Uuno continued, "Yep. We've made that very clear, hands-off, or else. This is why you should wear the patch. The red eyepatch with the Iron Golem logo is the symbol of our group."

Thorgrim picked up the patch.

"But, this patch doesn't have the Iron Golem logo on it."

"You're a recruit. When you've proved yer loyalty, you'll get one with the logo."

"I won't have to do anything illegal to prove my loyalty, will I?"

Uuno chuckled. "No! Well, technically yer already doing something illegal. You skipped out on the mines! Don't worry, we don't run around like mobsters breaking laws. We're a brotherhood. A unit. We're always looking for new recruits and let me tell you this. We don't take just anyone. I see something special in you . . . and apparently, so did Gary or he would not have sent you here."

Thorgrim shrugged. "Well, thankee, but can't anyone just put on an eyepatch and pretend they're part of yer group?"

Uuno offered a sinister chuckle. "Sure. The problem is, if we catch 'em, they'll never be heard from again. It's usually a non-issue. Everyone in the city knows this."

Thorgrim put on the eyepatch and looked around. "But, I can't see a thing!"

"Open yer eye!" replied Uuno.

Thorgrim grinned. "Oh, I guess that would help. Sorry, I had the wrong eye closed."

Uuno laughed. "I have to be honest, that concerns me! But anyway, I know it'll seem strange at first, however, you'll get used to it. And you don't have to wear it all the time; just when yer out in public."

"Oh, I understand," said Thorgrim as he removed the patch.

Uuno stood from his chair and said, "Okay, I'll put together yer papers, but it will take me a couple of days."

"What about muh job at the library?"

"The library opens at nine in the morning, so go there first thing tomorrow and ask for the head librarian. Her name is Gertrude. Tell her Uuno Kanto sent you, and she'll make a comment about the weather in the Brimger Valley. You'll reply, 'In the valley of the blind, the one-eyed dwarf is king.' Got that?"

Thorgrim repeated Uuno's words a few times, then said, "Yes, I've got it."

"Good. Don't forget it and don't share that with anyone else."

"Okay," replied Thorgrim with excitement etched all over his face.

"Gertrude will take it from there. She'll put you to work, likely cleaning the garderobe, but at least it's a start. Just make sure you don't let me down."

"I won't let you down, I promise! And, cleaning the garderobe or not, I'll enjoy working there. It's a dream come true!"

"That's the attitude I like to see. Okay, let's get to work on yer appearance."

"Now?"

"Ya got anything better to do?"

"No, I don't think so."

"Good. Head back down the hall and knock on the last door on the right. Festus should be in there. He'll cut yer hair, beard and then color it all to make you look a little older. Tell him I said black. He'll then do a good drawing of yer face, so I can use it on yer paperwork."

Thorgrim ran his fingers through his long beard, pouting as he went. When his hand found Blinky, the kitten woke again and purred.

"Shem, I'm a dwarf, so I know what yer beard means to you. You must understand that cutting yer beard is for yer own good. We're not going to cut it all off . . . maybe half. Someday, you can grow it back, but it may be a long time before that day comes."

Tugging on his beard a few times, Thorgrim replied, "My beard is like an old friend. But I understand. I'll just have to get used to it."

"That's right. Now, you'll have to keep cutting and coloring yer hair and beard every month or so. It's a pain, but we need to completely disconnect Shem Lybree from Thorgrim Longbeard."

Thorgrim nodding, understood.

Uuno offered a brief chuckle. "By the way, where did you come up with a name like Shem Lybree? It's unusual, to say the least."

"A few days ago, someone asked me muh name and I didn't want to use muh real name so I picked the first thing that came to muh mind. The Library of Shem. So, I flipped it around and said muh name was Shem Lybree. Kinda stupid, probably."

"No, as I said, I like it. I'll say it's kinda funny that you chose an elf library for yer name!"

Thorgrim grinned. "Yes, I guess it is funny. Never thought 'bout that. You've heard of the Library of Shem?"

"Oh, yes. Actually been there once . . . mmmmm . . . I'm thinking maybe thirty years ago."

"You've been there?" said Thorgrim excitedly. "Is it as big as they say?"

"A huge building. Many books, too. Over twice as many as what we have in the Supreme Library of Mharrak."

Thorgrim's mind went wild envisioning all of those books. He said, "Why did you go to the Library of Shem?"

"I went to Calibut to do a show."

"A show?"

"I'm a singer myself, you know. That should be obvious with all of the lutes hanging on the walls in here. I used to do a few shows here and there and that's how I met J.R. Moolah."

Thorgrim shook his head. "I can't sing at all. I don't think I could carry a tune in an ore wagon."

"You can't sing? Don't you ever sing when yer using the garderobe or taking a bath?"

"No."

"Shem, anyone can learn to sing. You should try it."

"Maybe someday," replied Thorgrim with a shrug.

"There are some books in the Supreme Library on how to sing. Since you'll be workin' there, you should read them."

Thorgrim smiled broadly. "I may do that!"

"Okay, so head on down and see Festus. Tell him I said to get right to work on you. It will take two or three hours to get everything done. You can start staying here tonight."

"I have a place to stay tonight, would it be alright to start staying here tomorrow?"

"Sure. Starting tomorrow, you can stay here for as long as you like. Uh, within reason of course. I don't want you to think that you can retire here! As I said, save yer money and you'll be able to afford yer own place soon."

"Okay, I will save every copper I can."

"Don't forget. Tomorrow, go to the library and talk to Gertrude about the weather like I told ya. I'll give the papers to ya when they're ready. Meanwhile, stay out of trouble. Lay low. I don't want anyone asking you for yer papers before you get them."

"Okay. Thankee, so much."

"Get down there and see Festus."

Thorgrim smiled, stood and reached out to shake Uuno's hand. While doing so, he asked, "If ya don't mind, I have to say that you and Gary must be special friends in order for you to go to all of this trouble every time he sends someone to see you."

"Gary never sends anyone to see me. You're the first."

"I am?"

"Yes, and you could say that Gary and I have a special relationship," replied Uuno. "You see, Gary is married to muh sister."

"Ah, I get it," said Thorgrim. "But you said you help people all the time in situations like mine. Aren't you worried that you might get caught and prosecuted?"

"Not at all. You've certainly heard of King Muechenberg?"

"Yes, he's our king."

"Many years ago, when the King was a young, teenage prince, he got into a lot of trouble, and I got him out of it. I'll leave it at that. Well, he never forgot my kindness and let's just say, I'm protected. At least, as long as I don't commit any major crimes, anyway!"

Thorgrim smiled again, and with Blinky's head poking out of his beard, he walked towards the office door.

Uuno said, "Shem, uh, before you let Festus cut yer beard, if I were you, I would take the cat out first."

"Oh, of course!" replied Thorgrim with a giggle.

Uuno laughed. "I would hate to see what Blinky would do to Festus if he accidentally clipped him with the scissors."

Thorgrim opened the door and left the office, closing it behind him. He looked down the long hall towards the door where Festus was supposed to be.

He paused, thinking about the future, wondering if he should really plan to stay in the capital, living a new life with his new identity.

Then, from beyond the door, in Uuno's office, Thorgrim heard a lute strumming. Soon, he heard a deep, calm bass-baritone voice singing.

It was the voice of Uuno Kanto.

"And I heard, as it were, the noise of thunder:
One of the four ogres saying: "Come and see."
And I saw.
And behold, a white, dwarven horse.

There's a dwarf goin' 'round takin' names.
An' he decides who to free and who to blame.
Everybody won't be treated all the same.

245

Moridon's golden beard reaching down.
When the dwarf comes around.

The hairs on yer beard will stand up.
At the terror in each sip and in each sup.
Will you partake of that last offered cup?
Or disappear into the potter's ground.
When the dwarf comes around.

Hear the trumpets, hear the pipers.
One hundred million angels singin'.
Multitudes are marching to the big kettle-drum.
Voices callin', voices cryin'.
Some are born an' some are dyin'.
It's Alpha and Omega's Kingdom come . . ."

Thorgrim listened to the lyrics of the beautiful song and understood them. Mesmerized by the music, he slowly walked down the hall, listening until Uuno ended the song. Then he rapped on the door and waited for Festus to answer.

Inside his office, with the song finished, Uuno put the lute back on the wall, sat down behind his desk and lit his pipe. Looking up, he stared at one of the drawings of the Dwarf in Black, for a moment. Shaking his head briefly, he smiled.

After taking a big draw from his pipe, he released a perfect smoke ring and watched as it floated lazily in the air. He thought, *A smoke ring. Hmmmm. Ring of smoke? No, boring.* Noticing the burning embers in the bowl of his pipe, another idea occurred to him. *Ring of . . . fire, Yes, fire!* He said aloud, "Ring of Fire. That would make a great name for a song! Hmmm, I'll have to come up with a melody and write some lyrics for that someday."

Pulling out a stack of paper from his desk, he dipped his quill and started to work on Thorgrim's identification documents.

XII. The Supreme Library

At approximately 9:00 p.m., Thorgrim arrived back at The Scalded Dwarf Inn, a new man. Riding into the stable, at first, the two stablemen did not recognize him. His hair and beard, formally long and auburn in color, were now much shorter and dyed black. He also wore a dark-red eyepatch over his left eye.

Although Thorgrim was tired after a long, eventful day, he was also feeling exhilarated. Not only had Uuno Kanto promised him a job working in the Supreme Library, but he had also told him, that having identification papers that matched his alias, Shem Lybree, there would be no reason to flee the country. Of course, there were risks. However, with his altered appearance and using the ID papers that Uuno would soon provide for him, he could safely remain in the city.

Another benefit of staying was that Thorgrim would not be far from his family in Vog. If he left the country, he might not ever see them again. He hoped that one day, hiding behind his new identity, that he might be able to return to Vog and see his family from time to time.

Fortunately, the ride from the pub to the inn had been without incident. However, Thorgrim did manage to fall on his rear while dismounting Nugget inside The Scalded Dwarf's stable. The mishap caused the two stablemen to roar with laughter. This time, Thorgrim, in a good mood after his visit with Uuno, laughed along with them.

Having noticed a line of rainclouds earlier in the day, he had hoped to avoid getting caught in a downpour during his return trip to the inn. Luckily, the timing of his arrival could not have been better. A soft rain began to fall the moment he approached the door to The Scalded Dwarf.

Norton was standing behind the counter working his usual evening shift when an intimidating-looking character opened the inn's front door and entered. The visitor wore a red eyepatch over his left eye and had a medium-length, black beard, and short hair.

Not recognizing Thorgrim, Norton said, "Good evening, sir. If you would like a room, we have some available."

Before Thorgrim could respond, Norton did a quick, double-take. "Uh . . . Mr. Lybree? . . . Mr. Lybree, is that you?"

"Yes, it is, of course," Thorgrim replied. "Is there a problem?"

"Uh, no, not at all. Um, yer room is ready and waiting. Don't forget the café closes at two-thirty, and if you have any laundry, just set it outside yer door as before."

"Thankee. I'm starvin', but I'm going take a quick bath and change muh clothes. Been riding most of the day."

"Oh, sure. I understand. Please enjoy your stay!"

"Uh, Norton, do you happen to have a small, shallow box? Maybe a foot square and a few inches deep? I need to fill it with some sand or loose dirt."

Norton was slightly puzzled. "I can probably manage that. Forgive me for my curiosity, but can I ask you what you're using it for?"

"I came up with a great idea today. Muh cat needs a place to go to relieve himself, and instead of having to take him outside all the time, he can use a box full of sand or dirt. Otherwise, he might have an accident in the room, if ya know what I mean."

Norton pulled on his short, pointy, red beard. "You have a cat?"

"Yes."

Thorgrim reached into his still, massively thick, though much shorter beard and pulled out tiny Blinky.

"This is my little friend, Blinky Eyes. I usually just call him Blinky."

Norton stroked the kitten's furry head. "Oh, he's a muplet, isn't he? Uh, sure. I'll find a box and fill it with some dirt for you. Ya know, that's a great idea! A garderobe box for cats. You might become famous for that idea one day!"

"Famous for inventin' a poopin' box for cats? Hahohaha. We'll see. You know, this is my last night at the inn, and when I leave tomorrow morning, you won't be here. I want to thank ya for yer hospitality. I'd like to thank Mooky, too. Is he around by chance?"

"You're very welcome, Mr. Lybree. No, Mooky's usually gone by five. I'll pass that on for you the next time I see him."

***

With the exception of the brief rain shower and flashes of lightning, the night would be uneventful. Following a huge supper, Thorgrim took another hot bath and then went to bed around midnight. Blinky, deep inside Thorgrim's beard, fell asleep almost immediately, though it took the dwarf awhile to drift off.

The excitement of spending the next day in the library and the Grand Hall kept his mind busy. Although he had no idea what either place looked like inside, his imagination ran wild with images.

Eventually, with his little friend's rolling purrs helping, Thorgrim Longbeard fell fast asleep, snoring so loud that even Nugget could hear

248

the annoying rumbling sounds all the way from the stable. Needless to say, so could everyone else trying to get some sleep at The Scalded Dwarf Inn.

***

Thorgrim was up early but before getting ready, he checked and sure enough, Blinky had used the little box of dirt kindly provided by Norton.

"Hmmm, maybe something will come of this cat box idea after all!" he mumbled while getting dressed.

After a big breakfast, he loaded up his backpack with his belongings, extra food, and fresh, water flasks, then put it on. It seemed heavier than ever. With Blinky, as usual, nestled away in his beard, Thorgrim took a final look around his room and then closed the door.

At the front counter, Goober had replaced Norton for the day shift. Thorgrim turned in the room key and again asked that his appreciation be passed on to Mooky.

In the stables, Thorgrim also thanked the stablemen for taking good care of Nugget. Happily, he successfully mounted his horse and rode out of the stable.

It was 8:05 a.m., Monday, July 22. Thorgrim halted along the narrow dirt path that led to Central Avenue from the stable. For a few moments, he became lost in thought, wondering if the authorities were now aware he had shirked his obligation. Of course, his father, with the help of Dr. Thacker's note, had bought him more time, but Thorgrim had no way of knowing this.

For Thorgrim Longbeard, each passing day brought with it more worries about getting caught by the authorities. But now, he was relieved by the fact that his appearance had been altered dramatically, and that soon, he would have ID papers that matched his alias.

Seeing his reflection in the mirror earlier that morning had shocked him. His hair and beard, now dark black, were less than half their usual length. With the eyepatch and the changes to his beard and hair, he hardly recognized himself. He hoped that if he ran into anyone who knew him as Thorgrim Longbeard, they would not recognize him either.

Before riding out, he looked up and down Central Avenue. Unlike yesterday, the avenue was buzzing with many dwarves who were working or on their way to work in one of the various businesses in the city.

The ground was damp from the previous night's rain, but fortunately, it remained overcast and the weather was cool for the second day in a row. Excited, he rode Nugget slowly out, onto the busy avenue and headed south towards the library.

Uuno had mentioned that the library opened at 9:00 a.m. Wanting to arrive before then, he gave Nugget a light nudge with a knee, and the horse obeyed, increasing his pace to a trot. At the faster speed, barring any delays, Thorgrim was confident that he would arrive at the library with time to spare.

While riding, he remembered the homeless he had encountered yesterday and began to worry that they might try to swarm him again. However, this time, when he arrived at North Thirty-Fifth Street, the transients were nowhere to be seen.

Puzzled, he thought, *Maybe they've moved on to another part of the city.*

With the exception of a couple of panhandlers who were being interviewed by a policeman, not one homeless person was seen anywhere.

I wonder what happened to those poor souls?

Although Thorgrim was relieved that he did not have to deal with the crowd of transients, he still worried about their fate.

Could the police have rounded all of them up overnight? Where would they take them . . . to jail? If I ever have the chance, I'll help people like that, someday.

He continued riding at a steady pace, simply going around slower travelers when possible. Occasionally, due to bouncing in the saddle, he had to reach up and adjust his eyepatch. The patch was uncomfortable, and it limited both his depth perception and peripheral vision. He hated it and often felt like taking it off, but remembering Uuno's advice, he kept it on.

As he trotted down the avenue, again heeding Uuno's advice about avoiding any attention, Thorgrim decided it best to mind his own business unless someone greeted him. In that case, he would return a friendly smile and wave. It seemed the natural thing to do, especially if he would encounter the police.

***

Having reached the corner of North Second Street and Central Avenue, due to heavier wagon and foot traffic near the City Center area, he decided to slow Nugget to a walk. He remembered that at the next corner on the left, was the monument of the Forgotten Miner. Concerned that he might again feel shame if he viewed the giant statue, he instead, tried to focus his attention on the huge torch sitting atop the Royal Castle, a couple of blocks further ahead on his right.

He knew that the Supreme Library was across the street from the castle, and the anticipation of finally getting to see the inside of the library, caused him to tremble with excitement.

After a couple of minutes of riding, Thorgrim halted in the middle of the avenue near the Heart of the City intersection. His timepiece read 8:41 a.m. He had arrived with plenty of time to spare.

The area was packed with dwarves going about their business, and as they traveled past, many swore at him for blocking traffic. However, he was lost in a daze. Still wearing his eyepatch, he could not take his lone eye off the Supreme Library of Mharrak.

It was not long before a policeman approached on horseback and warned Thorgrim to move along or face the consequences. The firm tapping of a heavy baton on Thorgrim's leg confirmed that the club-head meant business.

Embarrassed and cursing himself for gaining the attention of the police, he apologized, then steered Nugget across the avenue and onto the library's grounds, where he halted again.

Seventy-five feet from the front of the building was a long watering trough for horses, stacks of fresh hay kindly provided by the city, as well as plenty of hitching posts. There were several horses already tied to posts along with a few mule-drawn buggies and carts, parked next to them.

A couple dozen dwarves loitered near their horses, chatting while waiting for the library to open. Much to Thorgrim's surprise, he noticed several halflings and even a few togglins among them.

Thorgrim rode up, stopped near a hitching post, and prepared to dismount. By this time, the group of people began walking up to the library. Once there, they formed a single-file line in front of the entrance door.

Dropping the mounting block was easy. Everything thereafter was the difficult part. Taking a deep breath, Thorgrim looked down towards the block, while Nugget slurped up some water from the trough.

"Ready Blinky?" he asked his kitten, who was purring deep inside his beard. Placing a hand over his beard to protect the little cat in case of an accident, holding onto the pommel, Thorgrim pulled his right boot from the stirrup, swung his right leg over the saddle, and eased himself down. After both boots found the block, he sighed. He had done it, and to relish the moment, he closed his eyes, took a deep breath and pumped his fist.

251

Then he lost his balance, fell off the block and landed flat on his butt. He was embarrassed, despite being unsure if anyone had witnessed the disaster, though he thought he heard a few chuckles.

Thorgrim slowly stood, then checked his clothes for any mud or dirt while whining about either getting longer legs or a shorter horse.

He felt his beard for Blinky. The kitten was gone. Slowly looking up, squinting with his one eye, he found his tiny cat right where he expected. On the saddle, purring, and tipping his head back and forth while blinking his big orange eyes.

"But, I had a hold of you! How did you . . . oh, never mind. Good for you, my little friend."

Retrieving Blinky from the saddle, Thorgrim put him back inside his beard. Next, he hugged his horse around the neck. After giving him a carrot treat, Thorgrim said, "I love ya, Nugget. I may be awhile. Enjoy the break, my friend."

Wearing his backpack, with only his pride injured by the fall, Thorgrim began walking up the tiled path towards the library entrance.

Flanking the path were life-size, marble statues honoring famous dwarven authors, philosophers, and scholars. Similar to the Royal Castle, a wide assortment of colorful flowers decorated the front and side grounds of the Supreme Library.

Thorgrim was the last person in a group of about two dozen people who stood in line waiting for the library doors to open. Checking his timepiece, it read 8:55 a.m.

While waiting, he looked across the street at the Grand Hall of the Dwarves. Although the Supreme Library must come first, he looked forward in excitement and anticipation of getting to visit the Grand Hall, something that he was planning to do later in the day.

As he stood in line, Thorgrim was reminded about his horrid experience on Saturday night while trying to get into the city. So far, waiting to get into the library was much more enjoyable. The weather was cooler, he wasn't surrounded by feisty, sweaty, half-drunken dwarves, nor were there any vampire mosquitoes to deal with.

Promptly at 9:00 a.m., the door opened. The line flowed smoothly, and in a matter of seconds, Thorgrim reached the entryway. Before entering, he turned to make sure all was okay with Nugget. Much to his satisfaction, his horse was happily munching on the hay. As he looked on, several other dwarves and a few halflings had arrived and were already working their way up to the library entrance.

"Excuse me, sir," said a soft female voice. "Are you going to come in?"

252

Slightly surprised, Thorgrim turned around to discover, that the soft female voice belonged to a pretty, redheaded woman who was probably in her mid-twenties. Dressed in a green skirt and top, she wore a silver, heart charm necklace, and a flower-decorated, curly beard.

Caught off guard by her beauty, he turned a light shade of red and replied, "Yes, I'm coming in, thankee."

Thorgrim took a couple of steps inside so she could close the door.

"Sir, welcome to the Supreme Library. My name is Ruby. Feel free to browse through the Museum. If you have questions about any of the exhibits here in this room, please let me know."

Ruby then offered Thorgrim the warmest smile he had ever seen. Her radiant blue eyes twinkled as she smiled.

She pointed to a set of large doors at the far side of the room. "When you're finished in the Museum, the main library is through those doors over there."

"Thankee, Ruby."

Thorgrim adjusted his eyepatch and surveyed the Museum, which was a rectangular room about forty feet wide and thirty feet in depth. The Museum contained smaller versions of the statues that were on display outside, as well as other works of art that were sitting on pedestals or hanging on the walls. The floor was a checkered pattern of gold and silver tiles, while the walls and flat ceiling were finished in white oak. Having only a few narrow slits for windows, the place was illuminated by multitudes of candles and torches, all hanging on wall sconces, and a few small chandeliers.

Though the desire to see the collection of books and meet with the head librarian was overwhelming, Thorgrim appreciated all forms of art and managed to control his emotions long enough to examine a couple of the statues.

The first statue he encountered was that of the great scientist, Charles Dwarvin. The stone statue was of an older, balding dwarf with a medium length beard. On the statue's base was a small name plaque that read: 'Charles Dwarvin, scientist. 1809-1882.'

"Charles Dwarvin believed that dwarves are the descendants of a short, prehistoric ape-like creature," commented the same, soft female voice.

Thorgrim, unaware that Ruby had been standing behind him, was startled with she spoke.

"Oh! I didn't know you were behind me," he said, his face slightly flushed.

"Sorry! I didn't mean to surprise you, sir. I'm in charge of the library's museum. I hope you don't mind, but I'm supposed to walk around and discuss the artwork or answer any questions regarding them. Kinda boring, really."

"That's okay. I appreciate you sharing yer knowledge . . . uh, you said yer name is Ruby?"

She batted her lashes. "Yes, that's right."

He smiled. "Nice to meet you, Ruby. Muh name is, uh . . . Shem."

Ruby returned the smile. "And, it's nice to meet you, Shem."

A flash of light caused him to shield his lone eye. The silver heart charm, that Ruby was wearing, reflected a bright light from a nearby set of candles.

She noticed and covered her charm. "Sorry about that. This charm is like a mirror."

"Yer heart charm is beautiful."

Ruby looked down and touched it. "Thank you. My father gave it to me the day I was born."

"That was nice of him. I'm sure it's very special to you."

"Oh, yes. It's my most treasured possession."

Turning back to the statue of Charles Dwarvin, Thorgrim crumpled his brow a bit. "Ruby, ya said that this guy believed that we came from apes?"

She nodded. "Yes, in fact, his proposition is that all species of life have descended over time from common ancestors."

"I remember learnin' somethin' about Charles Dwarvin in high school," he replied. "Apes, huh? Well, there's an old sayin' that I just made up. Better to come from apes than elves!"

Ruby whispered, "You know, Shem, not all elves are bad. There are certain types of elves who are actually very good people. I even know a few of them."

"I was always taught to not trust any elf, because of the war and all. I mean, they stole the hammer. When I leave here today, I'm heading over to the Grand Hall to see where it had been displayed."

"But not all elves should be held accountable," she replied softly. "The grey elves are to blame for the theft of the hammer and other crimes. They are the ones who snuck into the Grand Hall and stole the Aurumsmiter Hammer. Worse, a week later, hundreds of greys infiltrated our border, killing people and stealing gold to fund their civil war against the Alacarjian Queen. As you know, the Dwarven Clans declared war soon after."

"The Great War," said Thorgrim.

She nodded. "Yes. A terrible bloodbath. No prisoners were taken."

"I guess to me, an elf is an elf," he commented. "I was taught that an elf is not to be trusted."

"I'm sorry you feel that way. The wood elves from Sherduin are honorable. So are the moon elves. Remember, that during the Elven Civil War, the grey elves tried to overthrow the Alacarjian Queen. She was a moon elf, a close relative of the wood elves, so it's of no surprise that the wood elves fought against the greys."

He nodded.

Ruby continued, "Well, the wood elves helped us fight against the grey-skins. The terrible thing is that the greys were once among the kindest of all elves until the dark elves of the deep woods corrupted them. Some say the dark elves used a magic spell to turn all grey elves evil."

"A magic spell? Ruby, do you believe in magic? I don't mean the kind where someone pulls a possum out of a hat. I'm talkin' about real magic."

"You mean arcane magic," she asked, twirling her hair. "Like magic wands, spells and enchantments?"

"Yes."

For the past few days, Thorgrim had been telling people that he was almost forty years old. Now, he believed that the change in his appearance helped his ruse by making him appear a bit older and thus more experienced. He thought it was a good time for a test.

Chuckling, he continued, "Oh, I've heard plenty of stories about wizards and sorcery. But, in muh forty years of livin', I've never seen anyone hurling fireballs from a so-called magic wand." He finished with a big smile.

Smiling softly, she replied, "I can't say that I've ever seen real magic either, but I see it in your smile and I like it."

"There's magic in my smile?" he replied shyly.

"Yes. Please, don't take this wrong, but has anyone ever told you that you have a wonderful smile?"

No one had ever said something like that to Thorgrim before in his entire life. He was speechless and his cheeks turned a shade of pink.

Ruby, realizing that her comment may have embarrassed him, took a step back. "Oh, I'm sorry. I don't know why I said that! How unprofessional of me. I didn't mean to embarrass you, and I don't want you to think that I . . ."

He quickly recovered and said, "Oh, it's okay and thankee for the compliment. That was very nice of you."

"You're welcome, Shem," she said, her eyes twinkling like diamonds.

"Ruby, I'm very impressed with yer knowledge of our history. You see, history is sort of a favorite subject of mine. I assume that because you have access to all of the books in this library, you've done a lot of reading."

"Yes, and I also have a degree in history from the university here in Bur Dhulgren."

He raised his brow, saying excitedly, "A degree!"

Although he hated lying to anyone, especially this young, pretty redhead (she was actually five years older than he was), he had no choice but to do so.

"Unfortunately, my family couldn't afford to send me to a university. So, right out of high school, I started working in the mines for my obligated twenty years of service."

Several other dwarves, who were milling around in the Museum, overheard Thorgrim. Embarrassing him even further, a bunch of them thanked him for his service as a miner, and a few even applauded.

"Yes, thank you for your service in the mines," said Ruby. "Twenty years is a very long time."

Forced to lie in order to protect his identity, he was still riddled with guilt by pretending to be a veteran miner. Unable to look anyone in the eyes, he replied, "Sure, of course, you're very welcome."

Thankfully, Ruby changed the subject.

She asked, "What brings you to the library today? Have you ever been here before?"

"No, never been here before. I came here to see this massive library because I come from a small town, and the library there is tiny compared to this one. Maybe only a few hundred books there and I've read most of them. Sadly, very few history books to read, but I loved the classics."

"We have probably fifty thousand books here."

Thorgrim tried to envision what fifty thousand books, all sorted neatly on shelves, might look like.

His lone eye widened. "Fifty thousand books? That's unbelievable. I can't wait to see them."

"As I said earlier, when you're finished in the Museum, you'll find those books in the main library right through those doors," Ruby replied, pointing again to a set of double doors on the other side of the room.

"I'm lookin' forward to it, thankee!"

"Would you like to move on to another exhibit?" she asked, gesturing with a slender hand.

Thorgrim nodded and walked over to the next statue.

"Who is this?

"That's the famous author, Mark Caboose."

Thorgrim's single eye became as big as a coin.

He joyfully announced, "He's the author of one of my all-time favorite books! The Adventures of Huckleberry Dwarf!"

He read the small plaque that sat in front of the statue.

'Mark Caboose, author. 1835-1910.' Quote by Mark Caboose: 'Never tell the truth to people who are not worthy of it.'

Thorgrim read the quote again and thought, *Lately, I don't ever seem to tell the truth to anyone, worthy or not.*

Shame was written all over his face and Ruby noticed it.

"Are you okay, Shem?"

Thorgrim sighed. "Yes, I'm fine, thankee. I suppose I better get into the library and look around. And also, I have to meet with Gertrude, the head librarian. Do ya know where I might find her?"

"Yes. Gertrude has an office behind the main circulation desk. You can't miss it."

"Nice to meet you again, Ruby, and thankee for the brief tour!" he said, with a sparkle in his eye.

Her eyes sparkled in return.

Thorgrim took two steps towards the big double doors that led to the main library. A hand grasped his arm, surprising him.

"Shem, I didn't want to say anything earlier but, I think you should know that—"

Thorgrim interrupted her and offered another magical smile. "Let me guess, there's a cat living in muh beard?"

Ruby snickered and twirled her curly, red beard. "No! I wanted to tell you that I find your eyepatch exciting. My father wears one sort of like yours." She blushed again. "Oh, maybe you don't want to talk about it, I'm sorry, I shouldn't have mentioned it."

Although Thorgrim knew Uuno Kanto would advise against it, he flipped up the eyepatch, revealing his other eye.

"Shhhh. Don't tell anyone! I only wear the patch because it looks cool."

Ruby batted her eyelashes. Giggling, she said, "Your secret is safe with me."

Thorgrim sensed a genuine attraction for Ruby. Although he had a few girlfriends in high school, he had no experience with adult women. *She's cute. But with this disguise, she can't possibly be attracted to me.*

Thorgrim was wrong.

He gave her a quick nod and again started towards the library doors. Just as he reached them, as before, Ruby grabbed his arm.

Giggling again, she said, "Sorry to keep bothering you, but, did I hear you say that you have a cat living in your beard?"

"Yes, I do as a matter of fact. Look in the middle of my beard. Do you see him?"

Ruby looked. After a moment, she said, "Oh, my gosh, I can't believe it. Yes. A tiny kitten. I can see its big orange eyes staring at me."

"It's muh battle panther," he said, winking with his one eye. "A real ferocious beast, let me tell ya!"

Blinky poked his head out and meowed.

"Blinky, meet Ruby."

Ruby gasped and brought her hands to her mouth. She exclaimed, "When the day finally comes when I can say that I've seen it all, I know that I will be telling the truth."

Thorgrim laughed and as he turned to open one of the doors, he thought, *I hope that one day, I'll be able to tell the truth, too.*

He paused, took a deep breath, and opened the door. Taking a few steps into the main library, he stopped dead in his tracks, stunned, staring in silent wonderment of what was before him.

The last thing Thorgrim remembered was seeing endless rows of twenty-foot tall bookshelves all stocked to the top with countless books and scrolls . . . then the room began to spin.

***

"Oh my! What happened to this poor dwarf?" cried an older female halfling.

"He fainted, I think," replied a male dwarf.

The female halfling exclaimed, "Well, for crying out loud, can someone throw some water on his face?"

"Yes, hurry. He's blocking the doors," said another.

Someone threw a glass of cold water on Thorgrim's face.

When he awoke a moment later, groggy, he was partially lying on his backpack, his face was wet, and so was Blinky, who was not too pleased. The kitten had fled the beard when the splash of water landed and was now standing next to Thorgrim, shaking his fur, trying to dry off.

"Where'd the kitten come from?" asked one of the librarians. "Is that one of ours?"

Ruby gently picked up Blinky, helping to dry him off with a fresh, dusting towel. She said, "This kitten belongs to the man on the floor."

258

A second splash of cold water thrown on Thorgrim's face completely revived him. He opened his eyes and sat straight up. When he realized that he had fainted, humiliated he tried to apologize.

"I'm sorry! I don't know what happened. I saw all of those books, and I guess I just lost it."

Ruby handed Thorgrim his kitten and said gently, "Are you okay, Shem?"

"Yes, I'm fine. I just—"

"No need to explain. You gave everyone quite a fright, though."

Slipping Blinky back inside his beard, he replied, "I'm so sorry."

"Shem, it's okay. Do you think you can manage from here?"

"Yes, I think so."

Ruby was about to help him to his feet when the head librarian, Gertrude Fizzlewhooper, approached.

"Ruby, what's going on here? Does this gentleman need a doctor?"

"No, Mrs. Fizzlewhooper, he's okay now. He's just overly excited about visiting the library, that's all."

With Ruby's aid, Thorgrim finally managed to get to his feet. "Yes, I'm fine. I'm sorry again, but visiting this library has been a life-long dream of mine. I just let the excitement get the best of me."

Gertrude laughed, causing her red beard to shake. "Well, I used to get excited about this place, too, until I found out I had to dust and keep track of all of these damn books."

Thorgrim looked around again and could not believe his eyes. The area of the room was over six thousand square feet. Most of the nearly eighty-foot long walls had shelves full of books. The center of the room contained plenty of tables and chairs available for anyone who wanted to study. It was a bibliophile's paradise.

Gertrude said, "So, are you okay then? I've got work to do. Ruby, keep an eye on him and if he faints again, take him outside and call a doctor. He's causing quite a disturbance with the visitors."

Ruby beamed. "I'll be happy to take care of him."

Gertrude raised her brows and said, "I'm sure you will."

Thorgrim, on a hunch, said, "Excuse me, does yer name happen to be Gertrude?"

"Yes," Gertrude replied. Her cat-eye glasses slipped from her nose and hung by the thin chain that was around her neck. "Why do you ask?"

"Uuno Kanto sent me to see you."

Ruby uttered a slight gasp.

Gertrude stared, pursed her lips but said nothing. Finally, after several seconds, she raised the corner of her manicured eyebrow, sneered, and replied, "Oh, is that right? Ruby, I'll take it from here. You better get back in the Museum."

Ruby nodded and said, "Bye, Shem. I hope you'll be okay."

"I'll be okay. Bye, Ruby."

Ruby offered Thorgrim a quick wink, then left to tend to the Museum.

Gertrude spun around. "Follow me, sir. My office is this way."

Her long skirt flowed behind her as she led the way to her office. Thorgrim, with his kitten in his beard, followed close behind. Occasionally, he stumbled over his own feet because he was busy gazing at all the books instead of watching where he was going.

The inside of the main library was flooded with light. Not from the few candles that burned but rather from the massive, overhead glass skydome.

He said to Gertrude, "From the outside, the library looks like a two-story building. But it's only one story?"

Reaching the door to her office, Gertrude opened it and gestured for Thorgrim to enter.

She replied in a firm voice that reminded him of his arrogant and sometimes angry, high school teacher back in Vog.

"If you count the skylight dome, it's two. Come right in here, please."

It was obvious to him that Gertrude was not happy that Uuno had sent him, though he had no idea why. Excited, though apprehensive, he waited for her to talk about the weather in the Brimger Valley as Uuno told him she would do.

Gertrude's office was rather stuffy and small at ten feet by twelve feet. The room had a desk stacked with several thick books, a couple of chairs, and a few framed paintings. Several burning candles mounted on wall sconces provided the only light.

"Sit there, please," Gertrude sternly said, pointing to the chair in front of her desk.

He nervously complied.

Pushing a few books away, she sat on the edge of her desk, looked at him with a deep scowl and said, "So, uh, what is yer name?"

"Shem Lybree," he replied, still not liking the heavy tone of her voice.

"Okay, what can I do for you, Mr. Lybree?"

Hesitating, he replied, "Well, like I said, Uuno Kanto sent me to see you and—"

"Oh, is that right?"

He blinked a few times before replying, "Uh, I think you already said that earlier."

"Yes, I did."

Thorgrim felt extremely uncomfortable. The room seemed to be getting smaller and warmer the longer he sat in front of Gertrude's desk. Her eyes seemed to burn right through him. Beads of sweat appearing on his forehead rolled down his face and onto his beard.

She uttered a long sigh. "Let's see . . . I'm supposed to talk about the weather in the Brimger Valley, and then you're supposed to come back with something witty about a one-eyed dwarf king?"

Thorgrim, not knowing where this was heading, slowly nodded.

"Well, Mr. Lybree I can also guess that you're looking for a job here at the library?"

He swallowed hard and nodded again.

"If I may ask, what kind of experience do you have with books?"

He raised his monobrow and replied, "I like to read 'em."

"That's it?" she said, tapping her foot, and twirling her beard.

"Ya, I do love books, though." Thorgrim became excited. "If you can hire me, I promise, I will take good care of the customers and of course the books! I'll protect them with muh very life!"

"We don't call them customers, they're called visitors."

His excitement intensified. Rising from his chair, he said, "Okay, I'll take good care of the visitors, and like I said, I'll protect the books with muh very life! If the place ever caught on fire, I would run in here and risk muh beard to save every last book. Not only that, I'd—"

"You're hired," she yelled, trying to talk over Thorgrim's excited yapping.

Out of breath, Thorgrim dropped back in his chair. Blinky, curious about all of the commotion, stuck his head out to see what was happening.

Almost speechless, unable to believe his own ears, he managed to whisper, "I'm hired?"

"Yes. But you won't be on the main floor . . . at least not until you prove yerself and yer trained. You'll be working in the garderobe that's for sure. You'll also be spending time in the basement, cataloging books that have been donated. And there are boxes and boxes of them."

Excited again, he stood. "Okay, whatever you say! Can I ask, how much does it pay?"

"You'll start out at one gold per week. If you can prove yerself, I'll double it. If you can make it to the main floor, you could make three gold in a week."

"Oh, I can't thank you enough! You have no idea, but this is a dream come true for me."

"Working in a musty library is a dream come true? Sorry, but I can't imagine. Yer shift is five days a week starting tomorrow. The hours are nine to five. Don't be late!"

Thorgrim could not believe that, thanks to Uuno Kanto, he had landed a job in a library that had over fifty thousand books. Choking back a few tears, he managed another, "Thankee."

She pointed to his beard. "Uh, and that cat in your beard thing that you've got going on there. I'm not sure it's a good idea."

"I promise, Blinky won't be any trouble."

"Well, we'll give it a try, but if there's a problem, you'll have to keep him at home. We have enough cats here already. I swear, every time I turn around, there's another one."

Gertrude rose from her desk and started towards her door. "I've work to do. Feel free to explore the library. Just try not to faint again, please."

Thorgrim followed behind her like a zombie. Numbed by the fact that he was now an employee of the second largest library in the entire realm.

Gertrude opened her office door but stopped him when he was about to exit.

Again, using a stern tone, she said, "Oh, one more thing. I'm just guessing, and I can't imagine why, but I think Ruby likes you."

"Well, I like her, too."

"No. I mean she **likes** you. I can see it in her eyes and hear it in her voice. Do you understand?"

Thorgrim understood and blushed. "Well, I' guess so, but—"

She squinted. "But, nothing. Not only do I not allow employees to date, I certainly won't allow you to date my daughter, whether you work here or not. No offense of course."

He stumbled back a step. "Ruby's yer daughter?"

"Yes."

"But, she addressed you by yer last name."

"We're all business here. So don't forget that or what I said about dating my daughter, or fainting spells will be the least of yer problems. She's off-limits . . . end of story."

"Oh, Mrs. Fizzlewhooper, I promise that you'll have nothin' to worry about."

Glaring over her cat-eye glasses, she replied darkly. "Let's hope so."

Exiting the office, he turned, reached out to shake Gertrude's hand and said, "I can't thank you enough for this opportunity. Like I said, it's a dream come true! I just can't believe it!"

Sticking her head out of the office, Gertrude said heavily, "Trust me, I can't believe it either. But don't thank me, thank my ex-husband."

"Who's yer ex-husband?" asked Thorgrim naïve and puzzled.

"Uuno Kanto," she replied gloomily.

He said, "But, yer last name is Fizzlewhooper."

Closing her door, she said, "I remarried."

He frowned and stared at the closed office door. He thought, *I wonder if Uuno is Ruby's father? Hmm, well, marriage sure sounds like a big pain. I'm never gonna get married. May muh beard fall off if I ever do!*

Turning, he again looked into the face of the second greatest collection of books the realm had ever seen. Taking a deep breath, thrilled, he quickly walked towards the closest trove of volumes.

∗∗∗

For the next six hours, Thorgrim sat at a table, though no one could see him, because he was completely hidden behind several towering piles of books. A few lay open, bookmarked with a small piece of paper. Sometimes, he would jump up and probe several shelves until he found what he was looking for. Then, with the new book in his hands, he would return to his desk and continue reading.

Thorgrim had a bad habit of reading aloud, and several times the librarian on duty and others chastised him for the disturbances. After an apology and slightly embarrassed, he would return to his reading, making every effort to do so, quietly. Unfortunately, he would soon forget himself and the process would repeat. Thorgrim was finally cured when he was threatened with eviction unless he could control himself.

Twice, during that time, Thorgrim had to stop reading to take Blinky outside to do his number. Of course, Ruby tried her best to catch Thorgrim's attention as he came and went through the Museum. Though he would have loved to visit with Ruby, he was worried about Gertrude's warning regarding her daughter. Therefore, instead, he only offered her a friendly wave as he passed through.

Much to the chagrin of the library staff, Blinky happily made his deposit in the garden next to the walkway, unearthing a few flowers as he finished.

During Blinky's escapades in the flower garden, Thorgrim was able to check on his horse. Both times, he found Nugget fast asleep with a full belly of hay. While returning from his second trip outside, he checked his timepiece. It read 3:25 p.m.

263

As he approached the library entrance, he glanced across the street at the Grand Hall. The many horses and carriages parked in front of the complex meant that it was a popular attraction. Though he could only guess, he suspected that it closed around the same time as the library at 5:00 p.m. Despite having a lot of fun with the books, he decided it was time to leave and visit the Grand Hall of the Dwarves.

Once back inside the library (after an awkward exchange of smiles with Ruby as he transited the Museum), Thorgrim hurriedly replaced the four dozen books he had removed from the shelves and then approached the circulation desk.

"Hi, my name is Shem. I'm leaving now, but will you please let Mrs. Fizzlewhooper know that I appreciate her hiring me? Tell her that I'll be here first thing in the morning."

The surprised librarian, a young blonde girl said, "You're working here?"

Thorgrim was ecstatic when he answered. "Yes! Isn't it amazin'?"

The librarian shrugged. "Uh, I guess so. You seem very excited. Well, congratulations, and we'll see you tomorrow."

"I can't begin to tell you how excited I am. First, I get hired to work in this incredible library, and now I'm on my way over to see the Grand Hall of the Dwarves!"

She shrugged again. "Have fun, sir."

"I will! Oh, by the way, when I was looking through some of those magnificent books, I found a signed, first edition copy of Moby Dwarf. It's probably worth a fortune. I would pull it and put it in yer rare book section, under lock and key, if I were you."

The librarian's jaw dropped.

Thorgrim smiled and went for the doors. Before leaving, he glanced around looking at all the books one more time. Taking a deep sigh he opened one of the doors and then ran straight into Ruby, who was about to enter the library from the other side.

Standing almost nose to nose with Thorgrim, she said, "Oh! I'm sorry, Shem! I was just coming in to take a break. It's been a long day. When we only have a few visitors, the day seems to take forever, you know."

Being this close to Ruby caused Thorgrim to blush. Surprised by her sudden appearance, he said, "Oh, hi Ruby, nice to see you again. I'm on my way over to visit the Grand Hall. Ummm, I'm sure the day drags from time to time. I may have to get used to that. Did you know that I work here now?"

"You do! My mother hired you?"

"Yes," he replied excitedly.

"She never said a word, although she did say that there was something she wanted to talk to me about later. She's probably going to tell me she hired you."

"Could be," he replied, in a slightly depressed tone, suspecting that her mother wanted to warn her to stay away from him. However, Thorgrim still found it difficult that this pretty girl might be attracted to him.

She continued, "We have not had much luck with new hires, but I'm sure you'll be the exception. Congratulations!" Then she whispered, "No worries, I won't breathe a word about your fake eyepatch."

Nodding, he said, "Thankee. You know, I was surprised when Gertrude told me she was yer mother."

"I'm sure you were surprised. I'm sorry, I should have told you, but I didn't really have a chance."

"That's okay, Ruby."

"When we're at work, I don't call her mother. It might make everyone else feel awkward. My mother would not want other employees to think she would show me any favoritism. In fact, she's probably stricter with me than she is with anyone else!"

"I do understand. Well, thanks again for helpin' me earlier. I'm still kinda embarrassed about faintin'."

"No, don't worry about it. I'm just glad that you're fine."

"Again, many thanks for your help," he said, gently smiling. "Uh, I suppose I better get goin'."

Wearing a mischievous expression, Ruby would not move out of the way, though it was obvious Thorgrim was trying to leave. He could open up the other door and try to go that way but felt it might seem rude.

Somewhat embarrassed, he said politely, "Excuse me, Ruby, I'd like to stay and visit, but I've really got to get going. I want to get over to the Grand Hall before they close."

"Oh, sure! I'm sorry," she replied, her cheeks painted with a hint of pink.

As she did a half step to her left, Thorgrim stepped to his right. Ruby smiled and responded by stepping to her right, but he was already heading that way. They danced back and forth a few times until both of them laughed.

Then he heard the unmistakable shrill sound of Gertrude's voice as she approached.

"Ruby!"

He anxiously said, "Ruby, I've got to go."

Ruby stepped away, and as Thorgrim slipped by her, she managed to plant a big kiss on his cheek.

He was numb from head to toe. The next thing he knew was that he was sitting on top of Nugget in the middle of the entrance grounds of the Grand Hall of the Dwarves complex.

Thorgrim had no recollection of leaving the library, let alone having mounted and then ridden a horse across a busy street.

The spot on his cheek where she landed her kiss, tingled.

***

Meanwhile, over a hundred miles away in Vog . . .

Luthor was exhausted both emotionally and physically. A rarity, he left work early, complaining about a migraine headache. Arriving home three hours before his usual time, he surprised his wife, while she was in the middle of doing her afternoon housekeeping.

Marjorie dropped her duster. "Luthor! Oh, you startled me! What are you doing home so early?"

His brow furrowed deeply, Luthor approached his wife. "Where are da kids? I don't want dem to hear dis."

Luthor was heavily clipping his words, so Marjorie knew her husband was extremely upset about something.

"Out in the backyard playing," she said nervously. "Should I sit down? What's wrong? Please, don't tell me they caught Thorgrim."

"No, dey don't even know he's missin', yet."

Luthor handed her Dr. Thacker's note regarding Thorgrim's condition.

Frightened, his wife asked him a series of questions, "Did they read this? What did they say? They don't believe it, do they."

Luthor placed his pickaxe in the corner of the room and set his lunchbox on the counter. He said, "Yes, dey read it. And yes, dey believed it. What's not to believe? Everything Dr. Thacker wrote in da note is true. Da only thing we are not tellin' dem is dat our son left town five days ago to flee da country."

Panicked, she fired another barrage of questions. "What's going to happen? Why are you upset then? They said something I don't want to hear, didn't they. Tell me, please."

He managed a quick smile. "You can read me like Thorgrim reads one of his books, can't you, Margie."

266

Sitting down in his favorite chair, Luthor tugged hard on his beard and said, "Dey appreciated da note, but considerin' Thorgrim's unacceptable attendance record, dey want a second opinion regardin' his condition. Dey are sending a company doctor tomorrow at noon to see Thorgrim."

She gasped. "What? But he's not here! What are we going to say when that doctor arrives?"

"I don't know. Now you know why I'm home early. I've been worried sick about dis all day."

"Luthor, when they find out the truth—"

"By da time they find out anything, Thorgrim will have six or seven day's head start on dem. Hopefully, he'll be far out of da country by da time da authorities can react."

She started to sob. "We'll never see him again, will we."

Playing tag, Thurston and two of the younger kids came racing through the back door but stopped when they saw that their mother was crying.

"What's wrong, Mama?" asked Thurston.

Calming himself, Luthor took a deep breath and said, "She's fine. Now, Thurston, you go back outside and take those two with ya. Please, stay outside until yer called, okay? Tell da rest of 'em the same thing."

"Okay, Papa," replied Thurston.

After his son left with his two siblings, Luthor continued. "Margie, we've discussed dis. It breaks muh heart too! But, it is what it is."

Still sobbing, she nodded her head. "I know, but I miss him so much."

"My own father once told me to always appreciate what you have in da moment. You never know when da moment will end. Nothin' stays as it is. Nothin' lasts forever. Things change and we have to accept it. But, never say never. I believe in muh heart that one day, we'll see him again."

In a shuddering voice, she said, "Will you be here tomorrow when that company doctor arrives?"

He put his arm around her. "I will. I would never let you face that alone. The Vog Silver Mine will do fine without me . . . at least for a day."

She suddenly had an idea. "When that doctor comes tomorrow, we can say Thorgrim went out for a walk, but we don't know where!"

Luthor raised his brow and slowly shook his head. "Good idea, but I'm afraid it won't work. The company made it very clear that Thorgrim is to be made available tomorrow at noon. If he's not here, he'll be officially charged with avoiding service. I already think they suspect somethin'."

Marjorie dropped her head, tears still falling.

Luthor took a deep breath. "We have no options. We can't tell any lies. Well, unfortunately, I guess we'll have to tell a partial lie. When the company doctor comes tomorrow, we'll tell him that when Thorgrim heard he was comin', he panicked and fled sometime in the mornin'. We just don't know where he went."

He gave his wife a big hug and held on to her.

She trembled. "There's nothing else we can say?"

"No," he replied, grimly. "And Moridon help us if they ever find out that Thorgrim really left five days ago. They might hang us out to dry."

XIII.   The Grand Hall of the Dwarves

The area in front of the Grand Hall of the Dwarves was packed with people and horses, some coming and some going. Even during the workweek, the Grand Hall was bristling with visitors from all parts of the realm. Even humans from as far away as the Theocracy of the Abbir have made the long, arduous trip to see the famous historical museum.

Although on a larger scale, the entrance grounds were laid out much like the Supreme Library, having plentiful hitching posts, several watering troughs, and fresh hay available for the horses.

Thorgrim was astounded by the sheer size of the complex. Beautiful water fountains and towering stone columns flanked the two hundred foot long, forty-foot wide, polished marble, entrance walkway.

The museum buildings were divided into four sections. The main entrance had a quadruple set of solid oak doors that opened into a sixty-foot wide, candlelit, windowless foyer called the Welcome Center. Here, a tour guide would greet visitors. At no charge, the guide would lead groups of up to twenty-four people through the entire complex, answering questions or telling stories about the exhibits and artifacts.

The Welcome Center led to the first of three rooms that were called 'halls.' Each hall was one hundred feet long, twenty-five feet wide and twenty feet high. The halls were candlelit and windowless, with the exception of a five-foot-wide skylight that ran the length of the room. The three halls were connected to each other in a zigzag pattern and if viewed overhead, would look like a three hundred foot long lightning bolt.

Each hall had a unique name. The first was called the 'Hall of Tears,' the second, the 'Hall of Heroes' and the third, the end of the lightning bolt pattern, was called the 'Hall of History.'

The Hall of History was connected to the main structure and namesake of the entire complex: the Grand Hall. The Grand Hall was a massive, two hundred foot in diameter, sixty-foot tall, star-shaped building, topped with a pointed, multicolored, art glass skylight. With the exception of the skylight, the Grand Hall was windowless with an exit door at the far end.

Originally, the complex consisted of only the Hall of History and the Grand Hall, but after the Great War, two more halls were added and a Welcome Center built.

Soon, Thorgrim would see for himself why Dr. Thacker had said, 'When yer in the Grand Hall, be sure you spend a lot of time in the Hall of Tears. What you'll see in there will shock you.'

***

Thorgrim, still disgusted that he could not consistently mount or dismount Nugget without a disaster occurring, had accepted that it was a fact of life and decided to stop worrying about being embarrassed.

Earlier, when he had tried to dismount Nugget, one of his boots became entangled in a stirrup. Hanging upside down, Thorgrim struggled briefly and then fell on his head. Some people, who were walking towards the entrance to the Welcome Center at the time, witnessed the incident and howled with laughter.

Once Thorgrim had entered the Welcome Center, he found several people still chuckling about his dismounting debacle. Ignoring them, he was adjusting his eyepatch, when someone wearing a silver and gold jumpsuit approached.

"Sir, my goodness. I hope that when ya fell off that giant horse of yers out there, you were not badly injured," said an elderly dwarf, one of the Grand Hall tour guides. "I happened to be outside getting some fresh air when I saw what happened! My, that was quite a fall! Are ya sure yer okay there, young man? Ya landed right on yer noggin!"

"I'm fine. Uh, muh timepiece says it's ten minutes to four. God forbid, but is it too late to see the place?"

The guide waved his hand and said, "Oh, there's lots of time. We stop taking visitors for tours at four in the afternoon. We officially close at five and ask that all visitors leave the complex by six. We're assembling a group for a formal tour now if you want to wait a few minutes, or you can go ahead on your own and explore. There are plenty of placards in each hall that provide information about everything here."

While the tour guide was talking, Thorgrim ruffled though his backpack, pulled out, and then bit off a piece of sausage. While chasing the meat with a big swig from a water flask, he glanced around at the rest of the visitors, several of whom were still laughing about his mishap.

Miffed, Thorgrim said, "Thank you for the offer to join the group tour, but I think I'll do this on muh own."

"Certainly. If you have any questions, feel free to ask any of the other employees here. Ya can't miss 'em. They're all wearing the same silly-lookin' silver and gold jumper that I'm wearin'."

Thorgrim replied, "Thank you, again, Mister, uh . . ." Thorgrim leaned over to read the older dwarf's nametag. It read 'Thorgrim.'

"Yer name tag says, Thorgrim." he said, somewhat stunned.

"Yes, sir."

"Why, that's muh name!" Thorgrim, realizing his mistake, caught himself and began to stammer. "I mean, that's muh name of a good friend of mine. . . I mean that's **the** name of a good friend of mine!" Thorgrim turned red. "Sorry, sometimes the words just don't come out right."

The old tour guide smiled. "That's okay, youngster! No need to be embarrassed. I'm a hundred and seventy-nine years old. When you get to be muh age, nuthin' ever comes out right. The good thing is that you'll forget it happened a minute later and won't remember being embarrassed about it either!"

Thorgrim was still studying the guide's nametag when a strange thought crossed his mind. Raising his monobrow, he said, "Wait, just curious. What's yer last name?"

Dreading that the old dwarf's last name was, by some strange coincidence, Longbeard, Thorgrim held his breath.

"It's a pity, but muh last name is Shortbeard!"

Thorgrim's jaw dropped. "Shortbeard? Tell me yer kiddin'?"

"Nope, wish I was. A pathetic last name for a dwarf, don't ya think?"

Thorgrim was practically speechless.

The old dwarf leaned closer and said, "Ya said yer friend's name was Thorgrim? What's **his** last name?"

Thorgrim's head felt like it was in a vice. "It's Longbeard . . . oh, uh, I meant to say Lybree. Uh, I mean, uh, his last name is . . . Knucklehead. Ya, that's it, Thorgrim Knucklehead. He's a good friend, but a real idiot sometimes, trust me."

"Really? Ha! Thorgrim Knucklehead . . . now that name sucks a mud malt if ya ask me! Now I don't feel so bad 'bout muh last name!"

An arrogant voice shouted, "Hey, old man, are you going to take us on a tour of this place, or would you rather spend all day chatting with Mr. Graceful Dwarf?"

The comment caused a wave of laughter from the rest of the group.

Thorgrim, doing his best to ignore them, fumed inside.

Mr. Shortbeard continued, "Well, looks like the group is ready for me, but I've got to use the garderobe, first. Dang prostate givin' me the fits today! Have fun exploring the museum! Oh, hey, did ya know that ya got a cat in yer beard?"

Thorgrim shook his head, "No, I didn't know that, but thanks."

271

As Mr. Shortbeard hurriedly walked to a door marked 'Public Garderobe', Thorgrim turned and walked past the waiting group of visitors; a mixture of about twenty dwarves, halflings and togglins. As he went by them, several snickered.

Then Thorgrim remembered what Uuno told him about one-eyed dwarves. Stopping, Thorgrim turned and stared straight at the group. The group, still gossiping, looked back at Thorgrim.

Thorgrim curled his lip and gave them his best, one-eyed glare.

The group, now intimidated by the eyepatch-wearing dwarf, became very quiet. Some of them shifted their feet and looked away.

"What's so funny?" asked Thorgrim heavily.

Reaching up, he grabbed the flap of his eyepatch. "Hey! Want to see something really funny? How many of you would like to see me flip this eyepatch up so you can see the big, black, bloody hole where muh eyeball used to be? Hahahohahoha! How about a show of hands?"

The group was stunned.

Thorgrim grinned. "Well, looks like the ayes have it! No pun intended! Here goes, take a good look!"

Thorgrim grabbed his eyepatch and started to lift it up.

Several cried out, "No, no, please! We're sorry!"

Thorgrim yelled, "Too late! Look really close! You can see my brain in the socket!"

Several of them fainted flat on the floor, and a handful of the others beat it to the exit, running at full speed for their horses.

Nodding, Thorgrim said to the remainder, "Just kiddin' Have a good day, then!"

The rest, aghast and speechless, looked like zombies. Several of them were busy trying to revive those that had fainted.

Thorgrim cursed himself for risking an incident with the crowd, which could have escalated into a fight, which in turn, could have gotten the police involved. Vowing to be smarter until he received his ID papers, he was satisfied. For the first time, he was proud of his eyepatch.

Looking ahead, Thorgrim saw a set of double doors. Above the doors was a sign that read: 'The Hall of Tears.' Grinning because of the incident in the Welcome Center, he exited the room, then entered the Hall of Tears.

Once inside the first hall, Thorgrim paused. "The Hall of Tears," he mumbled. "This was the place Dr. Thacker told me to make sure I visited. Hmmm. Wonder why they call it the Hall of Tears?"

Thorgrim looked down a straight, empty hallway. At the end, a hundred feet away, stood a single door. The hall was constructed of finely polished blocks of white marble, quarried from the Mountains of the Ancients. It was brightly lit by a hundred white candles that were mounted on wall sconces. The room was comfortable and likely cooled by a dry ice system similar to the one used in the Pretzel Brewery and Inn.

The floor was richly carpeted in a checkerboard pattern of alternating silver and gold squares. Looking up at the ceiling, he saw light from the afternoon sun shining through the skylight.

A large placard sitting on a wooden stand, read:

The Hall of Tears

In remembrance of the innocents who were killed
during the Great War with the Grey Elves, 1798-1800.
Let us never forget

The walls glimmered. Thorgrim squinted his one eye but was unable to determine what was causing the light show. Cursing under his breath, he flipped his eyepatch up and took a long look.

On both walls, from the floor to the ceiling, reflecting the flickering light of the many candles, were hundreds of gold plates. Each of them, one-foot square, had writing etched on them.

Thorgrim approached the first one on his left and read it.

'Durum Joopan, wife, Noonie, two children, Jasp and Rollo.

Thorgrim read the one below it.

'Gustov Foyt and wife, Mildred.'

Then, another one.

'Baby, unknown.'

"My God, all of these people died during the Great War?" Thorgrim said aloud.

"There's one thousand, nine hundred and six in here," said a soft female voice. "That's all they could find, anyway. Dozens were never found."

Thorgrim knew the voice. He turned around and smiled.

It was Ruby.

She continued, "All of them murdered when hundreds of grey elves crossed the border looking for gold to help finance their civil war against the moon and wood elves, in what was then called the Kingdom of Alacarj. Dozens of villages and farms were pillaged during what is known as Hell Week."

Thorgrim spoke in a whisper. "You said there's one thousand nine hundred and six in here?"

"Yes."

"What do you mean, in **here**?"

Ruby stepped up and stood beside him. "This is their tomb. All of them were cremated and brought here. Eventually, their ashes were poured into the blocks of marble that make up this hall. Now, you know why it's called the Hall of Tears. This hall and the next were added to the original buildings after the war."

Thorgrim grimaced. "This is a cemetery?"

"Yes."

"I was never told this in school. Never had access to any books about it either."

"It's sad but true," she replied.

Thorgrim looked at another plate. It read: 'Baby, unknown.' He looked to the right and saw that several more also said, 'unknown.'

"Unknown. Why?"

"They were either mutilated or no one was left alive to identify them."

"My God," he replied, stunned.

Thorgrim furrowed his brow so low that his flipped up eyepatch popped off and landed on the floor. Now angry, he bellowed, "Ya mean to tell me these people were murdered by a bunch of worthless, no good, god damned elves?"

Ruby nodded. "Shhh, not so loud. Grey elves, anyway. Remember, I told you that some elves are good."

Still upset, he said, "I don't care. I can't say I've ever heard of a good elf."

"I understand, but please don't be angry in here. This is a hallowed place."

Realizing that she was right, he gained control of his emotions. "Ruby, I'm sorry for yelling, and I'm also sorry for swearin' in front of a lady."

"That's okay. Shem, you really hate elves, don't you."

"Well, in truth, I've never met an elf before. Grey, wood, moon, dark or what have you. Don't know if I could tell 'em apart anyway."

Ruby bent down, picked up the eyepatch and handed it to Thorgrim.

Thorgrim put the patch in his pocket. "I can't see a thing in here with this thing on."

Hearing a commotion behind them, she said, "Hey, it sounds like there's a group of visitors coming for a tour."

Nervous he replied, "Hopefully, they're not going to kick me out of here. Let's get moving."

"Why would they kick you out?"

"Let's just say I had a little disagreement with a few of those people a while ago. I'll tell ya about it later. You know, a friend of mine told me to spend a lot of time in The Hall of Tears. I've seen enough. Get me outta here. These poor murdered victims . . . in the walls! I don't think I can read another one of those plates."

Ruby said, "I understand. Come on, Shem. Follow me."

She took Thorgrim by the hand, her little hand fitting perfectly in his and led him down to the end of the Hall of Tears. As they exited into a much smaller version of the Welcome Center, behind them, the old tour guide, Thorgrim Shortbeard, led what remained of the original group of visitors into the Hall of Tears.

Inside the new room, Thorgrim did a quick inspection.

The small candlelit foyer was empty with the exception of several benches intended for those that needed to rest. Ahead, was a large set of double doors that led to the next hall.

Above, was a sign that read: 'The Hall of Heroes.'

Ruby pointed to the doors. "This way."

Thorgrim glanced at his timepiece; it read 4:30 p.m. He said, "Ruby, it's nice to see you, but what are you doin' here? The library doesn't close until five o'clock. Aren't you supposed to be workin'?"

She smiled. "Yes, but it's kind of slow over there, so I asked my mother for the rest of the day off. I knew you were coming here, and I wanted to join you. I hope you don't mind."

"No, I don't mind. Thankee. I'm glad you came over. You've been here before, no doubt, so you can be my personal tour guide."

"I would be happy to be your tour guide," she said, batting her eyelashes. "And, yes. I've been through here several times. Once you've visited this place, it sort of grabs you and won't let go."

"The friend who told me to spend a lot of time in that last hall? He said it would shock me. He was right. After walking through there, I can really see why dwarves still hate elves, even hundreds of years after the war."

"Shem, it has been a long time ago. Almost five hundred years. Everyone from that time is long dead. I mean, what is the point in this continued hatred towards a race of people who had nothing to do with the Great War? Maybe it's time to forgive and move on and that's been long overdue."

"Maybe that's already happening. You know, they didn't tell us much about the war in school. I was really not aware of the savagery against those innocents that now reside in the Hall of Tears."

She said, "Then why do you hate elves so much?"

"I don't know. I was always taught that elves are bad. I never questioned it."

"Who taught you that?"

"My family and friends, I guess."

"Did your teachers in school claim that elves are bad people?"

"Not that I can remember. But I know my father was taught to hate them when he went to school."

"That's a shame," she said, shaking her head.

"Ruby, do you suppose that now the authorities don't want future generations to know what the elves did? Do you think that the schools no longer teach the ugly truth about the war, so we can forgive and move on, as you said?"

"It's possible. I think it's a good thing. Why teach young people to hate an entire race for something that happened almost five hundred years ago?"

"I agree, but a friend of mine once said that those who do not study history are doomed to repeat it. He was trying to teach me that if we ignore the truth of our history, cover it up, or change it, then we are likely to repeat the same mistakes of the past."

"Those are wise words, Shem."

"I'll tell my friend the next time I see him. You know, I've only seen the first hall, and I already feel very sad and angry. But angry or not, I'm still glad I came here."

She smiled warmly. "I'm grateful that you're allowing me to share this moment with you."

Pointing ahead, he said, "What is the Hall of Heroes?"

"I'll show you."

Ruby grabbed Thorgrim's hand, and as he blushed, she led the way to the next set of doors, then entered the Hall of Heroes.

As in the previous hall, a large placard sat on a wooden stand. It read:

The Hall of Heroes

In remembrance of those who faithfully served and paid the ultimate sacrifice during the Great War with the Grey Elves, 1798-1800.
Let us never forget

The second candlelit hall was nearly identical to the first one. This time, instead of gold plates on the walls, the names of the military personnel who died in action were etched into the marble. At the end of the hall were busts of the officers who also died in action during the war.

Thorgrim, ever wary of spooks, was creeped out.

"Is this also a tomb?" he whispered.

Ruby shook her head. "No. This hall honors the heroes in the Army and Navy who fell in battle during the Great War. No one is buried in this hall. They're all in the National War Cemetery.

Thorgrim looked closely at some of the etched names. "How many war deaths?"

"Over eight thousand, almost all of them from the Army. Though they're not listed here, there were thousands more wounded or missing in action."

Thorgrim was appalled. He shook his head and then followed Ruby, slowly down the hall, occasionally stopping to read some of the names. Soon, they reached the marble busts of the officers. Then Thorgrim recalled stories that his father had told him about his sixth-great grandfather, General Vog Longbeard.

Thorgrim's father had mentioned that the general's son, Otum, founder of the mining company and the town, had named both after his beloved father, Vog Longbeard. Thorgrim also recalled his father telling several bedtime stories about General Longbeard; how he had fought with distinction in the war with the elves but was killed in action when he engaged a group of trolls near a place called the Troll Glade. Of course, Thorgrim did not believe in trolls and always thought his father was making it all up.

There were at least thirty marble sculptures, and Thorgrim hoped that one of the busts was that of his famous ancestor. Worried that he might be asked to leave if the group following saw him and complained about his earlier behavior, Thorgrim hurriedly tried to find General Longbeard's bust before they arrived in the hall.

Ruby said, "Who are you looking for?"

He replied, "Ever heard of General Vog Longbeard?"

277

"Yes, in fact, I have. He was a famous and brilliant general. I recall reading that he was killed in battle fighting trolls."

"Trolls? Hardly. Well, he's my sixth-great grandfather. Help me find his bust before we run out of time."

Both of them searched each bust, looking at the nameplate below it. Thorgrim exclaimed, "Ha! Look at this one. What's with all of this troll B.S.? It says, Colonel Totum Hammerstein, 1688-1800. Slayer of the troll that killed General Longbeard at the battle of Minervia, 1799.' Troll or not, it looks like Colonel Hammerstein died during the last year of the war. Where's Minervia? Never heard of it."

Ruby replied, "Minervia used to be a small town west of the Troll Glade, on the Tambi River in Alacarj. Just ruins now. The trolls wiped it off of the map, and the elves never rebuilt it."

"No such thing as a troll," he commented, still searching.

"Sure there are."

"I've never seen one."

"I have, or at least I think it was a troll. Once, when I was a little girl, my father took me to see his parents in a town called Florence. The town is on the edge of a vast woodland called the Haunted Forest."

Thorgrim, still looking through the remaining busts, mumbled, "The Haunted Forest? Doesn't sound like my kind of place."

Ruby continued, "My grandparent's hovel was on the edge of the woods, and of course I wandered into the forest with a cousin who was also visiting. We were playing, but suddenly I heard a grunting sound, and when I looked up, I saw this big green creature with red eyes watching me from behind a thick grove of trees."

Thorgrim looked at Ruby and listened, now entranced by her tale.

"It spoke to us. It said in a gruff voice something like, "Hey, you dwoves. Git outta awe home, oh we wiw wip yo awms off un eat you."

Thorgrim's eyes bugged out. "You're kiddin'. What happened after that?"

"I think I heard a couple of them, but I only saw one. We dropped our toys and froze. The thing stepped forward and growled. It was humongous; maybe over twelve feet tall. Rippling with muscle, it had long arms that hung almost to its knees."

Thorgrim raised his monobrow and dropped his jaw. Her description of the event was frightening.

Ruby continued, "I think it was about to attack us, but before it tried, my father swooped in, grabbed us both and ran as fast as he could towards the hovel."

Thorgrim whispered, "Did it follow you?"

278

"No, thank God. Of course, we got in a lot of trouble for wandering into the forest. Later, my father told me it was a troll. I'll never forget those blood-red eyes."

"Ruby, I don't doubt yer story, but if trolls are real, how come no one had never found a dead one and put it in a museum somewhere?"

She shrugged. "Maybe someone has. There are lots of museums in the realm, you know."

Despite her story, he was still skeptical. "It wasn't a troll. Maybe it was a bear or mountain gorilla, but not a troll. People claim trolls can regrow entire limbs if they're cut off. Think about how absurd that sounds."

"Shem, some reptiles can regrow tails if they lose them. Besides that, I know a bear when I see one, and what would a mountain gorilla be doing in the woods, over thirty miles from the nearest mountain?"

"I don't know, maybe he was looking for bananas?"

She giggled and playfully tugged on his beard. "It was a real live troll, I'm tellin' ya!"

Thorgrim chuckled and was about to reply, but the sound of visitors entering the Hall of Heroes, surprised him.

"Here they come again," said Ruby. "We better get moving."

He quickly checked the last two sculptures.

"Wait! Look, it's General Vog Longbeard," he said excitedly.

The white marble bust was that of a middle-aged dwarf who wore glasses. A huge pipe, with a bowl the size of an apple, jutted out of his mouth. Thorgrim quickly read the nameplate.

General Vog Longbeard, 1671-1799. Hero to all, wood elves included. General Longbeard died in action while unselfishly saving the lives of a wood elf family after a group of trolls attacked his command post in the elven town of Minervia.

"Hmmm. He actually died defending some elves," commented Thorgrim.

"See, I told you some elves are good. Apparently, your ancestor agreed."

"Yes, it would seem so."

Laughing, she said, "And it says he died fighting trolls."

Thorgrim joked, "They were probably fighting a bunch of mountain gorillas, but maybe everyone was so drunk that they only thought they were trolls."

Laughing, she said, "Shem, you're impossible!"

Thorgrim heard the group of visitors chatting. One of them said, "Hey, isn't that the eyepatch wearin' troublemaker up there?"

Worried they might confront him about the incident in the Welcome Center, Thorgrim said to Ruby, "Let's get out of here and away from these people before there's trouble.

She grabbed his hand and pulled him quickly towards the exit.

He asked, "Okay. What's the next hall?"

"The next one is called the 'Hall of History.'"

Thorgrim raised his monobrow high. "Oooh, can't wait to see that one! Let's get in there!"

Ruby led Thorgrim into another small foyer. Identical to the previous one, a pair of doors led to the third hall. Over the doors, a sign read: 'The Hall of History.'

Anxious, Thorgrim led the way through the doors and into the next hall. Again, another wooden stand held a large placard. It read:

The Hall of History

Relics from our ancient past.

This hall was identical in size and shape to the previous two, but there were no busts, paintings, drawings, or nameplates on the walls. Instead, several roped-off areas flanked both sides of the hallway. A large, rectangular stone box was on display at the far end.

"What's all of this stuff?" said Thorgrim, squinting in the dim light. "The stone tablets? And, what's that up there at the end? A box?"

Ruby replied, "Yes. The stone tablets, scrolls, and sarcophagus that were found in the Cave of the Winds by goat herders two thousand, two hundred and forty-eight years ago."

Thorgrim grinned. "Amazing you can remember all of those details. Let me guess . . . you read all of this from books in the library?"

"Yes, and from my classes at the university."

He said, "Let's take a look before those idiots show up again."

Walking slowly down the hallway, they passed by dozens of pieces of stone tablets of various sizes and shapes. All of them had unusual inscriptions etched on their faces.

After a few minutes, they approached the roped-off sarcophagus. Next to it, on an iron table, were more stone tablet fragments, scroll parchments, various pieces of pottery and ancient hand tools.

280

Thorgrim looked closely at the closed, stone sarcophagus. Deeply etched into the lid was the ancient symbol of the dwarves.

Thorgrim whispered, "Is there a corpse in that box?"

Ruby chuckled. "No, just bones."

"Same thing as far as I'm concerned. Who's bones?"

"No one knows. It is assumed to be someone of great importance, of course. Probably a leader of some kind. Maybe a holy man. We may never know."

"Could it be a king?"

"Possibly. As you can see, many of the tablets and scrolls were badly damaged. What we have tells only a tiny part of the story of the early history of the first dwarves."

Looking at the tablet fragments, Thorgrim shook his head. "Look at those strange markings. How could anyone figure out what those symbols mean?"

Ruby replied, "Experts studied the markings for years. Somehow, they managed to decipher most of it."

Thorgrim shook his head again. "Those markings look like they were scratched into the stone by a drunken cat."

Blinky stuck his head out of Thorgrim's beard.

"Meow."

"No offense, Blinky."

"Meow."

Ruby reached over and stroked the kitten's head. "I almost forgot about him. He's been really quiet."

"He's been sleepin' since I got here."

"Meow, meow," cried the kitten.

Thorgrim's eye popped out and he raised his brow. "Oh, oh. I think muh cat has to do his thing. Any flowerbeds around here?"

"Yes, inside the Grand Hall. The place is full of flowers."

"Would it hurt to let muh cat do that in there?"

Ruby laughed and said, "I don't think anyone would mind, but just in case, we probably shouldn't brag about it."

"Okay, let's get in there before, God forbid, Blinky decides to use my beard instead, or do it on one of those tablets. Besides that, it's almost five-thirty. We only have a half-hour. The tour guide says they kick everyone out at six."

Exiting the hall, they entered yet another small foyer. Again, a pair of doors awaited them. Above the doors, in big letters were the words: **'THE GRAND HALL.'**

Upon entering, Thorgrim instantly stopped and gazed in stunned silence. Inside the star-shaped building, beneath a gigantic, sixty-foot high, multicolored skydome, thousands of colorful flowers bloomed. The beauty of all of those flowers and the floral scent in the room was hypnotic.

Blinky also noticed the scent and proceeded to jump out of Thorgrim's beard. In two bounds, the kitten disappeared into the blanket of flowers.

Thorgrim turned white, hoping no one noticed that his kitten was kicking up dirt and dropping a smelly steamer in one of the nearby flowerbeds.

Ruby covered her mouth, trying her best not to laugh.

When Blinky finished, he jumped straight into Thorgrim's arms and ate the treat his master had waiting for him. After finishing, he returned to his beard-bed, purring at first before resuming his usual snoring.

Thorgrim surveyed the magnificent room. The windowless, white granite walls sparkled like diamonds. The walls were bare, with the exception of various golden candleholders and torch sconces, which were used during periods of heavy overcast, or on rare occasions when the complex was open at night.

Three dozen visitors mingled in the building, all of them making every effort to make as little noise as possible.

One hundred feet away, in the center of the building, Thorgrim saw an altar that was surrounded by a ring of unlit, silver candles. There was something on top of the altar, but he was too far away to determine what it was.

In front of the altar, a dozen dwarves stood in line, waiting for their turn to kneel before it. Some were in tears.

Thorgrim whispered, "Why do some of those people seem to be crying?"

"They cry because the Holy Hammer is gone."

"That's where it was? Up there on that altar" asked Thorgrim, his voice shaking with excitement.

She replied, "Yes. Follow me."

Ruby took Thorgrim's hand and slowly led him to the center of the room.

When they arrived, they got in line behind those who were waiting their turn to approach the roped-off altar.

Designed by King Oakenhorn himself, the ancient altar that once held the golden Aurumsmiter Hammer was constructed of solid oak and had a half-inch thick top forged from pure, dwarven silver.

The altar, measuring six feet wide, four feet deep and five feet tall, weighed over six thousand pounds. The large size was intentional so that all dwarves who viewed the Holy Hammer must look up at it.

While waiting for his turn, Thorgrim studied the altar. Glyphs, matching those found on the stone tablets were hand-carved into its face. In the center of the altar's front, within a gold relief, was the diamond-encrusted, ancient symbol of the dwarves. The silver-colored candles surrounding the sides and rear of the altar looked very old. Most of them were sagging and a few were missing.

Thorgrim then took a good look at the object on top of the altar. It was a six-inch thick piece of polished, heavy steel, three feet long, that had wide, 'V' shaped pieces of solid oak mounted on each end.

Puzzled, he looked at Ruby.

"What is that on top of the altar?" he whispered.

"The cradle that held the hammer," she replied softly.

Thorgrim gazed upon the altar and imagined what it would have been like to see the Aurumsmiter Hammer sitting on the steel cradle.

An information sign stood in front of the altar. It read:

'This altar, designed by King Authumus Oakenhorn and constructed in the year A.F.D. 4, once held the Aurumsmiter Hammer of the first dwarves.

The greatest and most beloved of all dwarven relics, and a gift from the first dwarves to our Father God, Moridon.

Let it be known that Moridon's Holy Hammer was stolen by the grey elves on, June 14, 1798. The hammer has never been recovered and is presumed lost to the ages.'

Thorgrim did the math and realized that the hammer had been stolen four hundred and fifty years ago and has not been seen since.

Below the sign was a row of marble blocks. Etched into the blocks, flanked by the symbols of Alpha and Omega, were six-inch tall, diamond-encrusted golden letters:

A* The Aurumsmiter Hammer of the First Dwarves *Ω

A series of large paintings of the hammer, made by the famous artist, Leonardo dwarf Vinci, stood on a rack behind and to the left of the altar.

The first painting was of the ancient dwarven smithies forging the Holy Hammer. The second showed the jewelers working as they mounted the diamonds into the engraved, ancient symbol of the dwarves on both sides of the sledgehammer's head. Dwarf Vinci's final painting depicted the dwarven people presenting the Aurumsmiter Hammer to Moridon as a gift. His hand, reaching from the heavens, grasped the handle.

To the front and right of the altar were several, full scale, colorized drawings of the hammer.

The drawings revealed that the Aurumsmiter Hammer was much larger and heavier than a normal sledgehammer. The handle, made of a gold plated steel alloy, at four feet, was a full foot longer than that of a typical sledgehammer. The head, made of solid gold, was as big as Thorgrim's own head. Thorgrim guessed that the Aurumsmiter weighed two hundred pounds.

Soon, it was Thorgrim and Ruby's turn to approach the altar. Kneeling, both of them bowed their heads and offered a prayer to Moridon. Before rising, Thorgrim looked up and again imagined the hammer still in its place on the cradle.

After a minute, a few impatient dwarves, who had arrived in line behind them began to grumble. Thorgrim and Ruby quickly stood and walked away towards the exit door at the far end of the Grand Hall.

When they exited the backside of the Grand Hall, both of them, hand in hand, returned to the front of the complex using a beautiful, multi-colored marble path. By the time they walked to where Nugget was tied, Thorgrim's timepiece read 6:10 p.m.

Stroking Nugget's neck, Thorgrim said, "Ruby, this is my horse Nugget and yes, he's an elven horse. I know." He chuckled briefly. "Who would think . . . me with an elf anything. I'll explain it to you sometime."

Ruby giggled.

Then his expression darkened. "You know, Ruby, seeing the nameplates of those murdered victims really bothered me. I'll never forget it. I mean, they're buried inside those walls. Time may heal that, but the missing hammer will always be a reminder of the evil committed against us."

"Shem, I totally understand your feelings."

He said, "The Aurumsmiter Hammer. It's gone forever. How did those thievin' bastards steal it?"

"No one really knows, but we have a good idea. One night, a week before the raids started, a half-dozen eyewitnesses reported seeing a team of two horses hurriedly pulling a wagon away from the back of the Grand Hall and then east on South First Street. It was dark but they said they saw three elves riding in the wagon. Well, the next day, the authorities discovered that there had been a break-in and that the hammer was missing.

"But how do we know for sure that grey elves stole it?"

"For two reasons. First, an elven dagger, a type commonly carried by grey elves, was found near the altar, apparently dropped by one of the thieves."

"Now, I'm not tryin' to defend any elves here, but maybe that dagger was planted by the real criminals? Even dwarves can be thieves."

"That's possible. Except, there is the second reason. It clearly implicates grey elves."

"What's the second reason?"

"Three days after the theft, and four days before the raids, about halfway between the city of Brimger and Jasp, a local farmer encountered a group of three grey-skinned elves who were working on a wagon near the side of the road. The wagon had a broken wheel and the farmer offered to assist them."

"But Ruby, why would any dwarf help an elf?"

"Remember, this was before the war started."

"Okay, I understand."

"Anyway, the farmer suggested they unload the wagon so they could raise the carriage and pull the wheel. He reported that the elves seemed very nervous, but agreed. The three elves removed a few big boxes and a large, blanket-wrapped, heavy object."

"The hammer?"

"Yes. When the elves placed the object on the ground, the blanket fell open and the farmer saw the Aurumsmiter Hammer lying there. He recognized it immediately because he had seen it in the Grand Hall when he was a boy."

"Did the grey elf bastards kill him?"

"No. Apparently, they were not aware that the farmer had seen the hammer because he was on the other side of the wagon, working on the wheel. The elves were chatting in Elvish, but the farmer, having lived close to the Alacarjian border his entire life, understood some of it. He swore he overheard them talking about melting the hammer down as soon as possible. They were also bragging how the gold would help them win the war against the hated moon elf Queen. In addition, he also heard one of them complaining that he had lost his dagger. After the wheel was repaired, they loaded up the hammer and away they went."

Thorgrim scowled. "Never to be seen again."

"Concerned, the farmer rode past them and then continued to Jasp, where he reported the incident to the police. At first, they thought he was crazy, and by the time they believed his story, it was too late. The elves got away. They probably went off-road, crossing the border near the elven village of Reahalian."

"But what if the farmer made up the story to help the real thieves?"

"You've read too much fiction," she giggled.

Thorgrim said in a depressed tone. "I suppose yer right about that. So, the hammer was melted down by a bunch of skinny elves."

"No one knows for sure. Since the war, many stories have circulated about the hammer. Some claiming to have seen it. Others believing that the grey elves considered the hammer a war prize and still have it hidden away somewhere. We may never know the truth."

Still miffed, he said, "My God, the hammer. What a loss. It's irreplaceable. The bastards."

"Knights have searched for it. It's considered the most famous of all lost treasures."

Interested in such matters, his anger began to subside. "You know, I'm fascinated by lost treasure chests and ancient relics."

She replied, "The library has several books on the subject if you're interested."

The mention of books excited him. Completely forgetting his anger towards the elves, he beamed a wide smile.

"Shem, like I told you earlier today. You have a wonderful smile."

Thorgrim, though blushing, replied without hesitation, "Thankee. And, Ruby, you have the cutest, curly red beard!"

Ruby also blushed. "Thank you, uh, it's naturally curly, too!"

For some time, Thorgrim and Ruby talked about the weather, how long she had worked at the library, her time at the university and a few other random things. Hoping to avoid too many personal questions about his past, he did his best to keep the focus of the conversation off himself.

Eventually, he noticed that the sun was getting low in the sky. A glance at his timepiece revealed that it was almost 7:15 p.m.

"Ruby, I've enjoyed our conversation, but I have to ride to the Iron Golem Pub before it gets dark. I'll be stayin' in a room there until I can afford muh own place. You know, being new to the city and all. Plus, I'm starvin' and so is my kitten."

286

Nugget took another bunch of hay into his mouth, crunching it loudly. Ruby laughed. "You and your cat might be hungry, but I'm sure your horse has eaten a ton of hay already."

Thorgrim patted Nugget on his chest. "He'd eat all day if I'd let him."

"Shem, did you just say you're going to the Iron Golem Pub?"

"Yes."

"That's my father's place."

"Uuno Kanto is yer father? He's been helping me out."

"Yes, he's my father."

"I wondered about that because yer mother said Uuno Kanto was her ex-husband. But I wasn't sure if Uuno was yer father, and I didn't want to ask. It's none of muh business."

"Please tell him I said that I love and miss him . . . and to come see me sometime."

"You don't see each other much?"

"No. He and my mother . . . well, you can imagine. You know, I think she's still in love with him, but she won't admit it."

Thorgrim nodding, replied, "Oh, sure, I think I understand. Uh, I'll certainly tell him what you said."

"You said that you're staying in a room at the pub? That's over an hour ride every day to and from the library."

"I know. Two hours if I take my time. I'll have to live there until I make enough money to afford muh own place. Yer mother said that if I do well, she'll give me a raise. In the meantime, you know the sayin' . . . it is what it is."

Ruby's eyes twinkled. "I'm sure you'll get a raise in no time. Shem, have a safe ride and thank you for spending the afternoon with me."

"Sure, I enjoyed it!"

With her eyes still twinkling, she said, "Can we do it again sometime?"

"I would love to, Ruby. However, yer mother is not in favor of us spending time together. I'm not sure she really likes me . . . I don't know, maybe it's the eyepatch."

He put the eyepatch on and flipped it up and down over his eye several times causing Ruby to giggle. He said, "Besides that, she said that employees can't date."

"Well, who said anything about dating?" she asked, batting her long lashes. "Can't we just be friends?"

"Oh, now I really feel embarrassed. I thought you were wanting to . . . well, sure we can be friends. Absolutely."

Ruby leaned over and gave Thorgrim a warm kiss on his cheek. She held her lips against his face for what seemed like an eternity.

287

"Shem? Are you okay?"

Thorgrim was in a daze and unable to respond. The cheek Ruby kissed, tingled as if it had been struck by lightning.

Finally, a wet lick by Nugget across Thorgrim's face roused him from his trance.

Thorgrim blinked his eyes. "Huh?"

Ruby giggled softly. "Are you okay?"

"Uh, ya. I don't know what happened. I must be tired or somethin'. As soon as I get to the pub and eat somethin', I'm headin' straight to bed. Don't want to be late to work in the mornin'."

"Before you go, I want to introduce you to my little donkey, Penelope."

Thorgrim watched Ruby unhitch a black and white, five-foot-tall, miniature dwarf donkey that was secured to a post next to Nugget.

"That's yer horse? Uh, I mean donkey?"

"Yes. What do you think of her?" She brought the donkey over to him.

Reaching out, he scratched Penelope's little ears. "Aww, she's a muplet if I've ever seen one."

Ruby smiled. "Yes, she is! You know, your elven horse is so big, you should consider getting one of these miniature donkeys. It might be easier for you to get in and out of the saddle."

"Well, I have been struggling with that. Nugget is an amazing horse though. Be tough to ever give him up."

"Shem, please don't be embarrassed, but I saw you fall this morning in front of the library when you arrived. I also saw you hanging from yer stirrup this afternoon when you arrived here at the Grand Hall. I'm surprised you didn't hear me scream! I was afraid you were going to break your neck!"

He laughed. "You're not the only one who was afraid I might break muh neck!"

Ruby mounted Penelope and said, "I know you need to get going. Be careful during your ride. See you in the morning."

Thorgrim untied Nugget and placed the mounting block on the ground as usual. Stepping up, he said, "Yes! I can't wait to start tomorrow."

"Don't worry about my mother, okay?"

Thorgrim dropped his head. "If you say so."

Ruby smiled. "Remember, we're just friends."

"Yes, friends."

"Don't forget to tell my father what I said, okay?"

"I won't forget. Are you going home now?"

"Yes, it's not far from here. I'm in one of the new apartments a few blocks west of the university on Middle Street. They have some for rent and they cost only six gold per month. After you earn your raise, you might consider getting one for yourself."

Thorgrim smiled. "I would like to have muh own place."

"You deserve one."

"Thankee, Ruby."

"You're welcome. Hey, do you want me to help you get up on your horse?"

"Thankee, but I can manage. Here goes, wish me luck!"

Taking a deep breath, he launched himself up and made a perfect landing in the saddle.

Ruby clapped her hands. "You did it!"

"I did it this time. I got lucky."

Ruby purred. "Mmmmm, maybe you made it because of me. I know how boys always like to show off in front of girls."

Thorgrim's cheeks flushed cherry red. Pulling the block up, he fastened it and then checked on little Blinky. The kitten was sound asleep.

Steering Nugget away from the hitch, Thorgrim looked down at Ruby.

He tugged his beard, heaved out his chest and playfully replied, "You think I was showing off? Madam, I have not yet tried to show off. When I do, you'll know it."

The time was now 7:40 p.m. With a nudge, Thorgrim sent Nugget trotting onto Center Avenue and then south, en route to the Iron Golem Pub.

Glancing over his shoulder, Thorgrim could see Ruby slowly riding her little donkey down Middle Street. Though she did not see him, he waved, watching her until she blended in with the many dwarves who were moving up and down the street.

Who is this girl? I do like her, and though I want to, I can't get involved. Besides, maybe she really meant it when she said we were just friends. But what kind of friend would kiss someone's cheek like she kissed mine? If she would find out the truth about me . . . find out that I've been lying to her about who I really am, she'd hate me. No matter what, I don't want to hurt her. I hate lying to her, or anyone else for that matter.

✳✳✳

With Nugget alternating between a canter and a trot, Thorgrim reached the so-called 'unsavory south' at sunset. As he rode through the nearby, troublesome neighborhood full of hoods, he pulled the patch over his eye and displayed the meanest face he could muster.

Uuno was right; everyone ignored him. With the exception of a couple, random curse words, not one of the hoods seemed interested in bothering him. However, eyepatch or not, Thorgrim was still worried that someone might shoot another arrow his way, so he rode Nugget at a gallop until he reached the pub, about five blocks away.

It was dusk when Thorgrim tied up his horse in front of the Iron Golem Pub. The place was crawling with noisy dwarves who were enjoying the pub's frosty ale and hot food after a hard day's work.

Horses were parked everywhere, and some wandered around freely. Their alcoholic owners, thirsty for cold ale, did not bother to tie them to a hitch. Instead, they jumped off as soon as they arrived, running straight into the pub with their personal mugs in hand.

Unfortunately, Thorgrim fell again while dismounting. This time he sat on the ground next to the upturned mounting block for a few moments while his frustration simmered. Luckily, with the exception of his pride, he was uninjured.

Checking his beard for the little kitty, amazingly, this time Thorgrim found his furry friend still sleeping deep inside. Apparently, Blinky was getting used to Thorgrim's mounting and dismounting accidents.

Two inebriated dwarves, who had just stumbled out of the pub after drinking a large quantity of ale, had witnessed Thorgrim's fall.

One of them bellowed, "Hey, buddy! Looks like you've had way too much to drink!"

The other roared, "Ya, if yer drunk, you better not try to ride that big horse of yers, or ya might end up riding off into the Mharrak River!"

"Ya, dat's right! They'll never find yer body! Hahahaahohahaho!"

Thorgrim ignored their drunken ramblings. Rising, he said to Nugget, "It's not yer fault, my friend."

Nugget responded with a whinny.

Thorgrim reached up and rubbed the horse's muzzle. Looking into Nugget's dark eyes, he studied them for a moment. Something inside those eyes told Thorgrim that his horse was depressed. From that moment on, he began to worry about Nugget's health and thought he should talk to a veterinarian as soon as possible.

Thorgrim waved at Moocher and Booger who were on the porch greeting customers as they entered. They returned the wave.

Thorgrim was one of the gang.

As he walked through the open gate, he saw Bone Grinder suddenly run off to hide in the bushes.

"How's Bone Grinder?" Thorgrim asked after he walked up on the porch.

"He's fine," moaned Booger.

Leaning in close to Thorgrim's beard, squinting, he said, "Hey, where's dat hellcat of yers? Is he hiding in dare?"

"He's in there, alright. Don't get too close, or he might take yer nose off with a swipe of his razor-sharp claws!"

Booger jumped back, startled.

"I'm just kiddin', Booger," said Thorgrim chuckling.

Booger sneered, "Very funny."

"God almighty, doesn't he get hot inside there?" asked Moocher.

"Probably, but he likes it in there. Maybe he feels safe."

Booger shook his head. "Ya think yer cat feels safe while he's inside yer beard? Dat thing is a miniature tornado with fur. What does he have to be afraid of?"

Thorgrim, grinning, shrugged.

Moocher said, "Go on in. We're open for business, so dare's no need for da secret knock."

***

"Mr. Kanto, that's the best skunk tail casserole I've ever tasted! Reminds me of muh mother's cookin' back home! And oh, boy, do I miss that!"

Uuno smiled. "Thank you. I forgot to tell you that we have a full kitchen in the back of the pub. Uh, I hope you don't mind eating in muh office. It's kinda' busy downstairs, and I wanted to talk with you anyway in private."

Blinky lay curled up on Thorgrim's lap, purring because of a full belly. "I'll sleep well tonight after that meal. I'm full to the top and so is Blinky. I also want to thank you for taking good care of Nugget. Those stables in the back are amazin'! Like a grand hotel for horses!"

"Yes, an extra benefit for being part of our little group. Uh, just so ya know, we're open 'til two in the morning. I'll provide ya with some earplugs or you'll likely not get much sleep 'til the last boozers head for home."

291

Thorgrim said, "I understand. After all, this is a pub, not an inn! But, how can these guys drink like that and then work the next day?"

"Well, they don't get wasted. That's what the weekends are for!"

"I have a question. Does muh horse have to wear an eyepatch, too?"

Uuno laughed and shook his head. "No."

He continued, "With the exception of a few small details, yer paperwork is complete, and I'll give everything to you in the morning before you leave."

Excited, Thorgrim smiled ear to ear. "Thankee, so much, Mr. Kanto."

"Glad to help. So from now on, you are officially, Shem Lybree, from Dartag Bur. It's extremely important that you fully accept that, and forget everything about Thorgrim Longbeard. Do you understand?"

Thorgrim nodded his head, though in his heart he felt deep regret.

"I have created a complete history for you, and after you get the paperwork, I want you to review all of it, closely. If there are any problems, let me know, and I'll correct them. You will also need to study it in case you're ever asked any questions. It's important to be consistent with yer answers."

"I understand."

"Remember, if you get caught with false papers, even I can't help you. In the least, you'll be sent off to the Kronk Prison, and if they find out you're on the run from the mines, they'll likely double yer prison time."

Thorgrim's eyes grew as large as the bottom of an ale mug.

"Keep yer patch on when in public, but you don't have to wear it now. Sometimes I wear mine in the pub, sometimes I don't. But, I always wear it whenever I leave here."

Thorgrim took his patch off. "I'm having trouble getting used to wearing it, but I'll heed yer advice."

"Shem, the first thing you told me when you arrived tonight, was that muh daughter, Ruby, loves and misses me. So, let's talk 'bout muh little girl. How is Ruby?"

"Ruby is doing fine. She is an amazin' woman and very smart, as well."

"Yes, I need to get up and see her more often. I don't want her coming down here, for obvious reasons."

"Sure, I understand."

"And how's her mother? I'm sure that you discovered that Gertrude is my ex."

"Yeah, she told me. She also said she had remarried. Her last name is Fizzlewhooper?"

Uuno leaned back in his chair and laughed. "Hahahahaaho! I know. Quite a name, isn't it? I've met her new husband a couple of times. He's one of the jewelers for the King. Freddy Fizzlewhooper! He has a crazy name, but he's a really nice guy, though."

Thorgrim chuckled. "Fizzlewhooper is an unusual name, fer sure."

Uuno commented, "I'm glad my ex found someone to make her happy. I really am. However, I'm afraid that her marriage will eventually . . . fizzle out!"

Uuno paused, waiting for Thorgrim to laugh, but the joke went right over his head.

Finally, Uuno burst out in laughter. "Fizzle out, get it? Hahahahahohoaha! Her name's Fizzlewhooper and her marriage will eventually fizzle out. I just made that up, pretty funny, huh?"

Thorgrim, doing his best not to offend Uuno, tried to laugh, but after a few phony chuckles, he gave up and said, "No, I'm sorry, Mr. Kanto, I didn't quite get that."

Uuno raised his brow. "That's okay, and for the sake of a pipe that's fully packed with rare, Abbirian tobaccee, will you please call me, Uuno?"

Thorgrim nodded. "I'm sorry. Sure, Uuno."

"And stop apologizing all the time. There's no need for that. You know, a person can be too polite!"

"Oh, I'm sorry, I'll do my best."

Uuno rolled his eyes. "Well, anyway, Gertrude and I were married for thirty years, and we had Ruby ten years before we divorced. I was away from home a lot, on the road workin', and I guess she was lonely. I really can't blame her. Today, we remain friends of sorts, but she's still bitter. She only tries to get along with me for the sake of Ruby."

Thorgrim could see that Uuno was depressed and tried to change the subject. "I'm sorry, Uuno. I feel for you. Anyway, I suppose I should get to bed, because—"

Obviously, Uuno was not finished talking about Gertrude. "Ya know, I still love the woman, but the hardest part was missing out on so much time with muh little girl. Now, Ruby's twenty-five and all grown up."

"That must be tough," replied Thorgrim somberly.

"Yes. I came home one day after being on the road for a few weeks and found the divorce decree posted on muh front door. That's all it takes. The husband or wife wants a divorce, all they have to do is go down and pay a few gold and post the sign. It's official immediately."

"That seems too easy."

"Well, there are consequences. You can't remarry for ten years, and of course, the government will not tolerate non-married dwarves living together. It's against the law."

Thorgrim shook his head. "I'll never get married. Ever."

Uuno smiled, shook his big index finger and said, "Don't say never or ever!"

"Okay, I'll try to remember that."

"Hey, when ya get to the library tomorrow, give Ruby a big hug, and make sure ya tell her mama, hello for me, too."

Thorgrim replied, "I'll do that."

"I would appreciate it."

"Mr. Kanto, Uh, I mean, Uuno, it's the least I can do to repay just a bit of yer kindness."

"No need to repay anything."

Thorgrim yawned. "Like I said, I should probably get to bed. I'm not sure where muh room is, though."

"Yer room is down the hall on the left, directly across from Festus' room."

Opening his desk, Uuno pulled out a large skeleton key and a pair of earplugs, handing everything to Thorgrim.

"Here's yer key and some earplugs. When you get to yer room, you'll find some new clothes hangin' in the closet. The garderobe is downstairs, but your room has its own private bath."

"New clothes? Wow, thankee! Thankee, very much."

"We have a basin in one of the rooms behind the bar that we use to wash our clothes. You'll find containers of lye in a cabinet right next to the basin. After you've washed your clothes, you can hang them to dry in front of the heating stove."

Having never had to wash his own clothes before, Thorgrim cringed.

Uuno noticed and laughed. "What's the matter? Never had to wash yer own clothes before?"

"No."

"You better get used to it! Your momma ain't here to do it for ya!"

Thorgrim smiled and said, "Ya, I've been spoiled, I guess."

"Well, when yer ready to wash yer clothes, ask anyone down there to show you how. Okay? Feel free to use the washroom anytime you want."

"Sure. And, Thanks again."

Goodnight, Shem."

Placing Blinky back in his beard, Thorgrim exited Uuno's office. Out in the hallway, Thorgrim listened and as he had expected, Uuno began plucking one of his lutes. Soon, his rich bass-baritone voice resonated from beyond the office door.

"Love is a burning thing
And it makes a fiery ring
Bound by wild desire
I fell in to a ring of fire

I fell in to a burning ring of fire
I went down, down, down
And the flames went higher

And it burns, burns, burns
The ring of fire
The ring of fire."

Uuno stopped singing and said, "Hmmm. Not too bad. It's a good start, anyway."

Thorgrim smiled and walked down the hall to his room. It was almost a half-hour to midnight and he had to be up no later than seven-thirty in the morning in order to get ready and make it to work by 9:00 a.m.

When he reached the door to his room, he entered and lit a few candles. Looking around, he saw a comfortable-looking bed, a closet full of new clothes, and a small table and chair. In an adjoining room, Thorgrim found a bathtub.

Thorgrim then dropped his backpack and placed Blinky's ready-made potty box on the floor, along with a dish of dried fish and another with fresh water.

After doing his usual hygiene routine in a small bowl, Thorgrim carefully checked for mattress possums. Happily, he found none. Although his room was on the second floor, he still looked out of the window to check for any nearby tree branches . . . or random kittens. Fortunately, he found neither.

The rowdy noise from the late-night partiers in the pub below him was annoying, so he wasted no time using the earplugs Uuno had given him. Exhausted, though excited, with Nugget in the stables, and his beloved kitten snuggled in his beard, he slid under the covers of the bed and soon joined both of his animal friends in dreamland.

Part Two

"A New Life."

Author's Notes for Part Two

U sing the alias Shem Lybree, Thorgrim Longbeard would live and work in Bur Dhulgren for twenty-five years. Unfortunately, due to the damaged texts, only a few details have survived regarding his life in the city.

Although little information is available, Part Two will cover certain events that occurred in Thorgrim's life during the time that he lived in the capital, between the ages of twenty and forty-four.

Of the many books and scrolls found in the vault by the underwater archeologists, perhaps fifty percent survived intact, with the scrolls suffering the worst. Only a few of the three dozen scrolls were legible, most of them having been crushed by the heavy books, then disintegrating to dust during attempts to unroll them. Sadly, this includes various sections of the twenty-four volumes containing over ten thousand pages of Thorgrim's detailed notes and diaries. The diaries seem to have suffered the least damage, but they only contain minimal information in the entries.

Oddly, nowhere in Thorgrim's notes does he mention that he ever kept a diary. Nevertheless, several exist.

The reader will have already learned that nineteen-year-old Thorgrim Longbeard, suffering from severe claustrophobia, was unable to fulfill his legally mandated obligation to work in the ore mines. In order to avoid prosecution, he left his home in Vog in an attempt to flee the country and start a new life.

With a goal of traveling to the Great Kingdom, Thorgrim's escape route would take him to the capital city of Bur Dhulgren. Once there, he originally intended to spend only two days in the city in order to fulfill a dream of visiting the Supreme Library, and the Grand Hall of the Dwarves. But this soon changed.

During this time, he met with a one-eyed dwarf by the name of Uuno Kanto, who was able to help him in several ways. In addition to finding him a job at the Supreme Library (a dream come true for Thorgrim), Uuno altered Thorgrim's identity by cutting and coloring his hair and beard, giving him an eyepatch to wear, as well as providing false identification papers.

Uuno suggested that Thorgrim, now living under the alias, Shem Lybree, would not have to leave the country after all.

Though concerned, Thorgrim happily agreed to stay.

Thorgrim's fragmented records reveal that during this time, between the ages of twenty and forty-four, he was, for the most part, happy and content. We learn that Thorgrim fell deeply in love with a certain female dwarf by the name of Ruby Kanto and they eventually married. It was also during this time, due to a tragic event, that he developed an addiction to ale.

The documents mention that regrettably, because of an unfortunate incident that would expose his true identity, Thorgrim Longbeard, wanted by the authorities, would be forced to leave the capital and once again attempt to flee the country.

Thorgrim was consistent when recording the dates, time, and locations of the events in his notes and diaries, but in some cases, these are missing. Any dates, time, or locations that were not available, are presumed and noted as such.

XIV.   Twenty-Five Years

[Author's Note for Chapter XIV:]
Thorgrim's story continues five months after the end of Chapter XIII. We find that he is secretly dating Ruby, but has not revealed his true age or identity to anyone. We also discover that Blinky and Nugget are still with Thorgrim. He continues to work at the Supreme Library, has moved into an apartment in the same complex as Ruby and now enjoys drinking ale.

The scene is a popular nightclub on the evening of New Year's Eve, one day before Thorgrim's twentieth birthday. Due to his deception, he has everyone else convinced he is turning forty years old.

***

Date: Sunday, December 31, 2248
Time: 10:15 p.m.
Location: Grumbler's Pub and Nightclub, corner of North Third Street and West First Avenue, Bur Dhulgren.

Ruby tried to shout over the noisy party. "Shem, you're a New Year's baby! Happy birthday, and happy New Year!"

"Thank you, honey," replied Thorgrim. "But muh birthday is not until after midnight. I still have about two more hours to go."

Concerned, she said, "Are ya having fun? You seem uncomfortable."

Thorgrim took a big draw of ale. Glancing at the people dancing and drinking, he replied, "Ya know, I don't mind anyone else knowin' we're dating, as long as yer mother doesn't find out. It's bad enough that I'm livin' in an apartment in the same complex you are. If she finds out we're seeing each other, I'll likely be blowin' ya kisses from the moon!"

She grabbed his beard and gave it several playful tugs. "I would go to the moon to be with you, ya know."

Her eyes widened and she quickly released his beard. "Oh, sorry, I keep thinking that yer cat might be in there!"

Thorgrim chuckled loudly. "That's okay. I'm sure he's probably still lying on muh bed sound asleep," he said, ending with a big smile.

Ruby leaned in and said, "Hey, did I ever tell you that you have a wonderful smile?"

"What?"

Inside 'Grumbler's, the northern district's most popular nightclub, the inebriated crowd of New Year's Eve celebrators had become so loud, that it was almost impossible to even hear the music from the band.

Ruby leaned in closer and tried again. "I said, did I ever tell you that you have a wonderful smile?"

Thorgrim shook his head. "I still can't hear ya. Get closer." He turned his head so Ruby could talk directly into his ear.

She moved in close to his ear and tried again, "I said, did I ever —"

Before she could finish her sentence, Thorgrim whipped his head around and gave her a big kiss right on her lips.

Of course, though surprised, she returned it.

She beamed. "Wow, that was a slick move, Shem!" She dropped her brow and jokingly said, "Hey, who else have you tried that on?"

Thorgrim grinned and adjusted his eyepatch. "Yer the first! Well, I'm not counting all the girls I dated in high school." He flipped his eyepatch up and winked. Still lying about his age he said, "That was over twenty years ago and doesn't count."

She giggled and gave him a little push. "Hey, do you really have to wear that eyepatch every time you're out in public? I mean, you have both of your eyes. I want to see both of them. They're beautiful!"

"Like I told you, yer father is the one who gave me this patch. He told me to wear it because it would help keep me out of trouble with the undesirables in this city."

"I see yours has the Iron Golem initials on it now."

"Yes. Call it a promotion of sorts."

"My father and his crazy ideas. Well, I really don't mind the eyepatch because I know that you only have an eye for me."

He laughed. "Hey, dat's funny! Have I ever told you that you have a wonderful sense of humor?"

She cupped an ear. "What?"

He said, "The noise in here is terrible. I said, have I ever told you that you have a wonderful sense of humor?"

She leaned in close, placing her ear next to his face. "What? I'm sorry, I still can't hear you."

Thorgrim shook his head. Yelling, he tried again. "I said, have I ever told you that—"

Ruby whipped her head around and planted a big kiss on his lips.

After the long kiss, he said, "I knew you were going to do that."

She laughed. "Pretty good, huh? You know, I've had a lot of practice doing that trick. I remember a few years ago, back in my university days when I—"

300

He interrupted. "Oh, ya?"

He picked Ruby up and spun her in a circle. "You only get to practice that on me from now on!"

Again, they shared a long kiss, oblivious to everyone and everything around them.

When they finished the kiss, Thorgrim purchased a mug of ale and a glass of wine from a passing barmaid. Handing Ruby the wine, he said, "Hey, I forgot to ask yer mother last week if the library is open tomorrow on New Year's Day."

"Yes, we're open. We never close for holidays except on the King and Queen's birthdays."

He took a big draw of ale. "Well, I should probably back off the ale then. Muh head's already floatin'. By the time I get to bed, I won't get much sleep, and I'll be groggy tomorrow."

Ruby took a sip of wine. "Fortunately, groggy or not, you won't have to ride an hour to work like you had to do when you lived in my father's pub."

He nodded. "True."

"Look at the benefits of living near the library! You can walk to work in ten minutes! You don't have to ride Nugget!"

"But, I like to ride Nugget to work, and I can get there in only a minute." He leaned over and kissed her cheek. "That way, I can get to see you sooner. Even a few minutes away from you, seems like forever."

Glowing, she replied, "You're so romantic. Have I ever told you how romantic you are?"

He grinned. "What? I can't hear you!"

"Shut up, goofy, and kiss me."

Of course, he did.

After another long kiss, Thorgrim gazed at his pretty, redheaded girlfriend. As he looked at her, once again, everyone else in the noisy room seemed to fade away to nothingness. The screaming, yelling, laughing, even the music was gone. It was just him and Ruby.

He was in love . . . deeply so.

Watching Ruby as she stood before him, Thorgrim dreamed of the day when he could tell her the truth about who he really was. Doubting she would understand or forgive him for his deception, he feared he could never tell her. He was terrified that if she found out, he had been lying to her all of this time, she would walk away forever.

***

301

[Author's Note:]
The remainder of the surviving material from Thorgrim's notes regarding the events on New Year's Eve focuses on his growing distress regarding the lies he had to keep telling Ruby.

Other than knowing that Vog Longbeard was a distant ancestor, there was not a single thing about the real Thorgrim Longbeard that Ruby knew. Unknown to her, everything was a lie. His name, where he grew up, his parents, siblings . . . all of it, a pack of falsehoods created by Uuno Kanto in order to hide and protect Thorgrim from the authorities.

Thorgrim's heart ached because he was forced to continue to lie to the person he loved and trusted more than anyone else in the realm.

Approximately one year later, we learn that with the help of Uuno Kanto, Thorgrim had been exchanging letters with his parents.

In accordance with Uuno's instructions, he would write a letter and not sign it. He would give the letter to Uuno, who would then have it delivered through his network. Thorgrim's parents were instructed to address all letters to Uuno Kanto and not use Thorgrim's name in the letter. Once Uuno received a reply letter, he would have an associate deliver it to Thorgrim.

Uuno had warned Thorgrim that exchanging letters might put him at risk and warned him that in no way should he tell his parents his alias or reveal where he was living. Following Uuno's good advice, in his first letter, in an effort to throw the authorities off his trail, Thorgrim told his parents that he was somewhere deep in the southern part of the Theocracy of the Abbir.

Luthor and Marjorie were thrilled to discover that their son was okay. When their first reply letter arrived, Thorgrim learned that although his father had tried everything he could, he was officially wanted by the authorities for not fulfilling his obligation of working in the mines.

One Sunday, in the year 2249, Thorgrim's alternate reality almost fell apart.

Ruby had stopped by Thorgrim's apartment to spend their day off together. While he was getting dressed, she found an open letter from his parents lying on a table.

Naturally, she wanted to know why the envelope was addressed to her father and how Thorgrim had acquired it. Thorgrim had to think fast and using another lie, he saved the day. He told her that, over a year ago, when he was staying with her father at the Iron Golem Pub, the envelope had accidentally been mixed up with some of his personal things.

Of course, Ruby read the letter. Had she checked the date recorded in the letter, Thorgrim's lie would have been exposed. Afterward, she wondered what connections her father had with people in Vog and the Vog Silver Mine Company, or why the letter was signed, 'love, Mama and Papa.'

He shrugged and told her that he had no idea who the people were. Another falsity and he continued to hate himself for it.

Luckily, it seems she believed him and apparently never brought it up again.

***

[Author's Note:]

Although most of the details regarding Thorgrim's twenty-five years in the city are lost to the ages, we do have some information regarding several events that occurred between 2250 and 2253. A couple of broken sentences mention, that sometime in the year 2250, Thorgrim was recovering after a serious bout with the flu. In addition, an incomplete paragraph dated April 14, 2251, tells us that regrettably, he suffered a broken wrist after falling from his horse, Nugget.

Luckily, more details survived regarding the years 2252 and 2253. Although the exact date is unknown, the story resumes in the autumn of 2252, when Thorgrim is twenty-three years old (pretending that he is forty-three), living under the alias, Shem Lybree. He continues to work at the Supreme Library, now as a librarian. He is still dating Ruby, however, her mother is now aware of their romantic relationship. There is no evidence that Thorgrim had revealed any truths to Ruby or anyone else, regarding his real identity.

We find that Blinky, now a full-grown cat, still enjoys hanging out in Thorgrim's beard. Thorgrim learns the likely cause of Nugget's occasional bouts of depression. Finally, in the autumn of 2253, Thorgrim will experience a joyous event when he is greeted by unexpected visitors at the library.

***

Date: Autumn, 2252.
Time: Unknown.
Location: The Supreme Library of Mharrak, Bur Dhulgren.

Frowning, Gertrude leaned over and whispered, "Shem, how many times have I told you that you can't have that cat hanging around in yer beard while yer working? Someone complained about it again."

Thorgrim, now a librarian, was busy putting books back in their proper places on the shelves. Without stopping, he growled, "Do you know what drives me the craziest? People who don't put books back where they belong when they're finished with them. They just throw them in any old place, or leave them scattered on the tables."

Tapping her foot, she said, "Did you hear a word I said?"

He had one book to go. Before placing it in its assigned slot, he replied, "Yes, I'm sorry. I did hear you. Someone complained about my cat?"

"Yes, they did. I've told you that people find it unsettling when they see a cat sticking its head out of yer beard."

"Unsettling? Most people chuckle when Blinky pops his head out of muh beard. They always say it's adorable."

"They chuckle? Did you ever stop to think that they might be laughing at you instead? Besides that, and please don't be offended, but most of them are intimidated by that eyepatch that you wear. Now, on top of that, add a black cat that's crawling around inside yer beard. What would you expect them to think?"

"Well, I can't do anything about the eyepatch, but everyone knows libraries have cats, and there are five or six cats running around loose in here. Blinky has been stayin' in muh beard since I found him four years ago. I can't just throw him out."

Gertrude sighed. "Frankly, I can't imagine how he can be comfortable inside all of that hair. My God, doesn't he get hot in there? What about you?"

He laughed softly. "If it bothered him, I would imagine that he wouldn't go in there. As far as myself, I'm used to it, I guess. When you have a beard like mine, a little more hair doesn't matter much."

"Okay, okay. Just do yer best to keep him hidden when people are checking out books. If I get any more complaints, you'll either have to leave him at home or let him run with the other cats."

He slipped in the last book, hesitated, then pulled it back out and said, "Gertrude, have you ever read this children's book?"

He handed the book to her.

She read the title. "The Cat in the Hat. Yes, when I was a child, why?"

"I may write a similar story and call it, 'The Cat in the Beard.' I mean, if there can be a cat in a hat, why not one in a beard?"

Gertrude smirked and put the book back on the shelf.

Thorgrim said, "By the way, just so ya know, that copy of The Cat in the Hat is extremely rare. It's signed by the author. Dr. Goose's signature is on the inside of the front cover."

Gertrude's eyes widened. She pulled the book out again, opened it and looked. Sure enough, it was signed by one of the all-time greatest authors of children's books.

She shook her head in disbelief. "Shem, that's the fifth signed book you've found since you started working here. How do you find these, when no one else seems to notice?"

"It's the sixth, to be exact. Easy. I actually read books from cover to cover instead of skimming them like most people do now. I think people have become lazy in our fast-paced society. Many have forgotten how special it is to slow down and smell the flowers and listen to the crows . . . and of course, actually read a book. Next time yer outside, take a look at those autumn leaves. When was the last time you actually noticed them change from summer green to autumn gold?"

Thorgrim turned and headed back to the circulation desk.

Gertrude followed and said, "I agree, and I'm guilty of it myself."

"At least you can admit it, Mrs. Fizzlewhooper."

"You're very wise, Shem. How old are you again?"

Thorgrim, living the lie . . . lied. "Uh, forty-three, ma'am, and thank you, I read a lot . . . cover to cover."

"Hmmm, I'm not much older than you, though when I look into yer eyes, you don't look a day over nineteen."

Thorgrim, worried that Gertrude might be on to him, turned away and started to walk over to assist a visitor. "Thankee," he replied as he left. "Easy livin', I guess."

"Wait," she said.

He stopped and turned towards her.

"You do know that I'm not completely in favor of you dating Ruby."

Wearing a blank expression, he looked down at his feet, nodding slowly.

"But you always seem to come up with reasons for me to change my mind about you. Thank you, for reminding me to slow down a bit."

He gave her a huge smile. "You're very welcome. My Grandpa Pistachio always used to say, 'Like us dwarves, life is short . . . uh, umm, hmmm . . . darn it, I forgot the rest, but it was pretty wise and cool, too."

Gertrude could not resist a chuckle.

***

305

Date: Late autumn, 2252.
Time: After 5:00 p.m.
Location: An unknown veterinary clinic, most likely in Bur Dhulgren.

Thorgrim furrowed his monobrow while petting Nugget's neck. "What do you mean, my elven horse belongs with his own kind? Are you making that up because you hate elves?"

The veterinarian, a middle-aged, male dwarf by the name of Dr. Thomas Bitterbelly, shook his head.

"It has nothing to do with the fact that I don't care for elves, sir. To be honest, I don't know too many dwarves who care for elves. Do you know any that do?"

Thorgrim relaxed his brow. "Maybe a couple. But, I don't care for them muhself, of course."

Dr. Bitterbelly then took a bite out of a Sourfish sandwich. Munching on the food, he chased it with a gulp of tea.

He said, "Sorry about eating in front of you, but I've been very busy today. Believe it or not, this is my lunch. It's after five o'clock and most people are having their supper by now."

Thorgrim smiled. "No problem. Enjoy yer dinner."

Sniffing and examining the doctor's food, he said, "Hey, is that one of those Sourfish sandwiches?"

The doctor took another bite, food spraying out of his mouth when he spoke. "Yes, it is. My wife went to McDwarf's and bought me a Value Meal. It includes one Sourfish sandwich, a medium order of fried rat toes and a medium mold weed tea for only one silver!"

Ever hungry, Thorgrim's watering mouth dropped. "Hmmm. Look at the size of that sandwich! Is the head included with that?"

"Yes, head, tail and some spicy sauce. No bones or scales either."

Thorgrim smacked his lips. "Wow, the smell of that makes me hungry! All of that food for only one silver piece? I'll be stopping by there on the way home!"

Nodding, Dr. Bitterbelly crunched on a river rat toe and said, "Ya, use the 'ride through window', it's faster and you can take it home and eat it. Anyway, as to your horse."

Placing his sandwich on the table behind him, the doctor checked Nugget's teeth again. He said, "Other than he's depressed, this elf horse is fine, and not only that, it's very young. This horse is maybe ten years old, at best. Do ya know these elven horses can live over two hundred years?"

306

"Two hundred? Really? No, I didn't know that."

The doctor sneered. "Find an elf, and they'll be sure to remind you that their horses live almost twice as long as ours."

"Twice as long as ours? I didn't know that either."

"Our miniature dwarf donkeys are an exception. Have ya ever considered trading this elf horse in on one? They can live to be two hundred years old, as well!"

"Two hundred. That's a long time."

"Yes, it is. You know, I'm serious. You should really think about trading your horse for one of those donkeys. Just take a look at how tall your horse is. He's built for fast running, endurance, and jumping. He's so tall that I almost had to use a ladder to listen to his heart!"

Thorgrim laughed.

Dr. Bitterbelly continued, "Now, the donkeys are only a bit over five feet tall, so it would be much easier for you to mount and dismount. No offense, but ya looked pretty foolish hanging upside down from the stirrup when ya stopped by this morning after you tried to dismount."

"I know, I know," replied Thorgrim. He looked up at Nugget and gave him a couple pats on the cheek. Reaching in his backpack, he grabbed a fresh carrot and gave it to his happy horse.

"Well, anyway, that's my diagnosis. Yes, your horse seems depressed and since he is in perfect health, the only answer I can give you is that he naturally desires to be with elves . . . or in the least, other elven horses."

"He's been somewhat sad since I first got him a few years ago. I'm worried because winter will be here in a few weeks, and he really gets depressed when it gets cold and snowy."

Dr. Bitterbelly could see the love between them. He patted Thorgrim on the shoulder and said, "Don't get me wrong, Mr. Lybree. I'm sure Nugget loves you, and I can see that you also love him. But it's all about the natural order of life. I mean, how would you feel if you were stuck living in a city full of elves?"

Thorgrim crumpled his face. "Ugh. You've gotta point there. Live in a city full of elves? I'd rather shovel out latrines."

"I'm not saying that today you should cross the border and set him free in the Alacarj, but if you really want this horse to be happy, you might have to do it one day. Maybe you could find an elf who can love him as you do. Either way, because you do love him, it won't be easy for you."

Thorgrim sighed deeply. "I understand."

The doctor grinned and held out his hand. "I'm sure you'll also understand when I tell you that your bill for my services is three gold pieces."

Thorgrim reached in his coin purse and flipped the doctor three golds plus a silver.

"What's the silver for?" asked Dr. Bitterbelly, puzzled.

"Muh cat, Blinky Eyes . . . just ate yer Sourfish sandwich. Blinky, get over here! Sorry about that, doctor."

With part of the Sourfish sandwich in his mouth, Blinky jumped across the counter, into Thorgrim's beard where he nestled and purred.

***

Date: Early autumn, 2253.
Time: Sometime in the afternoon.
Location: The Supreme Library of Mharrak, Bur Dhulgren.

Ruby and Thorgrim were down in the library's basement, cataloging new books that had recently arrived.

Thorgrim opened up another box of books. "Ruby, the leaves outside on the trees have changed and match yer red hair."

She smiled, her eyes sparkling like a galaxy.

He said loudly, "Have I told you lately that I love you?"

Ruby put her finger to her lips. "Shhh! Not so loud or my mother will come down here and chew us out!"

"She'll get over it. If you've noticed, she likes me now."

"Yes, she does. And she no longer complains when you show up with me at family functions."

"Well, Ruby, I do love you! I want to climb to the top of . . . what's the name of that big mountain down in the Theocracy of the Abbir? Um, the one with that strange abbey full of monks, and the Oracle's shrine and stuff."

Ruby giggled. "Mount Ukjente Hoyder. The mountain of unknown heights. You'd really climb that for me?"

Thorgrim jumped on a box of books and opened his arms wide. His voice boomed. "Yes, I would! And, I'd shout to the entire world that I'm madly in love with a girl named Ruby Kanto!"

"Shhhhhhh! Please! My mother's going to get mad!"

He laughed. "Okay, sorry. Making yer mother angry is probably not a good thing, even if she does like me. Hey, speaking of the entire world,

308

do you ever wonder what else is out there? I mean, our entire realm seems to be surrounded by water. Don't ya think there's more land out there? Other people?"

Before Ruby could answer, her mother stormed down the steps and looked around the corner, offering them both a death stare.

"Excuse me, uh Shem. Although you have not yet told the entire world that you're madly in love with my daughter, you have, however, managed to tell everyone in the entire library. Would you please stop shouting? You know this is one of the reasons why I don't allow employees to date each other."

In the course of a few seconds, embarrassed as hell, the color of Thorgrim's face became pinkish-red.

"Sorry, I'm sure sorry," he sputtered. "Won't happen again, I promise."

Gertrude's eyes continued to blaze. "If you keep shouting, you're going to be walkin' down the street talkin' to yerself. Do you understand what that means? Now, please get those books cataloged, you two, or I'll find someone who is not head over in heels in love, to do it."

"Yes, mother," replied Ruby, trying to restrain the impulse to giggle.

"Yes, what she said," commented Thorgrim, still embarrassed.

Gertrude grumbled, then did an about-face and went back up the stairs.

Thorgrim pouted. "Sorry, Ruby."

"Hey, goofy, I love you, too," she replied softly. She moved in close and wrapped her arms around him. Before giving him the kiss of the century, she looked down at his beard.

"Blinky?"

"No, he's upstairs chasing the other cats."

"Good," she replied, with a devilish grin.

Ruby pounced on Thorgrim, rolling with him across a few boxes, down the side, and onto the floor. There, she landed on top of him and smiled coyly, her eyes twinkling even in the dim light. Now, hidden from her mother and the rest of the world, deep behind piles of books and boxes, in the basement of the second greatest library in the realm, they loved.

***

A half-hour later, both of them were sound asleep and still hidden behind the books. A voice woke them. It was Ruby's mother.

"Shem, will you come up here and fill in for me at the front desk? It's getting late and I've got some paperwork that I need to get finished before the end of the day.

Thorgrim panicked, fearing Gertrude would come downstairs and catch them. Jumping up, he put on his clothes and said, "Yes, I'll be there in a minute!"

"Please hurry! Ruby, you might as well come up too. There are a lot of visitors that need help finding books.

"Okay, Mother!"

After several, hectic minutes, both Ruby and Thorgrim were upstairs doing what they had been asked to do. Thorgrim took a seat at the front circulation desk, while Ruby wandered around the library offering assistance.

Blinky, tired of chasing the other cats, seeing Thorgrim, scurried over and jumped into his beard.

***

As usual, about thirty minutes before closing time, in front of the circulation desk, people began to get in line to check out books before the library closed.

Today, the line was exceptionally long.

In turn, each person would approach the desk with the books they wanted to check out. The limit was three books for library members. Non-members could get a temporary card but could only check out one book or scroll at a time.

Thorgrim was so busy that he barely had time to look up at whoever was checking out books. The line flowed smoothly and at 4:45 p.m., Thorgrim wearily glanced up and gratefully noticed that there were only a few more people waiting their turn.

A middle-aged halfling stepped up with three books in his hands.

"Name?" said Thorgrim, routinely.

"Harvey Aledrinker."

Thorgrim glanced up.

"Aledrinker? Yer kiddin'. You're a halfling. Do ya like ale?"

"Who doesn't?"

"Right. Uh, okay, what books are you checkin' out, today?"

"Three books. The entire Beard Wars trilogy. Beard Wars, The Elves Strike Back, and Return of the Dwarf."

"Oh, I've never read them. Ya like the sci-fi stuff, huh?"

"Yes, can ya hurry, please? The missus is waitin' outside and she's starvin'."

"Sure, sure. Can I see yer library card, please."

Thorgrim checked Mr. Aledrinker's card, then had him sign for the books.

"Next!"

Another apparent bibliophile approached with a big stack of books. "Name?"

"Juniper Snowdrift."

"Books?"

"I have six, but I know that you are only allowed to check out three."

Thorgrim looked up and saw a female dwarf in her late fifties.

"That's correct. I'm sorry, but rules are rules. I'm sure you understand."

Juniper dropped her head. "I know. It's just, my two little kids are sick at home and not doing well. I can't afford to buy them a new toy, so, I thought I would come down to the library and pick out a few books to read to them. Maybe it will make them feel better."

"Yer kids are sick? What's wrong with them?"

"The doctor doesn't know. I, um, it's okay. I understand. I'll take just three, then. I'm sorry for asking you to break the rules, sir. Here's my library card."

Thorgrim smiled. Juniper's love for her children reminded him of the unselfish love that his mother had for him. He said softly, "You don't have to call me sir. My name is Shem. You can take all of these books, and may Moridon bless you and yer children."

Tears welled in her tired eyes. "Thank you so much, sir. I'll never forget your kindness."

Reaching into his pocket, he found what he was looking for. In his mind, he heard Gary of Tuckerheim's words. 'Someday, I want you to do the same for someone in need, okay?'

Thorgrim smiled and handed her a gold piece. The same one that Gary had given him over four years ago in a little town called Stug.

"Ma'am, I want you to have this. It's very special to me. A friend gave it to me a long time ago to help me out when I was in need. Fortunately, fate smiled upon me and I never had to spend it. Please, go buy a couple of toys for yer kids. It would mean a lot to me if you would."

Juniper was stunned. "Oh, I can't take this!"

He grinned ear to ear. "Yes, you can. The toy store on West Third Avenue and Middle Street is open until eight o'clock, tonight."

"Shem, thank you so much! I will never forget your kindness!" Tears flowing, she turned and walked away with her six books and the shiny gold coin.

The next person in line placed two books on the circulation desk in front of Thorgrim. Without looking up, Thorgrim read the titles aloud.

"Oh, good choices! The Adventures of Huckleberry Dwarf, and The Dwarf and the Ring. Probably, my two all-time favorites!"

Thorgrim looked up.

Time stopped.

The person checking out the books, smiled and said, "Hello, Son."

Thorgrim could not breathe and the room began to spin.

"Son, are you okay?"

"Papa," whispered Thorgrim, his heart pounding in his chest.

Luthor nodded, continuing to smile, his eyes glistening.

Thorgrim slowly shook his head unable to believe his own eyes. His voice cracking, he said, "But . . . how?"

"Thorgrim . . . or should I say, Shem? I suspected and hoped this is where you've been the whole time. Of course, I wasn't sure, but I had to stop and check. You know, that was very nice of you to help that poor woman with the sick children. Your mother and I raised you well. I'm proud of you."

"When did you get here, Papa?"

"I recently bought a horse and carriage. I loaded everyone up a few days ago and headed this way. I thought it was time for a vacation and decided on taking a trip to the capital. You know, I have never been to this city before."

"Everyone came with you?" asked Thorgrim, glancing around.

"Oh, yes. They're running around in here, somewhere."

Thorgrim stood, his eyes welling with tears. He saw Ruby and signaled for her.

Ruby walked over. She noticed that Thorgrim seemed upset.

"Shem, what's the matter, are you okay?"

Thorgrim wiped his eyes and said, "I'm fine. Ruby, I want you to meet my father, Luthor."

Ruby looked at Luthor and said, "Mr. Lybree, it's a pleasure to meet you."

Luthor was caught off guard when Ruby addressed him as Mr. Lybree, but his wisdom spoke. Understanding, he replied, "And it's a pleasure to meet you, Ruby."

Thorgrim smiled and proudly said, "She's muh girlfriend."

His father smiled. "Oh, of course."

At that moment, a couple more dwarves jumped in line behind Luthor.

"Hey, excuse me, it's almost five," one of them said. "I really want to check out this book before the library closes."

"Ruby, will you please take over for me? I need to visit with muh father."

Ruby gave Thorgrim a quick peck on his cheek. "Sure, you go spend time with him. I've got this."

Sitting down, she hollered, "Next, please."

"Do you really want to check out those two books, Papa?"

"No, Son. Those are the two you left behind for Tadder. He wanted to bring them and thank you. Heh, he's still too young to understand those stories, but one day I'm sure he'll love them, as you do."

"Where is Tadder? I can't wait to see him. He's five years old now. The last time I saw him, he was a newborn."

"He's with yer mother. She's out in the Museum."

Thorgrim and his father walked together towards the entrance to the Museum. When they were a few feet away, the doors burst open and in poured Thorgrim's twelve siblings and his mother.

Marjorie instantly became a melted ball of boo-hoo.

She cried, "Thorgrim! Oh, my God, it's been over four years. We've all missed you so much!"

Luthor whispered into his wife's ear, "Shhh, not so loud. We can't use his real name. Remember, the police are after him. Call him Shem. I'll explain later."

Luthor cradled his wife who was doing her best to remain upright. "Margie, you promised me that you could handle this."

Sobbing, she said, "I know, I'm sorry. I just never thought I would ever . . . uh . . . —"

"See me again?"

Whimpering, she replied, "Yes."

"I know. Please, Mama, it's okay."

Thorgrim hugged his mother. After a few minutes in his arms, she calmed down.

Then, the entire family gathered around Thorgrim.

Luthor took this time to inform his family that they are not to use Thorgrim's real name and should call him Shem, instead. Everyone understood.

Thorgrim exclaimed, "I can't believe how big you all have gotten! Who's this big guy over here?" he said, pointing to Thurston.

"Thurston, is that really you?"

313

"Yep!"

"He's nineteen now and out of school," said Luthor.

"And workin' the mines, I presume?"

Luthor nodded. "Oh, yes. He's doing well there."

"Do ya like workin' in the mines, Thurston?"

"Ya, I get kinda dirty, but it's fun."

"Good for you!"

Thorgrim spent a few minutes with each sibling, going down the line from oldest to youngest. Finally, he said, "Where's Tadder?"

"Standing right behind you," replied his mother, still misty-eyed.

Looking down at his leg, Thorgrim found a five-year-old child with a fuzzy pile of bright-red hair on top of his head. The little boy was hanging onto Thorgrim's pants, looking up and grinning at his older brother.

Thurston cracked, "Lucky for Tadder, Thor— I mean, Shem didn't fart while he was standin' back there!"

Thurston's joke caused everyone to laugh. Even Marjorie giggled, though she said, "Oh, stop with the fart jokes! They're disgusting!"

Thorgrim grinned. "Same ol' Thurston. I suppose I better check to see if my wallet is missing before you leave here!"

"And yer pipe," replied Thurston.

"You don't smoke, do you . . . Shem?" asked his mother.

"No. Oh, I played around with it, but I didn't care much for it."

Bending down, he picked up Tadder and looked into his eyes.

"So, you're Tadder."

Tadder nodded. He held a six-inch tall, wooden toy dwarf in his hands.

"Is this yer toy?"

"Yesh."

"It's a dwarf?"

"Yesh."

Thorgrim examined the little hand-carved toy.

"Is it supposed to be a famous dwarf? Like a hero?"

"Yesh."

"Really! It's a cool toy."

"Papa made it for me," replied Tadder, smiling. "He said it's a special dwarf."

"A special dwarf? Who's it supposed to be?"

"It's you," replied Tadder.

Thorgrim's heart jumped into his throat. Swallowing it, he kissed his little brother on the cheek, then placed him on the ground.

Thorgrim glanced at his father, who returned a quick wink.

Tadder looked up and signaled for Thorgrim to lean down so he could whisper something into his ear.

Thorgrim bent over and said, "What is it, Tadder?"

Giggling, Tadder whispered, "You have a kitty in yer beard."

[Author's Note:]

Unfortunately, the remainder of the text regarding this event in Thorgrim's life was heavily damaged. What little information survived, indicated that Thorgrim left the library with his family to go somewhere in the city, but it is not clear where.

***

[Author's Note:]

After the surprising though joyful experience of reuniting with his family, very little is known about Thorgrim's remaining twenty years in Bur Dhulgren. Perhaps ninety-nine percent of the texts are unusable, beginning with the time after he meets his family in the library in 2253, through to the year 2273, when, due to a tragic event, he is forced to leave the city at the age of forty-four.

It appears that Thorgrim traveled out of the city on several occasions but when, or to where, we do not know. One seriously damaged paragraph mentions he rode Nugget to see Gary of Tuckerheim in Stug, but the date and purpose are unknown.

We do not know if he ever saw his parents or siblings again during the time he lived in Bur Dhulgren.

Madly in love, Thorgrim and Ruby eventually married. The wedding date is unknown, though there is some evidence that it occurred around 2260. Sadly, only a few, fragmented sentences survived regarding the wedding. We know that a ceremony was held in the flower gardens inside the Grand Hall and that family and friends were in attendance.

Thorgrim mentions in his diary that several times before they were married, he thought about 'coming clean' with Ruby.

His mentor, and Ruby's father, Uuno Kanto, advised against it. He warned him that if she accidentally said something to the wrong person, it might lead to his arrest. Several times in his diary he mentions his concerns about being imprisoned for years, unable to see Ruby.

Equally frightening and still of concern, was that there was no way to know how Ruby would react when she found out that Thorgrim had been lying to her all of those years. Maybe she would leave him. It was obvious that he was not willing to take the risk to find out.

Overall, despite the lost text covering his time in the capital, it appears that Thorgrim happily lived a normal life doing what he enjoyed: working with books. Thorgrim Longbeard was the ultimate bibliophile, and with the possible exception of a young female elf he would meet later, no one loved books more.

Thorgrim seemed to be happy, though his life was shrouded in sadness because he could not truly be himself.

Thorgrim loved his books, but he loved Ruby more than anything.

Tragedy would strike Thorgrim in a way that would change his life and attitude, forever. The exact date is uncertain, possibly in the late 2260s, some of the fragments mention that Thorgrim's beloved wife Ruby, died, along with their baby boy during a difficult childbirth.

We can guess that this shocking episode brought back the terrible memory of his mother's perilous experience during the birth of his youngest brother, Tadder.

Despite minimal information, it is clear that Thorgrim was devastated by their deaths. In his middle and later years, he would often brag that he had been 'married a dozen times' and that he had 'fathered thirty or forty kids.' The truth was that he would never marry again until much later in his life, and as far as the surviving records indicate, he never fathered another child.

Ruby Kanto was his only true love, and she was no doubt irreplaceable to him. As expected, her loss and that of his infant son was overwhelming, causing bouts of depression that lasted for years. Although by his early twenties, he occasionally drank ale, it was during this time, after the loss of Ruby and his son, that Thorgrim developed an addiction to the malted beverage.

More tragedy would strike. This time, details gleaned from several, intact pages from his notes and cross-referenced with his diary, reveal that Thorgrim became a victim of being in the wrong place at the wrong time. This unfortunate event, occurring almost twenty-five years to the day he left his home in Vog.

***

Date: Sunday, July 17, 2273.
Time: 6:03 a.m.
Location: Thorgrim's home in Bur Dhulgren.

Despite the intense summer heat, at dawn, Thorgrim decided to ride down to Old South Mharrak and spend the day exploring the city. Of course, his cat Blinky came with him, riding deep within his, once again, auburn, knee-length beard.

Battling depression, he hoped the trip, and the excitement of visiting a place he had never seen before, would ease his troubled mind.

Due to the heat, the ride would take longer than normal. After a four-mile journey south from his home in central Bur Dhulgren, it was another twenty-four miles to his destination.

At first, the idea worked. The trip down was uneventful, but when he reached the outskirts of Old South Mharrak, ice-cold ale called his name. The downhearted, thirsty dwarf decided to stop for a few drinks at the first place he could find. Then, he remembered it was Worship Day and likely, everything would be closed.

Disappointed, cursing himself for not bringing any ale along, he entered the main street on the north side of the city.

Looking down the street, he could not believe his luck. The first building on the corner had several horses tied up in front of it. It was a ramshackle establishment called 'The Cracked Mug Tavern.'

An 'Open' sign hung in the window.

Pleased, Thorgrim displayed a very wide, toothy grin. "If there's an ale god, he's smilin' upon me today," he said aloud.

Before directing Nugget over to the closest available hitch and a water trough, he put on his dark-red, Iron Golem eyepatch and then checked his timepiece. It was 10:00 a.m.

There, Thorgrim's life would change forever, due to a chance meeting with a couple of miscreants, who had recently been released from the Kronk Prison.

***

[Author's Note:]
The Cracked Mug Tavern was crumbling and probably should have been torn down years ago. Even the wood roaches hated the place. In its heyday, now over a hundred years ago, the tavern was the hottest place in Old South Mharrak.

The small city had seen better days as well. Originally, before the unification of the eight clans, Old South Mharrak was simply known as

317

'South Mharrak' and was the sister city to the provincial capital of Mharrak Bur (Mharrak City).

After the unification and creation of the Dwarven Kingdom, Mharrak City was renamed 'Bur Dhulgren' or 'City of the Dwarves.' The residents of South Mharrak refused to change the name to 'South Bur Dhulgren, but as time passed, the city became known as 'Old South Mharrak.

***

The bartender adjusted his glasses and said to Thorgrim, "Hey, buddy. Since ya got here, I've been wantin' to say yer tan horse is sure a tall one."

Thorgrim, in a gloomy daze, slowly nodded. Staring straight ahead, he only half-heard the heavily tattooed, rotund bartender.

The bartender waved his hands in front of Thorgrim's one eye. "Hey, buddy . . . you okay?"

Thorgrim's single eye gave the bartender a quick glance. "I'm fine. Sorry, just tired and daydreamin' after muh ride. Top off my mug with yer coldest ale, please. It's hot out, and I'm just grateful that yer open on Worship Day."

"Sure, buddy," replied the bartender, tipping a tankard of frosty ale into Thorgrim's mug. "We're always open, year 'round."

"I'm very grateful for that."

"Ya know, buddy, this is yer sixth mug of ale in a half-hour."

After taking a big slurp, Thorgrim grinned. "Only six? I lost count. Tell ya what. I'll keep drinkin' em, un you keep countin' em."

"Sure, buddy," replied the bartender. Pointing to a wide door past the bar, he said, "Uh, no doubt, you'll be needin' to use the garderobe, soon. It's right through that door over there."

"Thanks. I was about to ask ya about dat. In fact, I'll use it now. Be right back."

Thorgrim wobbled around the bar to relieve his bladder, which by now was overfilled with some of the coldest ale he had ever tasted. Ten minutes later, he returned to the bar to resume his drinking.

While filling the mug of another dwarf, the bartender said to Thorgrim, "Hey, buddy. That's a nice mug, ya got there. It's huge. Biggest I've ever seen. What does the letter 'T' ('T' in the Dwarven alphabet) stand for on the front?"

Thorgrim became lost in thought.

318

***

[Author's Note:]

The mug was a wedding gift from the Iron Golem Pub's bartender, Scootz McDonald, who had promised Thorgrim an ale mug of his own the day they met. Stating that 'No dwarf should be caught dead without his ale mug,' Scootz finally fulfilled his promise years later on Thorgrim's wedding day.

When Thorgrim took the large copper mug to an engraver to have his name etched on the front, he accidentally told him that his name was Thorgrim instead of Shem. While watching the engraver work on his mug, Thorgrim realizing his mistake became horrified and stopped the process.

Luckily, only the letter 'T' was completed. Thorgrim apologized to the engraver for the mistake and would take the mug as is.

Thorgrim told the engraver that he would think of something when anyone asked him what the 'T' stood for. Before long, he had the perfect answer.

***

"Well, buddy, what does the 'T' stand for?"

"Thirsty. It stands for thirsty. Dat's me. I'm very thirsty, in fact. Keep it filled, un keep it filled to da top, un overflow it if ya want. I'll lap up any dat ends up on the bar."

"Uh, sure, buddy. Whatever ya say."

Thorgrim was drunk, but like most dwarves, he could handle his ale. However, even dwarves have their alcohol limit, and Thorgrim had started to slur his words after the sixth emptied mug.

Still depressed, Thorgrim sighed, then took another big drink. Glancing around the shanty, wishing he were alone, he watched a dozen other dwarves as they sat at their tables, happily chatting, drinking beer or nibbling on bar food.

"Hey, buddy—"

"What?" interrupted Thorgrim, irritated. "Will ya please, stop calling me buddy, all the time?"

"Sure, I'm sorry. I . . . well, I just wanted to ask you if yer cat would like some milk? I see him pokin' his head out of yer beard and figured he might like some."

319

Thorgrim felt ashamed. "I'm sorry for bein' so rude. Please, forgive me. Uh, I didn't catch yer name?"

"It's okay. Muh name's Bubbers but everyone calls me Toad."

"Toad? How did ya get that nickname?"

"Well, ya gotta admit, I'm kinda shaped like one!"

Thorgrim chuckled. "Okay, I get it. Uh, yes please, it would be nice if muh cat could have some cold milk. Dat's very nice of you, Bubbers . . . if ya don't mind me callin' ya by yer real name."

"That's fine," replied Bubbers with a big smile.

Placing a saucer on the counter, Bubbers filled it to the brim with ice-cold goat's milk. Thirsty, Blinky instantly slid out from Thorgrim's beard and happily drank from the saucer.

Bubbers replaced the milk decanter in the dry ice box and said, "Hey, bud— um, I really like yer eyepatch. What do the initials IA stand for?"

Thorgrim took a sip of ale. "Iron Golem. It's a pub in Bur Dhulgren."

"Iron Golem Pub? Never heard of it."

Thorgrim removed his eyepatch and laid it on the bar.

He took another drink, smirked, then looked at Bubbers. "Who am I foolin'? I don't need dat eyepatch."

Bubbers was surprised. "You have both yer eyes? Why wear an eyepatch, then?"

"I don't know. I guess 'cuz it's supposed to make me look tough or somethin'."

"Well, I thought it looked pretty cool, and to be honest, it does make ya look a bit intimidatin'."

"It really does? Okay, I'll wear it then."

Chuckling, and beyond tipsy, Thorgrim picked up the eyepatch and put it back on, covering his left eye, as usual.

"Bubbers, would ya mind givin' muh cat a refill of milk? And, while yer at it, top me off, too."

"Sure thing."

Thorgrim looked at the tavern's wall clock. It was 11:45 a.m.

While Bubbers was filling Blinky's saucer, without warning, the front door of the tavern crashed open. Two shady-looking dwarves, with scruffy beards and dirty clothes, stomped in. Their rough appearance hushed the entire place. Looking around, they glared and sneered at everyone, then approached the bar, both taking seats to the right of Thorgrim.

The first dwarf said in a gruff voice, "Hey, chubster. Get me and my friend here a cold one, and make it quick. We got out of the big Kronk yesterday after serving eight years of a twenty-year sentence! We want to

320

celebrate our parole! We've been hitching since then, and we're ready to drink every drop you have in the place!"

The second dwarf grinned and said, "Ya, we're ready to drink every drop you have in the place!"

Thorgrim, again wearing his Iron Golem eyepatch, took a quick glance at them and then resumed his drinking.

"Who's flea-bitten cat?" asked the first dwarf, with a scowl.

"Mine," replied Thorgrim.

He smelled trouble brewing.

The first dwarf wasted no time in saying, "Oh, really? Sorry, but I find it rather disgusting to be sharing a bar with a filthy animal. I'll ask ya nicely once, to get it outta muh sight."

Thorgrim was not in any mood for these ass-hats.

Carefully, he picked up Blinky and put him back in his beard.

The first dwarf laughed. "By God, you actually park that cat in yer beard? If that ain't the dumbest thing I've ever seen!"

Thorgrim shrugged.

The second dwarf said, "Who's giant horse is that out there? The thing is a freak if ya ask me! Why, you'd need to be lowered into the saddle by a rope to even ride it."

Thorgrim stared straight ahead. "The horse is mine."

Both ex-convicts laughed. "Hahahahoahaho!"

Bubbers placed two mugs of icy-cold ale in front of the ex-cons.

The first dwarf picked up his mug and downed it in only two gulps. Slamming the empty mug hard on the bar, he elbowed his friend, who proceeded to do the same thing.

After the second dwarf gulped his ale and slammed his mug on the bar, the first one said, "Refills for both of us and make it quick, fatty!"

The second dwarf leaned over and said, "Ya, fill 'em up and make it quick, fatty!"

"Sure, whatever you guys say."

Bubbers filled both mugs and again both of them drank every drop in a matter of seconds.

While Bubbers was refilling their mugs a third time, Thorgrim decided he had had enough of these two boisterous fellows.

"Bubbers, what do I owe ya?"

After doing some quick math, Bubbers replied, "Fourteen coppers should do it."

"Here's a gold. You deserve it. Thankee for yer hospitality."

Bubbers smiled and grabbed the gold piece. "Thank you, sir. Hey, buddy, I didn't get yer name?"

"Shem. Shem Lybree."

"Pleasure to meet ya, Shem. Where ya headed?"

"I rode down from Bur Dhulgren to see this city. Never been here before. I suppose that I'll look around a bit and then head back home."

Bubbers smiled. "Not much here, really. Couple of ancient forts on the south side that are kinda fun to explore, but that's about it."

"Thankee. I just might go take a look at those forts. That kinda stuff is right up my alley."

Bubbers was about to reply but was rudely interrupted.

The first dwarf yelled, "Hey, fatty, I said keep our mugs filled. Quit yappin' with cat-face there, and do yer job before ya piss me and my friend off."

Thorgrim turned and glared at the first dwarf, who simply grinned in return.

The first dwarf, still sitting on a stool, leaned closer to Thorgrim. "Hey, cat-face. Ya think that eyepatch is goin' to intimidate me? My friend and I just got done doin' eight years hard labor for armed robbery, kidnappin', and attempted murder!"

The second dwarf looked over the first dwarf's shoulder and said, "Ya, We just got done doin' eight years hard labor for armed robbery, and attempted murder."

The first dwarf sneered at his friend. "Dummy, you forgot the kidnappin' part."

"Oh. Ya, that, too!" replied the second dwarf wearing an arrogant grin.

Thorgrim raised his brow and bit his lip. As he stepped off the stool, he swung his massive beard around in front of him. The beard, now back to its original color of dark auburn, hung past his knees.

Both of the ex-convicts noticed the incredible beard. As Thorgrim started to move towards the door, the first dwarf, his eyes as big as coins, quickly jumped off his stool and stepped into Thorgrim's path.

Thorgrim stopped and shrugged his shoulders. "What do ya want? I'm leavin', please get outta muh way. I don't want any trouble."

The first dwarf, wild-eyed, his mouth hanging agape, looked Thorgrim up and down for a moment.

"Holy buckets of river rat heads!" yelled the first dwarf. "Ya said yer name is Shem something or other? I smell tree ostrich shit if you ask me. Tell me, Shem, have you seen any red diamonds, lately?"

Thorgrim was speechless.

The first dwarf leaned in close, almost nose to nose with Thorgrim. As he did, the second dwarf jumped off his stool, equally wild-eyed and wearing a big grin, stood behind his friend, watching.

"Beardby! How ya been?" shouted the first dwarf. "What's the matter? Did the cat get yer tongue? Hahahahaaaahoha!"

From out of Thorgrim's haunted past, it was none other than Zippy Borknoi and Rumbler McGeever.

"Lookie here, Rumbler! It's our old friend, Beardby!"

Rumbler laughed. "By Gawd, can ya believe it, Zippy? It's really him! The summa-bi-atch who got us fired from the silver mine!"

Zippy said, "Ya, and don't forget his papa had to come and fight his battles for him too! Hey, Beardby, did ya know that yer father put us both in the hospital for several weeks?"

Thorgrim growled, "You both left me deep in that mine alone. I could have died in there."

Zippy sneered. "Oh, you could've died, is it? Ya know, I think we should try that trick on him again, Rumbler."

Turning to the bartender, he yelled, "Hey, fatty, ya gotta heavy cloth bag I can borrow?"

Bubbers shook his head.

With the obvious about to happen, several dwarves scrambled out of the tavern's side door in an effort to avoid any fighting.

Zippy saw them and yelled, "Hey, where ya all goin'? Did I say you could leave yet? You're goin' to miss all the fun!"

Bubbers pleaded, "Hey, buddy, come on, yer drivin' muh customers out!"

"Shut up, you fathead!" roared Zippy.

Rumbler yelled, "Ya, Shut up, you fathead!"

Thorgrim, though worried, chuckled. "I see Rumbler still copies everything you say. Kinda like a parrot, isn't he?"

Zippy leaned in closer, pushing Thorgrim's nose, forcing his head back an inch.

"You can shut yer mouth, too, Beardby. Hey! Now that I think about it, yer wanted by the law, aren't you?"

Rumbler leaned over, "Ya, Zippy, he's wanted for skipping out on the mines, remember?"

Zippy laughed. "Yep! I remember. Well, Beardby, here's what's gonna go down. First, me and Rumbler are gonna drag yer butt out back and beat the tar out of ya. Then, we're gonna tie ya up un throw ya on the back of that freaky horse out there. After that, we'll haul yer sorry ass up to Bur Dhulgren and then turn you in to the police! Why, I bet we'll get a big reward for capturing you!"

Rumbler leaned in again and said, "Ya, we'll probably get a big reward for capturing you!"

Zippy spun around and said, "Rumbler . . . shut yer hole, will ya?"

Zippy turned back to Thorgrim. With a malicious expression, he leaned in close, and when his nose again touched Thorgrim's, Blinky, screeching like a banshee, with fangs and claws slashing, leaped out of Thorgrim's beard and onto Zippy's face.

Zippy screamed and went down onto his rear, frantically grasping at the cat, who now had its teeth and retractable claws firmly embedded in his face. Blood and beard hair flew everywhere.

"Ahhhhhhh! For the love of God . . . Rumbler, get this crazy thing off me! Help, help!"

Rumbler tried to grab Blinky and when he did, the angry cat screeched and bit him deeply on the hand causing blood to spurt from several pointy wounds.

"Ahhhhhh, that freakin' wildcat bit me! I'm bleedin'! I'm bleedin! I'm gonna die! Whaaaaaaaaa!"

Blinky continued his attack, while Zippy's hands flailed in all directions, trying to defend himself. Rolling under a table, still screaming, Zippy sat up and started to punch the cat.

Thorgrim, fearing his cat might get hurt or possibly killed, yelled for him. "Blinky, stop it! Blinky, come here!"

Panicking, in a desperate effort to dislodge Blinky from Zippy's face, Rumbler picked up his ale mug then started to swing it around in order to strike the cat with it.

In one graceful move that would even impress an elf, Thorgrim again yelled, "Blinky!" while simultaneously sprinting over and pulling his cat from Zippy's face, which was now a bloody mess.

At the same time, Rumbler's heavy mug found its mark, only the cat was no longer there. Instead, it smashed into Zippy's blood-smeared face, knocking him out cold.

A split second after the mug impacted, Thorgrim, swiftly moving towards the exit, managed to land a solid kick into Rumbler's nards as he passed by him on the way to the door.

When he reached the exit, Blinky was already safely back in his beard. Before leaving the tavern, Thorgrim took a quick glance behind him and saw Zippy lying flat on his back, out cold, his face covered in blood. Rumbler was rolling around on the floor, moaning, and from behind the bar, Bubbers was giving Thorgrim the 'thumbs up' sign.

Outside, he took a chance. Racing to Nugget, Thorgrim untied the rope from the hitch and then somehow managed a perfect mounting without using the block. Trembling, he took off his eyepatch, looked at it for a moment, then shoved it into his front pocket.

With a big nudge, he sent Nugget galloping out of the city, onto the main highway and north towards the capital. Nugget could only gallop for a mile or so in the heat. Slowing to a canter, he pressed onward.

Thorgrim was half-way to Bur Dhulgren before he realized he had left his engraved ale mug behind. Now he was frightened. Two enemies from his past had discovered him, and he knew that they would not waste any time contacting the authorities to expose him.

Thorgrim now had no choice but to do what he had set out to do twenty-five years ago. He would have to leave the country.

***

[Author's Note:]
Fortunately, almost all of Thorgrim's records detailing his second attempt to escape from the Dwarven Clans survived intact.

***

Thorgrim understood that his false life of living as Shem Lybree was about to end, and oddly, he felt a strange sense of relief. Frustrated, he wished he could see Uuno Kanto to seek his advice, but Thorgrim had no time to contact anyone to tell them he was leaving. He also realized that it was in his best interest not to reveal his intentions to anyone.

He realized that Zippy and Rumbler would be able to hitch a ride to Bur Dhulgren within a matter of hours and report Thorgrim to the police. They knew his alias was Shem Lybree. They were undoubtedly angrier than ever, and Thorgrim knew they would stop at nothing in an effort to exact revenge upon him.

Time was short. The first thing he had to do was to get home as soon as possible. There, he would gather up a few important things and then stock his backpack with food, water, and other necessities.

It was fortunate that the afternoon temperature had dropped because he had to push Nugget very hard to get home as soon as possible. Though it was still quite warm, he managed to make the nearly thirty-mile trek in just under three hours. At 3:30 p.m., disappointed, angry, and terrified, Thorgrim arrived at the home he had shared with Ruby on West Third Avenue and South Fourth Street.

While he let his weary horse drink some water and eat, he ran inside his home to gather his things.

Having little time to sort through things, he filled a leather bag with his personal savings of one hundred thirty-two gold, along with some hygienic items, his false ID papers (which he may need to use in order to cross the border), and the letters from his parents.

Next, he hurriedly stuffed his original, high school backpack with food, fresh, water flasks and several changes of clothes.

Finally, he opened a dresser drawer and retrieved his most prized possession: The silver heart charm Ruby had been wearing the day he met her. After giving it a kiss, he attached it to the gold chain around his neck.

Making sure Blinky was safe inside his beard; Thorgrim took a last look around his home. "Goodbye," he said, his heart heavy.

Wearing his backpack and with the leather bag in his hand, he ran as fast as he could outside to Nugget. There, he paused before mounting him.

"My God, where do I go?" he said aloud.

He remembered facing this dilemma when he left Vog, twenty-five years ago.

He knew which way he had to go. It was the only option.

∗∗∗

[Author's Note:]

Ironically, Thorgrim faced many of the same issues that he did when he left Vog, twenty-five years ago, so it did not take him long to figure out that there was only one choice. Going to the sea was out of the question, because likely, he could not take Nugget on any ship.

Heading north, a distance of at least four hundred miles, would take too long. South was an option. But unless he went cross-country (exposing himself to bandits and other problems), the only way to the Great Kingdom border traveling south was back through Old South Mharrak. Traveling near the ancient city would be risky because it was very likely that Zippy and Rumbler had already shared their information with the city police.

Thorgrim knew that Zippy and Rumbler were not the brightest torches in the realm, but they were street smart and would know how to spread the news about their discovery quickly. Worse yet, the Dwarven Clans had in the past year redoubled their efforts to hunt down wanted criminals.

Criminals like Thorgrim Longbeard.

The maximum punishment for skipping mandatory duty without cause had been increased from five to ten years in the Kronk Prison. In addition, Thorgrim faced another three to five for using false identification papers.

The safest and shortest way was east over the Delaware River, through a strange place called the Haunted Forest, then across the border into the elven Republic of Alacarj. Another option was that after he crossed the Delaware, he could also stay on the main road and travel through the city of Brimger. Next, he would turn east again, going cross-country through the various farms south of Jasp. It would be a longer distance, but he could avoid the creepy sounding, Haunted Forest. Either way, he would have to eventually enter the land of the elves.

***

Taking a deep breath, he thought, *Better to walk with elves then live here and go to prison.*

After tying the leather bag to his saddle, with Blinky snuggled safely deep inside his massive beard, he mounted Nugget (luckily, the second time in one day with no mishap). He then raced away from his home.

Taking a final glance at the beautiful little bungalow, tears forming in his eyes, he thought, *So many memories, Ruby, yet, so little time together. I miss you.*

When he reached Middle Street, he turned east and slowed to a trot, not wanting to draw any unnecessary attention to himself.

Encountering little traffic, passing the University and the Royal Castle, Thorgrim traveled through the Heart of the City: the famous intersection of Central Avenue and Middle Street.

Just past the intersection, Thorgrim reached the Grand Hall and the Supreme Library for quite possibly the last time. He halted and looked towards the entrance to the front of the library, recalling the moment Ruby first spoke to him twenty-five years ago. In his mind, he once again heard her voice.

'Excuse me, sir. Are you going to come in?'

Heartbroken, he cried loudly, "Ruby! Oh God, how I love you and miss you! I'll love you . . . forever and a day!"

Thorgrim's tears flowed like little streams down and onto his beard. Openly weeping, he signaled his horse and rode onward.

The time was 4:10 p.m.

With his mind spinning from anxiety, Thorgrim went east, down Middle Street at a canter, slowing only if he saw police in the area. As he rode in the heat of the summer afternoon, he thought of Gertrude and wished that he could say goodbye to her. He also considered seeking the help of Uuno Kanto, Mooky, or some of his other friends, but there was no time to spare.

Regrettably, and most painful of all, he would be unable to stop at the Bur Dhulgren Cemetery to spend a few moments with Ruby and their son. The cemetery was a few miles northwest of the city on the road to Juht, opposite of the direction that he needed to go.

Soon, Thorgrim approached one of the Middle Street bar and pub districts. Had this been a Saturday, Thorgrim would have encountered the typical crowds of afternoon partiers, as well as the squads of club-heads who would have been out in force struggling to control them. Thankfully, with the exception of some party debris and a few pedestrians, the street was empty.

Thorgrim hurried Nugget along and by 4:30 p.m., the east gates were in sight. The gates were wide open for daytime transit, so he had no reason to stop.

Picking up speed, Thorgrim flew past the guards and out the gates without a wave goodbye. When he approached the Mharrak River Bridge, he was slowed by a crowd of people who were crossing the bridge on their way to the city.

After pushing his way through the chaos, he made it over the bridge, but unfortunately, a short distance east of the span, Thorgrim had to stop due to a traffic jam of vehicles and horses caused by a large, overturned wagon. There was no way around because the ditches were full of murky-looking water from the previous night's rain. As he impatiently waited, along with dozens of others, for the road to be cleared, he repeatedly glanced back to see if he was being followed. Then, grabbing his attention, he heard the call of a bugle off to his right, about a half-mile south of the highway.

When Thorgrim looked, he was astonished at what he saw unfolding before him.

In a large field, a battalion of cavalry was practicing maneuvers and charges. However, the sword-armed soldiers were not riding regular horses. They were mounted on pure-white, miniature dwarf donkeys.

There were perhaps eight hundred of them packed tightly in a perfect triangular formation. At the sound of a bugle, the battalion thundered forward, soon reaching a surprising speed for such small animals.

"What's going on out there?" Thorgrim said aloud, hoping someone around him might know the answer.

Another dwarf on horseback, also waiting for the road to clear, said, "That's a battalion of the King's White Guard. They're training and practicing horsemanship. Isn't that beautiful? Those soldiers are riding miniature dwarf donkeys. I've always said that a battalion of those critters charging in formation is a sight to behold. Wouldn't you agree?"

Thorgrim could not believe his eyes. "Yes, they're beautiful. But, those are donkeys?"

"Yes. Miniature dwarf donkeys."

Still astonished, Thorgrim said, "Muh wife had one of those. They're just little donkeys and cute as hell. I mean, they are only four feet tall! Wouldn't dwarven horses be more effective?"

The mounted dwarf replied, "The cavalry uses dwarven horses, especially the lancers. Trust me, don't let the small size and cuteness of those miniature donkeys fool you."

After Ruby had passed away, Thorgrim had been forced to sell her little donkey, Penelope. He remembered how shy and docile the animal was. Thorgrim remembered others telling him about the amazing abilities of miniature dwarf donkeys, but he still could not believe that the Army was using dwarf donkeys as cavalry.

Thorgrim watched as the battalion swung around to reform and try again. "I just can't believe the Army actually uses those cute little animals in combat."

The mounted dwarf grinned. "Cute or not, when fully trained, those animals are particularly ferocious in battle. I've even seen them chase off trolls before."

Thorgrim, noticing that the road had been cleared, laughed and said, "Oh, come on. Donkeys running off trolls?"

The mounted dwarf said, "Yes, sir."

Thorgrim chuckled. "I don't believe those little critters could run off bunny rabbits, let alone trolls . . . which by the way, I don't happen to believe in."

As Thorgrim was about to leave, he looked back at the dwarf who was still watching the King's White Guard practicing another charge. The dwarf was wearing a gold, feather-plumed hat and a white officers' uniform.

"How do you know all of these things?" asked Thorgrim. "You must read a lot."

Pointing towards the White Guard, he replied, "I'm the commander of the regiment those boys are attached to."

Thorgrim took another look at the charging donkeys and then at his timepiece, which read 5:15 p.m.

Thorgrim said, "Thanks for yer service."

"No thanks are necessary. It's been my honor to serve this kingdom for over seventy years."

Thorgrim gave the officer another glance, then he looked back at the great city. "I'm on the run from the law. Have I no honor?" he said to himself in a whisper.

With a nudge, he directed Nugget down the road, east towards a small city called Croydon, some sixty miles away.

XV. An Occurrence at the River Boat Inn

Though Thorgrim hated the thought of it, there was no doubt that he would be arriving in Croydon well after nightfall.

Not just in the Dwarven Clans, but also in any country, traveling at night along roads could be dangerous, especially highways that led to larger towns or cities. Robbers and other criminals knew that anyone using such roads were probably involved with some type of commerce. This meant it was likely that the travelers carried gold or other valuables, making them excellent targets for theft.

Fortunately, such crimes were uncommon.

Dangers also awaited those nocturnal travelers who chose to avoid the roads and instead, journey cross-country. Especially in the plains and scattered woods south of the tip of the Brimgers, between Bur Dhulgren and the Delaware River. There, other horrors, such as wolves or mountain cats, stalked the night searching for their next meal.

Though the Army did their best, it was an impossible task to police everywhere. Signs were posted along the roads warning wayfarers of the risks. People were encouraged to carry a weapon with them at all times and to travel in groups, whenever possible.

Thorgrim was alone and weaponless.

Aware of the perils, he pushed Nugget hard. Riding at faster speeds for long periods of time, Thorgrim knew that he would have to often stop to rest, feed and water his horse. Also, the necessary delays would cost him valuable time and expose him to danger.

By 7:00 p.m., two hours since he resumed his journey, off to his left, amidst a large swampy area, he could see the ninety-foot tall Vumfumik smokestack pouring forth a steady stream of black soot. He had been watching the massive plume floating on the horizon for some time.

Around 8:00 p.m., with the sun hanging low in the sky, he found a field of lush grass and pulled over. As Nugget grazed, Thorgrim and Blinky shared some food from his bag. While everyone enjoyed the break, occasionally, several people on horseback or in wagons happened by, offering waves and friendly shouts of hello.

Thorgrim could not relax during his stops. Everyone he encountered, every sound from the trees around him, heightened his anxiety.

He also had other concerns. Though he was worried about thieves and wolves, he also suspected that the police were coming for him.

Thorgrim realized that it was now very likely that Zippy and Rumbler had informed the authorities in Bur Dhulgren of the situation. He cringed at the thought that detectives were already rummaging through his house searching for clues. He was not far from the truth. The regional police, tipped off by Zippy and Rumbler, were already hunting for him.

***

Earlier that day, around 1:00 p.m., about twenty minutes after Thorgrim had left The Cracked Mug Tavern, Zippy and Rumbler reported Thorgrim to a squad of mounted military police, who were riding through Old South Mharrak on their way to Fort Delaware. They gave the police a full description of Thorgrim and that he was living under the alias of Shem Lybree. The MP's suggested that the two of them should file a report in Bur Dhulgren as soon as possible.

Of course, both ex-convicts were eager to cause Thorgrim Longbeard as much trouble as possible. Anxious to get to the capital, hoping to get a ride, they stopped anyone and everyone who came through Old South Mharrak.

By 1:30 p.m., the two ex-convicts finally managed to hitch a ride on a delivery wagon that was heading to Bur Dhulgren. Both of them, still bleeding from Blinky's attack, cursed the cat all the way to the capital.

A few minutes before 5:00 p.m., Zippy and Rumbler entered a police station in the southern districts of the capital. They immediately reported that Shem Lybree was in fact, a wanted fugitive by the name of Thorgrim Longbeard.

While they were making their report, unknown to them, Thorgrim was only a few miles away to the northeast, halted by an overturned wagon. While the wreckage was being cleared, he was busy watching a battalion of miniature dwarf donkeys practicing battle maneuvers in a field.

After taking Zippy and Rumbler's report, the police quickly sent out mounted officers to search for Thorgrim. At the same time, they arrested the semi-drunk, ex-convicts for consuming alcohol while on parole. Crying and complaining, Zippy and Rumbler were led to their holding cells. The next day, both would be sent back to the Kronk Prison to serve several more years of their original twenty-year sentence.

When Zippy and Rumbler's cell doors were slammed shut, Thorgrim Longbeard had successfully escaped the city and was on his way to Croydon.

***

Despite the hot weather, Thorgrim continued to push Nugget hard, making every effort to arrive in Croydon as soon as possible. Nugget's long legs proved effective, and about two hours after dark, around 11:00 p.m., he rode his tired horse into the outskirts of the small city. It had been a long, strenuous ride.

It was Sunday evening, and Thorgrim was surprised to find revelers out in full force instead of respecting Worship Day.

As he traveled down Croydon's torch-lit, main street, the scene reminded him of Central Avenue in Bur Dhulgren, only on a smaller scale. The typical establishments flanked both sides of the street. Bars, taverns, public baths, latrines, and a few inns, to name some of the more common types.

Because it was Sunday, Thorgrim was shocked to see heavily drunken dwarves, well past their limits, stumbling around outside, singing, dancing, laughing or doing what they love to do best: fighting.

Due to his depression, Thorgrim had developed a strong love for ale, but the sight of the lewd behavior of some of the drunks on a Sunday, shocked and embarrassed him.

He muttered, "This is Sunday, for God's sake. There's nothing wrong with drinking some ale even on Sunday, but this is out of control and sad."

Blinky, having napped almost the entire trip, finally popped his head out and meowed. He was hungry.

As Thorgrim rode by on his tall horse, a few of the partiers offered a variety of comments.

"Hey, while yer up there, say hello to Moridon, will ya?"

"Be careful that birds don't hit you in the head while you're way up there, pal! Hahahohohoohooha!"

"I've either had too much grog to drink, or that's a dwarf with a cat in his beard, riding an elf horse. Either way, I'm done drinkin' for the night."

Thorgrim could only shake his head.

Thorgrim and Blinky's stomach rumbled. Hungry and tired, he knew he would have to spend the night in either Croydon or on the other side of the Delaware River, in Florence. Thinking it was best to put as much distance between him and Bur Dhulgren, he chose Florence.

Continuing down the street, he noticed that Nugget was struggling, extremely tired from the heat and the long, swift ride.

Sweating himself, he reached up and rubbed one of Nugget's ears. "Forgive me, my friend. You did well. We'll stop soon, so you can rest all night long."

Insects were becoming a problem, as well. Weary of swatting at giant flies, vampire mosquitoes, and some other weird bugs he had never encountered before, Thorgrim decided that he would stop at the nearest inn and spend the night in Croydon.

On the corner of State Road and Second Avenue, he spotted a small, white building with blue trim. Outside, a large sign read: 'Riverboat Inn – Fine Food & Cocktails' On the building, another sign read: Voted #1. Philly's Best Cheesesteak and Crab Soup.'

He mumbled, "What in the hell is a cocktail? Doesn't sound appetizing to me. Unless it's a rat, skunk or a fish tail, I wouldn't eat it."

Shaking his head, he read the signs again and continued to mumble. "What's a cheesesteak? Well, I'm starvin' so I guess I could eat one of everything they have. Maybe I'll try the crab soup as long as the crabs are raw. Could drink plenty of cold ale, too."

Near the side of the building, the area was packed with horses. All of them were tied up to hitches and feeding on some stale hay or drinking water from a rusty-looking trough.

Then he noticed a large, enclosed wagon parked nearby. Attached to a team of two horses, the wagon had a sign painted on it that read: 'Big Al's Traveling Flea Market – Buy, Sell or Trade.'

Thorgrim said aloud, "A traveling flea market? Someone actually runs around selling bugs? Hey, Nugget and Blinky, the sign on the wagon says he buys fleas. Maybe we can sell him yers?"

He took another good look at the River Boat Inn. Music, along with the chatter and laughter of a crowd of people resonated from somewhere inside the building. It was Sunday night, yet the place was about as noisy as any pub in Bur Dhulgren on a Saturday night.

"Blinky, how will we manage to sleep with all of that noise? Maybe this is a bad idea." His rumbling stomach thought otherwise, yelling at him to get inside and order some food.

Then the smell of food cooking caught his nose. "That smells amazin'. Yep, we're stayin' here tonight!"

Blinky smelled the food, too and could not have agreed more.

Again, Thorgrim managed a good dismount. "I'm finally getting' the hang of this, Nugget! Took me twenty-five years, though."

Thorgrim tied Nugget to a hitch near one of the water troughs. Still wearing his backpack, he grabbed his leather bag and then fed his horse a few carrots. After allowing Blinky to do his thing in a nearby dirt pile, the starving dwarf stuffed the cat back inside his beard, then stumbled into the Riverboat Inn.

When Thorgrim entered, the place was so busy that no one seemed to notice him. Glancing around the interior, he saw dwarves everywhere. They were walking around, seated at the bar or at several tables, all of them chatting, eating and drinking.

For entertainment, a two-piece band was playing on a small stage. Everyone in the room seemed to be having a good time enjoying the music, food, and drink.

The food smelled delicious. Eager to eat, Thorgrim looked around for a place to sit, but every seat seemed to be occupied.

Then he spotted an empty barstool at the end of the horseshoe-shaped bar. Famished, Thorgrim hurriedly walked over and sat down to the left of another dwarf, who was enjoying a mug of ale.

Directly across from them, on the other side of the bar, Thorgrim spotted two attractive female dwarves who seemed to be showing interest his way.

However, he was not interested. Though she was gone, he still loved Ruby. Depressed over her loss and that of his infant son, at this point in his life, he would not consider dating another woman. He politely offered them a smile and a nod, but they returned no response other than a few giggles. Unknown to Thorgrim, the girls' attention was focused on the dwarf sitting next to him.

Removing his backpack, he placed it, along with the leather bag, on the floor. While bending over, his right foot bumped against something. Looking down, he saw a strange-looking musical instrument that probably belonged to the dwarf sitting beside him.

Thorgrim tapped the dwarf on his shoulder and said, "Excuse me, sir. Is that thing down there on the floor, yers?"

The dwarf, preoccupied with one of the pretty girls sitting across from him, glanced at Thorgrim and said, "Huh? What is it, pal?"

Pointing down to the musical instrument, Thorgrim repeated himself, "I was curious if that thing was yers?"

The dwarf smiled and said, "Yes. That thing, as you call it . . . is an accordion."

"An accordion?"

The bartender approached and said to Thorgrim, "Excuse me, what are ya havin'?"

"A cold ale would be nice. Oh, and I'll take an order of some of that crab soup and one of those cheesesteaks, whatever they are."

The bartender shook his head and chuckled. "Sure, whatever you want. Oh, we have a full buffet over there, if yer really hungry. Price is only three silver . . . all you can eat."

"No, the crab soup and cheesy thing will be fine. Oh, and I want the crab still movin'. The fresher the better."

"Of course. We never cook the crab here!"

Thorgrim turned back to the dwarf next to him. "I'm sorry. You said that's an accordion?"

"Yes. It's like a piano, only you hold it in your hands."

"Are you a member of the band?"

"Not this band. You might say that I've played in a few other bands though. Hey, muh name's Al Brownstone, and just so ya know, I'm the only white Al Brownstone in Philly, and I like to say that magic and music is my game."

Thorgrim shook Al's hand. "Nice to meet you. Muh name's . . . muh name's . . ." Thorgrim paused and pondered for a second or two. Figuring it did not matter now, he decided to tell the truth. "Muh name's Thorgrim Longbeard."

Al nodded. "Thorgrim, da pleasure's all mine."

"Al, you said, Philly? Never heard of a place called Philly. Where's that?"

Al smiled. "Never heard of Philly? That's what we call the area around Croydon. There used to be a small clan called the Philly Dwarves that lived in this area over a thousand years ago."

Thorgrim raised his brow and nodded. "That's interesting. Only proves it's good to study history. Hey, if yer name is Al, that must be yer wagon outside? Are you Big Al?"

"Yes, that's me and that's my wagon."

"Al, can I ask ya a question?"

"Fire away, pal."

"Do you really sell bugs?"

"Huh?"

"The wagon says flea market. Fleas are bugs, aren't they?"

Al laughed while his thick brown and silver beard shook back and forth. "Yes, fleas are bugs, but I don't sell fleas . . . at least not on purpose, anyway. It's called a flea market because I sell used stuff and sometimes used things have fleas. But I check for them. I can promise you that you'll get no fleas with anything you buy from me."

Thorgrim took a long draw of ale from the mug the bartender just placed in front of him, and replied, "Well, there's nothing worse than gettin' yer beard full of fleas!"

Al nodded. "You're tellin' me! Uh, speakin' of getting' stuff in yer beard, are ya aware that there's a cat in yers?"

Thorgrim smiled. "Ya, he's one of my best friends. His name is Blinky. Hey, Blinky, stick yer face out and say hello to Al."

Blinky popped his head out, meowed and pulled his head back in.

Al was astonished, "That cat understands you?"

"Well, I don't think he speaks Dwarvish, but he's hungry and probably can smell the seafood in this place. He'll be happy when that crab soup arrives."

"Yer beard hangs almost to yer feet. Any other animals livin' inside there by chance?"

Thorgrim laughed. "No, just my cat."

Al motioned and asked the bartender for a refill. "Hey, Lenny, after you fill the mug, make sure that those two girls sittin' across from me get a drink, also."

Lenny smiled. "Sure 'nuff, Big Al."

Thorgrim leaned over and whispered, "Al, I think those two girls you just bought drinks for, have been checking us out."

"I'm certainly checking out one of them. Her name's Nancy. Met her a few weeks ago in here. Maybe you might be interested in her friend . . . unless yer married, of course."

"I was married. Lost muh wife several years ago."

"Not over her, yet?"

"No."

"Must be tough. I'm sorry."

"It's been hell. Lost muh son, too. They both died when he was born."

Al brought his brow down. "I can see the deep sadness in your eyes. Again, sorry to hear about that, pal."

"Thankee." Thorgrim took a drink from his mug and looked over at the band as they performed.

"They're pretty good. Who's the singer?"

"His name's Richie. He owns this place."

Across the bar, due to a misunderstanding, only one of the girls received a drink. It was Nancy and she smiled directly at Al.

Al noticed her smiling at him. He said to Thorgrim. "Listen, don't take this wrong, but if she comes over here, you're history."

Thorgrim smiled. "I understand."

A moment later, Lenny delivered Thorgrim's bowl of crab soup. He said, "Yer cheesesteak is coming right up. Uh, would you guys like me to top yer mugs off?"

Both Al and Thorgrim nodded yes.

Thorgrim took a slurp of the cold crab soup. Chewing on the raw, rubbery crab, Thorgrim nodded and smiled. "Mmmmmm, mmmm! That's the way I like it! River crab soup that's almost as good as my mama could make!"

Al took a big draw of ale and said, "Pal, you'll love the Philly, too."

Confused, Thorgrim's brow furrowed. "I'll love the what?"

"The Philly. The cheesesteak sandwich. It's the best in town."

"Oh, it's a sandwich! I thought it was a chunk of cheese stuck on a woodin' stake! The sign out front said cheesesteak, so I thought—"

"You're not from around here, are you?" asked Al with a smirk and a shake of his head.

Deciding not to lie about his past anymore, Thorgrim replied, "No. I'm from . . . well, originally from a mining town on the other side of the Brimgers, called Vog. Until recently, I'd been living in the big city for some time. Never got out much, though."

"Until recently? Where do ya live now?"

Thorgrim gave Blinky a bite of crab and said, "Good question. I haven't decided yet. I am thinking about moving to the Great Kingdom and finding some work there."

"What kind of work are you lookin' for?"

"Books."

"You're an author?"

"Not really . . . maybe someday."

Lenny delivered Thorgrim's cheesesteak sandwich. Setting the plate down, he said, "There ya go, bub. Enjoy."

"Thankee. Uh, Al, you said earlier that 'magic and music is yer game.' What does that mean?"

Al chuckled softly. "I'm a wizard and also a musician."

Thorgrim took a big bite from the sandwich. The melted, cheesy goodness flowed all over his fingers.

"A wizard? Don't you mean a magician? You know, card tricks, hocus-pocus, possum's out of a hat, levitating beards and other tricks?"

Al gave Thorgrim a serious look. "First, are ya a republican or a democrat?"

"A republican or a democrat? I'm a dwarf, does that count?"

338

"Never mind," replied Al with a headshake. "Okay then. I'm a real wizard, not some stage magician. Magic spells, magic wands, fireballs from my fingers, you name it, I can do it."

Thorgrim nearly choked on a piece of steak. "What? Ah, I'm sorry, I don't believe in magic, trolls or even dragons. I do believe in spooks, though."

"You don't believe in magic?" asked Al with a slight smirk. "Want to come out to my wagon? I'll show you some magical items that'll change yer mind."

"Can I finish my sandwich, first?"

"No, bring it with you. Hey, Lenny, me un muh pal are going outside for a bit. Don't let anyone take our barstools!"

"Not a problem, Big Al."

Looking over at Nancy, he winked and mouthed the words, "I'll be right back."

She nodded and continued to smile.

Al slapped Thorgrim on his back and said, "Follow me."

Al got up and started towards the door. Thorgrim put on his backpack, grabbed the leather bag, then followed.

Outside, both walked over to the back of Al's large wagon. Al removed a key from his pocket and used it to open a padlock. Once the lock was removed, he swung the wagon's big door open.

After Al lit a torch, they both looked inside. Thorgrim saw heaps of everything imaginable.

Crystal balls, wands, weapons, bags of colored powders, and vials of strange liquids. The walls had floor rugs hanging from them.

"What is all of this stuff," asked Thorgrim.

"My wares! Most of it is boring, regular, everyday stuff but some of it is magical."

"I don't believe in magic."

"I heard you say that earlier. You saw the look in Nancy's eyes when she was starin' at me? Now that's magic, pal!"

"I know that kind of magic. I had that with my wife, Ruby. I'm talkin' about wizard magic. Fireballs, levitation, sorcery and things like that."

"Let me show you that magic is real."

Al stepped up into the back of the wagon, dug around for a minute, then pulled out a white, crooked stick.

"Now this is a magic wand. Watch what I can do with it. Keep an eye on that tall horse over there."

"Wait!" exclaimed Thorgrim. "That's muh horse!"

"I'm not going to hurt him. Are ya afraid that I might change him into a frog or somethin'? Just relax and watch. I'm going to levitate the critter. Here, hold my torch."

Thorgrim took the torch. Holding his breath, he was mortified.

Al noticed Thorgrim's concerned expression. "What are ya worried about? I thought ya didn't believe in real magic?"

"I don't. But I'm not always right about stuff, so I'm worried."

"No worries. Just relax and watch."

Waving the crooked stick back and forth, Al hummed and mumbled some strange words, while Thorgrim continued to hold his breath.

"There!" shouted Al. "Did ya see that?"

"See what?"

"Yer horse, I levitated him!"

"No, you didn't. I was watchin'. He didn't move an inch."

Al frowned. "Did you blink yer eyes while you were watching?"

"Well, I suppose so."

"It happens very fast! I raised him a foot off the ground and back down in the wink of an eye. Now, I'll do it again, but keep yer eyes open this time!"

Thorgrim sighed and said, "Okay, okay. Just don't hurt him. He's very special to me."

"I won't hurt him, I promise."

Again, Al wiggled the wand and hummed, mumbling more strange words.

Nothing happened.

He tried again.

Still nothing.

Thorgrim shrugged. "Sorry, Al, but I don't think that wand would be fit to be a toothpick for an ogre."

Al, frustrated, tapped the wand against the side of the wagon. "What the hell! Damn thing must be out of charges."

Thorgrim shrugged again. "Well, show me somethin' else, then."

Tossing the wand back into the wagon, Al replied, "Okay, I will."

Al aggressively rummaged through his collection, throwing this and that out of the way. When he found what he was looking for, he yelled, "Yes, this will do!"

Thorgrim squinted. "What is that?

"Why, it's a magic scroll. If I read it precisely, an earth golem will appear and do my bidding!"

Thorgrim took a step back. "Huh? An earth golem? Isn't that some kind of a big monster? Sounds scary if ya ask me."

"Not a problem, pal. The golem is bound by the magic spell to do exactly what I ask of it."

"What are you goin' to ask it to do?"

"Maybe organize the mess in my wagon, while I'm inside spending time with Nancy!"

Al unrolled the scroll and started to read it.

Thorgrim interrupted. "Are ya sure it's safe to do this?"

"Yes! Now, don't interrupt me, or it could spoil the spell and maybe even ruin the scroll"!

Al began reading from the scroll again, uttering weird words and phrases from a long, forgotten language.

Nothing happened.

Thorgrim chuckled. "See, I told ya magic isn't real!"

Al angrily threw the scroll into the back of his wagon.

"It is real! Maybe I'm not pronouncing the words correctly. You know the language on that scroll is probably ten thousand years old."

While Al was making excuses, Thorgrim spotted something silver and shiny in the corner of the wagon.

"Al, what's that over there in the corner. It looks like a silver axe or somethin'."

"Oh, that's a magic axe," replied Al. "It's fer sale. Want to see it?"

"Sure, I guess. It would be nice to have a real weapon with me."

Al pulled the double-headed battle-axe out from the chaos in the corner. Trading the axe for the torch that Thorgrim was holding, Al said,

"What do ya think?"

Holding the axe with both hands, Thorgrim examined it closely. "It's cool, that's fer sure."

Al looked puzzled and touched the axe. "It's cool? It doesn't feel cold to me. Are ya kiddin'?"

Thorgrim chuckled. "No, I mean it looks cool. Cool is a word from my generation that means the same as nifty does in yers."

Al nodded. "Oh, Okay. Well, is it cool enough that you'd want to buy it?"

"Sure, maybe. How much?"

"Mmmmm, it's a magic axe and very special, uh, um, how about, oh say, fifty gold?"

Thorgrim's monobrow jumped. "Fifty gold? For this? Seems kind a spendy, if ya ask me. If it's supposed to be magical, what can it do?"

"Not sure. Someone traded it for an ice wolf hide and a pair of fireball scrolls. He told me it was a magic axe, but before I could ask him any details, he took off."

341

Thorgrim studied the large two-headed axe. It was surprisingly light for its size and the grip on the handle seemed a perfect fit for him.

He smiled. "I like it. Do it for thirty gold and I'll put in a good word for ya with Nancy."

"Sold!"

Thorgrim reached into his leather bag and paid Al the thirty gold. "Thankee! Hopefully, I'll never have to use this axe other than for choppin' trees!"

"You never know, pal. Just be careful where yer swingin' it! With that double blade, you could prolly take someone's head off on the backswing!"

"I've never used an axe like this one before. My father taught me how to use a pickaxe, but I imagine this would be different."

"Yes. It's a battle-axe. Now, if you were wearing an eyepatch and carried this axe around, I can guarantee you that nobody would mess with ya!"

"I do wear an eyepatch from time to time."

"Good! But do me a favor, will ya, pal?"

"Sure."

"When yer wearin' that eyepatch, don't be swingin' that axe near me, just in case I'm standing on yer blindside. I don't want an unexpected haircut, if ya know what I mean."

Thorgrim laughed.

Al's eyes became big. "Hey, Nancy's waiting. I better get back inside before some lucky fella steals her away from me!"

"I'll join ya. I'm in need of some refreshment anyway. Besides, I need to sign in and get a room. Come to think of it, I didn't see a reception desk. Where is it?"

While Al was locking his wagon, his brow scrunched. Confused, he replied, "Reception desk? What do you mean, 'get a room'?"

"Ya, a reception desk. All inns have them. I want to check-in and get a room for the night."

Al chuckled. "This isn't an inn. It's a tavern."

Thorgrim was baffled. Pointing to the sign, he said, "But, the sign says Riverboat Inn."

"I know, but it's only a name. If yer lookin' for a place to stay, there's several in town. You might try an inn called King George the Second. It's up the street on Radcliffe. It's a nifty . . . uh, I mean, it's a cool place. A very old castle converted into an inn. They also have an excellent stable for yer horse."

Al led Thorgrim to the tavern's door.

Thorgrim said, "Who was King George the Second? I don't recall seeing any King George listed in any Dwarven history books."

"He wasn't a dwarf king. King George the Second was a human king of the Great Kingdom about seven hundred years ago. Supposedly, or so the story goes, King George the Second was having an affair with the sister of his wife, Queen Henrietta. When the news of the scandal got out, George abdicated his throne, fled the country and came here, seeking asylum."

When they reached the door, Al tossed the torch on the ground and continued, "Our ruler during that time, King Ruthus Goldbringer, allowed King George the Second to live in what was called 'Mummers Castle.' Trying to be trendy, a few years ago, someone bought the place, turned into an inn and renamed it, King George the Second."

Thorgrim, always fascinated by history, asked, "What happened to King George after he moved in there?"

Al's brow went up. "Oh, that's where it gets interesting. Good 'ol King George was dead within a week."

"He died in that place? The inn yer recommendin' I stay at?"

"Yes, murdered. They found him in bed with his head missin'!"

Thorgrim turned a shade of white. "Someone cut his head off? Who would do that?"

Al shrugged. "Don't think they ever figured it out. Some say George's wife, Henrietta, had it done."

"But I'm sure King George had to be protected by guards. How could anyone pull off a murder like that?"

"He was protected. By our own King's Royal Guards. Obviously, the guards murdered George. I'm quite sure that Goldbringer ordered it done."

Al opened the Riverboat's door. "Come on, let's get inside, I want to sit across from Nancy, so I can make googly eyes and flirt and stuff."

Thorgrim pushed the door closed and said, "Wait . . . Why would King Goldbringer order the murder of a man he just gave refuge to?"

Al said, "Because Queen Henrietta asked King Goldbringer to have her husband, King George, killed."

Thorgrim was dumbfounded. "Huh? Why would our king do what King George's wife asked? Especially committin' murder?"

Al leaned in close to Thorgrim, winked and whispered, "Because King Goldbringer was having an affair with her!"

Thorgrim shook his head. Dropping his brow, he said, "I'll never get married again, and I ain't stayin' in a place that's probably haunted by a headless spook."

Al laughed. "You'll get married again someday, pal . . . and there ain't no spooks in that place. I know plenty of people who've stayed there without claiming they saw a ghost. It's the best option tonight unless you want to go over the bridge into Florence. I don't think you'll find a stable over there for yer horse, though."

Thorgrim sighed. "Gotta have a stable. Okay, I'll stay at the inn of some headless king. I don't have time to run all over the city trying to find an inn. It's either that or camp out somewhere and I'm sick to death of the bugs."

Al said, "Come on, Nancy's waitin'. I don't want to start any bad habits with her!"

Both of them entered and walked back to their barstools. When Nancy saw Al, she lit up like the great torch on the Royal Castle in Bur Dhulgren.

While setting his new axe on the floor next to him, Thorgrim noticed Nancy's expression. He leaned over to Al and said, "Hey, Al. I think Nancy really likes you, and I don't think it's just because you bought her a drink."

Al smiled at Nancy. Unable to take his eyes off her, he said to Thorgrim, "Yer right, pal. The feeling is mutual."

The place was still buzzing with activity, though the band was in the middle of a break. Thorgrim emptied what was left of his ale and then yawned. He was tired and Blinky had been out of it, snoring loudly for the past hour.

The tavern's clock read 1:20 a.m.

"Al, I need to get going and find that inn, so I can get some sleep. I have a long ride ahead of me tomorrow."

"Pal, I've been around for quite some time." Leaning over, Al whispered, "Kid, what are ya runnin' from, and where ya goin'?"

"I'm no kid. I'm almost forty-five."

"You're a kid to me. I won't tell ya my age. Let's leave it at that."

Thorgrim shrugged. "Okay, I have to get out of the country and fast. I'm tryin' to get to the Great Kingdom to start muh life over. That's all I want to say about it."

"I understand. In yer case, there is no easy way to get to the Great Kingdom. If ya go south, you'll likely run into the military police. They're all over the place in the southern part of the Brimger Province."

Pulling out his small map, Thorgrim replied, "I know. I'm thinkin' about going up the road, through the city of Brimger and then around the northern part of this huge forest that's to the east of here."

Al said, "You mean the Haunted Forest."

344

"Ya, that forest. Sounds spooky to me, so I don't want to go in there."

Al raised his brow and his eyes enlarged, "Do ya like snakes?"

Thorgrim crumpled his face. "Hell, no! I hate 'em almost as bad as spooks! The only thing I can imagine worse than a snake or a spook is the ghost of a snake. Now that would be downright frightening."

"Then ya better not go north on the road to Brimger. You'll have to pass by the Snake Swamps."

"The Snake Swamps?"

"Yes, the problem is due to the recent heavy rains, the Snake Swamps have flooded the main highway. There are snakes crawlin' everywhere up there. Some of 'em will kill ya with one bite!"

Thorgrim, wearing a terrified expression, shook his head. "No, no, no. Not going that way, then."

"Then, ya gotta cross the bridge over the Delaware River, go through Florence and then into the Haunted Forest. There's a trail you can follow, but it's seventy or eighty miles before you reach the other side! Sorry, but it's the only way."

Thorgrim could hardly breathe. "Well, I hate snakes, so it looks like I'll be ridin' through the forest. For the sake of Moridon's beard, why do they call it the Haunted Forest?"

"Oh, the forest is big and thick. Over the years, people have made up ghost stories and legends about the place. Most of those are just fiction, nothing more. You know how fiction stories are . . . usually just made up drivel and other nonsense. However, though I've never seen one, supposedly trolls have been spotted in there."

"I keep hearin' about trolls. Muh dear wife once told me she saw a troll when she was a little girl visiting her grandparents in Florence."

Al nodded. "Very possible."

"Bah, I've never seen a troll, so I can't say I believe they exist."

"Oh, they do exist, pal. There are other dangerous creatures in the forest, too. Wolves, bears and the like."

"I figured those animals would be in the forest."

Al gave Thorgrim an elbow. "Hey, you might get a chance to test that axe you bought from me!"

Thorgrim grimaced. "I don't want to think about that."

Al wore a serious expression. "You know, there's a legend that a dragon lives in the Haunted Forest."

Thorgrim chuckled. "A dragon?"

"Yes, an ancient, green dragon. They say it's over a thousand years old. When you ride through the forest, beware!"

Thorgrim sighed. "I don't believe in dragons any more than I do magic or trolls."

"Why don't you believe in dragons?"

"I've read stories about dragons, but I've never seen one. Until I do, I won't believe they exist."

Lenny interrupted, "Ale, either of you?"

Thorgrim shook his head.

Al nodded, and Lenny filled his mug.

Al then said to Thorgrim, "Well, I've seen dragons. They're real."

Before Thorgrim could reply, Al looked over at Nancy, smiled and said to Thorgrim, "Let me tell ya, pal, I've seen angels, too. There's one sittin' right across from me."

Thorgrim patted Al on the back. "Yes, she is. Al, I've got to go. Thank you for everything."

"Hey, no problem, pal. Enjoy the axe! Wait, you promised you'd put in a good word for me with Nancy!"

"Right. I'll do that."

Still wearing his backpack, Thorgrim stood, then reached into his leather bag and paid Lenny for the food and ale. After grabbing his new axe, he looked towards the stage and noticed that the band was getting ready to start their final set for the night.

Thorgrim walked over to the stage and introduced himself to Richie and the organist. He mumbled a few words to them and pointed towards Al and Nancy. Both musicians smiled and nodded. Thorgrim smiled in return and tipped them both a silver piece.

Thorgrim then walked back to the bar and introduced himself to Nancy and her friend. He whispered to Nancy, "That friend of mine over there? He's a great guy, and he really likes you. He's a bit shy, though. Why don't you go over there and ask him to dance? The band's gettin' ready to start."

Nancy's eyes sparkled. She said, "Sounds like a good idea to me. Thank you, Thorgrim."

Thorgrim nodded and gave Al the thumbs-up signal.

Having no idea what Thorgrim said to Richie or to Nancy, Al returned a blank expression.

Thorgrim walked over to Al and said, "Goodbye Al and God bless. She's a darlin'. I'm not a magic-user, and I don't have a crystal ball, but if you end up with her, you'll both be happy for the rest of yer lives. I'm sure of it."

"Thanks, pal. God bless you, too. You be safe on your journey to where ever yer goin'. Lock and load, pal."

"Lock and load?"

Al smiled. "Ah, just an expression I made up."

"I'll lock and load, then. Goodbye, muh friend."

Thorgrim gave Nancy another look and winked. When he reached the exit, she was already halfway to Al's barstool.

Thorgrim gave Richie a nod, then went out the door.

Outside, he stopped and listened.

The organist began playing the song Thorgrim had asked him to do; a love song that his father used to sing to his mother. Soon, Richie started to croon.

"Wise dwarves say, only fools rush in.
But I can't help, falling in love with you . . ."

Thorgrim peeked his head inside the door and as he had hoped, Al and Nancy were each other's arms, dancing in a room full of people. Yet, to Al and Nancy, they were alone, together, just the two of them. And together, forever they would stay.

***

Exhausted, around 2:20 a.m., Thorgrim checked into the King George the Second Inn, asking that he not be given the same room that George was murdered in. While Nugget was being ushered out back to the stable, Thorgrim was already in his room and in bed. It was not long before he and his cat fell fast asleep.

Monday morning, a half-hour before sunrise, Thorgrim awoke, though still tired, due to a night of interrupted sleep. Several times, he was disturbed by the sound of strange noises in his room.

Peeking from under the covers and terrified, he expected to see a headless spook wandering around. But it was always Blinky making commotion while getting a drink of water or using the makeshift potty box that Thorgrim had managed to put together for him.

Thorgrim also awoke hungry as usual. Prior to waking, he had been having a dream about his childhood days back in Vog. In the dream, he could smell his favorite sausages cooking in his mother's kitchen and could still hear her beautiful voice calling everyone to breakfast.

However, his childhood days were long ago. Now, when he dreamt, usually his mother's voice was replaced by Ruby's. Thorgrim loved to dream about Ruby, and he hated to wake from them. For it was only in dreams that they were together again.

Thorgrim, fearing he had little time to waste, was up and out the door in only ten minutes. He moved quickly, though he was groggy from a lack of sleep. The first thing he had to do was pay for his room and the accommodation of his horse.

At the café next to the castle, he scarfed down a quick breakfast, then over-stuffed his backpack with extra supplies at a nearby store. Nugget was patiently waiting in the stable with a full stomach of fresh alfalfa. Thorgrim again managed a perfect mount and then raced down the street towards the Burlington-Bristol Bridge that spanned the Delaware River.

Off in the distance, spanning the entire eastern horizon, he could see the vast expanse of the Haunted Forest. It seemed endless. Thorgrim was horrified that he would have to ride through those woods, but according to Al, apparently, there was no other good option.

After crossing the Burlington-Bristol Bridge that crossed the wide, Delaware River, Thorgrim rode Nugget through the smaller town of Florence.

Along the way, he asked a few people about the Haunted Forest and some of them confirmed that there was a narrow trail that he could follow that would eventually lead him through to the other side. Thorgrim's map revealed the distance to be over seventy miles just as Al had told him. The people also warned him about wolves, bears, trolls and of course, the dragon.

Once he was inside the forest, Thorgrim would have no choice but to keep his axe close by, ride as hard as he dare and be prepared for anything. Having no training in the use of a battle-axe, he was worried that it might be a hopeless situation for him if he had an encounter with a bear, or God forbid, a pack of wolves.

Thorgrim, not believing in trolls or dragons, shrugged them off. He was much more worried about wolves. Several times, when he was a boy living in Vog, he had seen wolves in action ferociously ripping apart cattle and even horses.

Following the directions given to him, he easily found the clearing and the trail that led into the forest. Stopping, he realized that the home of Ruby's grandparents might be nearby but was not exactly sure where. He had met them only once, at the wedding, and sadly, he and Ruby had never traveled to Florence to visit them.

Thorgrim suddenly felt depressed again . . . as he usually did whenever he thought of Ruby. He was both downhearted and anxious because he feared the law might be closing in.

He was right, at that very moment, hot on his trail, sheriff's deputies had crossed the bridge into Florence and were going house to house asking questions regarding him and a few other wanted men.

With a firm nudge from Thorgrim, Nugget raised his front legs and bounded down the trail, into the Haunted Forest. The time was 7:30 a.m. It was Monday, July 18, 2273. Exactly twenty-five years to the day when Thorgrim left his home in Vog.

As before, Thorgrim Longbeard was on the run again.

XVI. The Haunted Forest

Thorgrim had been told that a dragon lurked somewhere deep in the Haunted Forest. The very forest he had just entered.

However, Thorgrim simply did not believe in dragons. He was one of those people who would only believe in what he could see or touch. The Father God, Moridon, spooks, and air, were the exceptions.

As Thorgrim rode into the forest, he thought, *Do dragons exist? Who knows? Perhaps they do and so do trolls. Maybe, it's just because I've never run into one . . . yet.* He remembered reading a few books about dragons and other legendary creatures when he worked at the Supreme Library.

***

[Author's Note:]

The legend of the dragon begins with ancient Dwarven lore, written over one hundred thousand years ago on scrolls and stone tablets. Using elaborate pictographs and a crude version of Dwarvish, unknown authors wrote of the existence of a gigantic, majestic creature they called 'uslukh' or dragon. The texts mention that over a dozen species of dragons existed, each variety having its own color and unique abilities.

The writings of Dwarven antiquity also mentioned that dragons once ruled the world.

Other books on the subject, written during Thorgrim's time, offered many more details about dragons.

The books claimed that the Bronze, Yellow, Blue, Silver, Grey, Brown and Purple species had become extinct long before the appearance of the first dwarf. Purportedly, still in existence when Thorgrim lived, were the Black, White, Green, Gold and Red types. The books mention that a variety of other, smaller sub-species also existed.

Uncommon, if not extremely rare, dragons were highly intelligent carnivores whose power and majesty was without equal. Some were geniuses, with many able to speak several languages including those of humanoids. Because of their intimidating appearance and seemingly selfish behavior, dragons were accused of being evil and malicious. In truth, with few exceptions, most dragons were not evil, at least not intentionally so. However, dragons were hunted to near extinction due to man's natural tendency to destroy what he does not understand.

Most dragons were magical. Many could invoke powerful spells for use in attack or defense. A few could even control and read minds.

Dragons had lifespans that far surpassed any other living creature. Some lived to be well over one thousand years of age and those that did were considered ancient.

Thorgrim had been warned that an ancient green dragon awaited him in the Haunted Forest.

Green dragons typically inhabited the swamplands, however, some preferred to build their lairs deep within dark forests. Poison was their main weapon, by either bite or a spray of noxious gas. They could also change their color and hide among the trees like the chameleon to ambush unwary trespassers. Even more dangerous, some green dragons could shape-shift at will, taking on the form of virtually any nearby, animate or inanimate, like-sized object, including groves of trees, large mounds or even boulders.

All dragons, despite their large size, were surprisingly quick and agile. Although not as big as the great red dragons, adult greens weighed over sixty tons, were one hundred twenty feet long from head to tail, with a wingspan of over ninety feet. With their head fully raised, they stood almost forty-feet tall.

Although there were exceptions, most dragons preferred to avoid mankind, choosing to live out their lives and raise their families in the privacy of well-hidden lairs.

For an unknown reason, almost all dragons loved to collect golden trinkets and other valuables created by the hand of man. The ancient writings warned of dire consequences for those who foolishly dared to trespass into a dragon's lair in an attempt to steal anything from their cherished treasure trove.

What were the origins of the ancient green dragon that Al said lived in the Haunted Forest?

Legends say that over a thousand years before Thorgrim's time, the Alacarjian elves fought a war with the dragons of the realm. The war began when a dozen, angry green dragons attacked and poisoned the Alacarjian towns of Ennore and Arianna, killing hundreds of elves of all types.

However, it was an act of revenge.

A few days prior, groups of dark elf bow hunters destroyed several green dragon nests in the forests southwest of the capital city of Serinqua. Dozens of unhatched eggs were stolen or destroyed. Many dragon hatchlings were murdered; some even tortured by the vile, dark elves.

351

The Alacarjian Army was ordered by their king to hunt down and kill or drive out of the kingdom, every dragon they could find. Not a single dragon was to be spared.

At first, the dragons fought well but were soon overwhelmed, though many elves were killed in the process. Most dragons fled into the Dwarven Clans and the recently formed Great Kingdom, while others flew to the highest parts of the Kragg Peaks.

The legend goes on to say, that a baby green dragon was carried to safety by its mother to a large forest south of the Brimger Mountains in the Dwarven Clans. There, the baby's mother cared for him until her death a few hundred years later.

Formally known as the Brimger Forest, locals often called the massive, wooded area, the Haunted Forest because of the rumored sightings of giant beasts, eerie sounds and strange lights that emanated from the vast woodland.

Soon, stories of evil, man-eating monsters were told and then passed down through the generations. Even the elves who lived some thirty miles east of the Haunted Forest were terrified by the story of a malevolent dragon that killed anyone who trespassed near its lair, hidden deep within the forest.

The people called the dragon, Malumhepta (which means 'mischief-maker' in Dwarvish). Many said that the dragon was the son of 'Malivore,' the Dwarven god of mischief and mayhem.

Malumhepta's only desire was to be left alone, so he could live in peace. There, deep in the forest, next to the bones of his mother, he lived a quiet, lonely life. Except when someone disturbed his lair . . . or when he was hungry. He enjoyed fresh cattle, though he particularly loved to eat young people.

Over the years, cattle, horses, other large animals, and people had been reported missing. They were never heard from again, and no one ever discovered what happened to them. Because Malumhepta could shape-shift, no one ever actually witnessed a dragon killing anyone or anything. They simply disappeared without a trace.

Malumhepta was extremely intelligent, bordering on genius. His favorite technique was to hide among the trees, often posing as a grove of oaks. Then, when the opportunity presented itself, he would spray poisonous gas, which could incapacitate people or even the largest animal, in seconds. Once the dragon's victims were helpless or dead, and he was sure no one was watching, he would devour them.

On rare occasions, someone would see Malumhepta moving through the forest. If they were fortunate enough to escape the swift dragon, they would complain to the Dwarven authorities. The police always dismissed the reports of giant monsters, claiming they were the result of an over-indulgence of ale.

One day, several hundred years before Thorgrim was born, the Dwarven King's son and his small squad of guards vanished while on a hunting expedition in the Haunted Forest. The distressed king sent in the Army to investigate. However, other than finding plenty of common forest creatures such as deer, bears and wolves, not a trace of his son . . . or any monster was ever found.

Interestingly, during the Great War, the Dwarven Army moved infantry forces through the Haunted Forest on their way to the Alacarjian border. Soon after the Army exited the forest, a few men were reported missing. They were never heard from again.

Despite the rumors and stories, there was no solid evidence that a real dragon lived in the Haunted Forest. Many blamed everything on the grey elves. The sightings of monsters in the forest, missing people, all of it, nothing more than ghost stories propagated in some way by malicious grey elves who were doing all they could to cause problems for their hated enemies, the dwarves.

***

Thorgrim rode steadily along the narrow trail, taking him deeper into the Haunted Forest. The weather was cool, if not chilly. Expecting roasting heat and humidity, he was pleasantly surprised by the comfortable temperature.

The morning sun lit up the tree canopy overhead, but the leafy crowns, overlapping each other like massive shrouds, were so thick that light could barely penetrate to reach the ground. The glow of light above, combined with the darkness and haze below, created a creepy, shadowy environment on the forest floor.

Thorgrim was not in the least worried about dragons or trolls, but spooks and wolves were another story, thus, he did not intend to spend one night in the Haunted Forest.

It was approximately seventy miles to the clearing on the east side of the forest. Under normal conditions on a dry road, riding at a canter, he could make the journey in about six hours, including stops for rest.

Thorgrim quickly realized that due to the spongy condition of the ground, riding at any speed beyond that of a trot was almost impossible.

The terrain was rather hilly in places with many overhanging branches as well as fallen trees.

Great care had to be used when riding at a faster speed through any forest. Thorgrim could be unhorsed and injured, or Nugget could step into an unseen hole and fracture a leg. Either accident could have disastrous consequences. Forced to ride at the slower pace, including the usual stops to rest, meant it could take eleven or more hours to cover the seventy miles. Without lengthy delays, there would still be plenty of time to exit the forest by nightfall.

He rode on confidently. Despite his excellent, dwarven low-light vision, it was very dark in some areas and difficult to see the path. Fortunately, Nugget seemed to be aware that he was supposed to stay on the trail and was able to follow it instinctively. Thorgrim was amazed by Nugget's ability and felt as if he could almost release the reins and let him trot on his own.

Thorgrim said aloud, "Nugget, I betcha' know the way, don't ya. Get us through here safely, my longtime friend."

Blinky seemed to be enjoying the ride through the forest. Comfortably snuggled inside Thorgrim's beard, he rode with his head sticking out so he could watch. Having never been in a forest before, his big orange eyes were full of astonishment and wonder.

***

Two and half hours passed without incident. Ever wary of wolves or bears, Thorgrim occasionally felt for his battle-axe, which was lashed to the right side of his saddle. To avoid injuring himself or Nugget as they rode, he had wrapped the head of the extremely sharp, twin-bladed weapon in a thick leather cloth he had obtained in the supply store back in Croydon.

It was 10:00 a.m. and though he could not be sure, Thorgrim guessed he had ridden about fifteen miles. Though it was a bumpy ride, everything had gone well, so far. However, he was becoming concerned, because it seemed to be getting darker the further they went into the thick forest. If the trend continued, he would have no choice but to slow his pace.

In his haste earlier that morning, he had neglected to purchase a few torches or even a lantern and he cursed himself for it. Either would have proved invaluable in the dark. Thorgrim only had the two torches he had brought with him from Bur Dhulgren, but they were old and likely would not remain lit for more than a couple of hours each. It would be impossible to ride through this forest at night without some kind of light to see by. The thought of camping in a wolf-infested forest after sunset, especially without torches, horrified him.

Shrugging off his fears, he had no choice but to continue onward in hopes of exiting the woods before sunset.

Around 11:30 a.m., during a brief stop for rest, unknown to Thorgrim, nearby, hidden in the shadows of the trees, an odious, evil monster studied him while probing his mind.

Thorgrim was sitting on a downed tree trunk, watching Nugget graze on some clover when he noticed a pronounced, ringing sensation in his ears. Annoyed, he shook his head and rubbed his ears in a failed effort to provide relief. Fortunately, the ringing stopped after a few seconds, however, it was replaced with a brief bout of vertigo, followed by a splitting headache.

Blinky, sensing an evil presence, hissed, but Thorgrim did not notice, because he was preoccupied with the painful, throbbing sensation in his head.

Thorgrim stood and stretched. Dizzy, with his head pounding, he suspected that he might be dealing with a stomach illness or some other ailment.

He decided to mount up and as he did, he noticed that both Nugget and Blinky seemed extremely nervous. Concerned that his horse and cat sensed wolves nearby, frightened, he put his hand on his axe and quickly rode out of the area. As they continued down the trail at a trot, thankfully, Thorgrim's headache seemed to ease.

After Thorgrim departed, a lanky, humanoid creature, wearing a brown hooded robe, stepped out onto the trail behind him. There, while uttering a chittering cackle, it watched its potential victim ride away. Gleefully, the red-eyed, rawboned monster rubbed its gangly-fingered, clawed hands together, while displaying a crooked smile that revealed several rows of uneven, dagger-sharp, yellowed fangs.

Then, using a raspy, unearthly voice, the fiendish, black-hearted creature muttered a strange word, and with a twitch of its pointed head, magically vanished into the ether.

In an instant, the thing reappeared in the woods, next to the trail, a mile ahead of Thorgrim.

And it waited.

Riding along, as he had feared, the forest continued to get darker . . . and oddly, unpleasantly cold. Darker, not because of a storm or nightfall, but due to the fact that the forest's trees and foliage continued to get thicker the further into the woods Thorgrim rode. The trees were bigger, taller and more numerous. Many branches, encroaching over the trail like the tentacles of an octopus, caused several near misses to Thorgrim's head, forcing him to duck numerous times.

To be safe, he decided it best to slow to a walking pace and hope the forest would eventually thin out, so he could resume a faster speed.

He checked the time; it was almost noon.

Fortunately, his headache was gone, and overall, he was feeling much better.

Thorgrim could only guess how far he had traveled since entering the forest four and a half hours ago. Taking into account a couple of stops, and the somewhat meandering trail, he estimated that he had traveled twenty-five miles, with about forty-five to go. Thankfully, it seemed that he was on track to get out of the woods before dark.

When he rounded a narrow bend in the path, he spotted a mound in front of him about fifty feet away. The trail continued up the mound, which rose about ten feet above the area around it.

Without warning, Nugget stopped in his tracks, snorting, obviously frightened.

Blinky, riding with his head protruding from Thorgrim's beard, hissed and dug his claws deep into Thorgrim's shirt, causing him to wince.

Then, Thorgrim's sharp headache returned, and the hair on the back of his neck stood straight up.

Someone or something was out there, just ahead of them, beyond the mound.

Thorgrim cleared his throat and called out, "Hello?" While he waited for a response, he carefully removed the makeshift hood from his battle-axe.

Hearing nothing, he called out again, "Hello! Who's out there?"

No response. In fact, there was no sound, not a bird, or even the whistle of the wind. It was as if the entire forest had fallen asleep.

Nugget shifted uneasily beneath him, while Blinky cried the eerie moan of a cat that was about to do battle with another cat.

Thorgrim's heart pounded. Nervous and frightened, sweat rolled down his face.

My God, wolves? A bear?

Thorgrim was in panic mode. Concerned that the law might be closing in behind him, he could not retreat. Because of the dense and thorny foliage, he could not leave the trail and ride around. Regrettably, he had no choice but to continue forward.

Gripping his axe tightly, his crushing headache, causing his eyes to water, Thorgrim gave Nugget the signal to walk ahead slowly.

Nugget, noticeably trembling beneath him, still snorting in fear, refused to budge. Instead, despite Thorgrim's commands to walk forward, the horse retreated a few steps.

Thorgrim tried to swallow, but his throat was dry as a bone.

Then he heard a voice up ahead, somewhere beyond the mound. It was a soft, female voice.

"Shem."

Thorgrim turned white. He recognized the voice, but it could not be who he thought it was.

"Who's out there?" he asked, trembling.

"It's me."

Unable to believe what he was hearing, Thorgrim became angry. Raising his axe, he yelled, "Who are you? God damn it, show yerself!"

He saw movement. Slowly, from behind the mound, the outline of a humanoid figure appeared. It stopped on the dimly lit crest and spoke.

Thorgrim peered ahead and studied the shape, which stood within an envelope of haze and darkness.

When he realized who it was, his heart leaped into his throat, and he began to cry.

At that moment, breaking the silence in the forest and startling Thorgrim, overhead, in the trees, hundreds of crows began to caw. Without warning, they took to flight in all directions, their shrill voices echoing in the woodlands around them.

After the departure of the crows, the forest became tomb-silent.

Thorgrim wiped his eyes and looked again.

It was Ruby.

She wore an infectious smile and held out her hand towards him.

"Shem, my love. How I've missed you! Come to me!"

Nugget continued to snort and whine. Blinky hissed and growled. Thorgrim was oblivious to both of them, entranced by the beautiful sight of his lost wife.

Ruby spoke again. "Shem, come to me! I need your help! They took our baby boy, and I've been searching these woods for him."

Still unable to believe his eyes and ears, he tried to speak but could not.

"Shem, we have to hurry! If we don't find our baby, soon . . . he'll be lost forever!"

Thorgrim squinted. Clearing his throat again, he finally managed to speak, though he stammered.

"Ruby. But, uh, yer dead. I saw you die delivering our boy. Both of you died in muh arms."

She shook her head and smiled. "No, Shem. That was only a bad dream. Don't you remember? After we got home with our baby, someone took him from us."

"A dream?"

"Yes, you had a nightmare."

Thorgrim's pounding head nauseated him. Dizzy, he almost fell out of the saddle.

"You and our son are really alive?"

Ruby beamed and held out her arms. "Yes!"

Thorgrim released the reins and felt for Ruby's silver heart pendant beneath his beard.

It was gone.

"Are you looking for this, my dear?" Ruby grasped the necklace she was wearing, pulled up the heart pendant, revealing it to him.

Recognizing the special jewelry, he immediately felt a wonderful, inner peace. Thorgrim realized Ruby was right. It had all been a terrible nightmare.

Overwhelmed with joy, and without using the mounting block, he stepped down from the saddle like a master equestrian.

He gazed at his beautiful wife. Her long red hair draped over her shoulders, her skin, white as cream. Her eyes twinkling, she raised her hand, gesturing for him to come to her.

Ruby was really alive.

"Has anyone ever told you that you have a wonderful smile?" she said with honey dripping from her plump, red lips.

Thrilled, he instantly replied, "You're the only one who has ever told me that!"

"Yes, that's right. Come to me, my dear. Love me, then together, let's find our son."

His head aching, Thorgrim nodded and dropped his axe. He stumbled forward towards Ruby and began to ascend the mound.

She saw him approaching and smiled, exposing her pointy, white teeth. "Come."

Thorgrim's cat would have none of it. Blinky hissed and with a howling wail, jumped from Thorgrim's beard and onto the ground. With two bounds, he was up on top of Nugget's saddle, growling and hissing.

As he approached her, Thorgrim ecstatically said, "Ruby! I still can't believe it!"

"Believe it! I'm here! I love you, Shem Lybree."

When she spoke his false name, it struck him like a hammer. One of Thorgrim's deepest regrets was that he never revealed his true identity to Ruby. Now was his chance.

He came closer. When he was halfway up the mound, she stretched out her arms, reaching towards him.

Wincing from the agony of his brutal headache, he said, "Ruby, I need to tell you something very important. I've been keeping a secret from you all these years."

Ruby leaned towards him but did not step forward into the light. She said, "I know your secret, my love. I've known all along that your real name is Thorgrim Longbeard. It doesn't matter to me. I'll love you 'til the end of time! Forever and a day!"

Astounded by her revelation, he started to weep again. Only a few feet from her, he said in a cracking voice, "Ruby, I love you. I'm in trouble. The law is after me."

Ruby's eyelashes batted. "I'll help you. Kiss me, my dear. Everything will be fine."

Thorgrim finally reached out to Ruby's outstretched hands, interlocking his fingers in hers.

He stopped walking. "Ruby, you feel ice cold," he said, surprised.

"Come warm me, husband. This forest is cold like the grave. Kiss me and then let's find our son."

Her soft, red lips glistening, beckoned him.

She began to pull him towards her.

As he took another step forward, from somewhere behind Ruby, Thorgrim heard a 'swish' sound, and then felt her body twitch. Her expression changed from one of happiness to that of shock.

His terrible headache immediately disappeared, and everything around him seemed to move in slow motion.

Releasing his hands, Ruby, her eyes big and wide, grabbed for her throat. As she did, her head rolled off her shoulders, landing on the ground with a squish, before tumbling down the mound and bouncing into the short grass beside the trail.

As Thorgrim watched in horror, for a few seconds, the decapitated corpse remained upright, standing in a neck-spewed shower of grey-green blood. Its clawed hands flailed wildly as if frantically searching for its missing head until the cadaver finally collapsed with a thud in a gory heap upon the crest.

Speechless and aghast, Thorgrim stumbled back and fell, rolling down the mound, coming to rest face-up on top of his backpack.

Thorgrim slowly rolled onto his side. There, he lay on the ground in stunned silence with his eyes closed, unsure if what he had just witnessed was real or a nightmare. After a moment, he heard a man's voice.

"Are you okay down there?" asked the man, speaking in Avalonian.

Trembling, Thorgrim slowly opened his eyes. Looking up towards the top of the mound, he watched as a large figure stepped over the crest and into the light.

Still numb with shock, Thorgrim sat up and began to retreat, crawling back towards his horse as fast as he could. He needed his axe. Whoever this man was, he had just killed Ruby and would likely do the same to him.

Struggling to his feet, Thorgrim ran to Nugget and picked up his battle-axe from the spot where he had dropped it.

Turning towards the man, Thorgrim quickly studied him. He was a tall human, who wore a short, dark-brown beard, and was dressed in a suit of silver chainmail. In his hands, he held a massive greatsword that was painted with green blood.

Thorgrim spun his axe and yelled, "You bastard! You murdered my wife! I'm goin' to make ya pay for that!"

Realizing that Thorgrim was a dwarf, the man replied in perfect Dwarvish, "Wait! You don't understand."

The man sheathed the greatsword on his back and began to slowly descend the mound towards Thorgrim.

"No, you're the one who doesn't understand," roared Thorgrim. "If you take another step forward, I'll take yer head off like you did muh wife! You murdered her, you sonofabitch!"

The man, his hands held outward, stopped walking and shook his head.

Thorgrim began to weep.

The man said softly, "My friend, that was not your wife. Look closely." He pointed to the decapitated head that lay on the ground, next to the trail in front of the mound.

Thorgrim slowly turned his eyes. Instead of Ruby's head, he saw something hideous. This head was pointed, had a long, crooked nose, and dark-green mottled skin. Its mouth hung open exposing sharp, pointy fangs. It's red eyes frozen in a stare of death and surprise.

Perplexed by what he saw, Thorgrim shook his head in disbelief.

Again the man began to approach Thorgrim very slowly.

Regaining his senses, Thorgrim raised his axe and retreated a step.

The man held his hand up and smiled. "It's okay, my friend. That evil thing is dead. Look upon the mound."

Thorgrim glanced at the fallen body on top of the mound. Instead of Ruby, he saw the headless corpse of a thinly built, robed creature. Long fingers, ending in razor-sharp nails, were still grasping at its headless neck.

Thorgrim blinked his eyes in bewilderment. "But, that's impossible," he bellowed. Once again, he looked at the fallen head. It was not Ruby's, but that of a monster.

"It is possible," replied the man.

Thorgrim, though still confused, finally accepted what he saw. He said, "What in the hell was that thing?"

"That, my friend, was a wood hag. Some call them forest banshees. I've dealt with them before. You were lucky because they're very dangerous."

"A wood hag?"

The man stepped closer. "Yes."

Thorgrim, still nervous, retreated another step.

"It's okay. My name is Sir Steven of George. I'm a paladin from the Theocracy of the Abbir. My squire and I had been hunting that monster for a week."

"You and yer squire?"

"Yes. John, come up here and bring the horses."

Within a minute, another figure appeared on the mound. He was a tall beardless human, wearing blue and silver leather armor. A short sword hung by his side, sheathed on his belt. He held both horses by their reins.

Taking a few steps down the mound, he brought the horses forward. When they appeared in the light, they looked magnificent. One of them was a powerfully built, white abbirian stallion and the other, a slightly smaller, though just as sturdy, silver abbirian stallion.

Sir Steven introduced his squire. "Friend, this is my squire, John of Hildman.

"That's John of Hildman the Third," replied John. "Pleasure to meet ya, friend."

Sir Steven chuckled. "Oh, of course. John is proud that he can put a number at the end of his name."

"Yes, and if I have my way, one day there will be a John of Hildman the Fourth!"

"I'm sure," replied Sir Steven with an eye-roll.

Thorgrim said, "I'm sorry. I'm still shocked by what just happened. But, it's muh pleasure to meet you both. Muh name is Thorgrim Longbeard."

Sir Steven raised an eyebrow and said, "Thorgrim Longbeard. Well, I can say this. Your name certainly suits you! That's the longest beard I think I've ever seen, my friend."

Thorgrim looked down and proudly tugged on his knee-length beard.

Sir Steven said, "As I was saying, we had been hunting that wood hag for a week."

"What's a wood hag, anyway? I'd swear on Moridon's beard that was muh wife standing up there."

Sir Steven gestured. "May we approach, friend? Then I'll explain."

Although still upset by the horrifying ordeal, Thorgrim now felt that he could trust these men. Nugget appeared relaxed and Blinky was asleep on top of the saddle.

Thorgrim nodded. "Sure."

Sir Steven walked over to Thorgrim and gave him a firm handshake. The knight, at least six feet tall, towered over the dwarf. John followed with both horses in tow.

Sir Steven wore a grim expression. "You say that thing looked like your wife?"

Thorgrim nodded. "Yes, my deceased wife. It was her, I swear it."

"Wood hags are undead creatures that play mind tricks in order to kill their victims," replied Sir Steven, pointing towards the corpse. "They can read your mind, learn about you, and then make you see and believe almost anything. I'm curious. Did you have a headache earlier?"

"Yes, a splitting headache. But it's gone."

"When they read your mind, your ears might ring, but while they have control, you'll have a terrible headache."

Thorgrim sighed. "Mind reading? Mind tricks? Unbelievable, yet I saw what I saw. She played the role of my wife almost perfectly. What a diabolical creature."

"Yes, they are. Though their abilities are powerful, their tricks won't work if they're in direct sunlight. If you noticed, she always stood in the shadows. Thick forests like this one are dark and make excellent hunting grounds for them. That's why they are called wood hags or forest banshees."

Thorgrim glanced around nervously. "You said that a wood hag is undead? Like a vampire? Could there be any more of those things around here?"

"They're undead like a vampire, but thankfully, extremely rare. I've only encountered two in my forty-three years and have only heard of one other case. They could be hell-spawned demons, but some believe they are old witches who have traded their souls for an immortal, undead

362

existence. Personally, I think they are agents of the archlich Teserak, leader of the Bone Empire, sent by him to cause harm to humanity."

Thorgrim frowned. "That's all terrifying. The Bone Empire . . . the land of the undead. I've heard of it."

"Mr. Longbeard, had she kissed you, she would have absorbed your life, and needless to say, you would have dropped dead on the spot."

"Why would she want to absorb muh life?"

"Somewhat similar to a vampire, though in many ways more dangerous, instead of blood, wood hags need the life energy of other living creatures, preferably, humanoids."

"She wanted me to kiss her. I was about to do it, but you killed her, thank God. And also thank God I wasn't standing closer, or yer sword might have taken two heads instead of one."

"I'm sorry about that, but I was very careful with my swing," replied the paladin with a gentle bow of his head.

John added, "Sir Steven's the best swordsman in the Abbir. Maybe in the entire realm. He can sunder a fly in midair with that greatsword of his. I've seen him do it!"

Sir Steven offered a quick headshake. "Thank, you John, but as you know, pride is not one of the eight principles of good."

"Of course," replied his squire.

"As I had started to tell you before my squire provided some unneeded boasting about my swordsmanship, decapitation is the only way to destroy them. This one was particularly dangerous because she could teleport several times a day. It's almost impossible to find and destroy something with that ability."

Thorgrim glanced over at the wood hag's head again. Cringing, he said, "I can't believe that I almost kissed that hideous thing."

Sir Steven nodded. "It would have been the kiss of death!"

"What a sinister monster," moaned Thorgrim. "Thank Moridon you were here."

"For the past year, I've been taking my squire all over the realm, training him to become a paladin. We were camping in these woods when that wicked creature found us a week ago. While I was away from our campsite, she had John believing that she was an old girlfriend of his. Luckily, a wood hag can only fool one mind at a time. When I returned and saw her for what she really was, I ran her off before she could kill John. Had I arrived a few minutes later, I would now be in need of a new squire."

John chuckled. "I could have handled her. You didn't give me a chance."

"I'm afraid my squire fancies himself to be a cowboy."

John continued to chuckle, "I would have never kissed her. That old girlfriend as you call her, well, I dumped her over ten years ago. She'd be the last girl that I'd ever want to kiss!"

Sir Steven raised an eyebrow. "You would have never kissed her? Sure. I saw the whole thing. When that hag asked you to kiss her, you wore the expression of a teenager on his first date. Kind of the same expression you have whenever we happen to cross paths with any women."

John shook his head. "Well, I don't remember it happening that way with that hag. As far as running into other women, I can't help it. I haven't been with a girl for a year, because I've been following you all over the realm."

"You want to be a paladin, don't you?"

"Of course, but I'm not a paladin, yet! Just because you're not allowed to be with a girl, doesn't mean I can't."

Sir Steven slapped John on the shoulder. "You know that it doesn't work that way. Get used to it, my squire."

Thorgrim enjoyed the banter between the paladin and his squire, but he realized time was short. A quick glance as his timepiece revealed that it was 1:50 p.m.

Thorgrim reached out and shook Sir Steven's hand. "I need to be moving on. I'm on muh way to the Great Kingdom."

"Then you have some riding to do."

"Yes. I can't thank ya enough. What an experience. You know, I could sure use some ale right now, and a lot of it. You don't happen to have any, do ya?"

"No, I'm afraid not," Sir Steven replied with a smile. "Other than wine used for special occasions, Paladins are not allowed to partake in drink."

John leaned in and whispered, "Nor partake in women."

Sir Steven rolled his eyes.

Thorgrim, curious, dropped his brow. "You can't drink ale?"

"No."

Thorgrim shrugged his shoulders. "But, why?"

"Because alcohol can poison the body and cloud the mind. It's the drink of demons."

Thorgrim shrugged again. "Really. It doesn't cloud muh mind."

"Well, you're a dwarf."

Thorgrim beamed. "So, ya noticed! Thankee!"

With a nod, Sir Steven turned to his squire and said, "Come, John. We need to be moving along, too. We're done here."

Thorgrim asked, "Where are ya goin'?"

"Our destination is Bur Dhulgren. It's been a dream of mine to see the Grand Hall of the Dwarves."

Thorgrim smiled proudly. "Really! Been there a couple times muhself."

In an instant, Thorgrim's mind replayed the twenty-five years he had spent in the capital city.

Recalling the moment he first met Ruby, he said in a somber tone, "Sir Steven, you saved my life, but will you do me one more favor?"

The paladin nodded. "I would be happy to. What can I do for you?"

Thorgrim reached up and removed the silver heart charm pendant from around his neck. Kissing it, he handed it to Sir Steven and said, "When you get to Bur Dhulgren, will you please take this to the city's cemetery? It's near Lake Mharrak, a few miles outside the western gates."

Sir Steven looked at the pendant in his hand. Puzzled, he said, "The Bur Dhulgren Cemetery? I will do that for you. Can I ask, what do you want me to do with this pendant once I'm there?"

Tears brimming in both eyes, Thorgrim replied, "That charm was my wife's most treasured possession. Now, it's mine, but it belongs with her. When you get to the cemetery, find the grave of my wife. Her gravestone says 'Ruby Lybree and infant son, Luthor.' Please press this charm deep within the ground over them.

Carefully placing the charm in his satchel, Sir Steven slowly nodded. "Consider it done."

"Thank you," replied Thorgrim, still downhearted. "I will never forget your kindness."

"It is my honor."

As Sir Steven and his squire mounted up, Thorgrim grabbed Blinky and stuffed him into his beard. Next, he put the mounting block on the ground then stepped up, swinging himself into the saddle perfectly.

Sir Steven said, "That's a tall horse you have there, Thorgrim."

"I know. I don't know what I'd do without him."

Blinky's head popped out of the beard.

"You have a beautiful cat, too."

"Yes, that's Blinky Eyes. My favorite cat in the whole world."

Sir Steven waved, started to ride off and said, "Take good care of your friends, and they'll take good care of you. Be safe on your journey, Thorgrim, and may the Creator God watch over you."

Thorgrim smiled while replacing the leather hood on his axe. He was about to continue his ride when he thought of something.

"Sir Steven, uh, you didn't happen to see any dragons or trolls running around in this forest did you?"

The paladin halted and looked back at Thorgrim. "No. But, I've heard stories about them. We've been out here for over a week. Other than the typical forest animals and that hag, I can't say we've seen much else. Oddly, lots of crows though. Thicker than mosquitoes. There's also plenty of wolves, too. Never seen one, but we could hear them every night. Beware of them. They'll slaughter you in your sleep."

"Believe me when I say that I'm not spending one night in this place if I can help it."

"Good idea," Sir Steven said, waving goodbye. "Until we meet again."

Thorgrim watched as both of them disappeared down the trail towards Florence.

Concerned, he checked his timepiece. It read 2:25 p.m. Doing some quick math and a little guessing, things did not look good for him. Behind schedule because of the delays, it would be dusk, if not completely dark, by the time he reached the edge of the forest. He would have to risk riding at a canter, to have any hope of getting out before nightfall.

There was no time to lose. Terrified of being caught in the woods at night, Thorgrim gave Nugget a nudge to start forward.

First, they would have to slowly crest the mound and see what was beyond before resuming any kind of fast riding. As he approached the rise, he was horrified to discover that the head and body of the wood hag were missing.

Shocked, he yelled, "What in the hell!"

A firm nudge from both his knees sent Nugget running over the mound and down the path, deeper into the forest. Fortunately, for everyone, the path was clear. Behind them, nearby in the woods, hungry wolves feasted on the remains of the dead, wood hag.

***

To Thorgrim, the trees were so numerous that sometimes they seemed to form a solid wall around him, and of course, this roused his claustrophobia, which caused him occasional bouts of vertigo. But he knew the consequences if he let it get the best of him while inside this wolf infested forest.

366

It likely meant death.

Luckily, fear can be a cure-all for many things and it was fear that gave him the power to shrug off his claustrophobia. Anxious to get out as soon as possible, he pushed Nugget dangerously fast, though he could hardly see ahead of him. The obstructed sunlight, barely reaching the floor of the forest, gave the appearance of early dusk.

For almost an hour, he made good time, but he had been lucky. Twice he was nearly unhorsed by low, overhanging branches.

Racing around a bend at a canter, another branch banged him on the head and almost knocked him out of the saddle. It was a close call and the near-accident finally brought him to his senses. He decided it best to slow him down before he was unhorsed. If such an event happened and he was injured, the wolves would have an easy time of it. Having no choice, he gently tugged on the reins and reduced his horse's speed to a trot.

After a few more minutes of riding, he thought he heard the sound of a horse's whinny coming from somewhere behind him.

The police? he thought. Thorgrim was mortified when he realized, that if the police had been pursuing him through the forest, they would very likely encounter Sir Steven and his squire. The paladin did not know of Thorgrim's plight and would certainly mention that he had seen him.

Thorgrim, ever paranoid, was worried that if the police discovered they were close to him, they might redouble their efforts to catch him.

Adding to his stress as he rode, he thought he could hear an occasional rustling of leaves and crunching of twigs on either side of him.

Paranoia's voice convinced Thorgrim that wolves were the source of every sound he heard in the woods. On the other hand, maybe it was the police, or possibly a spook. Perhaps it was all three.

Rounding another bend, he was dismayed by what lay before him. Likely caused by recent storms, lying across the trail, as far as he could see, were entanglements of thick foliage and broken tree limbs.

As he carefully worked his way through the wreckage, several times he was forced to halt in order to figure out how to get around or through the fallen timber. Those were perilous moments because it would be a perfect opportunity for waiting wolves to launch an attack.

Now, because of the delays, it seemed certain he would not get out of the forest before sunset.

He cursed because of it.

After spending a long hour slowly struggling through the debris, thankfully, the trail now appeared free of obstructions. Pleased and relieved, Thorgrim gave the signal, and Nugget, once again, trotted forward.

Though still forced to duck beneath an occasional, overhead branch, Thorgrim made good time as Nugget moved along the path, cantering when possible.

The wolves, stalking him, barked and snarled.

Thorgrim heard them.

He then spotted something large and furry crossing the path in front of him. He became alarmed until he realized it was a brown bear. There was little to fear because brown bears are relatively docile unless you tamper with their cubs.

He heard more barking, and a howl, the sounds causing his blood to run cold.

The damn wolves. Able to strike fear in anyone, they had been on Thorgrim's mind since he first entered the Haunted Forest. In his mind, he pictured packs of the wild canine brutes swarming all over the woods. They, with their piercing yellow eyes, sharp fangs and insatiable appetites. All of them patiently waiting for a chance to attack and kill anything that happens by . . . such as a dwarf with a cat in his beard, riding on an elven horse.

The time was now 5:45 p.m. Rest, food and water were overdue for everyone, especially Nugget. Despite the risk of a surprise wolf attack, Thorgrim found a small clearing and halted there.

He grabbed his axe and then dismounted without a problem. Trying to lighten the mood, he joked, "I'm really gettin' the hang of this, Nugget! Didn't even use the block!"

Nugget foraged nearby while Thorgrim, axe in hand, ate some food from his bag and fed his hungry cat some dried fish.

Blinky begged for some milk but there was none.

Thorgrim chuckled. "Tell me about it. You want some milk, and I want some ale. I guess we'll both have to wait."

At that moment, everyone heard crunching sounds in the trees around them.

Nugget, still eating, snorted several times. A sure sign of trouble.

Thorgrim tightened his grip on the axe. "Nugget, we're done. We've gotta get out of here!"

Without using the block, and holding only the reins, aided by a rush of adrenalin, he easily hoisted himself up and into the saddle. Still holding his axe, he gave Nugget a quick nudge and the poor horse, munching on some wild clover, bounded off down the trail.

Nugget raced along the path, gracefully leaping over fallen tree trunks without losing a step. Though the ride was scaring the hell out of him, it reminded Thorgrim of the time, many years ago, when his wonderful elven horse jumped over an entire ore wagon.

Thorgrim let his horse run for a bit, but the overhanging branches persuaded him to slow down again.

"Good job, Nugget! You're a great horse, and I'm sorry ya have to do all the work. Ya know, if ya were a little dog, I would be happy to stuff you in muh beard, and I would carry you and Blinky around."

***

At 7:05 p.m., the sun, now low in the west, cast eerie rays of light through the heavy canopy above. With less than two hours to go before dusk, though unsure how many more miles remained, he was convinced he would not get out in time.

Thorgrim found it difficult to ride while holding his axe. Stopping briefly, he wrapped the head, then strapped it to the side of the saddle, though he would keep his hand near it, in case of trouble. With just a pull, the axe easily slid out of the strap and after removing the hood, was ready for action.

Once his axe was secured, he signaled and soon had Nugget trotting down the trail again.

Fifteen minutes later, Thorgrim thought he saw movement among the trees a hundred feet away on the right side of the trail. At the same time, the faint cries of wolves could be heard, though he could not be sure from which direction.

He slowed to a stop.

His heart pounded.

He studied the situation, though, because the light was dim, he could barely see. As he watched, it seemed that on the right side of the trail, several large tree branches were waving as if in the wind.

But there was no wind.

Then, a loud, thudding sound was heard somewhere ahead. He looked closely. It seemed that from the right side of the trail, a huge tree had fallen across the path.

"Damn, another obstruction!" he moaned.

Then he heard a persistent rustling sound coming from where the tree had just fallen.

369

He put his hand on the axe. His horse snorted several times, as he did earlier when they encountered the wood hag. Blinky sensed something, too. He popped his head out of Thorgrim's beard and growled like a tiger.

Nervous and frightened, Thorgrim held his breath while trying to figure out what was going on up ahead. He squinted, using every advantage his excellent dwarven night vision could offer. Again, a heavy branch moved . . . or at least it seemed to.

"I think muh eyes are playin' tricks on me. Come on Nugget, let's get movin'! Who knows, the law might be right behind us, or maybe wolves. Either way, I don't want to stay here."

Although he was concerned about possible trouble behind him, he was also unsure about what might lay in front of him. Cautious, his hand still near his weapon, he directed Nugget to start forward slowly.

After a minute, he arrived in the area where he saw the tree branches moving. Now that he was closer, he could see things clearly. As he rode through, Thorgrim, wearing a frown, studied the trees around him.

There was no tree blocking the road and additionally, nothing seemed out of the ordinary.

"Nugget, I know I saw some trees movin' up here. I swear that I saw a big tree fall down right on top of the trail, but nothin's here!"

Mystified and weary, Thorgrim shrugged, then signaled his horse to travel onward. After he left the area, a giant tree, lying next to some fallen cottonwoods, shifted slightly. The end of one of it's thick, leafless branches turned and pointed towards Thorgrim. Two, golden-colored eyes opened and watched the dwarf ride away. A mouth appeared and smiled.

Satisfied that the interloper was gone, Malumhepta shape-shifted back into his natural form. With a belly full of fresh cows and one angry farmer, the legendary green dragon continued on the way back to his hidden lair, deep within the forest.

***

Darkness was falling and the wolves had been howling for some time. Frightened to death, Thorgrim hoped that he was near the outer edge of the forest and tried to hurry along, but, once again, he was delayed by fallen trees.

He stopped briefly to pull out one of the old torches. He lit it and prayed to Moridon that it would keep the wolves at bay until he could get out of the woods. He also feared that the light might attract them, but he preferred a lit torch to darkness.

With the torchlight, he quickly checked his map. He could only shrug in frustration because there was no way to know for sure exactly where he was. A guess put him within five to ten miles from the forest's edge. The baying of wolves reminded him that he needed to get moving. Their cries were numerous, louder and closer.

He glanced at his timepiece. 8:41 p.m. It was early dusk. Folding the map, he shoved it in his pocket, then signaled Nugget, sending him trotting down the ever-darkening trail.

Nugget was aware of the nearby presence of the Brotherhood. Grunting and snorting in terror, on his own initiative, he increased his speed to a fast canter, sometimes dangerously galloping at top speed. Thorgrim feared the horse might bolt, throwing both him and Blinky to the ground. He pulled on the reins in an attempt to slow his elven horse, but it was of no use.

Nugget was in command now.

Reflecting the light of his torch, several sets of yellow eyes could be seen on his flanks. The Brotherhood had arrived, and they were preparing to attack.

Nugget thundered down the trail, while Thorgrim could do nothing more than hold on for his life and pray. Worried that Blinky might be tossed out, he regrettably had no choice but to drop the torch and use his spare hand to hold on to his cat.

"May God help us," he said aloud in a raspy, panicked voice.

Several snarling, grey shapes appeared ahead on both sides, arrogantly stepping up to the trail's edge in front of him, only to retreat when his big horse speedily approached.

But they were the younger, inexperienced members of the Brotherhood. Unknown to Thorgrim, a few big adults, all veteran killers, including the alpha, waited patiently in ambush, somewhere ahead. Though rare and the largest of their species, at seven feet long and two hundred pounds, they were the giant grey wolves of the Brimger Province. Having eaten little in the past few days, the wild beasts chomped their fangs, panting at the thought of the tasty flesh and warm blood feast that awaited them.

It was hopeless. Thorgrim could do little or nothing to protect himself or his friends and he knew it. Terror-stricken, he uttered a prayer to Moridon while Nugget ran at near, full speed. Several times, despite crouching as low as he could, hidden in the darkness, again, overhanging branches nearly took him off the saddle.

Barely visible in the low light of dusk, a downed cottonwood appeared on the trail, blocking his path. Thorgrim cursed out loud at the sight of it. Nugget, unsure if he could make it over safely, had no choice but to slow his approach in order to time his jump properly.

Then the wolves attacked.

Led by the alpha male, four grey killers flung themselves from the flanks in an attack of coordinated savagery.

Thorgrim saw them and screamed. Releasing his grip on Blinky, his hand was already on his axe.

But Nugget would not allow the snarling, bloodthirsty wolves to finish their attacks. As the slashing fangs of the wolves fell upon them, timing it perfectly, Nugget twisted and caught two of them with swift kicks from his rear legs, breaking their backs.

A third one missed, landing and then rolling into the trees on the other side. But the great, elven horse could not stop the fourth one.

It was a big alpha.

However, Thorgrim did. With a swipe of his mighty axe, he caught the alpha in midair, behind the forelegs, slicing it cleanly in half. The two halves of the carcass landed on the forest floor, where they lay in twitching, bloody heaps.

Thorgrim was astounded, having never experienced anything like it before in his entire life.

Nugget raced on.

The remainder of the pack, stunned by the loss of three of their brothers including their leader, quickly withdrew deep into the woods. Starving, they moved on in search of other sources of food.

A minute after the wolf attack, with barely any light to see by, Thorgrim saw a massive clearing ahead. He was beyond ecstatic. He cheered as he approached the end of the Haunted Forest. Standing in the saddle, he looked back where the wolves had attacked. With his axe held high, he pumped it once, then twice while yelling triumphantly.

"To hell with you wolves! Ha! See Nugget, there was nothin' to worry about! Just a few wolves and a stupid wood hag! No trolls or dragons! What a big bunch of smelly bison—"

Then his head struck an overhead branch, blasting him off the saddle, knocking him out cold. Tossed to the ground, he bounced three times before coming to rest, again on top of his backpack.

After a few minutes, Thorgrim was brought back to consciousness by two tongues that were licking his face. One of them was big and wet, the other small and rough. Nugget and Blinky were taking turns trying to rouse the poor dwarf.

"Oh, muh head . . . okay, okay, will you two stop licking muh face?"

He sat up and wiped the saliva from his cheeks and nose. "Thanks, both of you. Come on, we better get the hell out of here before those wolves come back."

After collecting his axe, though his head ached terribly, he managed a perfect mount. With Blinky safely back in his beard, he lit his last torch and hurriedly rode away from the forest, cross country, because no road was available.

Although the sky glittered with billions of stars and a thin crescent moon, it was very dark and hazy. Having no compass, he could only guess he was moving in the correct direction towards the border about twenty-five miles away.

Using the light of his torch, a quick look at his map showed that the dwarven village of Valley was ahead, and a mile or two beyond that was the Alacarjian border. Though Nugget was very tired, Thorgrim had no choice but to push him to make every effort to get over the border before any pursuing police caught up with him.

Thorgrim was unaware that the police had not bothered to enter the forest. Apparently, the legend of Malumhepta scared the wits out of them. Or maybe it was the wolves or trolls. Possibly even spooks.

By 11:30 p.m., Thorgrim could see torchlights burning in what he hoped was the village of Valley. A minute later, he found a sign that confirmed it. Instead of stopping there, in order to get out of the Dwarven Clans, he decided to ride around Valley and cross the border to spend the night in or near the elven village of Leshara.

Fifteen minutes later, he noticed a small sign near a shack on the outskirts of a small village. The sign was written in Elvish. Thankfully, he had studied Elvish as well as Avalonian while working in the Supreme Library.

The sign said: Welcome to Leshara.

He had finally crossed the border into elven territory.

Thorgrim Longbeard had escaped the clutches of the Dwarven Clan authorities.

At least for now.

He knew that the authorities routinely sent out special agents into other countries to hunt for wanted criminals. He was one of them. There was no doubt that he would soon be needing another new identity if he wanted to avoid them.

Excited, though hungry and exhausted, he managed to convince an older, elven farm couple (after he confirmed they were not grey elves), to allow him to spend the night.

At first, the elves hesitated, frightened by the sudden appearance of a dwarf (especially one who could speak Elvish), knocking on their door at midnight. However, they quickly agreed when Thorgrim offered them a shiny gold piece, but, they told him the only place he could stay was in the barn. An extra gold bought Thorgrim a bath before retiring for the night, as well as a washing of his clothes in the morning.

After a quick bath, he dressed, then led Nugget to the barn. While sharing one of his last pieces of jerky with his cat, he shrugged and mumbled, "A night in a barn? I'll be with muh horse and cat. How bad can it be?"

Once inside the barn, Thorgrim lit a lamp and removed Nugget's bridle, saddle, and blanket. While his hungry horse grazed on some grass outside, it was not long before Thorgrim and Blinky fell asleep.

Despite the humidity, Thorgrim slept well, though he had weird, claustrophobic nightmares about being smothered by a feather pillow.

***

It was Tuesday, July 19, 2273. Lying flat on his back, Thorgrim woke from a much-needed sleep. After he opened his eyes, he immediately became concerned, because he was having trouble breathing and his vision was blurry. After a few moments, he realized why. A plump hen was perched on his face, and he was looking directly into her butt.

Appalled, he waved his hand and swiped at the bird. Surprised, the hen jumped off and ran away, cursing Thorgrim in chicken language.

Still lying on his back, he looked down and noticed there was a big, chicken egg and few feathers sitting in the middle of his beard.

Blinky popped his head out next to the egg and meowed.

"Some watch-cat you are. Thanks a lot." Thorgrim carefully grabbed the egg and sat up. Nearby, there were several hen nests. He gently rolled the egg into one of them.

Stretching and yawning, though starving, and despite finding a feather in his mouth, he felt wonderful. His sleep had been extremely restful.

"Wow, Blinky, I feel like I just slept for a hundred hours! That was the best night's sleep I've had in a long time, even though I woke up with a chicken's butt in muh face."

He looked around the barn, but Nugget was nowhere to be seen. Looking over to the windows, the height of the sun's disk told him that it was mid-morning.

However, something was wrong. Thorgrim instinctively knew that the windows faced to the west. It was not morning, but late in the afternoon.

Checking his timepiece, he cried, "Oh, muh God. I overslept again!"

Grasping Blinky so he would not fall out of his beard, Thorgrim jumped up and saw that Nugget was grazing in the field out front. Thorgrim hurriedly slipped on his backpack. Cursing, he grabbed the horse blanket and his leather bag in one hand, and the bridle and saddle in the other. Overloaded, he raced clumsily to his horse and then readied Nugget as quickly as he could. Using the block, he sprang up and into the saddle with one jump.

The old elf couple, who had allowed Thorgrim to spend the night, approached.

The old elf man said, "Mr. Dwarf, where are you going in such a hurry? My wife washed your clothes. Don't you want them? Maw, go grab his clothes off the line, would you, please?"

His wife smiled and went to the nearby clothesline to gather Thorgrim's things.

While pulling up the block, Thorgrim said, "Yes, hurry! Bring me muh clothes, please. I overslept un wasted a whole day! It's five forty-five in the afternoon, for God's sake. I've been sleepin' for over sixteen hours! How is that even possible? For the love of floor-length beards, I thought I asked ya to make sure I was awake by eight this mornin'?"

The old elf man replied, "I tried, but I didn't want to disturb my hen. She mistook your beard for a nest and laid an egg in it. Ya see, Muffy gets pretty upset if you disturb her after she lays an egg. The bird about takes yer arm off if ya try to take it from her!"

Thorgrim rolled his eyes. "Muffy? You named yer chickens?"

"Oh, yes. All eighty-three of 'em have names. There's Muffy, of course, ya already met her. Then, there's Betty, Harriet, JuJu, Lou-Lou, Patsy Mary, Kathy, Michelle . . . and, —um, uh, Maw, what are the other ones' names?"

Thorgrim interrupted, "Never mind about yer chickens. I've got to get going because I still have a long ride ahead of me. Like I said, I wasted a whole day sleeping in that barn."

"But where are you going?"

His wife approached with two sets of Thorgrim's freshly washed and dried clothes.

As he shoved his clean clothes in his backpack, Thorgrim paused, thinking. "Uh, I don't really know where I'm goin', but it'll be somewhere in the Great Kingdom. Do either of you know if there are any famous libraries in the Great Kingdom?"

Both elves shook their heads.

"Well, I'll find out when I get there. Let me ask you another question. To get to the Great Kingdom, I plan on headin' southeast towards a town called Puchie. First, I need to stock up on some supplies before I go. Does Leshara have a supply store?"

"Yes, but the place is closed," replied the old elf man. "The owner is ill."

"Oh. Well, I saw a town on muh map that's called Elkhorn. They should have a supply store, shouldn't they?"

"Elkhorn is a large town," replied the old elf man. "They have a general store. Maybe two of them."

"Good, that's where I'm heading next."

"Well, you'll need to be careful. When you get to Elkhorn, stay out of the forest."

"Why?"

Wild-eyed, the old elf man said, "Well, they don't call those woods the Mean Man Forest for nothing."

Thorgrim smirked. "Hah, I just rode through the Haunted Forest. How bad can the Mean Man Forest be compared to that? Why do they call it the Mean Man Forest, anyway?"

"Because, supposedly an insane, serial killer known as the Mean Man lives somewhere in there."

"Oh, bah. So what. I just survived a wood hag, and a pack of killer wolves. I'm not afraid of some nut-job. Muh axe will fix him quick if I see him."

Both of the elves shrugged.

The old elf woman had been studying Nugget for some time. Wearing a gentle smile, she walked up to him and stroked his face.

"Mr. Dwarf, your horse seems sad. His eyes tell me that he wants to be with his own kind."

"How do you know that?"

"Elven horses are just that way, trust me. I'm an elf."

Thorgrim rubbed Nugget's ears. "I know, he should be with his own kind. I've heard that before."

She said, "Well, he looks very healthy."

"We've taken good care of each other, haven't we Nugget?"

Checking his timepiece again, Thorgrim said, "It's getting late. It's ten after six and I've got over a two-hour ride ahead of me, yet. I want to make sure I get to Elkhorn before dark. Thanks for everything. You know, you're the first elves I've ever met in muh entire life. I didn't catch yer names, though."

"My name's Adon and this is my wife, Fraeya."

"Muh name's Thorgrim. You know, you've given me hope that muh wife Ruby was right."

Adon tipped his head. "Right about what?"

"That not all elves are bad."

Adon smiled. "No, we're not all bad. I know all about the Great War. You know, there is good and bad in everything if you look hard enough."

"There's nothin' good about an empty ale mug. But, I'll try to remember what you said. Look, I would love to stay and chat, but I've really got to get goin'. I'm hopin' that I can find a general store that's open late. I'm almost out of food and I'm really hungry. In case the store's closed, would it be possible to buy some food from you?"

"I wish we could help, but we don't have much to spare. With our own general store closed, we've been living on eggs and bread for several days. I may have to ride to Elkhorn myself if our store doesn't open up soon."

Thorgrim sighed. "Okay, I understand."

"Uh, we can provide some water though. Do you have any flasks?"

"Ya, I sure do, and thankee."

Thorgrim gave Adon his collection of waters flasks and he proceeded to refill them from the nearby well. While Adon was working the well pump, his wife ran inside their small home and returned with a few slices of homemade bread.

She said, "I made some bread last night. Here, you can have some to take with you."

Taking the bread, Thorgrim replied, "Thankee! Very kind of you."

Handing the filled flasks to Thorgrim, Adon said, "We could send along a couple of chicken eggs if you like."

"No, thank you. I don't like 'em raw and they'd probably break before I had a chance to cook 'em."

"Suit yourself." Adon chuckled. "Thorgrim, I think one of the farm cats took up residence in your beard last night. Sorry about that. Why don't you hand it to me."

"That's okay. That's muh pet cat, Blinky."

Adon said, "Your pet? Oh, my mistake. Okay then, goodbye, Thorgrim. Stop and see us again, anytime!"

Pulling the gold coin out of his overalls, Adon bit down on it.

"No worries, it's a real coin," Thorgrim said, grinning.

Thorgrim waved and rode away. Starving, he grabbed some of what little food he had left and shoved some into his and Blinky's mouths.

His next destination, hopefully before nightfall, was the elven town of Elkhorn, twenty-six miles away.

Standing together, the two elves watched Thorgrim ride off.

"Maw, how do you think I would look with a beard like that dwarf was wearing?"

She laughed. "You would look very lonely."

"I would? Lonely?"

"Yes. I'd leave ya if you grew a beard like that!"

He returned a chuckle. Rubbing his chin he replied, "Lucky for me, we elves can't grow beards!"

Map of the southern and central Republic of Alacarj.

XVII. Italia

After an uneventful cross-country ride from Leshara, Thorgrim arrived near the outskirts of Elkhorn, at dusk.

As he wearily approached the large elven town, his first thought was to find food. His pack was nearly empty. It was almost 9:00 p.m. and he guessed that any shops that sold supplies were likely closed for the night. This meant either hunting for food or finding a friendly elf who might give or sell him some.

Thorgrim also needed a place to stay. He desired a comfortable inn but was unsure how a town full of elves would treat a dwarf riding an elven horse. Though he possessed his certificate of ownership, he feared that the elven authorities might assume he had stolen Nugget. It seemed camping was his only option for tonight.

Thorgrim noticed several torches had been lit for the night. Many homes, really not much more than large, pointed huts, had candles burning in the windows.

He saw movement in front of him about a hundred yards away. Concerned, he halted, watched and listened. A few elves were on horseback moving back and forth along the northwestern edge of town as if on patrol.

Thorgrim heard one of them shout an order. Another saluted, then rode off into town. It was obvious that they were a unit of the town's militia. Wanting to avoid any trouble, Thorgrim directed Nugget towards the woods southeast of the town. Soon, he found a suitable location to sleep next to a fallen tree near the edge of the Mean Man Forest.

Although he was almost out of food, he had plenty of water. He gave Nugget one of the last carrots, then emptied two flasks of water into his horse's mouth. After removing the saddle, all of them settled in for, hopefully, an uninterrupted night of sleep.

It was unseasonably chilly for a summer evening, but he could not risk using a campfire, because the light might gain the attention of the patrolling militia . . . or forest predators. Blinky kept him warm, and together they huddled next to Nugget after sharing what few scraps of food were left.

Thorgrim yawned and said to Blinky, "So, this is the Mean Man Forest? A killer is running around in here somewhere?" Thorgrim's bravado had increased since his battle with the wolves, so he bragged,

"Well, if he runs into me and my axe, they'll have to rename this the Dead Man Forest. But, I better get some sleep first. I'm wiped out."

Blinky was already asleep. Completely spent, Thorgrim soon joined his cat in snooze-land.

***

On Wednesday morning, July 20, Thorgrim was up at sunrise, and though his intense hunger gnawed at him, he decided it was best to wait until mid-morning before riding into town. Blinky, also battling hunger, was hunting around the area, looking for anything edible.

The sudden, high-pitched shriek of a woodland mouse meant that at least the cat would have a full belly.

Around 10:00 a.m., Thorgrim's hunger would not allow him to wait any longer. After putting on his eyepatch, he prepared to mount Nugget. Confident that he could consistently climb into the saddle without using the block, he gave it a try.

Holding the reins, he squatted low and performed a big jump. Timing it perfectly, he planted his left foot in the stirrup and pulled himself up and over. But he missed, landing hard on the other side of his horse. Rolling to his back, lying on top of his pack, he looked up and sure enough Blinky was in the saddle, waiting.

Thorgrim heard someone snickering from the trees nearby.

Thorgrim cocked his head and said, "Hello?"

He listened but heard only the singing of birds and the wind softly whistling through the leaves.

Shrugging, he stood and rubbed the top of his head for a moment.

"Okay, Nugget, let's try this again."

Throwing his beard over his shoulder, he placed his foot in the stirrup and tried again. He missed the saddle and went over, this time onto his butt.

As before, Blinky had jumped out of Thorgrim's beard and landed on the saddle.

Now, Thorgrim thought he heard giggling.

"Who's there, damn it all?"

Thorgrim sat on his rear and waited, but there was no response.

Struggling to his feet, he looked around but saw nothing. Even Blinky and Nugget seemed unaware that anyone was nearby.

"Hmmm. I guess my starvation's causing me to hear things! Nugget, I don't understand. I've had no problems the last several times I've mounted you! Now, I can't seem to do it!"

Thorgrim's pride was stinging, and because of it, he refused to use the mounting block.

"Okay, again. Here we go."

This time, Thorgrim landed fair and square in the middle of the saddle. Ecstatic, he yelled, "Yes, that's how it's done!"

An instant later, Thorgrim's eyes widened when his right foot slipped out of the stirrup causing him to slide off the saddle and onto the ground. Landing in a heap, his beard completely covered his face and head.

Blinky looked down from the saddle and meowed.

Loud, persistent giggling and snickering emanated from a thick bush nearby.

Thorgrim jumped to his feet. Angry, he marched over to the bushes and swept the branches back so he could see who was behind them.

He looked down and saw what appeared to be a young girl. Thorgrim studied her for a moment. She had long dark hair, wore glasses and appeared to be about ten or eleven years old. Her pointed ears confirmed what he had suspected all along. She was an elf.

Still giggling, she was sitting on the ground and had obviously been watching Thorgrim through the bushes.

Scowling, he bellowed in Elvish, "An elf! I'm not surprised. What's so funny?"

The young girl covered her mouth but was unable to stop giggling.

"Hey, I asked you what was so funny."

She continued to laugh while shaking her head.

He tugged his beard. "Well, ya can sit there and laugh and shake yer head if ya want. I'm starvin', and I need to get into town so I can find somethin' to eat."

He looked at her for another moment, waiting for any response. She offered none.

"Goodbye," he said, sneering. He released the bushes and started to walk back towards Nugget.

Softly laughing, the young girl stood and stepped out into the open. "You speak Elvish! And you do it quite well!"

Halfway back to his horse, he said, "Yeah, I speak Elvish. Through the years I also learned some Avalonian. Hey, ya still haven't told me what was so funny."

"I'm sorry. But I'm only laughing because you look silly trying to get on an elven horse. You're a dwarf, aren't you, sir? Shouldn't you be riding a shorter horse?"

"Yeah, yeah. Yer right on all accounts. I'm a dwarf. I'm sure I look silly un should probably be ridin' a shorter horse."

When he reached Nugget, Thorgrim turned around, but she was gone.

"Good riddance," he muttered.

Turning to face his horse, Thorgrim grabbed the reins and was about to try and mount again but was shocked to discover that the young elf girl was standing next to him, petting Nugget.

Thorgrim did a double-take. "Well, yer certainly a fast one, aren't ya?"

Nearly a half a foot taller than Thorgrim, she looked down at him and smiled. As she stroked Nugget's soft coat, she said, "This is a beautiful elven cremello. They're famous for running fast and jumping high. Where did you get him?"

"I bought him a long time ago," he replied. "You sure seem to know a lot about horses."

Pointing to the northwest, she said, "We have several horses just like yours in a fenced-in area by our house."

"Well, good for you. Now, if you would excuse me, I'm very hungry. I've got to get goin'."

Thorgrim grabbed the reins and put a foot in the stirrup.

"Mr. Dwarf, sir. Why don't you use your mounting block?"

Thorgrim smirked. "Because I don't want to . . . nor do I need to."

"You know, Mr. Dwarf, it might be easier if you took off that fake eyepatch. I know you don't really need it. You have both eyes. I saw them. So, why do you wear that thing?"

"Cuz, I like to wear it. Anyway, I can get up in this saddle just fine. Watch."

With a big pull, Thorgrim launched himself up, over and onto the ground with a thud. Blinky as usual, perfectly timed his exit from Thorgrim's beard, gracefully landing on all fours in the middle of the saddle.

The elf girl giggled again. "Mr. Dwarf, sir. Are you okay? You know, your cat is better at mounting that horse than you are."

Embarrassed, he replied, "Yes, I'm okay. Muh cat? Yes, he's got a lot of experience landing on that saddle."

The elf girl ran around and helped Thorgrim to his feet.

Dusting himself off, he said, "Thankee, young elf. Uh, I didn't get yer name."

"My name's Italia. What's yours?"

"Shem . . . Oops! Hahaoahoa! I mean, Thorgrim Longbeard."

She looked down at Thorgrim's massive beard. "That's a very lonnnnnnnnng beard that you have there, Mr. Longbeard."

He smiled proudly. "Thanks, Italia."

She giggled again and said, "That's funny. You have a very long beard, and your last name is Longbeard. You know, I have an idea. Have you ever thought about changing your first name to 'Very'? Your full name would be 'Very Longbeard.' What do you think?"

Thorgrim chuckled. Twirling his beard he replied, "You're quite the comedian, aren't you! As far as changing my name, I've tried that. It didn't work out so well."

He was beginning to like this young elf girl named Italia. There was an innocence about her that reminded him of his little sister, Hannah; back when she was about Italia's age, many years ago when Thorgrim still lived in Vog.

"Mr. Longbeard, you said that you're heading into town to find something to eat? You said you were starving?"

"Yes, I'm headin' in to town and yes, I'm starvin'. My horse has been feeding on some of the wild grass, but muh cat's probably starvin' like me. I also need to buy some supplies because I am traveling to the Great Kingdom. Oh, and please, Italia, call me Thorgrim."

She smiled. "Okay, Thorgrim."

At that moment, Thorgrim heard a rustling sound coming from the trees behind him. Nervous, he looked around and said, "Hey, what do you suppose that sound was?"

"Probably some kind of animal. After all, we are standing in the woods."

Thorgrim crumpled his brow. Concerned, he replied, "Hey, now that I think about it, what are you doing out here alone in the woods? Isn't this place supposedly the home of some crazy, serial killer?"

Italia covered her mouth and laughed. "Oh, that's just a made-up story to keep kids from wandering off and getting lost. There's no one living in these woods other than a few wolves and rabbit bears."

"Rabbit bears? Never heard of that animal. What is it?"

"It's a bear with ears like a rabbit and a big fluffy tail. They make great pets."

"Pets? A bear? No thanks. I'll stick with cats, and this very tall horse of mine."

Italia smiled again and said, "Hey, follow me. I have an idea." Grabbing Nugget's reins, as graceful as a gazelle, Italia flew up and into the saddle without using a stirrup.

Thorgrim was astonished.

"I wish I could do that!"

"It's easy if you have the right horse! Of course, it helps if you're an elf. Follow me, and I'll take you to my house. It's not far, just past these trees. If you're really hungry, my mother's the best cook, ever!"

"Yer house? She's the best cook, ever? Sounds good, but are ya sure yer parents will be okay with a dwarf stoppin' by?"

"Thorgrim," she said with an eye-roll. "You've got to get with it! Just because elves and dwarves fought in a war a bazillion years ago, doesn't mean we can't be friends!"

"But you elves stole our most prized treasure and murdered innocent people."

She nudged Nugget forward and he began to walk. Thorgrim, with his cat in his beard, followed alongside.

She said, "No, we elves didn't steal anything. What I mean is that there are no elves or dwarves still alive from the time of the war. Also, it was the grey elves who stole the hammer and murdered those innocent dwarves. I'm a wood elf, and Elkhorn is a wood elf community. Most of any remaining greys live up north."

Looking up at her in the saddle, he commented, "You sure know a lot about history for such a young kid as yerself."

Italia grinned. "I read a lot. You should see my book collection! Oh, and I love to draw and build things."

"You love to read?" Thorgrim smiled. "Elf, or not, I think I'm going to really like you."

It only took them a couple of minutes to exit the woods. On the other side, Thorgrim saw a long row of elven homes running as far as the eye could see from north to south.

Italia pointed straight ahead. "That's my house over there."

Thorgrim looked and saw a beautiful double-sized hovel. It was the last house on the edge of town and next to it, as Italia had mentioned, was a large fenced in field. Inside, four elven horses frolicked.

Nugget saw them and became excited. He whinnied joyfully.

Thorgrim said, "Those are yer horses?"

"Yes!"

"What are they doin'? They seem to be happy and having fun."

"They are playing. We call it horseplay."

"Horseplay? My father always used to yell at us kids to stop the horseplay, but we weren't doing anything like this. In fact, for years, I thought my first name was 'Good God.' My father was always yelling, 'Good God, will you stop with the horseplay?'"

Thorgrim winked.

Italia chuckled. "You're the real comedian."

"Not really. I kinda stole that joke from someone else."

Thorgrim's belly suddenly rumbled so loud that Italia, Nugget, and Blinky all heard it.

Italia looked down from the saddle and said, "Wow, I could hear that all the way up here! Come on, and I'll have my mother cook you something."

Thorgrim rubbed his stomach. "Thankee! That would be incredible."

Italia rode Nugget up to the fence, jumped off and seemingly floated down to the ground.

She noticed Nugget's excitement. "Thorgrim, would you mind if Nugget played with our horses while you're eating?"

"That would be great. I'm sure Nugget would appreciate spending time with other horses, especially his own kind! I better remove the saddle and bridle if he's going to be running around in there."

He placed his battle-axe next to the fence along with his backpack and leather bag. Next, he removed Nugget's saddle and bridle, setting everything on the ground in front of his weapon.

Thorgrim had been told that Nugget was lonely for his own kind. The world around him seemed to move in slow motion as Italia opened the gate. Without hesitating, the excited horse, whinnying loudly, ran at full speed to meet his new friends.

Thorgrim watched as Nugget frolicked in the field with the other elven horses. Nugget seemed like a different horse. He was finally, truly happy.

Thorgrim drifted off in thought . . . *Muh, God. Look at how happy he is out there. I guess I've been selfish all of these years. I truly love Nugget, but I should have found him an elven home a long time ago. But I can't just sell him. What am I going to ride?*

"Are you feeling okay, Thorgrim?" asked Italia. "You seem sad."

Somber, Thorgrim told a half-lie, "I'm fine. Just hungry."

"Come on in, then! I already ate breakfast, but I'm kind of hungry, too."

Italia opened the back door to her home, stuck her head into the kitchen and called out to her parents.

"Mother, Father, we have a guest!"

387

Thorgrim leaned forward and said to her, "Are you **sure** this is okay? I don't want to intrude, they might be really upset! I'm a total stranger, not to mention, a dwarf!"

"They won't be upset! My family is the nicest bunch of elves you'll ever meet!"

Within moments, Italia's parents and two youngsters strolled into the kitchen.

Her father said, "Italia, did I hear you say that we have a guest? Who?"

"Yes! His name is Thorgrim Longbeard," replied Italia. "He's a dwarf that I met out in the woods. And guess what! He speaks almost perfect Elvish!"

"A dwarf?" replied her father.

"Yes, he's really hungry and he has the coolest horse, ever. Oh, and he has a kitty that lives in his beard."

Thorgrim peeked around the corner of the door. Shyly, he said in Elvish, "I'm sorry for the intrusion. Uh, I'm just ridin' through and had been campin' out in the woods. I was about to head into town to get some food and other supplies when I met Italia. She kindly invited me to your home for breakfast. I hope that's okay."

Italia's father gave his wife a quick glance and said warmly, "You do speak Elvish! Uh, sure. We've already eaten breakfast but would be happy to cook you something."

Italia's father walked to the door, put his hand out, and said, "Please come in. My name is Mark Durant." Pointing towards his family, he continued, "This is my lovely wife Alejandra and two of our kids. My daughter, Dalia, who's twelve, and my son, Navor, who's eight. Our oldest, Astrid, is twenty-one, but she's not here. She's taking summer classes at the university up in Tranjia, studying to be a nurse."

Thorgrim nodded but hesitated to walk into the house. "As Italia said, I'm Thorgrim Longbeard. Pleasure to meet you all. I, uh, well, this is very awkward fer me. I guess where I come from; we're not as trusting as you folks."

They all saw his intimidating, dark-red eyepatch. Pretending not to notice the patch, Mark said, "Please, do come in. My wife will fix you something to eat."

"I'm hungry, too!" shouted Dalia.

"Me, too," yelled Navor.

Mark chuckled, "Okay, I suppose that includes you, too, Italia?"

"Yes, Father."

"You kids already had breakfast! You're going to eat me out of house and home! Italia, drag your new friend in here, and your mom will make another breakfast. Is that okay, dear?"

Alejandra smiled. "Of course."

As she walked by her husband toward the pantry, he tweaked her pointed ears and kissed her.

"Yuck! You guys are kissing, again!" complained Navor.

His father laughed. "Someday, you'll understand, Son."

Looking everyone over, Thorgrim realized that next to Navor, he was the shortest person in the room.

Alejandra spoke, "Mr. Longbeard. Do you like garden-fresh, vegetable pancakes? They're a favorite around here."

Before he could answer, Italia took Thorgrim's hand and led him through the door to a chair at the kitchen table.

"You can sit here, Thorgrim," Italia said, and then she sat down in the chair next to his.

As Thorgrim sat down, his stomach flip-flopped. He had forgotten that the elven diet was mostly vegetarian, consisting of weird combinations of vegetables, flowers, and even weeds.

Thorgrim's bushy monobrow went to his hairline. "Vegetable pancakes? You mean that yer pancakes are made out of only vegetables? Never tried that before in muh entire life, to be honest."

"Yes, well, there's flour and eggs in them of course. We call them 'veggie cakes.' We have some fresh butter and maple syrup to go with them, too."

Thorgrim looked pale. "Uh, sure. Ya don't happen to have any sausages, do ya?"

The kids moaned, "Oooooh! Yuck! You eat dead animals?"

Thorgrim half-smiled. "Well, mostly dead. Especially bison or pork sausages. I love 'em crispy."

The kids bellowed, "Gross!"

Thorgrim shrugged.

Mark said, "Children, let's be respectful of our guest. He comes from a different land, and they happen to eat weird food there. Mind your manners, please."

All three kids covered their mouths trying to stop laughing.

Mark caught himself, though a bit late. He blushed and said, "I'm sorry, Thorgrim, I didn't mean to say you eat weird food. I meant to say you eat different food."

Thorgrim cleared his throat and said, "That's okay, Mr. Durant. I completely understand. No need to apologize. I'm yer guest, and I'm sure I'll enjoy yer wife's delicious cookin'."

Mark nodded and then gestured for the rest of the children to sit. Along with their father, Dalia and Navor each grabbed a chair.

He said, "Honey, while you're at it, you might as well make me a few cakes also, please."

Alejandra replied with a smile and a quick nod.

Mark said, "Thorgrim, uh, that's your name, right?"

"Yes, Thorgrim Longbeard."

"You'll love the pancakes, trust me."

Thorgrim adjusted his chair and said, "Okay. What's that old sayin'? Beggars can't be choosy, or somethin' like that. I'm so hungry, I could probably eat boiled crapweeds."

Alejandra turned from the pantry and said, "Oh, those are delicious. Want me to make you some?"

Thorgrim, cringing, waved his hands. "No, no, the vegetable cakes are fine."

Mark said, "So, what brings you through Elkhorn?"

"I'm on my way to the Great Kingdom in hopes of finding a job there."

"I have to assume you are from the Dwarven Clans, correct?"

"Yes."

The sound of a sizzling skillet caught Thorgrim's attention. He visualized giant, juicy links of sausage frying, but when he looked up, much to his horror, he watched Alejandra drop a few carrots into the pan.

Again, his stomach danced.

"What kind of work do you do, Thorgrim?" asked Mark.

"I'm into books. I used to work at the Supreme Library in Bur Dhulgren. Ever heard of it?"

Italia spoke up, "Oh, yes. It's the second-largest library in the world. The Library of Shem up in Calibut has a bazillion more books, though."

Thorgrim chuckled. "Mr. Durant, yer daughter is amazin'. Smarter than most of the people I've ever met."

"Thank you, Thorgrim. Please, call me Mark. And, yes, she's a reader as well as an artist."

Italia added, "And an engineer . . . don't' forget, Father."

Proud of his daughter, Mark smiled. "Yes, you are quite the builder."

Turning to Thorgrim, he said, "She likes to make things out of cardboard."

Thorgrim was impressed. With a grin, he said, "An engineer, too? Italia, are ya sure yer not a dwarf?"

The comment hushed everyone but soon, they all laughed loudly.

Mark said, "Italia, when we're done eating, why don't you show Thorgrim some of your artwork."

Thorgrim nodded quickly. "I would love to see them. Hey, I noticed a big net sitting in yer backyard. There's a black and white ball lying inside of it. What is that?"

Mark smiled. "Oh, that's a game Italia made up. She likes to try to kick the ball into the net and her brother and sister try to block the ball."

"Sounds like fun!" commented Thorgrim. "Maybe I'll have a go at it before I leave."

Thorgrim noticed that Alejandra was busy pouring a green-colored liquid into the skillet. It looked horrible, but Thorgrim had to admit to himself that it smelled good.

Curious, Thorgrim asked, "What do you do, Mark?"

"Well, I'm on leave this week, but I serve full time in the Alacarjian Air Force."

"The what?"

"The Air Force."

Thorgrim was dumbfounded. "What's an air force?"

Mark laughed. "It's a new branch of the military. We use piloted, winged kites as scouts. We can just glide along over enemy positions and report what we see. We are working on a bigger version of the kite where we can carry rocks and things to drop on an enemy. It's kind of a secret, and I probably shouldn't be talking about it."

Thorgrim was incredulous. "You mean some of you elves actually strap yerself to a kite and fly around?"

"Yes. I'm surprised the dwarven military doesn't use the idea."

"Are ya kiddin'?" laughed Thorgrim. "They don't make a kite big enough to carry a dwarf! Besides, we dwarves don't like heights!"

Mark grinned. "I understand."

Alejandra walked over and placed a large plate stacked with thick, veggie cakes on the table. Next, she gave everyone a plate, a drinking cup filled with fresh orange juice, along with a knife and fork.

"The butter and syrup are coming up!" she said.

Leaning forward, Thorgrim carefully examined the steamy, green veggie cakes. Pieces of parsnips, broccoli, green beans, and lettuce were intermixed with some kind of cooked bread dough. Thorgrim's stomach hung in the balance between wanting to eat anything in sight and wanting to throw up.

Twice, he considered making up an excuse to flee the table, but his hunger and fear of being rude kept him in check.

He emptied his cup of orange juice and thought, *Thank Moridon that elves drink orange juice.*

During this time, Thorgrim noticed that Navor had been staring at his eyepatch. Whenever Thorgrim would catch him, the boy would quickly turn away. Timing it perfectly, he caught him again and when the kid was staring, Thorgrim made a scary face, at the same time, flipping up the patch to reveal that he had both eyes.

Navor's eyes bugged out as if he had seen a ghost. He jumped off his chair and fled out of the room.

While Thorgrim was laughing, Mark hollered, "Navor! Where are you going? Get back here and eat."

In a moment, the kid returned pouting and slumped down in his chair. His father asked, "What's the matter with you?"

Navor looked at Thorgrim and as he was about to tattle, Thorgrim reached up and started to lift his eyepatch again.

The boy, aghast, suddenly sat back and said, "Nothing's wrong."

Thorgrim chuckled.

Alejandra brought over a plate of fried carrots, a big bowl of fresh butter, and a large decanter full of thick maple syrup.

Thorgrim saw the decanter and said, "That looks like a dwarven ale decanter. Oh, you don't happen to have any cold ale, do you?"

"It is a dwarven ale decanter," replied Alejandra. "I'm sorry, but we don't have any ale."

Thorgrim moaned, "No ale?"

"No, sorry."

Shrugging, Thorgrim said, "Uh, I'm curious. How did you end up with a dwarven ale decanter?"

"We bought it from a traveling flea market a couple of years ago. The guy said it had a genie inside and Italia just had to have it."

Thorgrim sat back, grasping his chin. "A traveling flea market? A genie? By any chance, did the guy who sold that to you, happen to be a dwarf who goes by the name of Al Brownstone?"

"Yes, I think so."

"I know him. He's a good fella. I have a battle-axe sitting out there by the fence that I had recently purchased from him. He told me it was magical, too, but I don't believe in magic."

Mark nodded. "Italia is still hoping the genie will come out of it. I hope he likes syrup though because if he's in there, he's swimming in it."

Italia giggled. "He's in there, you'll see someday, Father."

Thorgrim noticed the plate of carrots. With bile rising in his throat, he asked, "What's with the carrots?"

"Oh, just put one on top of your cakes. They add the right amount of extra vegetable flavor."

Though woozy, Thorgrim jokingly said, "Oh, no thanks, I prefer green peas and beets on my pancakes, but thankee."

Alejandra sat down in her chair and said, "That's a good idea! I'll have to add those to the recipe next time."

Thorgrim swallowed hard. Starving, he took three cakes, then smothered them in a mountain of butter. Next, he poured a massive amount of syrup on his buttered veggie cakes and then filled his drinking glass with syrup, as well.

Everyone was stunned.

"Thorgrim, why did you fill your glass with syrup?" asked Alejandra.

"I like a lot of syrup, I guess."

Holding his breath, Thorgrim took a big bite of the cakes, chasing it with a big swig of pure maple syrup from his glass. Everyone watched, speechless.

Thorgrim feigned a smile and nodded while syrup dripped down his face.

Blinky popped his head out and started to lick the buttery syrup off Thorgrim's beard.

Mark laughed. "Oh, you do have a cat living in your beard! I thought Italia was joking."

Swallowing his mouthful of syrup and cakes, he said, "Yes, I do. Hey, uh, you don't happen to have any milk for him, do ya?"

Alejandra jumped up and grabbed some milk from the dry-ice box. She poured a saucer full, placing it on the floor next to Thorgrim.

Blinky could smell a drop of milk from a mile away. The happy cat was down on the floor the moment the saucer touched the ground.

Doing his best not to gag, Thorgrim was about to take another bite, when much to his shock, a miniature dwarf donkey strolled into the kitchen from another room.

Surprised, Thorgrim dropped his fork.

"That's a donkey," Thorgrim said, pointing.

Dalia said, "It's a miniature dwarf donkey. It's Italia's."

"What's a donkey doing livin' in yer house? Is that sanitary?"

Mark grinned and said, "That's Chloe. She thinks she's a baby dog, so we treat her like one."

"That donkey thinks it's a dog?" asked Thorgrim before taking a big swig of syrup.

In-between bites, Mark replied, "Hahaha, yes. But she's housebroken, and you can still throw a saddle on and ride her!"

Thorgrim forced down a chunk of veggie cake. Chasing it with more syrup, he asked several questions.

"But, she thinks she's a puppy? How can ya ride a puppy? Does she bark like a dog?"

Chloe walked over and started licking Thorgrim's elbow.

Mark said, "She doesn't really bark, but she can make a very annoying whining sound whenever she needs to go outside to go potty."

Alejandra took her last bite and said, "Don't forget, just like a dog, she won't let any of the cats on the bed when she's sleeping with us."

"That's right," said Mark. "She's in charge of the bed!"

Thorgrim could not believe it. "You let this donkey sleep in the same bed with you?"

Mark replied, "Sure, the regular horses are too big."

Thorgrim pursed his lips and nodded. Not only was he a bit shocked by the vision of a bed full of horses, but he also could not take another bite. Full of syrup and as much veggie cake as he dare eat, he pushed himself away from the table.

He turned and took a good look at Chloe. She had a cute button nose, big brown eyes, a white and tan fur coat with dark grey ears and a curly tail.

Thorgrim instantly fell in love with her. "Chloe is what we dwarves call a muplet."

Italia spoke, "Muplet means, cutie in Dwarvish."

Thorgrim looked at her and said, "Very good. You speak Dwarvish?"

Italia smiled and nodded. "Yes, among other languages."

Thorgrim winked at her. "Yer an amazin' kid."

Turning to Alejandra, to be polite, Thorgrim said, "Mrs. Durant, I can say that in all of my nearly, forty-five years, those are easily the best veggie cakes I've ever tried. Even better than my mother's recipe."

Alejandra beamed. "Why, thank you, Thorgrim!"

Young Navor said, "But, mother, the dwarf said that he'd never tried veggie cakes before, so why would he—"

Mark interrupted his son. "Uh, Navor, you've had enough to eat, why don't you go out and kick the ball into the net for a while."

Navor frowned but did not move from his chair.

Thorgrim started to lift his eyepatch again and said, "Hey, Navor."

Navor saw him and turned white. He then jumped off his chair and ran outside at top speed.

Mark said, "I've never seen that kid move so fast before."

Italia tugged on Thorgrim's arm. "Hey, Thorgrim, do you want to see some of my drawings?"

Glancing at his timepiece, he replied, "Sure, I have a little time. Uh, as soon as Chloe stops lickin' my arm, I think I can manage to stand up."

Thorgrim stood up, then reached over to rub Chloe's little ears. They were soft, reminding him of small hand towels.

Italia smiled and grabbed Thorgrim's hand. "My room is in here, come with me. Hey, you know, I think Chloe really likes you!"

Thorgrim let Italia lead the way into her room. Chloe followed behind him.

Italia's room contained a small bed, and a desk to draw or do her crafts. The walls were covered with all sorts of beautiful drawings of people and flowers. What especially caught Thorgrim's attention was the rows of books that lined several shelves.

Thorgrim put his arm around Italia. "I love yer drawings, Italia. You are really talented. Maybe one day yer artwork will hang in a museum."

She smiled, pointed ear to pointed ear. "That would be totally awesome!"

"You have a ton of books, too! Where did you get all of these books?"

"My father brings them back when he comes home from the Air Force. There's a book store on the base."

Thorgrim picked up a book and read the cover. "Tales of Arcadia? Never heard of it."

Italia glowed. "Oh, you should read it. It's awesome."

"I'll try to find a copy somewhere," he replied with a wink. "You're a wonderful kid, Italia. You have a great family. Promise me that you'll never take them for granted. Appreciate each moment with them, because one day, many, many years from now, you'll be glad you did."

She looked at him, her big eyes, full of life and innocence.

"You have to go, don't you?"

Rubbing Chloe's ears, Thorgrim nodded. "Yes, I have to get Nugget and go find some food and water to fill my supply bag. I have a long ride ahead of me."

"You didn't care for the veggie cakes, did you?"

He dropped his head, "Not much. But don't say anything, okay?"

"Okay, I won't. Thorgrim, I really, really wish you could stay longer, but I understand. You know, when you leave, if you go into town, you'll find a food store. They have some of the kinds of food you like."

His stomach rumbled. "They do? Oh, thank Moridon!"

She excitedly said, "Moridon, the great bearded, Father God of the dwarves. His beard is made of gold and he can drop it all the way to the ground from heaven."

Thorgrim, astounded again, could only say, "Yer amazin'.""

***

After bidding farewell and thanking everyone for their warm hospitality, Thorgrim stepped outside and called for Nugget.

Everyone followed, and of course, so did Chloe.

Thorgrim noticed that Nugget was still running around with the other elven horses and having fun.

Mark said, "That cremello is yours?"

"Yes. His name is Nugget."

"He has a beautiful, creme-colored coat," commented Alejandra.

Thorgrim whistled and called again, "Nugget, come on, we have to go."

Checking his beard and glancing around Thorgrim said, "Oh, muh God, I almost forgot my cat. Has anyone seen him?"

"Your cat's riding on Chloe's back," replied Dalia.

Thorgrim looked and sure enough, Blinky was lying comfortably and purring in the middle of the donkey's back.

Thorgrim could not resist a chuckle.

Looking around, Thorgrim could not find Italia. "Where's Italia? I wanted to say goodbye to her."

Turning to Dalia, Mark said, "Go get your sister, please. Tell her Mr. Longbeard is leaving soon."

After another whistle, Nugget finally made it over to the fence. Mark opened the gate but Nugget refused to come out.

"Come on boy, we have to go," said Thorgrim firmly.

The other horses were now walking towards the fence to join Nugget. When they arrived, they all took turns rubbing up against their new friend.

"Our horses sure like Nugget, Mr. Longbeard," said Alejandra.

Thorgrim, again somber, replied, "It would seem so. I think the feelin' is mutual."

***

—Italia Durant

At that moment, Italia walked out of the house. She went up to Thorgrim, then handed him a piece of paper and a book.

Surprised, Thorgrim said, "What's this?"

"A drawing I just made and a book for you."

Thorgrim looked at the drawing. It was a beautiful sketch of the moment, earlier in the morning, when Italia had jumped up on Nugget while he watched. Blinky can be seen poking his head out of his beard.

At the bottom of the drawing, she had written first in Elvish, 'To my friend', then in Dwarvish, 'Thorgrim!'. Finally, she signed it in Avalonian, 'Italia Durant.'

"Thank you. That's amazin', you know the Avalonian language, too?"

"Yes, and Abbirian! I even know some Orcish."

"Orcish?" he said with a slight frown. "Well, let's hope that ya never need to use it!"

While he continued to study the drawing, his eyes became misty. "Yer simply an awesome kid. I love the drawin' and I'll keep it forever."

Giving him a big hug, she replied, "You're amazing, too, Thorgrim."

He looked at the cover of the book. "Yer copy of Tales of Arcadia?"

"Yes, I want you to have it."

"This is all overwhelming. Thank you, once again. I'll read it and treasure it, always."

He leaned over and whispered to Italia, "Ya know, I've never liked elves much, but you've shown me that I can make exceptions." He ended with a wink.

For a couple of minutes, everyone watched Nugget and the other horses while they played a game of chase inside in the field.

With hooves thundering, Nugget raced by in pursuit of one of the other horses. It was obvious to everyone how truly happy he was.

Nugget's happiness was especially obvious to Thorgrim.

Thorgrim tried again. "Come on, Nugget, we've got to go!"

Nugget continued to run.

Mark commented, "Thorgrim, it looks like your horse is having a lot of fun and doesn't want to leave."

Thorgrim swallowed a lump the size of the Aurumsmiter Hammer. "I know," he admitted, brow low, eyes sad, nodding slowly.

Standing next to Thorgrim, Chloe licked the dwarf's cheek and nudged him.

He looked at the little donkey. *Those eyes, so beautiful.* he thought. They reminded him of Ruby's donkey, Penelope. Reaching up, he massaged the side of Chloe's face. The little donkey, enjoying it, responded with grunting sounds.

Misty eyed, Thorgrim said, "Ya know, muh wife, Ruby, used to have a little donkey like this one. Her name was Penelope. After Ruby passed away, I had to sell her."

"Sorry to hear that," replied Mark, somberly.

"Thankee."

Thorgrim thought for a minute, saying nothing. Finally, after a heavy sigh, he said, "Hey, did you say that Chloe can be ridden?"

Mark replied, "Yes, she's very calm and well trained. Surprisingly, very fast and powerful, too. Hard to believe by looking at her, considering how little she is compared to a regular horse."

"Curious, where did she come from?"

Mark replied, "That guy, Al, who has the traveling flea market? He sold Chloe to us a few years ago the first time he came through here. Al said he found her wandering alone in a field somewhere in the Brimger Province. He figured she might have belonged to the Dwarven Army and somehow strayed away."

Thorgrim rubbed Chloe's ears and the donkey, enjoying it, responded with more grunting, baby pig sounds. He thought, *Like Nugget, Chloe belongs with her own kind. I'm a dwarf, she's a dwarf donkey. I guess that's close enough.*

For a few minutes, Thorgrim watched Nugget, who was still playing with the other horses.

With another heavy sigh, he glanced over at Italia. She smiled and spoke to Thorgrim with a slight nod of her head.

He understood and made up his mind.

"You don't happen to have a saddle that would fit Chloe, do you?"

Mark said, "Yes, we do. Do you want to ride her?"

"I want to trade for her. I think Nugget belongs here, with other elven horses and a loving elven family like you folks. I love him with my whole heart, but he's not truly happy. He's been sad for many years, and I've been selfish in keeping him this long."

Italia immediately spoke, "Yes, please, Father, let him have Chloe."

"But, you love Chloe; how could you give her up?"

"Because, I know she's sad, too. She needs to be with dwarves. She comes from the land of the dwarves."

"Won't you miss her?"

The other kids said, "Yes, we will miss her. We all love Chloe."

Italia looked at her siblings. "How would you two feel if you had to go live with dwarves or humans? Would you be happy?"

They both shook their heads.

"Are you sure, Italia?" asked her mother. "Chloe seemed to take a liking to you since the first day we had her."

Italia nodded. "I'm sure I'll cry after she goes, but I know inside Chloe's heart, she's been crying for a long time."

"So has Nugget," said Thorgrim, sadly.

Mark sighed. "You okay with this, wife?"

Alejandra answered, "Yes, I guess so. I think Italia is right. Chloe would be happier if she was with dwarves."

Mark shrugged and said, "Okay, if that's what you want. Two of you, go grab Chloe's saddle."

***

After a half-hour, Chloe's saddle was installed, and she was ready to go. Thorgrim put on his backpack and tied the leather bag and axe to the saddle.

Thorgrim checked the time. It was almost 3:00 p.m. "I have to go now. Thankee for everything. I know you'll take good care of Nugget. I love him very much!"

Everyone approached Thorgrim and shook his hand. Italia hugged him. He turned a final time and looked out to where Nugget played. With a heavy heart, and tears in his eyes, he ran to the fence, calling once more to his long-time friend.

"Nugget, come here, my ol' friend!"

Nugget heard him and sensed what was happening. The horse raced across the big field, stopping on the other side of the ten-foot-tall, wooden fence. Sticking his head through one of the gaps, Nugget licked Thorgrim's face several times.

"I love ya Nugget. I love ya so much. Muh dear friend, I have to go now, but ya have a new family who'll love ya as much as I do. Ya have new friends to play with, too. No more runnin' through scary forests un getting' attacked by wolves."

Nugget somehow understood Thorgrim. The great horse whinnied, his beautiful eyes moist with tears.

"You go play with yer friends, now."

Two more licks to Thorgrim's face, then the horse started to turn away and run back into the field.

Thorgrim yelled, "Nugget!"

The horse stopped, turned and quickly returned to the fence, nudging Thorgrim's face with his nose.

Thorgrim pulled out the last carrot he had in his backpack, giving it to his beloved friend.

Nugget happily ate it. When he finished, he neighed a couple of times and again nudged Thorgrim's face with his dark muzzle, followed by a lick to the dwarf's forehead.

Thorgrim recalled the first time Nugget had licked his forehead when they had met, twenty-five years ago in Stug.

400

Holding his breath, he fought back the urge to cry, but, despite his best efforts, many tears fell.

Nugget shook his head, then, after a long whinny, turned, and hastily ran back to the other horses.

Thorgrim had to do everything he could to avoid breaking down like a baby in front of the elves.

All of the elves were deeply touched by the obvious love between Thorgrim and Nugget.

After a few minutes, gaining control of his emotions, Thorgrim turned back to look at Italia and her family. He noticed that he was not the only one who was crying. The elves were shedding their share of tears while saying their final goodbyes to Chloe.

Thorgrim waited for a few minutes, before slowly walking back to Chloe and the elves. He noticed that Italia was holding Blinky and petting him.

"Time to go, Blinky."

Thorgrim smiled and gestured to Italia. She then handed him his purring cat.

Thorgrim, his eyes still wet from tears, said, "Blinky, my boy, it seems you've made a new friend, but unlike Nugget, you won't be stayin' here."

Italia leaned in and whispered, "Thorgrim. Blinky is a girl."

Thorgrim was stunned.

Wearing an unbelieving expression, Thorgrim replied, "He is? I mean, she is? Are ya sure?"

Italia lifted one of her eyebrows. "Oh, yes."

Thorgrim looked at Blinky and said, "Okay. Well, how did I goof that up?"

Shrugging, Thorgrim grabbed Chloe's reins and then stepped into the stirrup. With little effort, he easily pulled himself up into the saddle.

"Look how easy that was!" exclaimed Italia. "I told you it would be easy if you had the right horse!"

"Yer right, my young friend. Wow, everything seems so much different now! I'm closer to the ground, that's fer sure! I'll get used to it, though. Thankee. Hey, I want to tell you, Nugget loves carrots, and I know you elves probably have gardens full of them."

Mark replied, "Yes, we have lots of carrots. Just so you know, Chloe likes cheese. She can hear the opening of a cheese wrapper from a hundred miles away!"

"A donkey that likes cheese," replied Thorgrim with a grin. "She really thinks she's a dog. Amazin'."

"Will we ever see you again?" asked Mark.

"Perhaps one day. I can certainly say that I'll be lookin' forward to it."

"Yes, please, come back soon!" Italia said with tears in her eyes.

Thorgrim gave her a thumbs up. "One day, we will meet again."

He then spotted Navor peeking out from behind his father.

"Hey, Navor, come over here," hollered Thorgrim.

The young boy shook his head.

"Come here, I have something for you."

With some prodding by his father, Navor timidly approached the one-eyed dwarf.

Reaching into a front pocket, Thorgrim handed the boy a dark-red object.

"What's this?" asked Navor, puzzled.

"It's an eyepatch like mine. You're now an official member of the Iron Golem Pub gang."

"I am?"

"Yes! Only really tough guys can be members. Wear the patch proudly."

"Thank you! I will!"

Thorgrim helped Navor put on the patch and patted him on the head. The boy wore a huge smile.

Thorgrim gave Chloe a nudge and she began to slowly walk forward. "Bye, everyone! Thank you!"

Waving, the elves followed him until he reached the side road that led into the main part of town.

As Thorgrim rode away, he said to Blinky. "So, yer a girl? Now, don't be havin' any kittens! There's no more room, even in **my** beard."

Blinky purred.

"Chloe, I hear you're an excellent ride. Can you outrun wolves?"

Chloe grunted.

"I also hear that you think you're a baby dog? Well, that will make things interesting, to say the least."

Chloe made another soft grunting sound.

Looking at the back of the donkey's furry head, Thorgrim rubbed one of her ears and said, "Yes, you're a muplet."

As he turned along the path to enter the town, he could still hear the sound of the horses as they played in the field over a hundred yards away.

Thorgrim took a final look and saw that Nugget had been watching him.

His heart skipped a beat and it hurt. With a final wave goodbye to Nugget, more tears flowed. Nugget reared up, swinging his front hooves and bade Thorgrim farewell with one last, beautiful whinny.

It took several minutes, but Thorgrim was once again able to control his tears. He would think of Nugget almost every day for the rest of his life and his heart would ache every time. But he knew the horse was now truly happy, and that in turn, made Thorgrim happy.

Wiping away his remaining tears, Thorgrim slowly traveled down the main street in Elkhorn. The town reminded him in many ways of Stug, only much larger, and instead of dwarves, he saw elves. Although a few of them stared, most seemed disinterested in him.

As he rode, Thorgrim looked left and right for the general store. Spotting it in midtown, he hoped that Italia was right when she said that the store had the kinds of food dwarves enjoy.

"Sausages! I'll take all you have and then more! Blinky, that's what I'm going to say to the guy at the register when I get in there."

Chloe growled like a dog.

Thorgrim said, "No worries, my muplet friend. I'll get you some cheese."

At 4:25 p.m., Thorgrim had entered the general store and as he had promised, he purchased every last sausage in the place. He also bought a special flask that kept liquids cold longer and a large packet of cheese for a certain donkey.

He filled his own flasks, though he was disappointed to discover that the closest source of ale was either in the Dwarven Clans or about fifty miles away in the city of Tranjia.

While he was inside purchasing his supplies, Thorgrim asked the halfling storekeeper what he thought would be the best and fastest route to the Great Kingdom.

The halfling, though intimidated by the dwarf's eyepatch, tried to make conversation. "What's the big hurry to get to the Great Kingdom?"

Annoyed by the halfling's rather invasive question, Thorgrim replied, "It's really none of yer business, but I'm going there because I'm in need of employment and a solid roof over muh head. The funds I have won't last forever."

"Why can't you stay here and get a job? There are a few places to rent, too."

Thorgrim scowled. "What elf is goin' to hire a dwarf?"

The halfling shrugged.

"Okay, so what do you think is the best way to get to the Great Kingdom from here?"

"Well, the Tambi River is out of its banks. It won't be easy, but I'm afraid there's probably only one way to get to the Great Kingdom."

Thorgrim was disappointed. "Yer kiddin'. Only one way?"

"Let's take a look at a map," said the halfling.

The halfling storekeeper pulled out a larger version of Thorgrim's map. Unfolding it on the table, the halfling showed him that the only practical route was through the Mean Man Forest, across the southern Alacarjian prairie, then through Troll Glade. From there, he could cross a bridge over the Tambi River, which was about twenty miles from the Great Kingdom's border.

Thorgrim was concerned that the bridge in the Troll Glade might be washed out from the floodwaters. The halfling told him that anything was possible. But he suggested that the area around the glade, being so near the mountains, was at a higher elevation and probably unaffected by the summer floods.

Thorgrim became heavily disgruntled when he learned that the flood season would not end for over another two months.

Thorgrim had no choice but to try the route the halfling suggested.

The only good news was that several trails went through the Mean Man Forest. The halfling told him that an often-used path went northeast through the narrowest part of the woods, a distance of about fifteen miles.

As the halfling started to warn Thorgrim about the hideous monsters he would encounter during his journey, Thorgrim waved his hand and said, "I have muh axe."

However, when asked about wood hags, the halfling shrugged and said, "If ya count my mother-in-law, I guess you could say I've seen a wood hag. Well, I don't know about the wood part, but she's certainly at least a hag. But lucky for you, she doesn't live in the Mean Man Forest or the Troll Glade."

Thorgrim raised the corner of his monobrow. "Oh ya? Where does yer mother-in-law live?"

"Unfortunately, with me and the missus."

A storm was brewing in the west, so Thorgrim decided to spend the night in Elkhorn. Although he missed Nugget, and it would be fun to visit with Italia again, he did not want to intrude on the friendly elven family any more than he already had.

He found a suitable inn and stabled Chloe in the back. The miniature donkey resisted fiercely because she wanted to stay inside like a dog, but the innkeeper would not allow it.

For supper, because the inn's café only served horrid, elven dishes, Thorgrim and Blinky indulged on some of the sausages he had purchased. Luckily, he was able to purchase some fresh milk for his hungry cat. Out in the barn, Chloe, despite believing she was a puppy, enjoyed a few buckets of fresh clover provided by the friendly stablemen.

By nightfall, Thorgrim went to bed with Blinky, who was, as usual, purring deep inside his beard. Unable to sleep, he began reading Italia's book, Tales of Arcadia. Nearby, he had Italia's drawing propped up so he could see it.

Sometime in the evening, with thunder booming overhead, Thorgrim, exhausted again, fell asleep.

Throughout the night, he dreamt of Nugget and of course, Ruby. Sometimes, he would wake up with his eyes full of tears.

Blinky, worried about Thorgrim, snuggled closer and purred loudly.

Although Thorgrim's heart was broken because of the loss of Nugget, there was something extra special about Chloe. Something he did not yet understand.

His inner voice spoke to him after a particularly emotional dream about Nugget. The voice, soft and comforting, told him that one day, the little donkey would become his all-time best friend.

XVIII. The Troll Glade

It was 8:45 a.m., Thursday, July 21, 2273. The weather was hot and humid, as it usually is after a summer thunderstorm.

Before leaving Elkhorn, Thorgrim decided to stop at the general store, once again, in order to buy a few torches, a compass, and more food.

While Thorgrim was selecting his items, the topic of discussion was about his planned trek across the southern Alacarj on the way to the Great Kingdom.

Thorgrim asked the halfling storekeeper if he had any more information that might aid him during his journey.

The storekeeper told him that during the summer months, in addition to flooding, the northern and central parts of the Alacarj were fraught with violent storms. This included large hail, heavy rains, and massive tornados. He warned Thorgrim that during his ride across the southern prairie, shelter would be minimal.

Thorgrim thanked the storekeeper for the information, then related the story of the giant twister he experienced while spending the night at the Pretzel Brewing Company and Inn, twenty-five years ago. Even after all of those years, the thought of the tornado still frightened him. While telling the halfling about the terrible ordeal, Thorgrim fondly remembered Mr. and Mrs. McNoogle and wondered how they were doing.

The storekeeper again tried to warn Thorgrim about the dangerous animals and monsters that wandered the Alacarjian countryside.

This time, after the halfling ran through his long list of possible encounters, Thorgrim replied sarcastically, "What? Trolls and werewolves made yer list, but no dragons?"

"No dragons that I know of, sir."

"Hmmm. No dragons, but you did say that I might run into swarms of fist-sized hornets, giant, three-headed snakes, and some eight-foot-tall, carnivorous squirrels? Is that right?"

"Yes, and don't forget the dire wolves. They're everywhere there's deer. And the deer are thicker than vampire mosquitos this time of year. In fact, when you get near the Troll Glade, the woods in that area are full of wolves. Even the trolls avoid them."

"How do you know these things? Have you ever been up there?"

"I've heard tales from travelers who come through here from time to time. Never been up there, myself, though."

"Oh, ya? Do you believe everything you hear?"

"Why not?"

"Heh, really? Let me ask you, with the exception of wolves, do you really believe in trolls and all of those other crazy monsters you were just telling me about?"

"Yes, I do."

"But, have you ever seen any of 'em?"

"No, I don't believe so."

"So, you admit that you've never seen a troll before?"

"Yes."

"Yet, you still think they're real?"

The halfling's eyes became large. "There be trolls, sir."

Grinning, Thorgrim bit off a chunk of bison jerky. Chewing it, he winked and slowly said, "Sure, there are."

"Sir, I've been told that when you get to the Troll Glade, make sure you stay out of the woods. Stick to the highway. If you ride on the highway through the glade in the daytime and during clear weather, the trolls won't bother you. They love to come out at night or anytime during stormy weather, and they'll attack and try to kill anything they see."

Thorgrim laughed softly. "Okay. Look, I know you mean well, so I'll say, thankee. And I promise, if I ever meet a troll, I'll give him yer regards."

Thorgrim grabbed his things and started to leave, but stopped after a step. He said, "Oh, I almost forgot, someone mentioned something about a serial killer running around loose in this so-called Mean Man Forest? What do you know about that?"

"That's just an old rumor. I don't know if there's a murderer hiding out there, but I do know that the Mean Man Forest has its share of trolls and other horrors."

Thorgrim abruptly ended the conversation by flipping a copper towards the clerk and then slamming the front door when he exited.

Riding to the eastern outskirts of Elkhorn, the ground soaked from the previous night's storm, Thorgrim halted Chloe and examined his new compass. Next, he studied his little map. When he looked to the northeast, a mile ahead, patiently waiting for him was the Mean Man Forest.

"We have to go through another forest," Thorgrim said aloud. "Isn't that just great?"

407

Rubbing one of Chloe's ears, Thorgrim said, "Well, Chloe, have ya ever been chased through the woods by wolves?"

Chloe did not respond.

"How about a wood hag?"

Still no response from Chloe.

"I guess that means no."

Reaching into his beard, Thorgrim stroked his cat's head. "Blinky, ready?"

Blinky popped her head out and looked around.

"Boy, uh, sorry, I mean, girl, aren't you hot in there?"

Blinky was silent.

Thorgrim joked, "I suppose like Chloe, no response means no. I guess you girls are all the same, animal or otherwise. You both remind me of my wife, Ruby. Whenever I wanted somethin' I really didn't need, she didn't respond, either. It always meant no." He sighed, and said, "God, how I miss her."

Thorgrim did a double-check of everything. His old backpack was stuffed with food and water supplies. His leather bag also had food and extra water. Italia's book and drawing were carefully tucked away inside, as well. His battle-axe was covered and strapped to the back of Chloe's saddle and next to it was a sling with three newly purchased torches.

"Okay, everyone. We have a long ride ahead of us. And, I mean a long one."

Thorgrim was not joking.

En route to the Great Kingdom, they would be traveling through the southern Alacarjian prairie, an area full of light to medium density woodlands and swamps. Other than dirt trails, there were no roads and only a few, widely spaced towns. The distance to the Troll Glade was about one hundred and eighty miles as the crow flies.

Despite the hot weather, he still hoped he could ride an average of forty miles a day, though he had no idea how Chloe would perform. If everything went well, he could reach the Great Kingdom in five or six days, perhaps sooner if the temperatures drop. He would have to test his little donkey who had probably never made such a long journey before, especially carrying almost three hundred pounds of rider, cat, and supplies. In truth, Thorgrim had no idea how far or fast Chloe could travel. For all he knew, the journey would likely take much longer.

Though concerned about Chloe, Thorgrim had been told numerous times about the abilities of the amazing, surprisingly powerful, miniature dwarf donkeys. On this journey, he would find out if the stories about these little animals were fact or fiction.

Thorgrim understood that they would have to camp in the wilderness several times along the way. Dreading the thought of camping in the open, or in a wolf infested forest, he hoped that he might get lucky and find a friendly village or farm instead.

The nerve-wracking, extremely humid, though thankfully uneventful ride through the Mean Man Forest, was very slow due to the spongy, muddy trail. Along the way, Thorgrim encountered only rabbits, deer, birds, and other timid creatures. Luckily, not a single dangerous animal was seen and he was happy about that. The last thing he needed was a confrontation with some monster, a spook, or more wolves.

When Thorgrim exited the woods, he laughed and said, "A serial killer livin' in that forest? Hehehe, maybe a troll ate him. Hey, serial killer! Serial kill this!" Thorgrim held up a middle finger towards the Mean Man Forest.

Watching Thorgrim from behind some trees, a tall humanoid, wearing ragged clothes, murmured while repeatedly cutting into his own leg with a very sharp machete.

By nightfall on Thursday, Thorgrim took a close look at his map. Due to the slow, nine-hour ride through the forest, he guessed that he had only covered about thirty miles. With not a single farm in sight, he reluctantly made camp near a small grove of oaks.

In the middle of the night, Thorgrim heard a growl and then a weird whistling sound. Worse, it seemed to be nearby. Panicking, he sat straight up and broke out in a cold sweat.

His heart pounding, Thorgrim grabbed his axe, cocked his head and listened. Relieved, he heard nothing.

A few moments later, he heard the strange sounds again; a long, drawn-out growl that was followed by an eerie whistling sound. It repeated over and over, though sometimes the noise would abruptly stop for a second or two, then resume.

Frightened, Thorgrim stood up and raised his axe. It was then that he discovered the source of the terrifying sounds.

Chloe was snoring.

When Chloe inhaled, she growled like a bear. When she exhaled, she whistled.

Thorgrim sighed and listened to her. Chloe lay nearby, and though with only the light of the stars and the thin moon, he could still see her innocent face.

"Yer damn cute, that's fer sure. Scared the crap outta me, but yer still damn cute. Yuh, little muplet."

***

On the morning of Friday, July 22, the second day out of Elkhorn, though it was still hot and humid, the temperature was lower than it had been on Thursday. Because of the milder weather, Thorgrim thought it was a good time to test his miniature donkey. For a couple of hours, he rode her at a steady canter, instead of a trot. Chloe's version of a canter was nothing like Nugget's, but she still managed decent speed and her stamina was excellent.

During a rest break, Thorgrim said to his donkey, "Chloe, I don't know how you can haul muh fat butt around, along with muh cat, and all of this other stuff and not collapse from the weight of it. You are simply amazin'!"

Thorgrim had been carefully plotting his path and noting his time on the map. By late Friday afternoon, ten hours into the day's ride, he estimated that he had covered about fifty miles, for a total of eighty miles in two days, and was now about twenty miles north of a place called the Nice Dog Lake.

"The Mean Man Forest and the Nice Dog Lake?" muttered Thorgrim. "What's with the strange names for some of the places in this elven country?"

Chloe was spent and luckily, Thorgrim found a farm owned by a friendly elf widower. The old guy happily fed and put everyone up for the night at no charge. It was obvious to Thorgrim that the farmer was lonely, living by himself out in the middle of nowhere and appreciated any visitors.

When asked about the unusual name of the lake to the south, the old man told Thorgrim that, a century ago, the lake was named after a little stray dog who perished trying to fight off a wolf. The wolf had attacked the Alacarjian King's son while on a hunting trip there. The nameless dog was buried with full royal honors on a small island near the west end of the lake.

The story melted Thorgrim's heart. His love of animals was incomparable.

***

On Saturday, July 23, Thorgrim had to deal with a series of savage thunderstorms. The halfling storekeeper back in Elkhorn was not joking when he warned that the storms in the area were violent. Several times, due to hail, they had to take shelter wherever they could find it. Needless to say, the journey had slowed to a crawl.

The region was covered in light woodlands but not much else. Trees offered the only protection from the hail, but they also attracted lightning.

When they finally stopped to camp at dusk, Thorgrim estimated that because of the terrible weather, he had ridden only twenty miles for the day. This brought his total up to about one hundred miles after three days of traveling.

The storms left the area by nightfall, only to be replaced by the howling of wolves. Although the Brotherhood's persistent cries seemed far way, Thorgrim stayed up all night, axe in hand, while Blinky and Chloe slept.

Unknown to Thorgrim, that night, many miles away, in the Great Kingdom's capital city of Eastfair, a baby boy was born to the royal family. The infant was the future King Elric.

One day, nearly sixty years in the future, Thorgrim would meet the Captain of King Elric's Royal Guard; a certain knight by the name of Sir Sebastion of Scot. A man who would change Thorgrim's life forever.

***

It was exceptionally hot at dawn on Sunday, July 24. Regrettably, the hotter weather meant a slower ride and thus more rest stops would be needed.

Thorgrim ate, fed his friends, and studied his map. He was tired from lack of sleep and sore from riding in the saddle every day since he fled Bur Dhulgren, one week ago.

Thorgrim calculated that he was about sixty miles from the bridge but only if he rode through the heavily forested areas south of the Troll Glade, to get there. The halfling storekeeper's words rang in his ears ' . . . when you get near the Troll Glade, the woods in that area are full of wolves. Even the trolls avoid them.' Not wanting to risk another encounter with wolves, he selected a different, though longer route.

Thorgrim believed it would be safer to ride around north of the woods and then travel down the highway to the bridge. He guessed the distance would be about eighty miles to the highway, twelve more to the bridge, and another twenty to the border.

It would be highly unlikely that he would be able to reach the border by Sunday evening. Today, due to the extreme heat, it would be impossible to ride faster than a trot without risking Chloe's health, nor could he risk riding more than eight or nine hours. At that speed, including extra stops for rest, averaging about six miles per hour, he would be lucky to manage fifty miles. There was no doubt that he would have to spend at least one more night in the wilderness. Of course, there was always the chance that he might encounter another friendly elven farmer who might put him up for the night.

At 7:15 a.m., he mounted up and rode northeast. It was so hot that Blinky chose to ride on Thorgrim's lap instead of inside his beard.

An hour after leaving camp, during a stop for rest and water, Thorgrim glanced towards the northwest and was horrified by what he saw. Along the horizon, menacing purple-black clouds were moving in rapidly. It was another powerful storm. This meant more delays and danger. Within the system, forks of lightning flashed and thunder rumbled.

No shelter could be seen in the area except for a few small trees and patches of thorny bushes and other shrubberies. He had no choice but to continue onward in hopes of finding some kind of protection before the storm arrived.

The storm was moving in fast, bringing with it cooler temperature. Thorgrim was aware that cooler air in front of a summer storm was usually a precursor to driving winds and dangerous hail. Frightened, he had no choice but to increase Chloe's speed to a canter in hopes of reaching the protection of some heavy oaks or a building of some kind.

By 10:30 a.m., having covered only about eighteen miles, the storm caught Thorgrim in the open. Thankfully, off to the south, about a half-mile away, he spotted the remains of an abandoned house. Peppered by hail and rain, he turned Chloe towards the building, increasing her speed to a gallop.

Her speed was astounding, though, by the time they reached the structure, she was almost exhausted.

The house was in rough shape and the remains of the roof leaked terribly. Already soaked to the bone by the downpour, the leaks did not matter to any of them, except Blinky, who, like most cats, hated being wet.

Though she was a miniature donkey, like a dog, Chloe seemed frightened by the thunder, shaking uncontrollably with each rumble. Concerned for his new friend, Thorgrim tried to calm her with some cheese along with a few hugs. The treat and the affection relaxed her, and she happily ate half of the cheese that Thorgrim had purchased back in Elkhorn.

It was during this time after he had shared one with her, Thorgrim discovered that Chloe loved the taste of bison sausages. "Yep, yer a dwarf!" he said with a chuckle.

By 11:30 a.m., the storm had blown over. Though it had been brief, it dumped almost two inches of rain in an hour. Before riding out, Thorgrim, using his timepiece and studying his map, calculated they had about nine and a half hours to reach the border before dark.

With the heat and humidity returning after the storm, such a trek seemed impossible. To make matters worse, the ground was soft and muddy from the heavy rain shower. Still, Thorgrim needed to move on towards his destination, in the least, hoping to find better shelter than the rickety house they were currently staying in. He feared wolves or possibly bandits might arrive tonight and enter the place, catching him in his sleep.

Chloe, despite having already traveled three hours, seemed fully refreshed after over an hour and a half rest. Thorgrim decided he would ride until Chloe decided when she had had enough. He rode out at ten minutes before noon. His plan was to find the closest farm or village and then spend the night.

**

The journey went without incident, though as expected, they were slowed by the mud. Fortunately, by early afternoon, the hot sun dried the ground out allowing Thorgrim to get Chloe up to a steady trot.

Amazingly, despite the pace, the miniature dwarf donkey showed no signs of giving up.

But even miniature dwarf donkeys have their limits.

By 7:00 p.m., Thorgrim was several miles north of the heavy woods that flanked the glade. At early dusk around 8:45 p.m., he had reached the main highway that led to both Calibut, far to the north, and the bridge that spanned the Tambi River to the southeast.

Oddly, there was not a soul anywhere. Not even a rabbit or bird. The main road seemed eerily abandoned.

He figured he was about twenty miles from the bridge with just over twenty to go after that to reach the border with the Great Kingdom.

With about forty-five minutes before complete darkness, Thorgrim had at least another two to three hours of hard riding to get over the border into the Great Kingdom where they might find refuge.

However, Chloe was exhausted. While they were stopped on the main road, she laid down on the ground and refused to move.

Thorgrim was worried he had pushed Chloe too hard. He sat next to her on the highway while she rested, cooling her with water from his flasks.

Out of the darkness, a few elven hunters on horseback rode in from the wilderness and asked Thorgrim if he needed any help. Again, he was surprised at the friendliness of the elves that he had met so far.

When he declined, they warned him to stay out of the glade, especially at night. They told him that there was no town nearby, but there were a few abandoned farms not far away to the north. With their torches blazing, the elves rode north towards Calibut, leaving Thorgrim with a final, dire warning to stay out of the glade.

It was very dark because the moon and stars were hidden by a heavy overcast. Around 9:30 p.m., Thorgrim lit a torch and urged Chloe to her feet. Leading her northwest on the highway, he hoped to find one of the old farmhouses that the elves had mentioned. Fifteen minutes later, he found a barn near the remains of a burned down farmhouse.

The barn was in rough shape, not much better than the old house he had taken shelter in earlier during the storm. It was obvious the building had not been used in many years. The wood siding was rotted, although the supporting oak frame seemed solid.

Inside the barn, Thorgrim removed Chloe's saddle and bridle, then gave her a good brushing while she fed on some long grass that he had collected for her. The little donkey, loving the attention, made grunting sounds with each movement of the brush on her back.

By 10:30 p.m., Thorgrim had decided to get some sleep. He was exhausted after the long ride across the prairie, battling storms and the hot summer sun. He longed for a refreshing bath but knew that would have to wait until he could find an inn the following morning after he crossed the border.

He realized that when he reached the border with the Great Kingdom, he would likely have to present his ID papers. It seemed that at least one more time, Thorgrim Longbeard would have to become Shem Lybree.

While drifting off to sleep on top of a blanket in the corner of the barn, he wondered who had lived on this farm before and why it had been abandoned. Tomorrow, he would learn why.

A beautiful dream about Ruby was interrupted around 2:00 a.m. by the terrifying sounds of a pack of wolves engaged in battle.

Sitting up, Thorgrim propped himself up against the wall and listened. Far off in the distance to the southeast, barking, howling, and growling sounds could be heard intermixed with what sounded like several people arguing and yelling in a combination of poor Avalonian and some other weird language. Thorgrim assumed it might be a local militia engaged in combat with a bunch of wolves.

The sounds grew louder. Shrieking, screaming, cursing, yelping, snarling, and growling.

It seemed the battle was moving in his direction. Not wanting to get involved, Thorgrim prayed to Moridon for help.

For over an hour, Thorgrim heard the yelping of wolves and several deep voices shouting in anger, again using a mix of very bad Avalonian and some other foreign language he had never heard before. Finally and thankfully, with the exception of an occasional curse word or the bark of a wolf, the night became silent. The battle apparently had ended.

Then, Thorgrim heard movement in the grassy fields behind the barn. Though brief, it was obvious that something was moving through the area.

Wild-eyed, he anxiously looked towards the barn's open entryway. The doors were missing, and he was now extremely concerned that wolves might be approaching. Grabbing his axe, he faced the entryway, sitting with Blinky and Chloe in the far corner of the barn. Together, they waited, trembling in fear.

However, exhausted, despite the threat of wolves, all of them eventually and unwillingly drifted off to sleep.

A few hours later, at sunrise, Thorgrim, tired, though excited for the day, rose and stretched. The first thing he did was curse himself harshly for falling asleep when he should have been on guard for wolves, although he knew little could have been done if the Brotherhood had discovered him and his friends.

After eating a quick breakfast, he led Chloe out of the barn so she could graze on the wild grass. The morning sun, now clearly above the eastern horizon, shown brightly in the cloudless sky. The weather was thankfully, surprisingly crisp and cool.

While Chloe enjoyed the grass, Thorgrim refilled his flasks from a nearby well. After a half-hour, he led Chloe back into the barn and gave her a good brushing. He was about to saddle his donkey, when the entire southern wall of the barn crashed in with a tremendous explosion, sending splinters of rotted wood and large sections of broken beams flying everywhere.

415

Thorgrim, shocked, covered his head as the debris rained down around him. He looked up towards the remains of the southern wall and saw a huge, humanoid creature standing there. At least twelve feet tall, it had dark green skin, red eyes, and a pointed, hairless head with an elongated face that was decorated with a crooked, oblong nose. It was extremely muscular, with thick arms that hung almost to its knees. A lot of dried blood was caked on the creature's body in various places. Some of the blood belonged to the creature, while some belonged to wolves.

The humongous beast looked exactly like what Ruby said she had seen in the Haunted Forest when she was a small girl.

There was no doubt that it was a troll. The thing was searching for the remainder of the pack of wolves that he and his brothers had battled in the middle of the night.

Thorgrim muttered, "Moridon's holy beard, trolls are real!"

Unable to believe what he was seeing, Thorgrim froze. Blinky hissed, jumped out of his beard and ran out of the barn towards some bushes. Chloe, snorting in fear, remained by Thorgrim's side.

In its right hand, the angry troll carried part of a tree branch that it had been using as a makeshift club. Glancing around the barn, unable to find any wolves, it roared in fury.

Then it spotted Thorgrim.

Insane with anger, it tipped its head back while releasing an ear-piercing, bloodcurdling scream.

Thorgrim, horrified, almost lost his bowels.

Though he wondered what good it would do, he looked for his battle-axe but it was propped up in the corner of the barn next to his backpack, near where he had been sleeping. Regrettably, there was no way to get to the weapon, without going through the troll.

"Almighty Moridon, please help us," he whispered.

Not wanting to aggravate the troll any more than it already was, and not sure that he could outrun the monster, Thorgrim cautiously retreated out of the barn, and Chloe instinctively followed him.

Without further hesitation, the troll quickly bounded towards Thorgrim and Chloe, its tree-club raised and ready to strike. It screamed, sending gobs of spittle flying everywhere. Then using a mixture of Trollish and broken Avalonian, it yelled, "Skevich! (Stupid!) I gonna boko (kill) you now, wittow, furry-face man!"

Though it used a mixture of very poor Avalonian and its own native language, Thorgrim understood every word.

***

[Author's Note:]
Over the centuries, trolls had learned the language of humans, oddly preferring it over their own native language.

***

"Chloe, run!" Thorgrim grabbed Chloe by her mane, then turned and ran out of the barn as fast as he could, pulling the donkey with him.

Grunting and yelling, with evil intentions the irate troll gave chase. The monster wanted to rip the dwarf apart, then catch and eat the little donkey. Bounding out of the barn, it was upon them in only a few seconds.

Still running hard, Thorgrim released his donkey and yelled, "Chloe! Run for the road and keep going!"

Chloe had already decided that heading for the road was the best choice.

Thorgrim turned and ran in the opposite direction, hoping the troll would follow him instead of Chloe.

As he started his turn, Thorgrim heard it coming . . . 'swooosh, boom!' The tree-club struck the ground, barely missing him.

Thorgrim covered his head and ducked, rolling into a ball, as the one-ton troll ran over the top of him, barely missing him with its big feet.

Thorgrim now realized that there was no way he could outrun the troll. There was only one option, but he needed his weapon.

With the troll behind him, he saw that the way to his battle-axe was open. Fearing that his life was now in grave danger, Thorgrim quickly stood up and ran toward the barn entrance. As he went, he looked around, and thankfully, Chloe and Blinky were nowhere to be seen. Concerned for their lives, he hoped they would remain hidden.

The troll, cursing, again gave chase.

Thorgrim sprinted to his axe. Hoping in the least, that he might be able to wound the troll and frighten it off, he picked up his weapon and removed the hood. Raising the axe, he turned around and looked up. He found himself staring into the face of the monstrous troll who was now only a few feet away.

A sudden backhand by the troll surprised Thorgrim, flinging him back into the wall. The blow nearly knocked him out and the impact with the barn caused him to drop his axe, which now lay at his feet.

417

Furious, the troll stepped forward, leaned down and roared in Thorgrim's face, spraying spit all over the front of the dwarf.

Barely a foot away from the dwarf, the irate troll breathed heavily; its breath, sour and rancid.

Woozy and beyond terrified, Thorgrim was trapped in the corner of the barn with his back to the wall and no place to run.

"You stoooooopid, stooopid. You da one who bwought da gwey, mean doggies here. Dey bite me. Dey bad doggies. I wiw pull yo wittow head off, wittow man wit furry face. Den, I wiw hunt down yo teeny howsee and kill it, too. I wiw pull it's wittow wegs off and use dem fo toot-picks. Tonight, me un my bwudders and maybe my seeesters wiw eat you all fo dinna."

Though fearing for his life, Thorgrim was now angry and his anger revitalized him. Scowling, using his sleeve, he tried to wipe the troll's saliva from his face.

Most sages would warn that it was unwise to spit on a dwarf. Considered a great insult by all dwarves, spitting on them roused their anger like nothing else. The same sages also warned that an angry dwarf was no one to mess with. Even when they were cornered or outnumbered, they would fight twice as hard.

Angry dwarves were also surprisingly quick thinkers. Thorgrim knew the troll was stupid, and that was the only advantage he had.

Thorgrim devised a plan.

Slowly reaching into his front pocket, he found what he was looking for and pulled it out. Carefully, slowly, he wrapped the dark-red, Iron Golem eyepatch over his left eye and tied it behind his head.

The troll paused, curious about the eyepatch. It tilted its head back and forth trying to figure out the strange behavior of the little, furry-faced man.

Thorgrim waited for the right moment. Although still horrified, his intense anger trumped his fear.

The troll noticed the glimmering, silver battle-axe on the ground near Thorgrim's feet and said, "Dat yo puny bwade? Hahaha. You goin' to twy to cut me wit dat?"

The thing leaned down closer and continued to breathe its sickening breath in Thorgrim's face, now at a faster rate which indicated the monster was about to attack.

Despite the odds, despite the fact that the troll was three times taller, eight times heavier, and ten times stronger than any dwarf that ever lived, Thorgrim furrowed his brow deep, squinted through his one eye and said in perfect Avalonian, "Yer breath stinks, friend."

The troll was stunned by Thorgrim's comment. It stood up and took a half-step back. Wearing a puzzled expression, it said, "It does?" The creature brought its free hand up to its mouth and breathed into it. Sniffing its own breath the troll said, "I don't tink it sm—"

The troll was interrupted when, moving as fast as an elf, Thorgrim reached down, grabbed his mighty axe, then struck the monster's left arm halfway between the elbow and shoulder, severing it.

The appendage, after dropping to the ground with a loud thud, twitched and wiggled as if searching for its owner.

The troll screamed in agony as blue blood sprayed out of the ghastly stump. Dropping the tree-club, the troll grabbed at the remains of his arm with its free hand, while blood gushed out of the massive wound. Wailing in misery, it staggered back a few steps, dropped to its knees and fell to the ground in a heap, writhing in pain.

Thorgrim fled out of the barn, and as he passed by, he whacked the monster again, this time on its right ankle, almost cleaving it with one blow, again spraying troll blood everywhere.

Stunned and in shock, the beast rolled onto its back. While still grasping at its gory, stump of an arm, it shook its injured leg, blood shooting from the deep gash.

Watching from a distance through the barn entrance, Thorgrim witnessed the monster struggle as it attempted to sit up. Failing that, the troll continued to cry out in pain, while at the same time, uttering various, badly pronounced, Avalonian curse words. After a few minutes, the creatures lay motionless and became silent.

Full of adrenaline, Thorgrim cautiously approached the barn entrance and peeked inside to get a closer look.

Thorgrim carefully studied the monster. With no sign of breathing or movement, the troll certainly appeared dead. Near the corner, its severed arm lay where it fell, though it no longer twitched.

Turning away from the barn, Thorgrim raised his bloody axe, yelling, "I killed that sonofabitch! Chloe! Blinky! Where are you! We need to get going before more of them show up!"

A hundred feet away, Blinky and Chloe reappeared from behind a few trees near the main road.

They both ran to Thorgrim and then suddenly stopped. Blinky hissed, turned and then ran for the bushes again.

Thorgrim heard heavy breathing coming from behind him. His mind flashed, *What the hell, another troll?*

Able to hear his own pulse pounding in his ears, turning, Thorgrim realized that it was not another troll.

It was the same one.

The monster looked at him and grinned diabolically. The atrocious arm wound had healed and the end of the stump was pulsating. Thorgrim watched in stunned silence as the troll's arm began to regrow right before his eyes. A quick glance at its nearly severed right foot revealed that the wound had already completely healed.

In another minute, the limb had grown back. The troll laughed and made a fist with his new hand. He shook it at Thorgrim and yelled, "Now, my turn, wittow man."

Horrified by what he had just witnessed, Thorgrim, cursing and retreating, tripped over a large stone, falling onto his back. Losing his grip on the battle-axe, the weapon flew several feet away, landing on the ground, out of reach.

The amazingly quick troll raced forward, grabbed Thorgrim by the midsection, then easily picked him up and held him ten feet off the ground. The creature's new hand, still growing, almost completely wrapped itself around the dwarf's stomach.

The troll brought its other hand up and grabbed Thorgrim around his chest.

Offering a sinister growl, the troll began to squeeze Thorgrim, causing him to grunt in pain.

Overwhelmed with terror, struggling in vain, Thorgrim kicked and squirmed in the monster's powerful grip. About to faint, in a last-ditch effort to free himself, Thorgrim bit a large chunk out of the troll's thumb, spitting it out into the beast's face.

Unaffected by the bite, the troll responded with a slow, eerie giggle. Then it squeezed Thorgrim tighter.

Thorgrim was helpless and he knew it. His only concern now was for Blinky and Chloe. Unable to breathe or speak, he prayed to Moridon to protect Blinky and Chloe.

Thorgrim's only solace was that he would be soon joining Ruby and their infant son. A son he named after his own father, Luthor.

The troll grunted triumphantly. Its face painted with a crooked smile of pleasure.

It squeezed tighter.

Thorgrim's ribs were at the breaking point.

As Thorgrim watched, everything became darker, quieter.

Now, moving in slow motion, the troll's head came forward, its face now wearing a surprised, contorted expression.

As if in a dream, Thorgrim felt as if he were floating, down, down, down.

When Thorgrim hit the ground he had already passed out, but the impact woke him.

Unknown to Thorgrim, Chloe had charged the troll, jumped up, and using her head, struck the monster in the midsection with incredible force. The miniature donkey's powerful blow stunned the troll, causing it to drop Thorgrim, who was only seconds away from being crushed to death.

Thorgrim shook his head, trying to catch his breath. What he witnessed next was unreal. Impossible. Incomprehensible.

With the wind knocked out of it, the troll fell to the ground and onto its back. Furious, unable to breathe, it struggled to get up, but from out of nowhere, Blinky leaped onto the troll's face and began raking its eyes out with her claws.

The troll screamed in agony. Grabbing Blinky, the monster pulled the cat off its face, flinging her away to the ground where she gracefully landed on all fours. But, it was too late. Now eyeless, the troll was completely blind.

After tossing Blinky aside, the troll finally struggled to its feet.

At the same moment, Chloe struck the troll again, this time in its chest. The shock of the impact knocked the sightless beast back into the barn, where it collapsed into a heap.

Blinky, by this time, had run back to Thorgrim who was still on the ground, in extreme pain and stunned by what he had just witnessed. When she arrived, the worried cat began to lick her master's face repeatedly.

In the barn, the troll stood again. Confused, moaning in pain and unable to see, it wandered aimlessly, stumbling over debris as it tried in vain to get out of the barn.

Then to Thorgrim's horror, another troll arrived. Unsure about what had been happening, the monster looked into the barn and saw its seriously wounded brother floundering around, unable to see a thing.

The second troll turned, and seeing Thorgrim lying on the ground, roared in anger. It started to charge the helpless dwarf, but Chloe counter-charged, smashing into its midsection, knocking it out cold with one blow. A few minutes later, when the second troll woke up and saw Chloe, it screamed in fear and retreated into the barn to join its brother.

The second troll soon reappeared with its injured brother draped over its broad shoulders. Exiting the barn, it tried to run away, down the main highway, east towards the glade.

Chloe pursued the trolls, chasing them down the road. After a quarter of a mile, the angry donkey gave up the pursuit, then bounding like a rabbit, quickly returned to Thorgrim.

Thorgrim was still on the ground, injured, though not gravely. Closing his eyes, he tried to rest. While he recovered, Chloe and Blinky stood guard.

After an hour, Thorgrim slowly sat up. Still dazed, he took a flask of water from his pocket, emptying it in only a couple of gulps.

A few minutes later, Thorgrim felt well enough to stand. He took another flask of water and poured some over his head. Chloe and Blinky were also thirsty, so he shared the remainder of the flask with them. When they were finished, he picked up his axe and slowly led Chloe back into the barn.

Though excruciating, Thorgrim installed Chloe's blanket, saddle, and bridle. Then, wincing in pain, he somehow managed to get his backpack on. Next, he covered his still bloody axe with the hood, grabbed his leather bag and fastened both to the saddle. Last but not least, he placed his purring cat beneath his great beard.

As Thorgrim mounted up, his cracked, throbbing ribs caused him to cry out in agony.

Riding out of the barn, glancing around, still wary of trolls, he hurriedly rode for the main highway in an effort to get away from the area. As he went, he praised his brave donkey and cat for saving his life.

"You both risked yer lives to save mine, and you did it out of love. I promise ya both, I'll always do my best to return it."

Blinky popped his head out of Thorgrim's beard and meowed.

Stopping on the highway, Thorgrim checked his map. He had known all along that he would be riding through the Troll Glade to reach the Great Kingdom's border.

But that was before he discovered that trolls really exist.

The halfling storekeeper back in Elkhorn had told him that if he stayed on the highway and rode through the Troll Glade only in the daytime during clear weather, there would be no trouble from the trolls.

It was mid-morning. The weather was calm and the sky was clear. However, the trolls were riled up because of last night's encounter with the wolves and now the incident with Thorgrim and his furry friends. Far off in the distance to the southeast, he could hear them screaming and raising hell.

To get to the Great Kingdom, he would have to run the gauntlet, but because the trolls were in a furious uproar, he would not risk it.

No doubt, they're pissed off and will be waiting in ambush for anyone that happens to dare ride through the glade. I could wait for them to cool down, but who knows how long that would take. Could be days or weeks!

Cursing, he looked at the map again.

I can't get to the Great Kingdom! I can't sit here and wait, either. But where to go?

On the map, he found a point of interest.

"Calibut?" he muttered. "No. Though I've learned not all elves are bad, still, the whole city is probably full of 'em."

Coughing, he grimaced in pain.

But the Library of Shem is there.

"Library or not, Calibut is over two hundred miles away," he mumbled to himself, shaking his head.

As he pondered his decision, Thorgrim pulled out a pipe that he had purchased at the Elkhorn general store. He thought it was about time he smoked, as most dwarves naturally like to do. After packing the long wooden pipe with some tobacco, he lit it. Taking a couple of puffs, he choked on the smoke, which made his ribs hurt, causing him to wince in pain.

Thorgrim shook his head. "Nasty stuff," he mumbled, "I'm sure it looks cool, but maybe another time." He snuffed out the pipe and put it in one of his pockets.

He considered his options for a few more minutes. Staring at his map, he thought, *It's the largest library in the world!*

Raising one side of his bushy monobrow, he folded up his map and shoved it into his backpack.

Though it hurt to laugh, Thorgrim chuckled. "Calibut. Hmmm. Why not? Better than going through the Troll Glade and becoming a dwarf sandwich! Come on Chloe and Blinky! We're going to a place where there's a lot of books! And I mean a **lot** of books! I just pray they have plenty of ice-cold ale in that city! I'm parched and could drink an entire keg!"

He directed Chloe out onto the main road, then halted. Thorgrim Longbeard, dwarf extraordinaire, with his cat purring in his beard, sat proudly in the saddle for a few moments, drifting off in thought.

Ruby was on his mind.

"Oh, my darling, I know you're here with me because I carry you in muh heart. Together, we'll begin a new adventure!"

Battling depression, tears began to form in his eyes, but he shook them off and forced a smile.

After a sigh and a nod of his head, he gave Chloe a light nudge with his knee, then the little donkey began to slowly walk forward on the road to Calibut.

Unless the trolls returned, there was no need to hurry.

His ribs hurt like hell, and every time he coughed or took a deep breath, he was reminded of the angry troll who tried to squeeze the life out of him.

For several miles, each time he felt pain, Thorgrim looked back in the direction of the Troll Glade and flapped the end of his very, very, long beard.

End of Volume One

"Thorgrim Longbeard at The Cracked Mug Tavern"

Original digital art by Steven Bogenrief.

A fragment of ancient parchment with what is believed to be a drawing of the Aurumsmiter Hammer. Note the diamond-encrusted symbol of the first dwarves on the hammer's head.

Appendix

The Ancient Dwarven Calendar

The days of the week, modern equivalents and definitions:

1. Moridon-alod. Sunday. Also called Worship Day. Named in honor of the supreme deity, Moridon.

2. Uthar Ducim-alod. Monday. First workday of the workweek.

3. Oakenhorn's-alod. Tuesday. Named in honor of the first dwarven king, Authumus Oakenhorn.

4. Midr-alod. Wednesday. Middle day. The middle of the workweek.

5. Erfidi-alod. Thursday. Toil day. Another workday.

6. Ulol-alod. Friday. Last workday of the workweek.

7. Stydja-alod. Saturday. A day to rest.

The months of the year, number of days, modern equivalents, and definitions:

1. Ir Id -31. January. New Year.

2. Akath's Ilrom -31. February. Winter's Peak.

3. Akath's Inir -30. March. Winter's Decline.

4. Ir Thunen -30. April. New Life.

5. Blomis -30. May. Flowers.

6. Omer -31. June. Green.

7. Isram -30. July. Summer.

8. Isram's Ilrom -31. August. Summer's peak.

9. Isram's Inir -30. September. Summer's decline.

10. Thatthil Golud -30. October. Autumn Harvest.

11. Thatthil's Inir -30. November. Autumn's decline.

12. Akath -31. December. Winter.

Thorgrim Longbeard's Paternal Lineage

6x Great Grandfather: **Vog**. 1671 - 1799 (128 yrs. of age).

5x Great Grandfather: **Otum**. 1721 - 1912 (191)

4x Great Grandfather: **Puck**. 1799 - 1961 (162)

3x Great Grandfather: **Ghorge**. 1851 - 2001 (150)

2x Great Grandfather: **Orbi**. 1940 - 2107 (167)

Great Grandfather: **Mosaphar**. 2042 - 2163 (121)

Grandfather: **Pistachio**. 2112 - 2285 (173)

Father: **Luthor**. 2174 - 2329 (155)

Thorgrim. 2229 - 2431 (202)

But, How Could He Know That?

Much of the information regarding details that Thorgrim could not have had direct knowledge of (such as conversations and incidents occurring when he was not present), were obtained from correspondence letters between Thorgrim and his parents.

Most interesting, according to Thorgrim's handwritten notes, is that a few events that would be impossible for him to know about, were revealed supernaturally to him, by a mysterious entity known as the 'all-knowing, most-wise Oracle.' (Read, *The Greatest Treasure in the World*,' for more information regarding the Oracle.)

The Discovery in the Cave of the Winds

Unfortunately, little was known about the god Moridon, or the history of the original, first dwarves. Most of the information that we have was gleaned by dwarven researchers from fragments of ancient stone tablets and several tattered scrolls that were found by goat herders in a mysterious cave at the highest peak of a small group of mountains. The cave and the historical contents were discovered over two thousand years before Thorgrim was born, during a time when the various groups (or 'clans') of dwarves bickered and warred with each other.

The dwarves named the cave 'the Cave of the Winds' because researchers noticed that their torches flickered in the breeze blowing from various crevices inside the cavern system. The wind also caused an eerie howling sound causing many to believe that the cave was haunted. Because of the historical discoveries in the Cave of the Winds, the dwarves called the local mountain group the 'Mountains of the Ancients.' (See the map on page six.)

Luckily, the dwarves recorded their discoveries and some of that material was found inside the steel vault recovered from the Atlantic Ocean floor in 2012.

While exploring the cave, the herders found dozens of broken stone tablets, each carved with strange glyphs and drawings. Deeper in the system, they found a large, stone sarcophagus. When the herders reported what they had found to the local clan chieftain, word eventually reached the authorities in Mharrak City. Immediately, researchers were dispatched to investigate the discoveries.

When the researchers arrived, they were stunned by what they saw. It was obvious that the items in the cave belonged to a very old, previously unknown, dwarven civilization. A strange glyph, shaped like an 'X' inside of a square, was marked on everything. This glyph would become known as the 'ancient symbol of the first dwarves.'

Deeper in the cavern, while investigating the sarcophagus, there was another remarkable discovery. After carefully opening the heavy stone lid (which was engraved with the symbol of the first dwarves), they found a diamond-encrusted, golden sledgehammer, along with a few scrolls and the bones of an unknown dwarf.

Dwarven scholars and engineers carefully moved the sarcophagus, the stone tablets, and the rest of the discovered items to Mharrak City, for study. After several years of research, the glyphs were eventually deciphered and the translated information shocked everyone.

431

Based on the information found on the tablet fragments and parchments, it was believed that over one hundred thousand years before Thorgrim's time, the ancient dwarves (or 'first dwarves' as they were eventually referred to), constructed a gold sledgehammer as a gift to a god they called 'Moridon.' The ancients called the hammer the 'Aurumsmiter' (smite with gold) and when the news was revealed to the dwarven public, it instantly became a symbol of pride for all dwarves.

The tablets and parchments said that although many gods existed, Moridon was the King of the Gods and the creator of everything. Moridon supposedly resided in a holy palace of gold and silver beyond the highest place in the sky and that he was a god of justice, honor, and love.

The writings also claimed that Moridon had a beard of gold that was so long, he could drop it from his palace in the sky and it would touch the ground. This led many dwarves to believe that when they died, Moridon would drop his holy beard to the earth and their spirit would climb it all the way up to join Moridon in his palace for eternity.

When the news of the discovery and successful deciphering spread, thousands of dwarves from all of the clans made pilgrimages to the city to see the tablets, scrolls, and bones and to touch the Holy Hammer.

The information found on the fragments and scrolls was incomplete, but still exciting for everyone. However, something else was found in one of the parchments that completely changed the lives of every dwarf in the land.

The writings claimed that in the middle of a bloody war between several clans, Moridon's hand reached down from heaven and swept the armies aside. The god then 'spoke from the sky in a loud, angry voice' and ordered that all dwarves must unite and serve under one king. Moridon warned that failure to do so meant that sometime in the future, a powerful, evil force from another land would destroy the Dwarven civilization. A bolt of lightning then struck a boulder, turning it into solid gold. After the smoke had cleared, an inscription was revealed. The text, written by Moridon's own hand, read specifically: 'One Land, One People, One King or Death to All.'

It was not long before the eight clan leaders wholeheartedly agreed. Soon, every dwarf was united under one king as proclaimed by Moridon and remained so until the end of the special land.

Identification 101 in the Realm of the Special Land

The reader may wonder how you could identify any particular dwarf or anyone else for that matter. In our modern civilization, photos are often used as a form of personal identification. However, photographic technology did not exist for the inhabitants of the special land. Instead, most of the humanoid countries (the Great Kingdom, Dwarven Clans, Republic of Alacarj, Theocracy of the Abbir and Sherduin) used a system that required anyone over the age of fifteen (this age varied in some countries) to carry identification papers.

These papers, (two or three pages of 5"x 7" sheets of paper) were stored in a small folder. The papers contained the person's name, date, and place of birth, current residence, details about their parents, a detailed physical description, a crude drawing of their appearance, and other personal information.

The system, the best available at the time, worked for the most part because anyone asked to present their papers would be required to answer specific questions regarding the personal information contained in the paperwork. Using false or stolen identification papers was harshly dealt with, usually resulting in a prison term along with hard labor.

Actually, in most countries, it was quite rare that anyone would be required to present their I.D. papers. The police or military doing investigations might ask to see them, but there were official reasons, too. For example, applying for a job, borrowing money from a bank, joining the military, getting married or, in Thorgrim's case, trying to cross the border.

Thorgrim had forgotten his identification papers back in Vog. Of course, this had advantages and disadvantages for the troubled dwarf. If he had his papers and was asked to present them, he likely would be sent on his way. However, if he was wanted by the police, he would be arrested and then prosecuted. On the other hand, if he was stopped without his ID papers, he would likely be arrested for not having any on his person.

Acknowledgments

My wife, Karrissa. Thank you for your incredible love, patience, and support. My princess bride, I love you. As you wish!

Italia Durant, this one is for you. Thank you for the great drawing of your character riding Nugget, with Thorgrim and Blinky watching.

Nancy Brown. Your editing help was priceless! Your love and support made this book possible. I thank you.

My loving, unselfish pets who waited next to me every day and night while I typed and typed and typed. Thank you.

Thank you to my friends for allowing me to use your names for some of the characters.

My dad. I miss you, daddy. Life is not the same without you. Empty in many ways. I look forward to seeing you again. Thanks for everything.

My children. There are no words to describe my love for you. Thank you for your love.

My former student, Steven Bogenrief, thank you for your amazing digital image of Thorgrim holding his ale mug at 'The Cracked Mug Tavern.'

For those of you interested in hiring Steven for any digital artwork, here is some info about him:

Steven was born and raised in Sioux City Iowa and is a current instructor at Western Iowa Tech Community College. Steven also worked for a high-level advertisement firm known as Threedium UK.
His lifelong goal is to bring a high-level modern advertisement/media company to the Sioux City Iowa/Midwest area where local artists can stay local instead of having to move away.
A link to his website: https://freckle.artstation.com/
Email: steven.chinn@witcc.edu.
You can find a full-color version of the image on my author's page:
https://www.facebook.com/TheGreatestTreasureintheWorld/

Cast of Characters

?

(as Thorgrim Longbeard).

Ron Thacker
(as Dr. R.E. Thacker).

Mark Krumwiede
(On the right, with the author)
(as Marko Krumwiede, day shift manager at the Vog Silver Mine).

Charla Tucker
(as Gary's wife, Charla).

Gary Tucker
(as Gary of Tuckerheim, owner of 'Tuckerheim's
Equine and Shoeing).

Nugget
(as Nugget, the elven horse).

**Licorice Stick Ninjitsu
(as Thorgrim's cat, Blinky Eyes).**

**Scott McDonald
(as the Iron Golem Pub's bartender, Scootz
McDonald).**

Uuno Kanto
(as Thorgrim's mentor, Uuno Kanto).

Nancy and Al Brown
(as Nancy and Al Brownstone).

**Steven Bogenrief
(as the paladin, Sir Steven of George).**

John Hildman III
(as Sir Steven's squire, John of Hildman III).

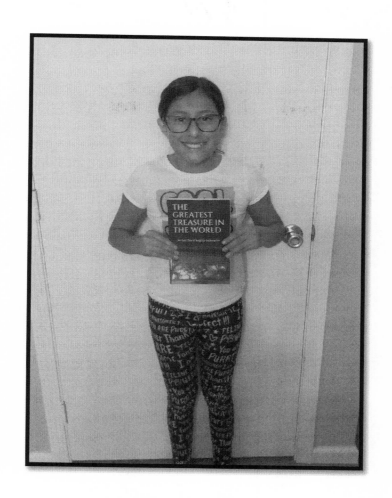

**Italia Durant
(as the elf, Italia Durant).**

Mark Durant (and family)
(as Italia's father, Mark Durant).

Chloe
(as Chloe, the miniature dwarf donkey).

Coming soon:

The Legend of Thorgrim Longbeard
"Dwarf Extraordinaire"

Volume Two. The Library of Shem

Made in the USA
Middletown, DE
06 January 2022

58005274R10267